Inside Straight

An Amber Farrell Novel
Book 6 of the
Bite Back series

by
Mark Henwick

Published by ***Marque***

Series schedule, reviews & news on
www.athanate.com

Bite Back 6 : Inside Straight
ISBN: 978-1-912499-18-2

First published in June 2016 by Marque

Cover design: CreativeEdge, Andrew Dobell
Cover model: Maria Askew

Author's note:

Asian names:
Throughout this series, I use the Western sequence (First, Middle, Last Name) to depict names, so as to match with the majority of characters in the books. Most Asian societies would put the Last Name first.

Series continuity:
The Bite Back series is a continuous story rather than a string of episodes. It's not advised to start anywhere but at the beginning, with Sleight of Hand, and read through in order.

There are three novellas between Bite Back 5 (Angel Stakes) and this book. Two are set in Michigan and explain the background to House Lloyd (The Biting Cold & Winter's Kiss), and one is set in New York (Change of Regime). It's not essential to read them before Inside Straight, but they do provide much more information on the side stories that feed into Bite Back at this point.

Acknowledgment:
For Joanne, whose simple request when we met in NM precipitated a whole character in my head.

Prologue

Midnight in the heart of the Painted Desert, and the tattered dead rise up like the dust of dreams behind her whispering feet.

Their features are blurred, the many dead; all the once-proud edges have been caressed into soft, uncertain shapes, the way stone is carved by centuries of wind and rain. Moonlight flows through them as if through troubled water, and they raise a million tangled, untold stories to fly like banners behind them.

They're called here, the dead, from their silent graves along the countless sorrowing trails. Here, where the mountains still breathe and the rocks talk. Here, where rain is a blessing on the seared earth, and the sun looks down on the yellow corn as it dances to the desert's tune.

Here, where they may find those who may listen, in this sacred place.

Tullah listens as she steps the circle through the cold depths of the night. Every night. It's her choice. Her atonement. In exchange, the dead swirl behind, obedient to the summons, and their spirits cloak the kiva in which her family and friends sleep underground.

She can *feel* the searchers she hides them from; great, blind monsters snuffling over the hills and through the valleys, flickering spirit tongues testing the city airs, cold spirit hands like spiders creeping across the plains.

As the days have crept by, there are more of them, instead of less.

Her family and the others are safe, so long as the legions of dead surround the kiva—around, above, below, and make it a place *between* the physical world and the spirit world. The searchers slide over them, oblivious, unable sense the kiva and the people within.

So far.

This masking is Chatima's working, a powerful working, shamanic and obscure to the searchers, and without it they would have found her long ago. It is a spell of strange and awful beauty, locked here around this place of power. Tullah maintains the working, treading the circle every night, and takes some pride that she does it well.

But it cannot last forever. They have reached a point of balance between the dangers of staying here and the dangers of moving.

She has discussed this with Chatima and with her parents. They've waited as long as they dare with the spirit world pressing in so close. Being with the spirits takes its toll: the sun-struck lethargy; the night-long, dreamy disconnection from the physical world; the feeling of being more spirit than flesh.

Not for the first time, Tullah thinks of the kiva as a grave.

Much longer inside and it *will* be; their spirits will untether from their bodies.

Even before that, the fragile tethers to spirit guides will part, and prevent her from ever getting Kaothos back.

The thought of that sinks claws into her chest, making it difficult to breathe. If that happens, she might as well become one with the spirit world.

But not the others. They shouldn't suffer.

It's *her* the searchers are looking for, because they think she still has Kaothos. Not that it would be a good idea to point out their error: being caught without Kaothos is even worse. They'll know that they could use her as a way to draw Kaothos into a trap. It would actually be safer for them to do it that way.

She has to leave. She has to evade the searchers. She has to return things to the way they were before.

The rest of them won't be in danger for long, once she's gone.

She must prepare herself. She can't perform Chatima's workings on her own, nor can this working be moved from this sacred place, but she has concealment spells of her own that might do for the time it takes to get back to Denver. Matt says that's where Kaothos and Diana are heading right now.

She must go soon. She must go alone. All thoughts of the deadly situation aside, her crippling shame is infecting everyone. Even Matt.

As the moon slips across the night sky, someone walks beside her on the circle path.

The dead sometimes do that, so it takes her a while to notice it's Chatima.

Whether she's in her body or she's spirit walking, Tullah is not entirely sure. Here, in the place *between*, it's not always possible to tell.

"There are many paths to go forward, but none to go back," Chatima says, as if she hears the thoughts in Tullah's mind about returning things *to the way they were before*. "And every path bears death and sorrow and pain and loss."

Amber's words.

Tullah's tears fall to the dusty path, to be lost among the dreams of the dead.

"All the things I've ever done," she whispers. "In balance with all the things I will do. I will make this right."

"The world is a maze, child. The way is never straight. But look up sometimes, for the sky remains pure."

Tullah raises her eyes. Chatima is right; the light of the crescent moon has a silver purity. It's calming.

The shaman Adept is no longer beside her when she looks back down.

"All the things I've ever done," she repeats to the listening dead. The words seemed so simple when Amber spoke them. She'd heard them with her ears, but she'd not felt them in her heart. The words had seemed so light.

Now they are like draglines on her soul.

The dead do not shy away from her shame. The dead stay with her.

Their thousand, thousand voices rustle like dry leaves. If she let them, they would leech the shame from her. It would be so easy; spirits hunger for the emotions of the living. Yes, it would be so easy to let them feed, but they would take all. And when they finished, she would be one of them.

Thoughts like that come to her. It's not a good place, this *between*, not for anyone, and especially not for her.

Alongside the thoughts, she sees visions and hears voices.

She sees Evans sometimes. The man she killed in the battle at Carson Park. Her hands tingle and she feels the *snap* as his neck breaks, all over again. The sickening, *appalling* moment of savage pleasure and the following flood of shame and recrimination.

It's not about him. He deserved to die. It's about you.

It feels as if Amber herself is speaking the words to her, and they do help.

Sometimes the visions are a comfort as she walks: the cougar, down off her lonely range; the bear, awakened from her sleep; the buffalo, up from the grasslands. The coyote. The fox. The snake. The owl. The raven.

Sometimes it's not a comfort: her dragon walks silently with her, a vision of all she's lost. And often, when the dawn breaks, the strange wolf will stand on the cliff with the rising sun behind her, a vision aflame. Chatima is uneasy about the wolf, though she tries to hide that. Openly, she says it signifies the hope of redemption, but in her heart of hearts, Tullah knows that for her, it's a vision of shame, and a symbol of forgiveness denied.

Chapter 1

"Amber. Amber. Wake up. Sorry. Phone call. You have to deal with this."

It was Pia whispering in my ear, shaking me awake in the small hours.

"From Tullah?" I mumbled, reaching out a hand.

I was dreaming of her... walking a circle... death and sorrow...

"No."

Alex was rising off the bed, hearing trouble in Pia's voice, imagining a threat, his eyes halfway to wolf already when Pia held up a hand to stop him.

Jen rolled over sleepily and tried to drag us both back.

"Athanate business," Pia explained. "It's a House Lloyd. I don't know her. She apologizes, but says it's urgent and private. I've transferred her to the phone in Jen's study."

I slipped on a bathrobe and frowned as I followed Pia out of the bedroom.

My House regularly 'borrowed' my cell and dealt with callers so I wasn't disturbed. A middle-of-the-night call from some House that I *had* to take myself meant trouble. And an *unknown* House?

"I thought you knew all the Houses," I said as we climbed the stairs. "Unless—she's not from Carpathia or the Empire, is she?"

That would open a can of worms that I didn't need right now.

"With a name like Lloyd?" Pia said. "No, she's American, from the slight accent. That's what's so strange—I thought I knew them all. But she's a real House; she spoke perfect Athanate and used all the correct protocol."

I thought that over. "Diazoun?" I suggested.

Pia's eyes widened slightly. "I hope not," she muttered.

So did I—that would be another squirmy, messy can of worms.

It had once been acceptable to be diazoun: to cut all ties with other Athanate, and live without getting involved in the squabbles of creeds, or the responsibilities of associations. It wasn't acceptable anymore. Skylur had declared every Athanate in the US had to be associated, directly or through intermediary Houses like me, to House Altau. *Diazoun* now had the same connotations as *epitre,* which, though it translated approximately as 'unorthodox', really meant 'unacceptable'.

Rogues were *epitre.*

Rogues were put down.

A diazoun House wanting my help would put me in a tricky spot, and however patient Skylur had been with me so far, there were limits.

Pia stopped at the study door. The caller had said private.

"I'll wait here," she said. "Speak cautiously. Call me if you don't feel you understand the political implications of anything."

The Athanate can be picky about how things are asked for and agreed on.

"You mean like the approved way to ask why the hell she's requesting an urgent, private conversation in the middle of the night while everyone's in bed?" I grumbled.

Pia just ushered me inside and closed the door behind me.

On the table, the sleek handset's 'hold' light blinked.

I sat down and, despite the hour, the last traces of sleepiness vanished.

I picked up the handset and punched the button.

"This is House Farrell," I said. My Athanate was still poor, so I spoke in English. Maybe that would cut down on any ambiguities about how things could or should be said.

I should be so lucky.

"Thank you for taking my call, House Farrell. I apologize for the hour. My name is Amanda Lloyd, House Lloyd."

Her voice was smooth, and despite what Pia had said, I thought it was nearly accentless, but it gave the impression of being tightly controlled. This sounded like a strong woman under considerable stress.

"House Lloyd," I said. "May I ask what's so urgent that you needed to speak to me in the middle of the night? Especially as my Head of Protocol is unfamiliar with your House."

I heard her take a breath, and then she said, "We're diazoun. From Michigan. House Farrell, I'm calling to beg sanctuary from you."

Shit!

I'd gotten it in one guess—a can of worms.

From what I knew about Athanate protocols, 'sanctuary' could mean either simple protection, or becoming a sub-House. It was all trouble, but the amount depended on which she wanted.

If—for some insane reason—I accepted House Lloyd's Blood oath and made her my sub-House, then all her problems suddenly became mine. But on the other hand, if I took her diazoun House under my wing *without* making her part of my House, it would mean I, too, could be declared epitre, along with my entire House.

In the usual, absolute, Athanate way, there was some balance applied to this situation: in asking for sanctuary, she was offering me the power of life or death over her and her House.

It wasn't a move to be considered lightly and I had no idea *why* she needed sanctuary—and from me in particular—but it couldn't be good.

I shivered. Athanate politics was deadly and complex. My impulse was to just say no immediately, but I'd already heard something in her voice that stopped me from rejecting her outright. I felt I had to at least listen to the woman.

Didn't mean I should go easy on her.

"Michigan. So, you're from House Prowser's territory," I said. "I have to warn you that I'm a direct sub-house of Altau, and House Prowser is a senior ally and close friend of House Altau. If you're on the run because you've offended or betrayed her in some way, I can't help you."

I was being less than diplomatic, especially by Athanate standards, but it *was* the middle of the night, and if she needed sanctuary, she was in no position to complain about my manners.

"We're not running from House Prowser," she said. "I don't believe she will contest our departure."

She *believed*. She didn't *know*. And she hadn't said she *wasn't* on the run—just not from Prowser. This wasn't sounding any better, and I was losing patience.

"Well then, who *are* you running from? And why are you proposing to come over a thousand miles to Colorado? There must be dozens of Houses between here and there."

She said nothing for a moment. Then: "House Farrell, I am desperate, and it can only be you."

That iron control was slipping, and a raw *need* was singing to me down the line.

"For heaven's sake, why?"

"Because Scott, my eldest kin…" she paused, a catch in her breath, and I could hear she was gathering herself, fighting to keep her voice level. "Because he's dying. I lost my other two kin in a car accident a year ago and I thought I'd lost him as well. I... can't. I can't lose him too. Not even now I have more kin. He's been with me all my Athanate life."

The sheer power of her simple words held a weight I could not turn aside, and the shock of emotions she'd let slip combined with my guilt over thinking this appeal had been all about Athanate politics.

I leaned forward over the phone, as if that movement would somehow make a difference to her.

"Can't you heal him?"

The question came quicker than I could stop it, but even as I spoke, it sounded heartless.

She didn't flinch from answering.

"Not from age, House Farrell. It's complex. We were separated for a year. If we hadn't been, I would have infused him while he was still strong so he could become Athanate. Now it's too late; he'd never survive crusis from an ordinary infusion."

Finally, her purpose and her need became clear to me.

Oh, damn!

"You want me to infuse him?"

Me, with my unique blood.

"It's his only hope," she said. "I'm told your infusion carries less severe crusis and he has a chance of surviving it."

I wasn't ready for this. Every time I thought about infusing someone I felt a leap of eagerness inside, immediately squashed by the fear that it would go wrong.

"My infusion hasn't been tested," I pointed out. "The rumor may have told you my Blood shortens crusis but it's just that—a rumor. It may kill him outright. Even if it doesn't, I guess the rumor also told you I'm hybrid Athanate-Were. My infusion may make him a werewolf and drive him rogue."

"It's better to hope than do nothing," she said. "Please, House Farrell. I'm begging you. Send us back to Michigan if you must. But please, infuse him first."

I hesitated. If Prowser wasn't after her, then Skylur might agree to my giving sanctuary. And there *was* pressure on me to test my infusion. Nothing like an order from Skylur yet, but definite reminders from time to time.

Could I use that as a reason for Skylur to agree to them staying?

Finally, I said, "Well, in any case, you understand I'm going to have to talk to others and ask questions before I can commit to anything?"

Skylur, House Prowser, Bian. There were a lot of people who had to agree if we were going to move forward.

"I understand, House Farrell. We're at the state border. May we come on to Denver? Please? I'm sure I can explain it all better in person." She faltered, and I got the sense she was working hard to speak calmly and evenly again. "If your final answer is no, I will understand."

I could feel how much that last comment had cost her.

The rest of it, staying outside the state border until I gave permission, was an Athanate courtesy. Strictly, she should have been requesting permission of Bian, not me. Skylur had transferred his whole Colorado territory to Bian when he announced Altau would be moving to New York.

In any event, the issue opened what I thought could be the deal breaker.

"House Lloyd, there's something you should realize before you cross that state border." I had to warn her, without giving any of Skylur's secret plans away. "Colorado is going to be closed to unauthorized Athanate movement anytime now. I don't want to go into details—it's all to do with House Altau moving his domain to New York and certain tests he wants to perform here. It could mean, if you end up denied sanctuary, you'd be imprisoned here instead."

It was immediately clear that nothing would change her mind. "I understand the risks you've described, and I take full responsibility, in my capacity as House Lloyd." She paused to gather herself. "In recompense, my Blood may also be of some value to you. My kin are unusually long-lived and while I was recovering from losing my other kin..." She paused again; her voice crackled with remembered pain. "During that year, I was able to survive without Blood myself."

That stunned me. *A year!* Normal Athanate would go into coma after a couple of weeks.

It put her into the same category of Athanate freak as me. It was possible my Blood could be valuable to other Athanate because it might reduce crusis. In exactly the same way, her Blood might be valuable because she didn't need to bite humans so often. Many Athanate would want to treat House Lloyd as they wanted to treat me: by locking me up and milking me of my valuable Blood.

Thinking of it that way broke something in me. I imagined myself in her situation, begging for sanctuary and having to offer my Blood in exchange to a House I didn't even know.

"House Lloyd," I said. "*If* I do this, I'm not doing it like some deal in a bazaar, based on what I think your Blood may be worth."

The line went quiet for a couple of seconds. She clearly hadn't been expecting that.

"Thank you. I truly appreciate that," she said, her voice lower. "You should still keep in mind what I have to offer. I'm not a wealthy House, and I cannot be proud: I offer Blood for Blood. Infuse Scott and my Blood is yours."

Her words were coming closer to the form of oaths that bound House to House. I didn't think I could take on a House without meaning to, but on the other hand, I'd taken Yelena into my House accidentally. I needed to be careful.

Before I could say anything else, she went on: "To be clear, this is not necessarily exclusive. The reason I believe that House Prowser won't contest my leaving Michigan is that I allowed one of her House to take Blood from me before I left."

"As I understand it, Amanda, Blood doesn't necessarily work that way, and it's not going to be the reason I agree or not, but I appreciate you telling me."

I had to admit to myself that I was trying to find a way to agree to her request. But she'd dodged my question earlier: there was still the little matter that she might be on the run. And I needed to make sure who I was inviting into my House, whether it was temporarily or permanently. More questions...

"So it's you and Scott, and...?"

"And my new kin. Two of them." Her voice slowed, tried to sound as if it were unimportant. "They're Adepts."

A thrill coursed through me and I sat up straighter.

Athanate and Adepts had very little to do with each other; Adepts as kin were almost unheard-of, and highly valued.

How the hell had this even happened?

"What coven did they belong to?" I asked.

"They're not affiliated, except to each other," she said. "They're shamanic."

My mouth dropped open. That was a whole new level of risk and opportunity, writhing around each other like snakes.

My Athanate wanted Adepts in my House. Any Athanate House would, but given I was some kind of latent and possibly shamanic Adept, I *needed* Adepts who could help me harness or understand whatever powers I had. To help me to get control of the Were ritual, for instance. Which was probably why my wolf side had started to take notice.

The rest of me wasn't so sure. Shamanic Adepts were not well regarded by the newer Adept communities. In fact, they were sometimes actively hunted down.

Oh. The pieces started falling together in my mind.

"Please tell me you're not on the run because of these shamanic Adepts."

She cleared her throat. "Not exactly on the run. But there would have been trouble if they had stayed in Michigan. Apparently, as shamanic Adepts they're outcasts from all the communities up there, both sides of the border, and there was a local group of covens that came after them at House Prowser. But we're not in their territory now, so I don't see that that's a problem, and it could even be another factor in Prowser being happy that I left."

Adept communities in the north cooperated with others? That was a new one on me—the Denver community didn't cooperate with anyone. Not even each other, from what I could tell.

But it was unlikely this northern group of covens would follow two shamanic Adepts halfway across the country. And yes, House Prowser might be glad they weren't part of her responsibilities any longer, if keeping them would have caused problems with the local Adepts.

I came to a temporary decision. "Okay," I said. "I'm inclined to look favorably on your petition. But here's the problem: all of it, *all* of it has to be passed up the chain of command. If you're really sure this is what you want, come on into Colorado, and come here." I gave her the address of Manassah. "It's the big place on the corner, looking out over the Country Club. There are guards on the gate. Meanwhile, I will make your case as strongly as I'm able, and if I can, I will infuse Scott, but I *will* have to do what Skylur orders me to do."

"Thank you, House Farrell. I understand. Whatever my House can offer is yours."

"Call me Amber. I'll see you in a few hours, Amanda."

I ended the call.

She'd sunk the deepest of hooks into my heart. I remembered only too well what her desperation felt like, from when Jen was dying of her wounds after the rescue at the warehouse in Longmont. I would have done anything at that time, if it meant saving her. It hurt to know so vividly what Amanda Lloyd was going through.

I was taking a big risk, encouraging her to enter Colorado before talking to Bian. But Amanda had accepted all the risks I listed and she was *still* coming. How could I turn that away?

Not to mention the fact that two shamanic Adepts came with her—practically tossed in my lap, just when I needed them most. It was almost as if it were meant to be.

Pia didn't agree when I told her everything that had been said.

"Diazoun!" she muttered, shaking her head. "You realize the potential problems? What if some Agiagraphos fanatics in the old Eastern Seaboard

Association decide that surviving for a year without Blood is epitre? Or what if she's wrong about House Prowser? Prowser might be happy those Adepts aren't her problem any more, but she's an old, proud House. What if she's offended by House Lloyd's refusal to be a sub-House? What if Prowser declares feud unless they're executed? What if Skylur demands you execute them?"

That shook me. I knew enough of Athanate rules that the scenario Pia painted was entirely possible.

"Do you really think he'd do that?" I asked.

Pia just gave me a look. "You've heard Skylur talk about Emergence. He'll do whatever he has to, to keep his alliances from falling apart. He has to think of all Athanate, not the individuals."

Her words brought me a memory of Skylur speaking to me in Los Angeles: *I don't care about Ibarre. I will kill him, or exile him, or forgive him, just so long as it does not hinder our plans for a safe Emergence. That applies to anyone and everyone. Nothing can be allowed to stand in the way of a controlled Emergence.*

Ibarre had been an old, well-connected Athanate House, but he'd put himself in Skylur's way, and paid for it with his life.

Yes, if the alternative was damage to the process of Emergence, Skylur would order the execution of Amanda Lloyd and all her House.

Would I do it? Execute a House on the basis they'd disobeyed a command from Skylur that I didn't entirely agree with myself?

If I didn't follow his orders, my House in turn would become outcast. We'd all be diazoun, and under sentence of death.

Which Bian would be responsible for carrying out.

Would *she* do it?

I didn't know. I hoped not, even at the expense of her own House.

But where did that stop?

Alternately, what if Prowser was okay with it, but Skylur wanted them for himself? An Athanate with potentially useful Blood and Adepts willing to work with Athanate. Why wouldn't he want them under his direct control?

I found I was really unhappy with the idea that Skylur might want to take House Lloyd and her Adepts from me. *Mine,* I wanted to snarl, just thinking about it. Even my wolf joined in on that.

However, there was no point in snarling at Skylur; I needed to present a case to him showing the benefits of House Lloyd being here in Denver, in my House.

As I'd warned Amanda, Colorado was about to become isolated from the rest of the USA for Athanate. The real reason for it was that Diana and Kaothos were coming here, and on no account could news of them leak to the Empire of Heaven, or the barely balanced political arrangement which had Skylur and the Emperor running the Assembly from the sidelines would collapse.

The reason Skylur would give, when the isolation directive went out, was that the potential for my Blood to reduce crusis was being investigated, and the control on movement was a sort of quarantine.

So... it would make sense for House Lloyd's Blood to be tested here, in the 'quarantine' zone. I could use that argument. At the same time, infusing Scott would show I was willing to do what Skylur wanted and it would support the reason for his directive.

What else? The shamanic Adepts might be useful to help get Kaothos transferred back from Diana to Tullah, and they might be able to help Tullah learn to harness her powers.

Also, since both Tullah and I were considered to have broken Adept community law, maybe a couple of Adepts in my House would provide some defense against the Denver community.

Not great arguments, certainly not knockouts, but a start.

And I needed to show I was willing to cooperate in other ways, by going through the correct channels and following protocol. Before I even got to making arguments, I needed to contact Bian and Skylur.

Bian first, simply because she was the only one with a direct line to Skylur at the moment.

Which meant I'd have to wake her in the middle of the night and admit to inviting House Lloyd into Colorado.

I winced.

Not a great beginning.

Chapter 2

So... I'm doing things the right way. For once. Go me.

It was still stupid o'clock, the *early* morning of Christmas Eve, with the sun sensible enough to be in bed, and I was out at Bian's house, Haven, Colorado's Athanate HQ.

So much for my Christmas vacation.

You and your House rest. Christmas with your family. Food and wine and television. Cards and presents: Down in LA, Skylur had *ordered* me to take the time off.

If it hadn't been so serious, I would have laughed, but even putting House Lloyd's petition to one side, it was becoming clear something had gone wrong out in the wider Athanate world.

As far as the rest of the paranormal world was concerned, Skylur was in mourning for Diana after her dramatic death in LA. In fact, Skylur, Alice, Diana and Kaothos had left LA in a magically shielded van to drive up here in the utmost secrecy. Only Bian, my House, and those four in the van really knew the truth: Diana's 'death' had been carefully stage managed by Kaothos, Tullah's dragon spirit guide, to divert the Empire from the truth about the dragon they demanded the right to control.

In keeping with the deception, Bian had gone through her protocol of sending out a request signal. She warned me we would have to wait for a response before opening a triple-encrypted connection.

But the request signal had been answered immediately. Bian opened the protected connection and Skylur was there, waiting.

And if that was the back of a truck on the road from LA, I was a pink flamingo.

What the hell is going on?

Skylur's eyes narrowed to see me there, but all we got was: "Bian, Amber. Hello. Quickly, please."

Bian went straight in.

"Amber's received a petition for sanctuary from a Michigan-based diazoun House. We've warned them that Colorado would be under quarantine, but that didn't dissuade them, so we've allowed them to proceed. They'll be with us in a couple of hours."

I got a rush from hearing that little lie, that 'we' had allowed them to proceed.

Bian had my back. We were sitting close together, facing the conference call cameras with poker faces, but this close, each of us felt the other's eukori and Bian would know how grateful I was that she'd taken my side.

"Ah." Skylur sat back and steepled his fingers in his familiar pose. "That'll be why I've had email requests for an urgent conference from Amelie through both Naryn and Tarez."

"She requested the same though me," Bian said. "No details, and it's in the hopper along with seventeen other Houses' requests of similar stated urgency."

Skylur smiled, if you could call the thin stretch of his mouth a smile.

"The rest will have to be passed to others to deal with. Plans have changed, as you can see," he said, gesturing at his surroundings. "I'm in New York already. Diana is coming directly to you in the van and should be with you tomorrow. Given what this involves, we have to deal with it, but none of us are going to have a lot of time to handle it, so make your suggestions succinctly."

If he'd left Diana in the van, there was a lot going on, but it didn't look as if he was going to explain it, and I couldn't get distracted by that at the moment. I'd made a gut-level commitment to House Lloyd and I needed Skylur's permission to make it formal.

Heart racing, I launched into my pitch, dovetailing arguments that we should actually be doing the things Skylur was going to establish the quarantine for, along with the security issues for House Lloyd herself. I followed up with Amanda's Adept kin clearly not being welcome in Michigan and potentially of great use to us here, so we wouldn't have to depend solely on Alice for magical protections or advice. I added that they might be able to teach me about my own Adept powers, which, I pointed out, he'd included in the list of things I should be working on.

Skylur asked a couple of sharp questions to establish that we didn't know what House Prowser was thinking about it, and certainly didn't know how powerful or useful these Adepts were.

He wasn't buying my arguments.

"I'm not sure you're thinking dispassionately about this," he said. "You appear to have made some level of commitment already."

"Yes," I replied, because I had to. "It was difficult not to identify with what she must be going through. I've acted on my gut instinct."

Bian was about to say something, but Skylur had gotten that brooding look in his eyes and she held off. I took my cue from her, much as I wanted to keep making my case.

The silence let other issues sneak into my thoughts.

Diana coming directly? Did that mean she'd already picked up Tullah? Why had he left them and gone on to New York?

Skylur sat back up. "Despite your emotional involvement in this, your instincts have worked well before. House Lloyd are proceeding to Denver on your responsibility. I'm not going to micromanage. Make your own decision whether to carry on with the infusion of her dying kin, using assistance from Bian and Pia, or Diana if she gets there in time. I'd advise you prepare yourself for the likely outcome."

I bowed my head. *Likely outcome. That Scott was going to die whatever we tried.*

"As you are clearly now prepared to test your infusion, you should also proceed with a more suitable test subject, but wait until Diana is there for that. As to the actual sanctuary—you have my support, contingent on agreement from House Prowser. I will not have a House as widely regarded as Amelie's at odds with me during this time. Plans for Emergence cannot afford it."

He waited as I nodded acceptance again.

His eyes became bleaker. "As you will have guessed, our trip back didn't go to plan. We lost our contact with Tullah and so didn't divert to Arizona to pick her up. That could be simply because she's taking more security precautions, but it's worrying. I believe your House may still have some ways to attempt to communicate. You should use them, and report to me."

I'd had some forebodings about Tullah—strange dreams and a general uneasiness. Now those feelings solidified into fear. Although Skylur had sent the Empire's Adepts away after the Assembly in LA, some of them were almost certainly back in the country. We might have tricked them about Diana, but I felt sure they didn't believe our lie that Kaothos must have died when we'd freed Diana from the Taos Adepts.

If they were searching for her, Tullah would be rightly scared, and she'd have hidden well.

I knew David had set up some emergency systems with Matt, but that was a long time back. I had no idea if they were still in use.

"They're old backup systems, but we'll try everything," I said to Skylur.

"Good. I will need to speak to Amelie now." He made a signal to someone off-screen. "Meantime, Bian, I have Naryn on the other line waiting to talk to me. Stay on the line, I'll patch him through to you while I call Amelie. I know you have some administrative issues that he'd be best placed to deal with."

Bian knew how much I wouldn't enjoy seeing Naryn again, even if it was only on a video conferencing screen.

"Go to the gym," she said quietly. "There'll be something to distract you. I'll be down as quickly as I can."

I left, already about as distracted as I could be, now worrying about Tullah as well as House Lloyd.

Tullah had to be here with Diana for her to reclaim her dragon. Even if there had been hints that reclaiming wasn't as straightforward as it sounded, I had hoped that once she and Kaothos were home, things would become easier.

Or at least easy enough for me to turn my attention to my family, and more specifically, my sister. It was only a couple of days since the shock of Agent Ingram's revelation to me, and I'd spent a lot of time thinking about it. All the time I'd been caught up in resolving what Forsythe had done to me in my last year of school, I'd completely missed that he'd done the same thing to my sister.

Initially, I'd thought I should come in like the cavalry and fix things for her, right away, using whatever Athanate powers would do the job. I'd wanted to erase every memory of Forsythe from Kath's head. Remove every trace of him. Scrub her clean.

That had been anger speaking. It'd been all about what he'd done to me. It was as if he'd done it all over again.

Alex and Jen had waited for my rage to burn out and held me while I cried and swore.

"Now let's make a plan," Alex had said quietly when I'd finished. "A plan for *Kath*. What *she* needs and how to do it."

And so Jen and Alex and Pia and I had decided that we needed to start very slowly—first I had to ease back into the family, and my relationship with Kathleen.

Which, crises about House Lloyd and Tullah allowing, started with Christmas Eve dinner at Mom's tonight. *Tonight, 7pm.* Fourteen hours' time. In pretty clothes and with my face washed. No excuses. No point turning up in any way that would give Kath something to get angry about.

Not that she needs rational or reasonable excuses.

I kicked myself. As Jen had put it, a lot of Kath's worst behavior was probably bottled-up, denied rage that had transformed itself into a different aspect.

I needed to be able to let the rages just wash over me without reacting, and start thinking about how to overcome the real problem behind them.

Starting tonight.

That was, of course, unless everything went to hell today.

No point thinking about that this morning, but it was as if my frustrations latched onto everything else I thought about. I wanted to get going and make progress with something and yet here I was waiting.

I understood Skylur's reasons for talking to House Prowser, but I'd spent ten years in Ops 4-10 and far too much of it had been hurry up and wait.

Still, what was bugging me seemed to be more than a mixture of frustration, apprehension and anger. I'd felt odd, ever since Pia had woken me from that strange dream of walking with Tullah. A 'fingernails on the backboard' feeling. Something had gone wrong, or was just about to.

But if it was real, where? Which problem? If it wasn't real, what was it?

Bian had suggested there would be something to distract me in the gym.

If there wasn't, I was going to hammer a punching bag until either it burst, or Bian came to calm me down.

But as it turned out, there *was* a distraction, even at this ungodly hour.

Chapter 3

It was Mykayla.

A few months ago, she'd been a happy-go-lucky Denver girl who liked raves, and had a crush on me and Bian, not in that order. Now she was Bian's kin, and an Aspirant—a human training to become Athanate. Diana had chosen Mykayla as the first person she wanted me to infuse, to test out whether my infusion would actually reduce crusis, or turn people into hybrids. Or something else entirely. Like kill them.

Mykayla, crazy girl, had actually volunteered.

She was training this morning; Aspirants go through a vigorous physical program, so that when their time comes to be infused, they're in peak condition. It helps them survive the dangerous physical stresses of crusis.

House Lloyd's kin was already dying. How could he possibly survive even a short crusis?

I pushed the thoughts away and concentrated on Mykayla.

I hadn't been monitoring her progress while I was away in LA, so I was surprised by the change. Her exercises on the training mats and the sleek look of her body impressed me. Let alone the dedication to get up this early to work out.

She wasn't alone. Haven was busy—even the gym, even at this hour.

Colonel Laine had recruited soldiers from our old battalion, Ops 4-10, after the whole Ops 4 group was disbanded. They'd started out based in Wyoming, but as of a few weeks ago, Haven was their HQ. They were working directly for House Altau now and they were taking their new role as seriously as I would expect from former Ops 4-10 personnel. It wasn't just people in the gym at strange hours; there was a new multi-channel comms system covering the area, patrols 24/7 with staggered shifts, biometric monitoring of active personnel and surveillance of the locality across the spectrum.

I could see they were just begging Basilikos to try attacking Haven.

It was intended that small teams of former Ops 4-10 would be sent from here to just about every House in North America. Skylur had declared that North America was his territory and he intended to strengthen his sub-Houses so that there was no weak point for Basilikos to exploit.

Colonel Laine looked to have that objective all in hand.

Keith had wandered off to find breakfast and any familiar faces from his days in Ops 4-10, leaving me alone when the training ended.

Mykayla came bounding over.

"Hi, Amber!"

We hugged.

"Hi yourself. You're looking good, girl."

"Yup! I'm ready."

I didn't need to ask what she meant she was ready for. The girl wanted to start the process of transformation by being infused by me.

"You're ready when Bian says you're ready," I said and sat back down on the bench.

"Come on! Tell me I'm not in top condition," she insisted. Her face got a little sly look to it. "Get a load of these abs."

She opened her *gi* and lifted her sweaty shirt.

Yeah, great abs, and an entirely intentional opportunity to appreciate the cutest little pink-nosed puppies too.

I snorted and grabbed her by her canvas training pants, lifting her up as she squealed and depositing her next to me on the bench.

I was laughing, and after a little pout, she joined in.

"Bian put you up to that, didn't she?" I asked.

"Sort of."

"Either she did or she didn't. Come on, Mykayla, spill."

"She bet me. Said if I got you into bed, she'd agree I was ready to be infused."

I laughed harder and gave her a hug. That was typical Bian, but Mykayla hadn't quite seen all of it.

"Could have been a double whammy," she said indistinctly and sighed, her face pressed against my shoulder.

"Congratulations," I said.

She leaned back and looked up at me suspiciously, as if I were teasing her some more.

"What do you mean?"

"Well, Bian might have a horrible sense of humor, but look at it this way: do you think she's irresponsible?"

Mykayla frowned. "No. Not at all. I don't understand."

"Hundred percent responsible?" I prompted her. "Ninety? Eighty?"

"Hundred, of course."

"So, let's say you aren't ready to be infused, but there was a chance, oh, one in ten, say, that we actually ended up in bed. That'd make her only ninety percent responsible, unless…"

Mykayla frowned again before suddenly it dawned on her. "Oh! Unless it didn't matter. Unless she thinks I *am* ready, and getting me to try and seduce you was a joke."

"Congratulations," I said again.

"Oh, Amber!" She leaped up from the bench and did a handspring followed by cartwheels in a complete circle so she ended up back in front of me.

"Today? Now?" She bounced on her toes.

My fangs were throbbing with anticipation, which was distracting, but I managed a shaky laugh. No matter how eager my Athanate was to infuse someone, I needed help to go through the process, and *I* wasn't in any hurry. No one knew what would happen when I infused someone. The thought of infusing Mykayla was scary enough. Now I had Scott to think of as well.

"When Bian sets it up," I told her, and sent her off to shower.

She disappeared, and on cue, Bian came into the gym, her brow furrowed.

I leaped up from the bench.

"What's up, Pussycat?"

She gave me a distracted hug.

"What we have here, Round-eye, the Empire of Heaven would call a crisis," she said. "That is, danger at a point of change. I think my first sword sensei would have called it a flying wakizashi."

I had to laugh. "I know the wakizashi is the short sword the samurai used. I've no idea what a flying one is."

"My sensei would toss the wakizashi in the air, so that it was spinning really quickly. You had to grab it. If you caught the handle, all was well."

"And if you caught the blade you might lose a finger or two. I see. Tough sensei."

"Hmm." She looked lost in thought for a moment.

"House Lloyd? Sanctuary? You mean that's the flying wakizashi?"

She blinked and came back into focus.

"Yes. House Prowser told Skylur she has given up any claim to House Lloyd as a sub-House and waived her rights to Blood payment or feud with you."

She didn't seem that enthusiastic.

"That's good, right?"

"Maybe. You did note, didn't you, that Skylur handed the decision about infusing Scott to us, or more specifically to you. He's done the same with the request for sanctuary. Our choice."

Which meant it would be our responsibility as well.

I felt a chill down my back.

It was my choice to take House Lloyd or not, but again, Bian had said 'our choice', meaning she was going to back me regardless.

But Skylur was distancing himself. Not entirely—Athanate oaths didn't allow for that—but enough that, if things went wrong, it was up to us to fix.

"Another thing House Prowser mentioned," Bian said. "You remember down in LA, when she passed on details she'd been able to find—that Forsythe was going to sell Tamanny at a slave auction."

"Yeah? Something about information from a criminal and a court case up in Detroit."

"Well, apparently Amanda Lloyd was the main person responsible for bringing that criminal to justice."

"So I already owed her. She had to know that, and she didn't try to cash it in. Why?"

Bian grimaced. "We can ask. From the way House Prowser put it, I get the sense House Lloyd felt she couldn't use that because it would imply she'd done it for a return, and that would be unacceptable to her, unless everything else failed."

"But..." I stopped.

"Complex person," Bian said. "Strong principles. Interesting."

There was a lot to think about and no time. House Lloyd would be here this morning.

I should get back to Manassah, but I needed to hear if anything else had been said.

"Any more on Diana?"

Bian shrugged. "We've no way to call her. It was deliberately designed for Skylur to be my only point of contact. Oh, there are things that have been set up, like posting something coded on social media that asks them to call us, but that depends on them stopping and looking, not to mention deciding if it's secure enough. She'll be here soon anyway."

Bian didn't seem worried about Diana. I guess, given that she had Alice and Kaothos with her, I shouldn't be either. I just couldn't shake this feeling of foreboding.

It wasn't just a matter of her safety. I needed Diana here. I really didn't want to try infusing Scott without my Mentor on hand. I was relying on Diana to guide me through the process, using eukori. Diana was the *Kumemnon*, the eldest living Athanate. If anyone had a chance of ensuring things didn't go wrong, it was her.

"That situation in New York that got Skylur to change his plans..." Bian said. "Apparently, there's a large group of diazoun Houses who've been hiding out in Brooklyn and the rest of Long Island."

I frowned. New York State had been the territory of the Warders, prior to their dissolution at the last Assembly. The Warders had claimed their domain as independent, while secretly cooperating with Basilikos.

A strong and secure Athanate House might decide to allow one diazoun House to sit on the edge of its borders. Two, if they were very quiet and respectful. But a 'large group' of Houses? Inside their territory?

"The Warders let them?" I asked.

Bian laughed outright. "Not really. Apparently, the Warders just didn't have a clue what was going on. Naryn stopped there on the way to his new domain in Boston, and the leaders of the diazoun presented themselves to him, figuring they'd never get away with hiding in Skylur's territory."

"They got that right. Well, I guess they all give him their oaths or go to Ireland. Simple. Isn't it?"

The Irish Athanate had declared themselves independent from all Athanate politics and Ireland itself was open to any as a refuge.

Bian wrinkled her nose. "If it's so straightforward, then why is it urgent for Skylur to go there rather than making sure Diana gets here safely?"

Good point.

"Skylur didn't explain?"

Stupid question. Bian snorted.

"It's made you uneasy," I said.

"I'm uneasy about a lot of things," she replied. "The security situation once Diana gets here, the dangers of your infusion, the fact I have to rebuild my own House from scratch while holding Haven, not knowing where Tullah is hiding out and why. Yes, I'm concerned that Skylur isn't briefing me more fully on New York. But this morning's uneasiness is about this morning's business: House Lloyd."

"What specifically?"

"House Prowser was complimentary about House Lloyd and yet took no persuading to cheerfully give up any claim. Put yourself in her shoes."

I swallowed. Athanate politics were prickly, especially when it came to sub-Houses and associations. Given my own response to thinking of someone taking any of my House away, I would have understood if House Prowser had declared feud.

So why hadn't she?

Maybe I'd gotten lucky. Maybe I hadn't.

Bian smiled one of those not-smiles. "Maybe she knows something about House Lloyd that we don't."

"Has anyone ever told you you're paranoid, Pussycat?"

"Yeah, lots of people, but they're all dead, because they didn't see it coming."

Chapter 4

Fifteen minutes later, as Keith drove us home, I was even more restless, twitchy and uneasy. The hairs on the back of my neck were standing up, and I still couldn't figure out why.

Not that I didn't have an entire buffet of things to worry about. Diana and Kaothos. Tullah. My promise to infuse an elderly, desperately ill kin who wasn't even mine, and who would almost certainly die from it.

And to top it off, there was Mom's dinner tonight, and trying to figure out what to say to Kath.

Oddly, though, it didn't feel like any of those things. It didn't even feel like Bian's flying wakizashi—or her paranoia. It felt like sensing someone looking over my shoulder, combined with a deep certainty something somewhere had already gone wrong.

I hoped I could figure out what it was before it blindsided me.

My cell pinged, startling me. A text message from Yelena.

Landed at Centennial. On way home.
No problems. Tove is a mess.

Yippee. I added that to the worry buffet. Yesterday I'd sent Yelena to make good on a promise I'd made in LA. She'd flown down to California to pick up Tove Johansen, another victim of Forsythe, who'd helped us catch him.

It'd been a promise made in the heat of the moment without being thought through—that Tove could come live with us to get her life back in order.

Yeah. Not thought through: all part of the after-effects of going rogue.

I'd spent months on the brink, before sliding all the way down that slope out in New Mexico. Wild fits of impulsiveness had been one of the symptoms.

They'd brought me back from the abyss—Diana, Bian and my House. Now it was time for me to figure out how to make good on the promises I'd made, and fix things. If I could.

So much for a relaxing Christmas holiday with my House.

I texted back.

We have a situation.
Diazoun House inbound, seeking sanctuary. With complications.
Talk to Pia.

I glanced at the clock on the dash. In twelve hours and change Kath would be at my parents' house in Aurora, everyone ready for Christmas Eve festivities. I was determined to be there, beginning the process of letting Kath know that she could count on me again, that I would show up for her and make her a priority. But this morning had its own urgent problems. Amanda Lloyd had called before entering Colorado. Given the time I'd spent getting Bian's response, Keith and I might arrive back home just as House Lloyd turned up.

As I saw it, I had three choices: drag her and her kin out to Haven and turn the decision over to Bian; offer simple sanctuary; or take her oath as a sub-House.

My fangs throbbed.

Who am I trying to kid?

I'd already decided, unless something went very wrong in the next hour: if she was willing to give an oath, I would accept it.

Which meant I had to start thinking hard about how much metaphorical baggage House Lloyd was bringing with them. Hopefully not a lynch mob of northern Adepts, or something subtle that would poison Athanate politics.

For example, House Lloyd was diazoun, an outsider, so she wouldn't have contact numbers for the Athanate territories she'd passed through, and, as diazoun, possibly didn't think it mattered if she passed through another House's territory.

I had to address these potential problems, because if I accepted her as a sub-House, they became my problems.

I knew highways were open to Athanate, but what if they'd stopped somewhere for food?

Or Blood?

I called Pia.

"If they stayed on the highways and she didn't feed, there's no issue," Pia said.

"Otherwise?"

"Well, unofficially, no harm, no foul. A written apology citing urgency would cover it. If she caused a problem anywhere that reflects on the resident House, all bets are off. And none of that covers House Prowser's claims. What did Skylur say?"

"That Prowser's okay with it," I said. "And we have the go-ahead to accept Lloyd as a sub-House and try out my infusion on her kin, if we think we're up to it."

Pia was quiet. Like me, she was probably adding up everything that could go wrong. She was my *zamenik,* theoretically in charge of the process around infusing new Athanate in my House and then guiding them through crusis. Pia would be the new Athanate's Mentor, and her kin would help provide the training on feeding. Once I bit House Lloyd's kin, he *should* become mainly Pia's responsibility.

And all of which assumed my bite would work. I had accidentally and partially infused David and that worked out okay, but he'd been infused by Pia before me. No one knew what would happen with a completely new infusion, let alone the complicating factor of a kin who hadn't gone through rigorous preparation, and was about to die anyway.

"Okay, Boss. Well, it's your call then." There was a noise in the background, David's voice, and Pia spoke again. "David's talking to House Lloyd now. They say they'll be here in five."

"Make them comfortable in the sunroom and leave them alone." I glanced out of the car. We were just coming up to the Platte River crossing on 6th, and traffic was quiet. "I'll be there in ten."

The cell was beeping, telling me there was a second call.

My mother.

"Hi, Mom."

"Hello, Amber," she said. "This is a pleasant surprise. I was expecting to get that rude foreign woman again."

"Yelena?"

"That's the one. Always telling me I can't speak to you. Has she got the day off?"

No. She's bringing a drug-addicted prostitute from LA to live with us.

I decided I wouldn't share that news with Mom.

And, yes, Yelena probably was a bit abrupt with everyone calling me whenever she took charge of my cell. She'd told Felix, the Denver alpha werewolf, to 'fuck off' once. I hoped she hadn't said that to my mother.

"Hello?"

"Sorry, Mom. Distracted. Is everything okay for tonight?"

"I was calling to make sure you remembered."

She was calling to make sure I turned up. She knew I didn't forget things, but family life had been difficult recently.

"Wouldn't miss it for the world," I said.

"Did I mention Taylor will be here with Kathleen?" she said casually.

It was anything but a casual comment. I'd made my feelings about the pair of them clear. Kath's fiancé had certainly gone along with her craziness.

"Good," I said, tamping it all down. "I've been wanting to... rebuild bridges."

It sounded lame, and it was. I could barely keep the tremble from my voice.

In my head, I was back at Jen's ranch, high up in the Rockies, looking at the videocassettes that Special Agent Ingram had just given me. The cassettes that Forsythe used to record his rapes. There was one cassette that recorded my rape, neatly labeled with my initials. And one more. In the lighting, the letters written on the front were dark, like blood under UV.

KF.

Kathleen Farrell.

I'd run away. I'd left my sister behind in Denver with that monster. Now I had to repair the result.

"Amber? Are you all right?"

"Sorry," I said again. "Mom, I'm going to be busy right up until it's time to come over."

She wanted to talk. Wanted to talk to me alone about Kath, but she was so nervous I'd make up an excuse not to come, she let me go. We'd have to talk sometime. Tonight, I'd be there with Jen and Alex. Kath would be suspicious if Mom and I disappeared off together, so it wasn't going to be tonight.

I could guess some of the things Mom might want to talk about: Kath's alcoholism, her erratic behavior, or the split between us.

I'd intended the split to be permanent: the last words I'd said to Kath had been designed to hurt.

I had a little sister once, I'd said. *I loved her with all my heart.*

And I'd walked out of her house, not wanting to see her ever again.

Justified? She'd tried to have me committed to a maximum security mental institution as a violent psychopath.

But as we'd talked it around, my team and I had finally decided her behavior was driven by the rage at what Forsythe had done to her—driven so deep she'd probably deny it—and a sense that I'd abandoned her.

I *had* left. That had been part of my way of dealing with my rage, along with near-suicidal risk-taking and impulsiveness. But not being there didn't mean what Forsythe did to her was my fault, any more than it was my fault what he did to me.

And yet, and yet. *I ran away. If I'd gone straight to the police...*

Then his family's lawyers would have made it look as if I were to blame. They'd have claimed I was drunk. That I wanted it. That I encouraged Forsythe and his sick friends.

But *Kath* would have believed me, back then. Without question. With the result that she'd never have fallen for whatever line he'd come up with.

So in a way, it *was* my fault.

But I couldn't have these conversations with Mom. I couldn't have them with Kath either.

Not yet.

My team and I had agreed—first rebuild the relationship, then review how to fix the damage.

How high was this mountain?

And why couldn't I think it through without feeling like I was going to burst into tears?

"Boss, Julie and I..." Keith stuttered, breaking into my thoughts. "We understand how this Athanate thing works. Sort of. I mean..."

He was floundering even more than I just had with my mom. Not usual for Keith. I raised a brow at him.

I knew the whole situation *was* difficult. Keith and I had been an item back in Ops 4-10, before I'd been bitten and infused. By the next time I saw him, he was married to my friend Julie, also Ops 4-10. And not long after, I'd nearly gone rogue and bitten him. Now he was part of my House. *Mine.* As far as Athanate rules went, I could have his Blood anytime I wanted. And by Athanate customs, his body as well. Same for his wife's.

Yeah. Made it a little awkward.

But the only reason he'd bring it up now would be to distract me from my thoughts spiraling uselessly. Obviously, my ex-boyfriend still knew me well.

Which wasn't going to stop me from teasing him.

"Your body is probably safe from me," I said, putting on a husky voice as I ran a fingernail down his arm. "I don't think I can manage much more in the bed at the moment. Your Blood, now. Hmmm."

He twitched and I watched the pulse in his throat pick up.

Joking aside, it made my jaw throb in time.

Keith stayed silent.

"Thing is," I went on, "the Athanate rules say I *should* bite everyone in my House to ensure they're bound to me."

Keith swallowed.

"But you and Julie are Yelena's kin, and she's bound to me, so I don't *need* to check the pair of you out..."

"Copy that," he said quickly.

"Course, I might do it for fun anyway."

He knew I was teasing him then, and he laughed. It was good to hear that sound. There hadn't been much of it back in LA.

"Yelena *has* bitten you, hasn't she?"

I walked my fingers up to his collar and edged it aside. No scars.

"Yes, Boss."

He was blushing already. That was *so* cute.

"Just not on the throat," I said.

He coughed. "No."

Not on the wrist either. The bite scars generally healed to invisibility in a week, but there had been none on display. I could *smell* he and Julie had been bitten by Yelena, but I wasn't going to say that.

"None of my business, really, where she bites you," I said, thoughtfully. "Might be your upper arm. She bit me there once, you know."

He went a shade darker.

"But, as I understand it, for a real... *intimate* bite there are only three places. Throat, wrist and—"

"Okay! Okay. Yeah. She bit us both on the thigh. Happy now?"

I smiled. *Oh, yes.*

Julie would blush too, probably even more than Keith, when I brought it up. And I *was* going to bring it up.

In the meantime, he'd successfully distracted me and we were back at Manassah, Jen's mansion, where the car Yelena had been using was parked alongside a Volvo with Michigan plates, brick-red under the road dirt of a long trip. House Lloyd's car.

Thank you, Keith.

Now. Back to the present. Mind in gear.

In the next few minutes I had to decide about House Lloyd and infusing her kin, based, as ever, on my gut instincts, which were being inflamed by Athanate desires I still didn't completely control.

And to do that with a clear head, I had to put aside this constant, looking-over-my-shoulder feeling that I was missing important things that had *already* gone wrong.

Chapter 5

They were waiting in the sunroom as I'd asked.

Yelena went in first. She'd caught a serious case of Californian biker chic from the girls of the Belles werewolf pack in LA. She was dressed head to toe in mean, sprayed-on black leather, with sunglasses pushed up onto the top of her head.

I was right behind her in my cowboy boots, jeans and an oversized winter jacket I'd 'borrowed' from Alex.

Probably neither of us was exactly what House Lloyd expected to be wandering around in Jen's upscale mansion with its elegant decor.

With Yelena in front of me, looking like that, it kept attention focused away from me, and gave me a chance to develop some impressions of them.

A jumble of sensations hit me with an unexpected shock.

Their scent. My nose flared, caught the usual Athanate copper base but overlaid with something floral and appealing.

House Lloyd herself had a sensitive, intelligent face, dominated by gray eyes that were wary and watchful. A hand's width shorter than me in height, maybe five-five. Blonde hair pulled back severely. Trim. Wearing casual clothes that suited her, and still looked good, despite probably being what she'd lived in for a couple of days.

She projected a sense that she was all tightly buttoned down.

The two men standing with her must be the shaman Adepts. I eyed them with interest. Both Native American, tall and dark and breathtakingly good-looking. They were dressed almost identically in jeans and handmade buckskin jackets. One had his hair braided up in a complex knot that ran in a thick rope back over the top of his head. As I studied them, I could *feel* the power flowing off them, like silk brushing against my skin. Not threatening, just watchful.

An older kin, another handsome man in a dramatic Old World way, lay on the sofa. He was unconscious. That had to be Scott.

He didn't look good. I had the feeling we didn't have much time.

I crossed the room and knelt next to him. "How is he?" I asked House Lloyd. He was still breathing, but his pulse was faint.

She shook her head, biting her lip. It was the first crack in her buttoned-up armor. She was desperately afraid for her kin.

A sensation filtered through my Athanate senses of Amanda Lloyd's age. I knew many older Athanate, but they toned it down. House Lloyd didn't. She was older than Yelena, Pia or Bian. I wasn't good enough to make an accurate guess. Not *really* old. Not like Skylur or Diana. Younger than Naryn or House Prowser. But a helluva lot older than me.

And her kin was old, too. I wondered how many years—decades—they'd been together.

"He's getting steadily worse," she said. "That's why we drove through the night and I had to call ahead when I did." The same smooth voice as the telephone call, but in person I could taste the whip of adrenaline, and elethesine, the Athanate equivalent.

I'd forgotten to introduce myself.

"I'm Amber Farrell, House Farrell," I said.

"Amanda Lloyd." She seemed to collect herself and added: "House Lloyd."

She stepped forward for the formal Athanate greeting, and we met in the middle, taking hold of each other's forearms.

She was shivering. Black swiftly chased the gray from her eyes.

The primary purpose of the Athanate *laimia*, the greeting by kissing each other's necks, is to allow both parties to gauge the state and mood of the other. I hardly needed that; I could see Amanda Lloyd was barely under control.

I couldn't blame her. I could imagine what she was feeling—I remembered kneeling by Jen, feeling her life slipping away.

But that didn't mean she and her kin were a good fit for my House. I needed to know how to handle this—whether to merely offer sanctuary, or to take this even further.

I kissed her neck, breathing deeply.

Coppery, as all Athanate marques were. I concentrated on the remainder: Gardenia. Springtime peony. As Athanate marques went, House Lloyd had one of the most attractive I'd ever come across.

Laimia greetings aside, the Athanate marque had deeper purposes. The pleasure two Athanate got from their perception of each other's marques were indicative of the potential benefits from an exchange of Blood.

My instincts were telling me House Lloyd's Blood was strongly compatible and complementary to mine. A powerful addition to my House.

Mine.

My fangs started to ache with need. They wanted to erupt and claim her for my House *now.*

Unable to stop myself, I took a second deep breath.

Amazing.

Also rude in Athanate manners, but Amanda wasn't complaining; her reactions mirrored mine, right down to the surprise.

Thrills chased over my skin and I felt a shiver in response from Amanda.

The intensity of it scared me—I was being rushed into decisions by reactions that worked at some deep level I couldn't control.

I forced myself to step a little back, cleared my throat in embarrassment.

"Thrice welcome," I said in Athanate.

My voice was hoarse.

She blinked a couple of times and then she swallowed. Her face steeled.

I opened my mouth to suggest we sit, but she moved before I could: she knelt at my feet, taking my right hand in hers, her head bent.

"House Farrell." She spoke quietly, her voice ragged. "I beg sanctuary for us, but first I beg—"

I pulled her back up onto her feet.

"We don't do kneeling for petitions here," I said.

My Athanate was responding to it though. *Mine. Mine. Mine.* My whole jaw throbbed in sync.

Behind me, Pia entered the room. I could feel her caution reaching out to steady me but I knew, deep down, that my instincts had just picked a direction and sent me on a runaway train. Every worry or reservation in my head was being battered aside by a conviction that House Lloyd and her kin belonged in my House.

"Yes," I said quickly, before Amanda could start again, or Pia could interrupt. "I grant sanctuary. I will also attempt to infuse your kin, if you are willing to accept responsibility for the risk."

She blinked again, her tightly-bound eukori opening.

"Please," she said. "It's why we came all this way. It's our last hope."

My eukori touched on hers, and sensed the way she was linked tightly to Scott, synced deeply with his vital functions. I got the feeling it was the only thing keeping him alive. If nothing else convinced me, that would have: I'd been warned it was possible to die, bound to your kin that way.

I took a deep breath. Suddenly, I was the one trembling.

"I'll do everything I can," I said as I reached out to Scott with eukori and sensed his heartbeat, the flow of his Blood, the weak pulse of life throughout his body.

I was no healer like Bian, but I could tell he was slipping away, and he was pulling Amanda with him. It was madness, but I had to infuse Scott right now. Waiting for Diana or Bian to help would take too long.

Linking with me through her eukori, Pia sensed my decision.

"I'll guide you," Pia said. She was the only one of us that had real experience infusing humans to set off the change that would result in them becoming Athanate.

On the other hand, we were going to throw out every tried and tested procedure she'd used in House Altau and rely on a blind roll of the dice.

We quickly cleared the area around the sofa and I knelt down beside it. Yelena tore Scott's shirt away from his neck. Pia knelt at his head and put a hand on my shoulder.

I was a confused whirl of emotion inside. After getting so aroused at the thought of biting Amanda, I was still hungry for Blood. I had no practical idea of what was needed to infuse someone. No idea of what would happen to Scott if I did.

What if I killed him?

"Take it easy," whispered Pia. "Just bite first."

I licked his neck. The pulse was faint and erratic, but it still called to me.

Amanda's scent filled my nose, overlaid with Scott's own.

Despite all my fears, my fangs burst from my jaw with such sweet anticipation that I groaned.

I sank my fangs into his neck, and the pleasure burned through me as I *pulled* on his Blood, sending it coursing down the taryma, the network of Athanate channels in my throat.

Even with my senses blurred with pleasure, I could feel my glands releasing bio-agents, flooding back through the taryma and out of my fangs. Nothing yet to do with changing him to Athanate, just a reflex.

Pia began to stroke my back, calling my attention to her.

Eukori communicates sensations and emotions. It wasn't easy for Pia to communicate clearly how my Athanate glands were supposed to produce the right bio-agents for infusion. Not even the Athanate had words that described what I needed to do in a way that told me how to do it. But generations of Athanate had learned by being guided through eukori, and that was how we were doing it too.

Pia's sensations and memories flooded into me. It was like walking down a long, echoing corridor. Each sensation carried a shadow impression: another person's memory, which in turn was overlaid by another, fainter memory, and another, all eventually fading away into whispers and darkness. All of them tried to guide me, evoking a state that my body could interpret and act on.

Sensation poured in: I tasted unfamiliar flavors in my mouth; images like doves flying up into clear blue skies and pale green shoots rising from ashes; a deep stirring in my chest; the feel of cool breezes in the morning and a clockwork spring slowly tightening. More and more. Feelings I had no words for battered me.

Was it the right response? The right bio-agents? The right strength?

"That's good," Pia said quietly in my ear. "Relax. Of course you won't harm him: you've accepted him as part of your House."

I felt more bio-agents flooding exquisitely through my fangs.

Whatever it was I was doing, it was as pleasurable as taking Blood.

"Gently, gently," Pia kept saying. She and Amanda were syncing with me, anchoring me to my task, keeping the sensations from sweeping me away.

In a minute or two we could feel Scott's reaction as well, as the infusion slithered through his body, reaching everywhere, seeping into his heart, his liver, his brain.

Waking deeply buried subconscious parts of him.

He went into shock; his heart failed and violent shudders ripped through his body, dislodging my fangs from his neck.

Amanda frantically supported him through her connection with his body, forcing his heart to work again.

Yelena joined us, sharing the load.

It was like teetering on a high wire suspended over a crevasse. One moment we leaned too far one way, the next, the other.

I felt the Adepts get tied in through their connection with Amanda. They were blind about what needed to be done, but they brought raw strength, freely given, that Amanda could use.

"Steady. Calm." Pia's trembling voice was in contrast to her words, but we steadied. Slowly, we steadied.

And Scott's reactions subsided. His heart re-started on its own, even if it was beating erratically.

At Pia's insistence, I bit him again. His throat was bloody and without Pia's help I wouldn't have been able to focus. Together, we were more careful now; bio-agents trickled into his body, spaced out with long pauses.

I lost my sense of time.

Gradually, his immune defenses were turned into allies, until finally, his body was tricked into treating the bio-agents as part of itself and to stop fighting. Changes rippled through him, each small, but building on the previous.

An hour, maybe two.

I was aware distantly that my knees hurt, but it felt as if I were floating in a pool until eventually, Pia whispered: "Enough."

My fangs retracted. I carefully licked his neck clean, sealing his wounds before resting my head on his chest. I could hear the weak but steady thump of his heart. His flesh was hot to the touch.

There was a feel about him. Too subtle to pinpoint, but we'd started with a dying human kin and at some stage, although he was no longer fully human, neither did he seem so close to dying.

"Did it work?" I asked.

"Far too early to tell," Pia said. "His body went right to the edge of death. It's now definitely undergoing the fundamental change of crusis... but..."

An ordinary Athanate, an Aspirant, fit, healthy and well-prepared by his mentors, might spend weeks or months in crusis. Scott hadn't been ready in any sense. He hadn't been healthy. He hadn't been prepared. No one knew what my infusion would do, even if he had been prepared. Scott might die from the crusis, whether or not my infusion was quicker and less dangerous. Or he might turn into a hybrid Athanate-Were. Or a plain werewolf.

We couldn't tell.

"Thank you," Amanda said. Her eyes were red, and she still held his hand.

I was going to tell her to thank me when it worked, but I bit down on the words before they emerged. She knew.

"He's probably going to sleep for a day after that, and you should be with him," Pia said to Amanda. "If you need someone to help, or take over for a while, I'll be somewhere in the house, no more than a minute away."

Amanda smiled faintly in thanks.

I'd withdrawn my eukori a bit, but I could still feel the warmth of Pia's offer, and a similarly warm acceptance of Amanda from Yelena.

From Amanda, I got the sense of bone-deep exhaustion and gratitude.

But our eukoris had bound together as tightly as they could to carry Scott through the process of infusion and I knew, under that gratitude and the love she had for Scott, there was more. Something about her other kin, the two Adepts I had hurriedly given sanctuary to.

Her eyes met mine, and I could see her flinch with guilt.

Chapter 6

Still holding on to Scott's hand, Amanda cleared her throat and started hesitantly. "Thank you for infusing him. You said you accepted my plea for sanctuary, but we need to explain—"

"Actually, sanctuary is a short-term solution," I interrupted her.

She flinched again.

"Thank you. I understand. Still, I should explain about Flint and Kane."

"I'm not sure you do understand. There's no obligation on you for Scott's infusion. Sanctuary has no cost either; I can tell you that House Prowser does not intend to pursue you or me. Still, sanctuary is not a long-term option if you want to stay in America; Skylur won't allow it. You're free to go–Ireland accepts diazoun."

I paused. "But I hope you won't. What I'm asking is for you to stay and become a sub-House."

Pia murmured. "Boss, taking on a sub-House should really be a process with a careful, informed decision. Discussion on both sides."

My words were sounding more and more clumsy to my own ears, but I pushed on. "Amanda, I want you as part of my House."

Her eukori was still twinned with mine. She'd know I was speaking the truth. She also knew as well as Pia that this wasn't the way Athanate normally handled these things.

"I'm honored," she said. "And I mean no discourtesy, but… why? Just because our marques... Well, you hardly know us, and there's all the..." She stopped and gave a short, embarrassed laugh. "I got all worked up to make my case and here I am rather arguing against it."

My Athanate desire to take her into my extended House was based on the balance of intangible Athanate perceptions and needs. I hadn't really thought about whether I would like her as a *person*, but I found I did.

Still, *why* was a good question for her to ask, and one that Pia answered for me, having given up on cooling me down. "My mistress relies a lot on instincts. They have served us well," she admitted.

She was right. Things *had* worked out okay.

So far.

We'd probably been lucky once or twice. Maybe even a few times.

The trouble was, it wasn't really a strong argument for House Lloyd to agree to become a sub-House, if all she had been readying herself for was to argue for sanctuary.

Unless it was good enough for her.

"Yes," she said, and I felt a fierce pulse of Athanate joy course through me and come to rest in my jaw.

Her eyes flicked to her Adept kin and she ducked her head. "But I still need to be sure you understand all the problems."

"You've told me these young men are Adept outlaws in Michigan," I said, looking the two of them over. They *were* attractive, but that wasn't quite so distracting that I didn't get a hint of unease coming off them.

Interesting.

"About that..." Amanda said.

I waited.

One of the Adepts cleared his throat. "It may not be just in Michigan."

It was the whipcord-wiry one, with the rope of hair running over the top of his head.

"I'm Kane," he said. "Thing is, we may have pissed them off one time too many."

"I can imagine." I smiled. "Any of these pissed-off people in Colorado?"

All three exchanged glances.

"We're not sure," the bigger guy said. "I'm Flint. Thing is, we've always found that just moving out of the area makes them lose interest. We've really moved this time. Never been this far south before, but..."

"Somebody's taking an interest down here," Kane completed the sentence.

I wondered if they finished each other's sentences all the time, and if it was something to do with their power linking together, or if they just knew each other very well.

"Local Adepts, or someone from Michigan has followed you?" Yelena asked.

They shrugged.

"Impossible to tell," Flint said.

"More a case of that someone-looking-over-your-shoulder feeling," Kane said.

Which was pretty much exactly the feeling I had as well, over the last day or so.

Was that what I was picking up? Some kind of Adept vibe?

As far as I knew, local Adept communities didn't really interact much. If this vibe was just the Denver community, well, they already had a beef with me, so taking on House Lloyd probably wouldn't make it a lot worse. But if I was going to be facing Adept trouble not just from Denver, but from groups of Adepts in Michigan that cooperated with each other, that was a different level.

I let it sink in, tasted the thought.

It needed investigation, but it didn't change my mind.

"I accept there may be some trouble from the Adept communities. We'll discuss it as a House, along with everything else," I said firmly. "Later."

Amanda had gone very pale, but she nodded once, short and sharp.

I could taste her answer in her eukori.

Yesss.

"Diakon Vylkove, Zamenik Shirazi, attend," I said. I needed witnesses.

I reached out and took Amanda's hand.

She was still in shock, but her voice was strong. "I petition, for all House Lloyd, association and acceptance to the mantle of House Farrell. I offer our Blood, lives, loyalty and obedience to House Farrell. We will honor the obligations and responsibilities of the House and submit always to the absolute rule of the House."

The words echoed through me. Fangs threatened to erupt again, but I needed to speak clearly first. I hoped I remembered the responses right. "Under the authority invested in me as House Farrell, I accept House Lloyd within my mantle."

Letting my hand go, Amanda reached out to her two Adept kin. "I swear, on my Blood, my House will honor this association, and return oath for oath, faith for faith, Blood for Blood, life for life."

"I grant the rights and privileges within my gift."

"My Blood is yours," she said.

"It is done," I finished.

"So witnessed." Both Yelena and Pia spoke softly.

With our eukori open, I could feel the oaths bind themselves around our hearts.

"Mistress," Amanda said.

"It's Amber," I replied.

"Or Boss." Yelena laughed as she and Pia enjoyed hugging the Adepts in welcome.

I wanted to enjoy an exchange of Blood with Amanda right away, but Pia moved in quickly.

She carried the unconscious Scott and led Amanda away to a bedroom. I could hear her telling Amanda that her kin would sleep for at least a day, and the best thing for both of them would be to sleep beside him.

Leaving me disappointed on one hand and both elated and eager on the other.

New members for my House. A possible first infusion.

Amanda needed to time to recover, which meant I needed to keep her other kin out of her hair.

"So," I hissed amiably at the new Adept members of my House, backing them into a corner. "What are they after you for?"

"We're not interested in giving up our shamanic magic...." Flint said.

"Just because they think we might do something wrong sometime in the future," Kane completed.

"And you've done nothing wrong?" I pressed them.

They glanced at each other. "We've killed," Kane said. "In self-defense. Never an Adept, to our knowledge. Unlike them."

"Even they'll admit that our fatalities were in self-defense, but they still have rules about it we don't follow."

Tullah's mother, Mary, had fallen foul of something similar down here, so I wasn't surprised.

Yelena and I were watching them like hawks; I knew they were telling the truth.

"Fine. You can tell me more about it some other time. Today, there's something bothering me. I've been noticing it all day. It was there when Amanda's call woke me, and it's still there. That itchy feeling. Someone looking over my shoulder, as Kane said. I've felt it before, when a shaman used a working to call me from miles away, down in Albuquerque. What exactly do you boys think it is?"

"Could be a Calling," Kane said. "But we wouldn't feel that if it was only for you."

"Not necessarily shamanic," Flint said.

Apparently, this speaking alternately *was* a habit.

"Not necessarily only for you, either."

"Don't know it's Denver's community."

"Doesn't feel right for Denver. Or Denver alone."

"You can tell that?" I asked.

Flint shrugged. "It's more northern style. Feels more modern. Not what we expected here."

They could tell the difference between modern and traditional workings? Northern and southern? That might be useful; I wondered if they could teach it to me. I put that away to investigate later.

"So someone followed you down and maybe they're working with the Denver community?"

Kane shook his head. "Not followed. We'd have felt them. This is like... they flew here. Got ahead of us."

"On a magic carpet?" Yelena said, leaning on my shoulder and raking the guys over with her eyes.

Kane snorted. "Delta, more like."

"So, let's assume it some kind of broadcast meant for both you and me, and it involves the Michigan Adepts... it kinda leads to the question, how did they know you'd be here?" I looked at Yelena. "Tracker on the car?"

"No." Yelena shook her head. "Is checked."

Yet another question to store up for later.

"But whoever came down from Michigan, they're working together with Denver?" That was a key point for me. I didn't feel overly threatened by the Denver community alone. They knew I was connected with both the werewolf and Athanate communities and would hesitate to come after me. But both Denver and Michigan together? Something regrettable might happen.

Kane waggled his hand. "Difficult to say. Can't even be sure they're from Michigan. If we got closer to the source we could probably tell."

"Dangerous to get closer?"

Kane smirked.

"They got close to you in Michigan," Yelena said.

"And they still couldn't lay a hand on us. Four or five covens trying to work together," Flint said.

"And just getting in each other's way," Kane completed. "They all tried to trap us in House Prowser's estate and we still got out."

"Truth is, the more they bring, the more inefficient they are."

"You see, their style depends on everyone working seamlessly together."

"Yeah. No practice, no good."

Yelena grunted, unconvinced, but both of us knew the two of them weren't lying—boastful or not, they believed what they were saying.

"Can you do stealthy?" I asked. "Can we get closer without them knowing?"

Flint waggled his hand. "Yeah, there's a way to go undercover, but then we can't sense them either."

"But every so often, we could pop up and sneak a peek before they realize it," Kane said. "Then disappear again."

A vivid memory of my old Ops 4-10 instructor, Top, came to mind.

Reconnaissance is never wasted, he'd said to us.

The idea took root.

"Well, I don't like not knowing who or what we're facing, so let's go scout," I said. "Find out a little more about what we're up against. I bet clever boys like you can do magical direction finding, can't you?"

Chapter 7

"Is stupid."

Yelena's blunt assessment of my plan for scouting seemed to gather weight as she pulled over and stopped the car at Kane's quiet request.

I was still undecided.

Flint and Kane had seemed as good as their boasts.

They put us into 'stealth mode' before we left Manassah, and that over-the-shoulder, being watched feeling had evaporated. We'd taken a tablet with a streetmap, driven south for ten minutes and then they'd cautiously uncloaked. As soon as I started to feel the sensation of being watched again, they'd cut it off.

Cloaked again, we'd gone west to Lakewood and repeated. Then north to Arvada, east to Park Hill, south to LoDo, and finally, at the centre of the spiral, we were now in Denver's RiNo area—River North.

People said that RiNo was Denver's next big up-and-coming place, as the rebuilding in LoDo came to an end. It was being marketed as the 'Art District' by the developers. I thought of it as the lost bit between the Coors Field ball park and the Blue Moon brewery, nestling in the armpit made by the intersection of I-25 and I-70. It used to be a lot of dust, scruff and old warehouses with the South Platte River and the railway yards running through it.

I had to admit, things had moved on since I'd last been this way. Long, low commercial buildings had pushed out the scruff, and pastel-colored apartment buildings had sprung up like mushrooms.

The thing was, part of whatever had been bugging me all day had gotten worse. Not the over-the-shoulder feeling, but the sense something was going wrong.

I looked around.

Snow was blowing in from the northwest, and streamers of it slithered down from the tops of the buildings, waving like white silk ribbons in the wind.

Yelena raised an eyebrow at Kane for further clarification, but it was Flint who spoke.

"Somewhere here," he said, waving a hand to indicate the block. "Probably easier to walk now."

"We're a lot closer, according to your instructions," I said, "but you still can't get a fix on who they are or where they are without walking around?"

Kane scratched his head. "It's weird. It's like they aren't even paying attention. It comes and goes."

"Like there's only a couple of them?" Flint said. "Fading in and out, being distracted. They're not local but it doesn't really feel like Michigan Adepts either."

"How dangerous?" I asked.

Flint's mouth twitched. "A couple of them, not even paying attention? Not at all."

Tullah's mother, Mary, had once told me sensing magic energy was like being on a huge trampoline. You could feel other users around you, especially powerful users. Two of them, fading in and out, didn't sound that dangerous.

Maybe if I still had Hana, my wolf spirit guide, I'd feel more. But she had gone, along with Tara.

It stabbed at me, that loss.

I still didn't know exactly what had happened to me back in that fight against the Taos Adepts in New Mexico, that caused Tara, my stillborn twin sister's spirit, and Hana, my wolf spirit guide, to leave me.

I was hoping that Tullah and Kaothos would be able to tell me—to help me find them again. But at the moment, I was bereft, depending on secondhand information from Flint and Kane.

The buzz I'd felt back at Manassah after infusing Scott had leaked away, leaving me feeling tired and depressed.

I mustered my energy and focused as best I could.

Yelena was looking at me for the go-ahead.

Flint and Kane seemed cautious, but not at all concerned, so I nodded and we got out.

"Two minutes and then we go home," I said.

The car doors closing sounded very loud. It was quiet, even given that it was Christmas Eve. There was no one else on this road. No moving cars, no pedestrians. Strange.

My unease was growing, but I still felt almost compelled to go forward. Whether it was the Calling or my instincts, I didn't know anymore.

We were parked in front of a new building which advertised itself as Schown Apartments—*A community of UPSCALE comfortable homes—HURRY!—LAST FEW still available.*

Popular or not, with its hi-tech aluminum columns and bold glass front, the Schown building looked as if it was designed for summer. It gave the impression it didn't like the snow much.

Kane and Flint turned left and walked slowly.

Yelena and I followed for about fifteen paces before I felt something change, as if my itch suddenly became a prickling over all my skin.

Not good.

We all felt it. Flint and Kane turned around, suddenly worried.

I looked back.

A shroud of snow billowed around the Schown building, so all that was visible was the gleaming top of the facade. The entrance, the sidewalk and our car had disappeared in a fine white mist.

Darkness moved where the sidewalk was, floating like a mirage, then resolving into a figure walking toward us.

A woman. Pale. Hair like ice. Even at this distance I could tell she had startling blue eyes. She was dressed in black, with an open leather duster and thin gloves, entirely unsuitable for the weather.

"Oh—" Kane started.

"Crap," Flint finished.

There was a feeling in my head like I was breathing in cold smoke. The Adept version of eukori. I clamped down, imagining shiny metal shields around my head. The soft awareness of Yelena and my two Adepts behind me chopped off abruptly.

The woman walked like Rita, the were-cougar, did—all slink and dangerous purpose. She came to a stop in front of me.

"Amber Farrell, House Farrell, I believe." Her voice was sharp, cutting the sentences up into isolated, breathy puffs. "I am Gwendolyn Enkeliekki, Hecate of the North."

"Alias Wendy Witch," Kane muttered. "Leader of the Michigan and Ontario Adepts."

Her cold lips stretched. I couldn't call it a smile exactly, but if she was upset by the nickname, she gave no hint. Her eyes never left mine. Their blue was deep and sharp, like cold fire. Electric neon.

"Pleased to meet you..." I said. *Hecate*? A title of some kind. I wasn't even going to try her surname. "Gwendolyn? Call me Amber."

The prickling intensified.

This wasn't a couple of Adepts fading in and out. This was raw power. Somehow, they'd disguised their strength, luring us down here by seeming weak and inept.

Even though I'd known we were being *Called,* I'd underestimated how much I was affected by it.

This was a trap—a clever, insidious trap.

I was aware of Yelena beside me, balancing on the balls of her feet. Flint and Kane pressing forward as if to protect me, the feel of defenses from them sliding around us like shutters. The wind buffeting all of us, wrapping us in a whirl of snow, isolating us in a white vortex until it seemed as if the whole world was nothing but the five of us.

The Hecate had turned up the collar of her duster, her only concession to the cold. It flapped against her cheek like a captive bird's wing.

Her lips curved up. That *was* a smile.

Hairs stood up on the back of my neck.

"Shit—" That was Kane.

My thoughts exactly. She was doing *something*. I reached out, but tripped.

We *all* tripped, and fell into the icy heart of a blizzard.

Chapter 8

I was lying in the dirt. I must have hit my head. Badly. Passed out.

I shook myself and stood up. No dizziness.

Also no Denver. No roads and buildings. No snow.

Strong, clear sunlight. Warm wind. Flat, dry scrubland, dropping away westwards to a barely visible river.

What the hell?

Yelena was standing next to me, blinking. She was dressed in old-time buckskin, her hair in braids, with a turquoise bead choker around her neck and moccasins on her feet.

From the way she was looking at me, I was dressed the same.

I almost wanted to laugh, except for the seriousness of what had just happened.

What the hell didn't seem strong enough.

There was no sign of the others.

"Flint? Kane?" I yelled.

A glossy raven floated down out of the impossibly blue sky and landed on my shoulder.

Flint. The Raven. I just knew it was him. I could sense him now.

Kane is near the river, watching her.

...and I could hear him, in my head.

"What the hell happened? Where are we?"

She tricked us. The raven shuffled its weight from side to side. *She has the elite team of her coven here.*

"Where?"

I looked around. There was no one else.

The raven danced some more.

Not here, exactly. In Denver, near where we were. We're physically here, they're physically there, but the worlds are spirit-close. I think they're in that apartment building we passed, shielding themselves somehow. Showing just enough of themselves to lure us down there.

"So where are we?"

This is the spirit world, as she has drawn it. A Denver without people. The same place, just... shifted a bit.

"In summer."

The bird gave a little half-flap of wings, like a shrug, like I needed to concentrate on important things.

"Can we get back?"

Yesss.

It wasn't the most confident of replies.

"Means no?" Yelena said. She was picking up stones. That was a good idea. Low tech but very unpleasant to be hit by a heavy, well-thrown stone. "Means Hecate-bitch can keep us here? Where is she?"

The raven cawed and flapped.

As soon as one of the coven falters, we can get back, he said. *Or we can undermine her channeling of the energy that weaves the spirit world here and pulls us into it. Until then...*

He faltered.

"What?"

This weave is hers. While she and her coven are fresh, and we're here, she's really powerful. She could have killed us all, the moment we got here. Still could, maybe. And...

"And what?"

We've figured out what must have happened. Up in Michigan, Wendy had the covens surround House Prowser's mansion, waiting for Prowser to hand Kane and me over. Amanda drove out the front with Scott while we sneaked out the back way. We didn't think Wendy knew that we'd become Amanda's kin, so when Wendy asked where Amanda was going, she just told her. Didn't seem any reason not to.

Which cleared up one mystery. Gwendolyn hadn't needed to follow them. She'd flown down, with her coven, in whatever comfort you could get on a short-haul airplane, arranged for an apartment and waited for House Lloyd to arrive. Then lured us here.

My stomach sank.

"Hecate-bitch is two steps ahead of you," Yelena said.

Not the real point, though. If she knew we were kin, she could have caught us in Michigan by taking Amanda hostage. And if she's gotten this powerful, she could have killed us there. Or she could have killed us here when she brought us here, into the spirit world.

"So... she hasn't killed us. Yet." I thought about it.

Did it mean she *didn't* want us dead?

Or she wanted to play with us a bit first?

I didn't voice that thought.

"Why?" I asked instead.

Kane and I think she wants to be here in Denver for some reason, and she wants to talk to you, House Farrell, more than she wants to kill us.

"And so we should see what she wants?"

The raven bobbed its head.

I had the feeling he was hugely embarrassed to have been tricked and kinda surprised to be alive. And very curious, which was a good thing, sometimes.

I sighed, trying to pretend this whole thing hadn't scared me. "Point me in the right direction. And you..."

The raven cocked his head, one beady eye fixed on me.

"Crap on my shoulder and I'll make a headdress out of you."

Kane was halfway to the river bank. His coyote fur was tan and orange, which matched the ground. He was almost invisible until he stood and gave himself a dusty shake.

She's sitting down beside the river, he said. *Just waiting.*

"Well, if she wants to talk, let's go talk." I kept my voice down. "But if you two can manage to get us out of here, I'd rather talk to her on my ground."

Understood, Flint said. *But...*

She may not hear us speaking like this, but anything you say aloud in the area, she'll be able to hear, Kane added.

"Great."

I walked on to where the ground dropped and became uneven. The river in spate had eroded the banks, leaving a margin of naked rocks and channels of collapsed earth.

This wasn't some half-imagined virtual world. This Colorado was, for want of a better description, *real*. Just without the city and the people.

The Hecate was close to the flowing water, sitting cross-legged, with her back propped against a large boulder, hands folded in her lap. She looked comfortable, her whole body relaxed. Not as if she was about to turn me into a toad and squash me.

I climbed down cautiously and sat opposite her, with Yelena on my right. Flint remained on my shoulder. Kane sat between Yelena and me, tongue hanging out and attention focused on the Hecate.

She was still wearing the black leather duster. It seemed she'd been waiting for us to join her.

As I watched, her whole appearance changed. Her skin became darker, her hair became light brown and wavy. The eyes warmed to hazel instead of that chilling, bottomless blue.

I'd seen werewolves' faces *shift* between human and wolf, and if they could do it, I guessed an Adept could as well.

Why would she do it, though?

The new face, although almost completely the same, was softer, less stiff. More... *human* somehow.

I imagined she thought it made her less frightening.

She was wrong. Whatever she looked like, there was an aura of eerie threat coming off her.

I'd been too dazed by being kidnapped so suddenly to be really scared, yet, but watching her change, watching her sitting so completely relaxed and in control made me realize how powerless I was here, even with a pair of Adepts and Yelena.

And in contrast, how powerful she was.

Not a good idea to let her realize how scared I was.

"We change clothes or bodies and you just change your face?" I asked.

Her lips thinned, slightly lopsided.

"This is just me, as I am, without the Aspect of my spirit guide," she replied. "As for your clothes, this substantiation of the spirit world is not purely mine. As I drew you in, three of you interacted with it, modified it a little to include some of you. What other forms would Raven and Coyote take but their own? And you, it appears, subconsciously mix your Native American heritage with your expectation of the spirit world."

Her voice remained the same, very quiet and precise.

"I've never been here before," I said. "I have no expectation."

"Not here exactly." She pursed her lips briefly again. "But I understand you've called up a substantiation of your own while helping the Were cubs who had trouble shifting. I'm impressed, by the way."

I shook my head to clear the memories she called up, of dancing through clouds of smoke from bonfires to the rhythm of stamping feet. That wasn't like this.

"I doubt I would magic our pistols away," I said.

"No. But things like that generally don't exist here." She paused. No fidgeting, no movement, other than her face. Complete, concentrated stillness. Disturbing. "And as for your valiant Diakon, with rocks in her pocket, I should point out I wouldn't even need to duck. I have you where I want you, and you cannot attack me here."

I heard the hiss of exasperated breath from Yelena, but she didn't unload the rocks. The Hecate claiming something wasn't the same thing as it being true.

"You've given sanctuary to House Lloyd, haven't you?" she said. "So you all come as a package now."

Her eyes flicked from Raven to Coyote.

"Yes. I've taken House Lloyd as a sub-House, which means that they're all under my protection, and therefore also under the protection of House Altau."

I needed to get that in. Flint and Kane seemed to think she could kill me here with no more effort than a blink of her eyes, but she wouldn't, if she made an enemy of Skylur by doing that.

I hoped.

Wind blew strands of hair across her face. She ignored them. Her eyes returned to hold mine.

"And when you took House Lloyd's oath, did she tell you her kin were under sentence of death?" she asked.

"Yes."

"They have explained I could have killed you all when I brought you here?"

"Which would have started a war with the Athanate."

"Maybe." Her nose flared. "Maybe not."

She didn't seem concerned about the thought of a war with the Athanate, which was chilling in itself. Or just maybe she regarded it as unlikely to happen. If all four of us disappeared without trace, what was Skylur going to do? Start a war with the Adepts in full view of humanity? On the suspicion some Adepts might have killed us?

The Athanate codes of behavior were written up in the Agiagraphos, the closest thing to a holy book the Athanate had. But in this instance, there were two rules that applied. One rule demanded that the responsibility for protection of members of a House was shared all the way up the chain of association. House Farrell was a sub-House of Altau, so Skylur was responsible for the safety of my House members as much as I was, and Skylur could command the entire Athanate population of North America.

But... the rule that overrode all other rules in the Agiagraphos was to hide our presence from humanity. Skylur was going to break that rule, but he wanted to break it when *he* judged the time was right, not when one of his inexperienced sub-Houses got caught up with Adepts who had their own rules and concerns.

Emergence was more important to the paranormal community than me and my House.

On the other hand, Skylur had a long memory. I was sure once Emergence was out of the way, questions would be asked and Athanate honor satisfied. Not that it would be much comfort to me if I was dead.

She surprised me with her next comment. "You don't approve."

What?

I scrabbled to work out what she meant. "You mean I don't approve of it being a death sentence for Adepts not joining in your covens? No, I don't."

"I see. Tell me, House Farrell, what the Athanate do with rogues?"

Given I had been a rogue, I really didn't want to talk about this, but I answered with the standard response that Athanate give.

"We kill them," I said.

"Why do you kill them? Why is it justified?"

I wanted to say to protect innocent humans, but I knew that was false.

"They threaten our existence."

"Yes. Your Agiagraphos laws. A rogue could go on a spree, killing humans indiscriminately, and leading humanity to discover the Athanate. Leading to an almost certain disaster for the rest of the Athanate." She sighed and looked upwards. "So it's justified to kill rogue Athanate."

"Make your point."

"You accept the justification for your treatment of rogue Athanate. Given you're a hybrid Were, I imagine you probably accept the same treatment of rogue Were. Yet, you don't accept that Adepts might have similar burdens and responsibilities put on them."

Damn. It was a good argument.

"Okay. But not in all cases, and not in this case. These guys aren't rogue. They're..."

I was going to say that Kane and Flint were the Adept equivalent of diazoun, that they were simply unaffiliated. But that was a trap, because Skylur had decreed that there were no diazoun allowed in North America anymore. And in the end, he'd enforce *that* the same way he had to enforce the laws on rogues. The Hecate could have some similar argument.

I changed tack. "They're not going around killing bystanders, like rogue Athanate or Were would."

"A valid point, if the purpose of the laws were to protect humans, but it's not, it's to protect the paranormal community."

Arguing with the Hecate felt like I was in quicksand. I had to admit, to myself, she was right. I'd accepted the laws about rogues with false justifications that made my human side happier.

Not only was she winning the argument, she was seriously unsettling me. She still hadn't stirred; apart from her face, she might have been a statue. *Everyone* twitches and gestures. As a human, I'd learned to read the body's movements and posture, which give me an insight into that person's thinking. Hell, I *depended* on those skills playing poker in the army. And now, as an Athanate, I could hear her heart beat, I could smell her stress levels, I could sense the changes in temperature of her body, but I was getting none of the information I depended on when dealing with people.

Her heartbeat was slow and regular, her temperature even, her bio-signs neutral.

It was *really* unsettling.

Worse, I suspected she knew it.

"We nullify or kill wild talent for the same reasons you kill rogue Athanate and Were," she went on. "An untrained or insane Adept has far greater potential to reveal the existence of the paranormal community, and is potentially far more dangerous to humanity than any single Athanate or Were."

"And yet, these two haven't offended, that I'm aware of," I said, hoping desperately that was true. I really should have interrogated them more before taking them on reconnaissance.

"Not excessively. Lucky for them. But in any event," she said, "I'm not here to discuss the politics of how Adepts govern themselves. Not in this instance anyway. Your House Adepts are safe from *me*, now that the Athanate rules about revealing paranormals to humanity apply to them. I'm not sure they thought this through yet, but they should start to worry about *you*."

Damn.

Again, she had a good point. If Flint or Kane behaved in a way that threatened to expose the Athanate, it had become my problem to deal with. Up to and including killing them.

Flint shuffled on my shoulder and Kane's head dipped.

I changed tack again. "You seem to know a great deal about me and about Athanate business. I know nothing about you. Who are you? Who do you represent? If you say they're safe from attacks by you, does that extend to the Denver community?"

"That's all one question. Or two, maybe. I won't answer for the Denver community, yet. I represent the Northern Adept League, what you'd think of as an association of covens in Canada, Alaska, the Great Lake states and eastern states of the US down as far as New Jersey." She paused and her hazel eyes sharpened until I could see the icy blue showing again. "You know nothing about us because we have chosen, until now, that the Athanate should know nothing."

The hairs on the back of my neck stood on end.

Hell, I have to warn Skylur. A whole Adept association right under his nose that we know nothing about?

"So what's changed?" I shrugged like it was no big thing. "All of a sudden you're going to talk to us? And you come to me?"

"Oh, yes. Very specifically to you. And here, in Denver. Not because we think Altau is here, but because *this* is where Diana and the dragon will return."

Shit! How the hell does she know anything about Kaothos?

"That's why I'm here. You and Diana may have fooled the Empire, Amber, but you haven't fooled us. The point is, you have no idea what you're doing and we *need* to meet with the dragon before..."

Beside me, Kane suddenly shivered and rocked backward and forward. His paws planted themselves on my thigh and Yelena's. I recognized the skin prickling. My Adepts were about to try to get us out.

Now.

The sensation was like diving into water from a height—a rush, felt over my whole body, my eyes blurring, pressure, disorientation and then suddenly it all cleared.

We were sitting on the bank of the South Platte, in the snow. In our normal clothes. Kane and Flint in their human bodies. Denver skyline behind us.

I leaped up. I could feel the weight of my HK in my holster, but I had a horrible thought that this might be *another* Denver. One that only looked the same.

"You got us back? This is home?"

"Yes." Flint looked pale. Whatever he'd done had taken a toll.

Beside us, just a pace or two away, air seemed to boil.

Yelena and I drew our weapons.

The Hecate appeared as we'd first seen her—the shock of white hair and those cold, cold blue eyes. Except this time she sort of ended at about the waist. Her legs were visible, but faded into a blurred shadow.

"Well done," she said. "I congratulate you on the acquisition of a powerful pair of Adepts, Amber. May you never regret it."

"Thank you, I guess."

Would a bullet kill her, if she attacks? Is she even there, or is it just a projection?

But she hadn't directly threatened me. I kept the HK Mk 23 pointed at the ground.

The Hecate not overtly threatening and even wishing my House well somehow scared me more than if she'd spat curses.

"I was nearly finished with you for today anyway. There's probably only so much you can take in at once. I have two last things for you to think about," she said, and her eyes seemed to glow. "First, I *demand* to meet the dragon, and I can back up my demands, so prepare Diana when she arrives. Second, you should know in the human myths, there are sometimes glimpses of the truth. Glimpses even of the nature of Adepts and Athanate and Were. And of dragons."

I gave a hum. More *I hear you* than actual agreement.

"Do you know the background of the name Dracula?"

That caught me by surprise. I laughed nervously.

"Yes. Dracul means *dragon.* Dracula means *child of the dragon.*"

"Indeed. There it is in the old Athanate, and filtered through the millennia into modern Romanian. I bet the dragon told you herself."

I nodded, wondering if this apparition could actually see me.

She could, apparently. "I also bet she didn't tell you the root of the word."

I frowned. "No."

"The oldest word, from which the others descend, is *drac.*" She faded, and her last words whispered through the air as she disappeared entirely. "And *drac* means *devil.*"

Chapter 9

I stared at the place where she had disappeared. With the Denver Adepts, I'd known what I was dealing with. This Hecate was a whole different ball game, and she seemed perfectly capable of enforcing her *demands.*

How had she known about Diana and Kaothos?

"Sorry," Flint said, breaking into my thoughts. "Our fault. She really caught us off guard."

"We need to move away," Kane said, helping his fellow Adept to his feet. "This is all in her zone."

We trotted back to where we'd left the car, increasingly nervous as we approached the Schown Apartments. There were people around now, cars, normal things. No witches appeared out of sudden snow clouds.

"What's the time?" I asked as we got in.

I had a clock in my head I could usually rely on, but being hauled off into the spirit world by the Hecate's coven had screwed with it. My head was telling me it was early evening, but it felt wrong.

Early evening would be another *major* disaster of a completely different type. It would mean I was late for Mom's dinner.

"It's five," Yelena said. "It feels wrong, no?"

"Time passes differently in the spirit world," Kane said. "Sometimes really differently. We need to check what day it is."

"Oh, God, no."

My cell said it was still today, but his comment spooked me.

Please, I'm not a day late for Mom's party. Please, please, please.

I dialed home.

Alex answered. "You okay?"

"Yeah. What day is it?"

"Same day it was a couple hours ago. You *sure* you're okay?"

"I'll explain later. We're on our way back."

Great. He probably thought I'd gotten a concussion or something. I could just see his expression when I told him I'd been transported to fairyland.

Traffic was light and Yelena was driving, leaving me to puzzle over what the Hecate had said.

Kaothos was a friend. A strange kind of friend to have, but still. Not a devil.

So what did the Hecate mean by that? And if she believed Kaothos was a devil, why was she so eager to speak with her?

Just as urgent, I needed another conversation with Skylur and I was not looking forward to telling him that there was a huge association of Adepts who'd been sitting quietly right under his nose.

Well, as I couldn't speak directly to him yet, I guessed that was Bian's problem.

Mine was to get Kaothos and Tullah back together before the Hecate had time to get any more involved.

I called David.

"Yes, Boss?"

"You still get occasional texts or calls from Matt?"

"Yeah. He's still in hiding I guess, and he doesn't trust they can't backtrack him, but he'll send something now and then."

Matt was the expert at untraceable. If he was worried about being tracked, I wasn't going to ignore that, but I needed to be sure about Tullah. That itchy feeling hadn't gone away.

"You have someplace you can put a text for him to see?"

"Yes."

"Put up that the boss needs to speak to her assistant and wants her back, ASAP."

"Okay."

"Gotta go."

Jen was calling. I switched to her.

"What's this about not knowing which day it is? You do remember—"

"We're off to my mom's. Yes. It was just some Adept weirdness. I'll explain later."

"Okay," she said. "I'm really calling to warn you Bian's here. I've tried explaining that we're due to go out, but she wants to know what's happening."

Good.

"I get to tell you both at the same time."

"Hmm. Going to happen while we're getting dressed then," she drawled. "We are not going to be late for this one, honey."

I swallowed.

My wife, my husband and I would be naked, in the same room as Bian. Who was my husband's one-time lover and who had, several times, told me *and* shown me, she was eager to get in my pants too. This was shaping up to be... awkward.

"Bian, darling, would you help me with the zipper, please?"

Jen was taking Bian's presence in her stride.

I guessed I was too wrapped up in talking about what had happened to be embarrassed.

Alex was suspiciously worried about removing the towel he was wearing like a kilt. And it didn't lie exactly flat.

Bian was... Bian. One moment she'd be all business, clarifying something I'd said, and the next she'd be casting smoldering looks at one of us, or even all three at the same time.

"Amber, your hair's still wet!" Jen said. "Could you help her, Bian? And which of these lipsticks do you recommend for tonight?"

Alex escaped back to the bathroom to put on his underwear. Bian picked a lipstick and then started on my hair.

It wasn't that wet. Barely a couple of minutes later Bian put the drier down, and started to brush.

I continued talking.

"If the Northern Adept League stretches from the Lakes down to New Jersey, then there should be some in New York," I said. "Skylur might be able to learn a bit more about them there."

Bian nodded. "Believe me, I'll make the point to him when I call later."

She stopped brushing my hair and rested her hands on my bare shoulders.

I tensed, expecting some of Bian's questionable humor, such as kissing me in front of Jen and Alex, but she didn't.

Her voice was serious: "Tell me again the Hecate's exact words about why she was here."

"She said: *Here, in Denver. Not because we think Altau is here, but because this is where Diana and the dragon will return.*"

"So she knows that Diana and Kaothos aren't dead, and that we put on a smoke and mirrors show for the Empire. *And* that Diana's coming back here. *And* she knows Skylur isn't going to be here. That's a lot of inside knowledge, Round-eye. A lot of very up-to-date inside knowledge. For example, Skylur took the decision to go straight to New York yesterday."

"Well, they're obviously powerful, this league," I said.

"More powerful than the Empire's Adepts? Really? Or do they just have better intelligence?"

I blinked.

"The gray pants, Alex, they show off your ass better," she said over her shoulder.

Jen laughed and handed Alex the gray pants. He put them on.

Wise choice; Bian was right.

I got dressed as I thought through what she was saying. I knew Bian well enough to follow which way her mind was working on the Adept league, ignoring the distraction about Alex's ass.

"Have I mentioned recently that you're paranoid, Pussycat?" I said.

"This morning, in fact. Come on, tell me what I'm thinking."

I sighed. "There is one person who is not Athanate, and not in this room, who knew exactly what was going on, and why, and where. The only person, apart from Diana, who knew Skylur was going to New York even before you did."

"Precisely. See? This paranoia is catching."

"I know you don't like her. You've always had reservations about Alice Emerson. I remember you telling me she deserved to get thrown off the *Mayflower*."

"So I've always been right. You blaming me for that?"

I had no answer. *I* liked Alice Emerson. And Alice was the Adept responsible for the magical shields that were hiding Diana and Kaothos from the Empire. My gut said she wasn't working against us, but that wasn't the same as not having any conflict of loyalty. And surely Skylur had bound her?

"Oh," I said, remembering something else. "Alice was working with the Warders before. Skylur sort of adopted her when they were expelled after the Assembly at Haven."

"You're getting there, Round-eye."

"The Warders' mantle was New York. It's a reasonable guess that's where Alice is from. Which would make it likely Alice is from the League, or has ties to them."

"You get your paranoia gold star." Bian clapped her hands.

"And we will lose all gold stars if we don't get out the door now," Jen interrupted.

"But we haven't talked about what the Hecate said about Kaothos—"

"Not my monkey. That's *your* domain," Bian said, urging me out of the bedroom. "First, you've got to get Tullah back, then deal with the Hecate. My domain is security and paranoia, and I have my hands full."

She demonstrated with Alex's ass, which he totally enjoyed, the traitor.

Chapter 10

My heart was in my mouth as I walked into my mom's house, ducking the bright and blinking Christmas decorations. My stepfather, John, had gone overboard to make it cheerful, but it wasn't working on me yet.

Tonight would be my first step to getting back into a relationship with my sister. And the first real opportunity for my mother and stepfather to meet Alex and Jen together.

I would have to explain the rings we wore, and that I regarded Alex and Jen as my husband and wife, and no, I wasn't changing to any polygamous faith, so there was no likelihood of a church service.

Heaven help me. Give me a weapon and people shooting at me every time.

To say the evening started slowly would be an understatement.

We came bearing gifts which Jen and Alex had somehow found time to buy, probably during my lost hours in fairyland. They went into a pile in the corner of the hall. Mom's rules: strictly to be opened after dinner. After depositing them and leaving our coats, we went into the living room. We were standing because there weren't enough seats.

John offered us soft drinks and Kath stared at the floor, knowing we were going without alcohol because of her. The family knew. I wanted to say something. Whatever she'd done, she was my little sister, and it hurt to see her hurting.

But the five paces between us felt like five miles.

Baby steps, Alex and Jen and I had agreed.

Mom saw the rings immediately, of course. Her gaze shot from my hand to Alex's, and her eyes widened in delight. Then she looked at Jen's hand. Her face fell and she quickly made an excuse about the sauce needing attention and rushed out to the kitchen.

Great start. Freaking A.

Well, it was bound to be a shock, even though she knew I was in a relationship with both of them. I just hoped she could manage to adjust.

I turned my attention to the others.

I hadn't actively disliked Taylor when I first met him; he'd just seemed a bit bloodless. Strange description for an Athanate to use, but it fit. That day last fall, talking about their engagement, he hadn't said he was in love with Kath, but that they'd become 'very close'. It just sounded so wrong to me, so weak, so... bloodless. Yet here he was, committing career suicide by taking time off to look after her.

Maybe I'd been too quick to judge.

He turned out to be the easiest to get talking and break the ice before we suffocated: Jen was a patron of the Denver ballet and Taylor loved the ballet. He was a little in awe of Jen. Kath stayed beside him and Jen spoke easily to both of them, talking about seeing the ballet in New York, comparing it to our own in Denver.

John succumbed next. We'd arrived in my Audi today, but John knew about Alex's little old Ford: *the* Mustang; a '69 Boss in Black Jade. They got talking about all the problems of keeping a classic in its original glory.

It *was* a cool car.

Mom came back from the kitchen, eyes a little shiny.

"Lovely rings, Amber," she said quietly, and then beamed a big smile around the room. "I think we're ready. Let's sit at the table. Kath, would you give me a hand, please?"

Alex charmed Mom at dinner, talking about all the local history he'd researched. Jen spoke knowledgably to John about the business he was in.

Kath wasn't talking. Her eyes seemed dull.

That left me with Taylor.

I'd threatened him, the same as I'd threatened Kath, to keep out of my way and not even talk to me. Now I needed erase all that and start again, using nothing but words.

"So, ah, Taylor. What do you think of Union Station now? Isn't it great?"

"Yes. I guess so. It needed something. For tourists and so on."

"And what they're doing to RiNo!" I burbled on, mindlessly. "Bound to lift the value of property all over Denver."

Shit. Taylor and Kath rented. How had I forgotten that?

I saw Kath grimace, but she still said nothing. She ate slowly, mostly looking down at her plate.

I plowed on, feeling worse every minute. I told the story about the couple that had both hired investigators to check whether the other was being unfaithful, only to find that the two supposed 'lovers' were each other's investigators.

That bombed.

I tried to get Kath involved, but she let every opportunity slide by her.

Until dessert and the conversations had paused for a moment.

"What do the rings mean?" she asked abruptly.

Head on, as usual.

"Symbols that we're in love and we're committed to each other," I replied. "All three of us."

She wasn't looking at me; she was looking at her own engagement ring which Taylor had produced that day I'd first met him. There had been talk of a spring wedding, but Mom would have made sure I knew of any date that had been set. Nothing had been said.

I bit my lip.

Trouble between Kath and Taylor?

Or just Kath?

"All three. Really?" she said.

"It's what works for us." Jen's voice was cool and firm.

"I'm sure it is." Mom. Meaning she hadn't a clue, but didn't want an argument.

"Not looking good for the Broncos," John said into the silence.

I knew they'd just been trampled by the Buffalo Bills and they'd need to win a wild card just to get into the playoffs, but that was the extent of it. I hadn't seen a single game this season and I couldn't think of a thing to say.

"Need a quarterback who can actually play quarterback," Alex said with a snort, and they picked the conversation up again. Kath went back to her food.

I breathed out quietly.

A few minutes later, Jen mentioned to Taylor that she was looking for a couple of lawyers from outside her company to do an independent analysis of some of the standard legal templates, given the increased size of the company and the latest legislation.

Contract work, flexible arrangements. Could work from home.

Taylor pursed his mouth and said it sounded interesting. He glanced at Kath, who showed no sign of hearing.

"I'll have to get back to you," he said.

Mom was about to suggest coffee when the doorbell rang, startling her.

"I'm sorry," I said. "That'll be for me."

That went down like the proverbial lead balloon.

Yelena had my cell and strict instructions to interrupt only in emergencies.

Or a call from Tullah.

I rushed to open the door and breathe cool, fresh air that didn't taste of tension.

I could feel Mom's eyes, like lasers burning into the back of my head, through me and right through Yelena.

"Ouch," Yelena said, speaking very quietly, but letting her accent bubble up. "Mother of beast, is also beast. Is old Ukrainian saying."

"Bullshit," I said, trying not to laugh despite everything. "Give."

"David says message from Matt. He will call, maybe with Tullah." She checked her watch. "In five minutes."

Staying out here was not going to be popular, and risked undoing even the little I'd achieved tonight, but I couldn't miss the opportunity to talk to Tullah.

I closed the door behind me and we stood waiting, watching the time tick down on my cell.

"Anything else?"

"Diana arrived at Haven with Adept Emerson half an hour ago," Yelena said. "Bian sent a text. No other information yet."

Oh, to be a fly on that wall when they'd arrived.

"I spoke to the pretty boys as well. Nothing from the Hecate since we left RiNo."

I had a feeling she'd probably called Flint and Kane pretty boys to their faces. And they'd liked it.

"Also, Scott, Amanda, Tove all asleep," she finished.

Pia had used pheromone-based pacifics to sedate Tove, and protect her from the onset of withdrawal symptoms.

Yes. I also need to decide what to do with Tove. Another urgent situation.

The cell beeped. Unknown caller.

"Tullah?"

"It's me, Boss." Matt's voice, speaking hurriedly. "Please don't talk, just listen, this connection will cut off if it detects tracking. They're getting better trackers on the web, and I only have a few seconds. Tullah got your message and she's heading back to Denver on her own. They were getting too close anyway, even with this cool spell hiding us. She says she should be okay, traveling alone. I hope she's right. Should be there in a few days. We may try a diversion. I may be able to get some better explanation through to you. Don't be too hard on her—"

The connection cut abruptly.

"Damn."

We stood looking at the cell as if the call might suddenly come back to life, but there was nothing.

Mom opened the door.

"Amber," she said. It was all she needed to say. What it meant was: why was I being rude, had she brought me up this way, and did I realize what disappointment I was to her?

"Nothing to do now. Enjoy the rest of meal," Yelena said. Her eyes slid past me briefly, and then she turned on her heel and walked back to the car.

I turned back.

"I'm sorry, Mom. One of our younger colleagues is travelling alone and we've lost contact with her. We're very worried."

She frowned, looking over my shoulder.

I imagined what it looked like to Mom: Yelena would have passed as the grim reaper in skin-tight leather.

"I don't like that woman," Mom said as I went back into the house. "I don't think you should employ her. There must be more professional people in security who would be far better. It's not as if the Kingslund Group are some seedy clubs in the—"

"No, Mom. It's not the Kingslund Group any more. It's Altau Holdings, including the Kingslund Group. And I love Yelena."

Mom's eyes widened.

"Not like that," I said.

"Thank goodness," she muttered as we returned to the dining room.

An image rose in my mind of me explaining to Mom that Yelena and I bit each other in the neck and really enjoyed it.

It was almost enough to make me laugh. Or cry.

That was nothing compared to what waited for me at table.

Kath had cleared the dessert plates and was bringing out the cups for coffee.

"It'll never change, will it?" She glared at me. "Always something more important than the family."

She might as well have been a different person from earlier. She stood straight and held her head up defiantly for the first time that evening. She looked energized.

"Kathleen," Mom tried to stop her.

Taylor touched her arm.

She ignored them.

"We've got two of Denver's business leaders at table, but it's the 'security chief' who has to take the call in the middle of dinner."

"That's not unusual at all," Jen said.

Kath ignored her as well.

"I'm surprised you didn't stay down in LA. That's the sort of place you fit in, isn't it?"

It made me angry enough that my wolf woke up and took notice.

I took a deep breath. Brandy. Seemed fair enough, given it was in the cake that Mom had made. But...

Oh, crap.

"Mom," I said quietly. "What did you do with the rest of the brandy after you finished baking?"

She didn't move. It was John who darted back into the kitchen, only to return with the empty bottle.

"Oh, Kath." Mom's voice was full of pain.

"Don't you dare fucking judge me, any of you." Suddenly Kath was screaming. "You have no idea."

Taylor stood. "Calm down," he said. Like that ever worked.

"Your fault!" She pointed at me. "Everything people expected from you! When you left us, I had to pick it all up. You never came back."

Taylor took her arm, tried to pull her back down to her seat.

"Get your hands off me. What's wrong with you?"

"Nothing's wrong with me," he said. "You're not yourself."

"Not myself? Who else could I be, asshole? What's wrong with you that you want this shit?"

She slumped back down on her chair. "You never came back," she said again, and then she dissolved into tears.

Taylor and John worked together to take her out to the car while Jen and I tried to comfort Mom, who was in tears as well.

Jen looked up at me, and I knew what she was thinking.

I gritted my teeth and ran out. This was the last thing I wanted, but if I didn't do it now, I'd never do it.

Kath was sitting silently in the passenger seat. Taylor was walking quickly to the driver's side. John tried to stop me, but I pushed through and opened Kath's door.

"You said I never really came back." I had to throttle that anger and force the words out. "Okay. I'll give you that, Kath, and I'm sorry. Now, I'm trying, I'm really trying to be back. For you."

She wouldn't look at me.

"I can't stop being different than the person who left Denver after school," I went on. "You've changed too. But can we start again? Can we try? Please? Put everything in the last couple of years aside?"

Taylor got in and slammed his door.

I wondered how long he'd stay after tonight. Kath would need someone.

She didn't respond, but I knew she'd heard me. She looked confused.

I closed the door gently and Taylor drove them away.

Shit.

"You're not the kind who gives up because the going gets tough," Jen said.

We'd left the house immediately afterwards. No opening of presents. Tearful, silent farewells and unspoken recriminations.

Merry Christmas.

I sighed. "What is it the shrinks say? You can make people better, but first they need to want to be better. I'm not sure she wants to be better."

I felt drained.

Everyone had agreed this was the way to do it, but I was looking at the size of the task and doubting myself.

Did I have the strength? The time? With everything else that was happening, could I really give Kath the attention she needed?

Or was it already too late?

Chapter 11

After Christmas Eve, Christmas Day wasn't the disaster that I feared.

I'd had no time to buy presents. It didn't seem a good omen to have nothing for anyone in my House on the first Christmas we'd spent together, but that was without reckoning with Pia. Even the late arrivals, House Lloyd and Tove, got some presents, from 'me', thanks to her.

How? I didn't want to ask.

The next bonus was a terse text from Bian—*Merry Christmas, Round-eye. Enjoy the day with your House & family. Sleep in tomorrow and then come out here in the evening. Not before.*

So, instead of apologies all around and a mad dash out to Haven, I got to wrap up in a bathrobe, sit in the living room, wander in and out of the kitchen, cook and share breakfasts with everyone, drink coffee, open presents, give and take lots of hugs and kisses.

Everybody was around at some stage in the morning except Scott.

Pia told me he'd woken briefly in the early hours, showered and shaved, eaten a meal, neatly hand-written me a lovely letter of thanks and was fast asleep again. Pia and Amanda were taking turns checking on him every hour and all they had to report was that his vital signs were good and he was dreaming vividly.

We still didn't know whether the infusion had worked, but it had certainly kick-started his body again. Dreams were a common symptom of crusis, as was prolonged sleep. Pia said she thought it was going well, but couldn't point to any specific reason for her optimism.

David had managed to get another message to Matt and received one back—*Problems. Empire putting a lot into tracking. She's on her way. She'll call if she can.*

You could read too much into text messages. I didn't want to ruin everyone's day, so I pushed it to the back of my mind, where it stuck like a small, dark cloud on the horizon. David and I kept our cell phones on. David posted another couple of requests for more information on DarkNet boards where Matt would look, if he felt it was safe.

At about 10:30, Pia's kin—Gary and Leon, the redheaded twins, and Irene—chased everyone out of the kitchen and announced that they were taking over the cooking of the Christmas dinner, and since we'd made such pigs of ourselves over breakfast, and hadn't got the turkey on early enough, we wouldn't be eating until late afternoon.

Back in the living room, the rest of my House sprawled over the furniture and floor.

Welcoming Amanda's two Adept kin had become something of an event. In the middle of the room, and urged on by Dominé and Vera, *of course*, Jofranka and Dante were experimenting on Flint and Kane, braiding their long, thick hair in different styles.

For some reason this had required the girls to take the guys' shirts off, and that revealed both of the boys had tattoos on their chests—their spirit guides, naturally.

Flint's raven went shoulder to shoulder, intricately styled, with silky feathers and a gleam in its eye that captured that mystic knowing look of the Raven from Native American mythology.

And on Kane's chest—the trickster Coyote, lean and quick, laughing at the chaos that followed him.

Very fitting. Both of them.

It also seemed the level of detail and artistry required that young Jofranka and Dante trace the tattoos' lines out with fingers. There might have been some flirting going on.

And then their tattoos had gotten Savannah interested, so she was sitting with them on the floor displaying her own ink—an unique blend of Native American totems and Celtic spirals wound around each other, down her arms and across her belly.

Flint and Kane found them fascinating, also tracing out the loops and swirls on her skin with their fingertips.

There was a *lot* of flirting going on.

I looked at Amanda, concerned about her reaction to the byplay with her new kin.

But House Lloyd was a mature Athanate and secure in her bonding. She smiled indulgently at them and returned her attention to Savannah's younger brother Claude, who was sitting talking to her.

I'd inherited Savannah and Claude the last time someone had approached me for sanctuary. That had been Larry Dixon, from New Mexico, before the last, ill-fated Assembly had been held in Haven. Larry had been killed by Basilikos, but that didn't affect my Athanate obligation to his kin once I'd agreed to his request. Savannah had been the last surviving one I'd rescued in Albuquerque, and I sort-of adopted her kid brother because, although he wasn't kin and hadn't been bitten or bound, he was in danger and he knew way too much about the Athanate.

They'd both been difficult to fit into the House. Savannah partly because she had to work through her grief at Larry's death, and partly because she was socially awkward. And Claude because he was young *and* awkward *and* difficult to get to open up.

Well, it seemed Christmas had brought me a couple of unexpected presents.

Savannah finished showing Flint and Kane as much as she was willing to show them of her ink, and returned to snuggle beside David in a way that reassured me *that* problem was solved. I should have seen they were made for each other.

And Claude was chatting animatedly to Amanda, one leg tucked under him and body turned toward her. Body language that I could read across the room. No one, not even Pia, had managed to get him to relax like that.

I caught a little raised eyebrow from Amanda to me. I guessed it was a polite query to ask if there was any reason she shouldn't be interested in him as kin or katikia, but I wasn't complaining—one less to worry about.

Having unbound humans in my House *was* a worry. Bian had made it very clear that House Farrell needed to look secure to her paranoid Athanate mind. She meant with all the members bound closely to the House. If Savannah was David's kin and Amanda took Claude, that left me with only two remaining concerns, the girls that I'd rescued from LA: Tove and Tamanny.

And if I got them sorted out, there was Kath, who I thought would need Athanate healing.

I need time and peace and quiet.

Tove was, as Yelena had said, a mess. She had to get her head straight and her addiction controlled before I faced her with any kind of a choice about becoming part of my House.

Tamanny was just too young, not to mention vulnerable after her experiences at the hands of Forsythe. Part of rescuing her in LA meant she'd become aware of the paranormal. She certainly would notice what went on here in Manassah if she stayed.

Not secure, Bian would say.

How much time would she give me to fix that?

Tove was sitting to one side, against the wall. Nick Grey, the skinwalker, was talking to her, radiating calmness in the way he did. It seemed to be helping, but her eyes were watchful and she had to be wondering what kind of place she'd landed in.

I wondered how long it would take for the magic of my Athanate House to work its way into her, giving her the same feeling of security and comfort that everyone else was getting.

Problems everywhere, inside and outside of my House. Big, difficult, frustrating problems. Small, complex, irritating problems.

What wouldn't I give for a magic wand to wave which would make everything better?

"Your hair!" Pia interrupted my fantasy, moving behind me with a brush. "Honestly, Amber, it's as if you don't look in the mirror."

She was right: I didn't like mirrors anymore, but I didn't reply to her. It was easier to sit back and let her rhythmic brushing and the positive vibes from my House seep into my subconscious.

Like Yelena, I was Carpathian Athanate—uncommon outside of the domain of Carpathia. One of the benefits it gave me was a longer reach for my eukori and so, as I relaxed, my eukori unwound and touched on everyone in Manassah.

Which was when I found that linking eukori with Flint and Kane allowed me to use their Adept senses and auras.

And how weird was that...

Chapter 12

I rush upwards. It's like an express version of one those glass-walled elevators, without the glass. I can see the Rockies, the high plains. Further. There's a storm brewing to the west. It's feeling its way through the mountains like a blind man. Clouds begin to slither through the high passes like spirit serpents. Lightning lashes the valleys. It stings like a whip. Winds batter at me. The scent of snow assaults my nose.

And beneath me, in Denver, clustered around Manassah: eyes. Dozens of eyes. Hundreds. Watching...

I snapped back so quickly, my heart stuttered.

"Sorry, Pia."

I jumped up and in three steps I was beside Flint and Kane, down on the floor with them, taking their hands to strengthen the eukori connection.

"Tell me you know what that is out there," I hissed.

My voice was wrong; it came out as slow as cold molasses.

Kane shook his head. His hair was still tangled in Dante's hands and the movement pulled it through like silk running through her fingers.

All so slowly.

Around us, my House stirred, aware that something was happening.

Vera came across and took Tamanny to help in the kitchen, before she noticed.

Dominé went and spoke to Tove, casually positioning herself to block Tove's view of us.

My House, operating smoothly, supporting me. I felt a surge of pride.

As Flint, Kane and I reconnected our auras, I wanted to rise again, to look outside, look harder, to see what was threatening us, but Flint spoke with a voice that pulsed with power: "Not that way," he said. "This way."

And he pulled us down. Down, down, down.

Our mixture of eukori and auras darkened to the gray of slate, of graphite, and still darker, until the only thing that separated the color from the blackness of space was a hint of movement like a river at midnight.

We sank into the earth beneath Manassah, into the welcoming arms of great sacred shapes, too big to comprehend. Shapes that waited silently in the cold and dark.

Our hearts do not beat, our lungs do not breathe, our limbs do not move. We become as slow as the passing of years, almost crushed by the weight of the land upon us, seeping up through the layers of time, and a century passes before we can reach up with jagged, broken arms into the sky. Now our breath becomes the rush of wind. Now our hearts beat to the pull of seasons.

In our reaching arms there are sparks and sharp sounds. Quick movement.

"Crows," says Flint, his voice become the creak of branches stirring.

He has named them, and now I see them as he does. All that flickering motion; each flash a single bird, a single heartbeat in a feathered chest, shivering warmth in the cold air.

It seems a lifetime ago, but I remember Felix Larimer, the Denver alpha, talking to me in the woods above his ranch, about spies and the abilities of some Adepts: "They can see through animals' eyes," he'd said, "listen with their ears. They like crows for it."

Adepts are watching Manassah, watching us, using a flock of damned crows. And we are watching them back, somehow, through the spirits of trees.

Kane laughs his Coyote-crazy laughter, echoing in the earthy darkness, and Flint the Raven reaches up to gentle the alarm of his little feathered cousins.

"If you can, don't scare them off," I say. "Just make them look the other way. I'd prefer whoever's watching us doesn't know we know."

Kane laughs all the more. "Done," he says.

And then we were rising again, like ghosts seeping back into our bodies, sitting on the floor in the living room.

A strange mixture of reactions were passing over the faces of Flint and Kane. They enjoyed this sort of thing, it pumped them up, but the first signs of unease showed.

Amanda was kneeling beside us, looked concerned.

"Nothing to worry about," I said. *I think.* "But your kin and I need to talk privately."

I didn't want to ruin the mood of the day for the rest of my House.

Flint and Kane seemed to understand and they got up quickly, disappointing Jofranka and Dante.

"I promise I'll let them come back," I said to the girls as the boys put their shirts back on. "I just need them for a short while."

I let Amanda come as well. Nick looked across at me from the corner where he sat with Tove. I nodded my head to call him, too. Pia, Yelena and the others I signaled to stay.

We went into the sunroom and I closed the doors behind us.

The contrast between Nick and the youngsters couldn't have been more dramatic. They all shared bronze hints to their skin, chiseled cheeks and the sleek hair of their Native American heritage, but Nick carried an aura of calmness and dignity about him, from his unhurried movements to the weight of his stare. He was centered.

Flint and Kane were manic fireworks in comparison.

I was glad Nick was here, and waited until he sat before I spoke to the two young Adepts. "What did we just do?"

Flint couldn't keep the laughter from bubbling up. "We just kicked some Denver Adept ass," he said.

"Without them even knowing we did it," Kane clarified.

I'd been synced with them; I'd tasted how much they *enjoyed* getting one over on Adepts. I began to suspect it wasn't any wonder they'd been chased out of the north. The mystery was probably why it hadn't happened earlier.

"What did you do?" I said.

Flint kept laughing. "Just made their connection to the crows more efficient, so they'll be maxed out with irrelevant stuff."

"I predict migraines," Kane said, and the pair of them high-fived.

The touch of steel in Amanda's voice brought them back down to earth. "Could you start at the beginning, please," she said.

They sobered. A touch.

"The Denver coven are watching us," Kane began. "They can spirit link into animals like crows and pick up impressions of what the crows see and hear. We'd never have noticed, but Amber's eukori..."

"Just gave us a boost," Flint said. "It was awesome! Flew us right out of the house and up into the sky."

"They're talking about aural projection," Nick clarified for Amanda. "Spirit walking."

"That was the first attempt," I said. "Am I right, after that, we did some kind of a spirit link into *trees*?"

"Yeah," Kane said.

"It's not the type of magic the modern covens understand," Flint added and stopped thoughtfully. "Well, at least not the Northern Adept League."

"You don't sound so sure it was the Denver Adepts linking into the crows," I said.

Flint shrugged. "Communities have styles. You get a feeling from the way they weave their magic, the traces they leave. This wasn't Wendy Witch, or any of her Northern Adept League group."

"So, *possibly* the Denver community. Possibly someone else entirely."

They sobered a bit more. They got points for realizing they'd made a huge assumption.

"Can you find out?" I asked.

I needed to know who was spying on me, especially if it wasn't the Denver community. Adept communities aren't really territorial. It could be anyone spying on me for all sorts of reasons. The Empire of Heaven, for instance. I shivered.

We can't let them find out about Kaothos.

"Amber." Nick raised a hand in warning and both the Adepts kept silent. There was a way he had, just speaking my name, that gathered attention and held it.

"Yes," he went on. "You could find out, but you really don't want to open a channel and look. Something like that can be used in both directions."

Flint and Kane looked at Nick with renewed interest. Other than a brief introduction, they really didn't know much about Nick, and I was betting they'd pigeonholed him as just another shifter. In fact the skinwalker was as much an Adept as he was a shifter.

Still, they were nothing if not confident in their abilities and they seemed inclined to argue the point.

"But the power boost we got from Amber—" Kane began.

"Is dangerous in itself," Nick interrupted.

I stopped them. This *was* something I wanted to talk about, just not today.

"If we do nothing more now, is there an obvious and immediate danger?" I asked.

Eyes met. Small shrugs, shaking of heads.

"No, not immediate," Nick spoke for all of them. "I can set up a working that will sense any change outside."

"Good. Then we won't do anything else yet. We'll go back and enjoy relaxing with the rest of the House. You three," I nodded at the Adepts and Nick, "will compare notes about what you know and what we might be able to do about the danger from Adept communities. Keep in mind, neither Tove nor Tamanny are part of the House yet. Then tomorrow, you come speak to me, and I have a *lot* of questions."

I was buzzing with a thirst to know about magic—though some questions they probably couldn't answer—but I wanted Christmas Day to feel as normal as possible for the House, under the circumstances.

They filed out, leaving me with Amanda.

"I'm sorry," she said. "They're impulsive. All too eager to make fools of stuffy Adept communities, without any regard for the situation. You really don't need that added to the mix of what's going on."

"Maybe, maybe not," I said. I took the opportunity of inhaling a lungful of her marque and savoring the anticipation of biting. "But if you think I regret bringing you into my House, you're completely wrong."

I was being truthful, and not just because I found her marque attractive. My gut instinct was insistent that I needed Adepts as well as shifters and Athanate and humans: I wanted a coven as well as a pack, all neatly inside my Athanate House.

Was this remotely normal for Athanate? No, I guessed not, but then I wasn't normal either: a three-way hybrid: an Athanate, a Were and an Adept.

I seemed to have little natural magical ability other than helping Were cubs through their first shift. And today's surprise: that I could hitch onto Flint and Kane's auras and spirit walk. But with Kaothos back with Tullah, and Nick, Flint and Kane in my House, surely I would be able to find my lost spirit guide and Tara.

Then maybe that idle fantasy of fixing things magically wouldn't be so idle.

I growled, just thinking about it.

Amanda looked away and flushed.

My newest Athanate was still not quite sure of how my House ran. I thought she might be worried I was growling at her. I touched her to reassure; my hand on her arm, my eukori brushing hers.

"So, it looks as if Claude might end up as your kin," I said, changing the subject. "From what I could see earlier. He seems fascinated by you."

"I wanted to ask you about that..."

"I'm delighted," I said. "What about the other side of the coin? Are you all right with the attention your kin are getting?"

"Yes," she said. But up close, the image of cast-iron confidence was less convincing, and I couldn't resist the temptation to tease her.

"And you personally? You're going to be popular, you know. You're working a lot with Pia, are you sharing her bed?"

"No, I'm not." She was still avoiding eye contact. "I... prefer my own bed."

I let a hint of chill come into my voice. "Is that going to be a problem, then?"

"No, Mistress."

But now she looked back at me and saw I was barely able to keep a straight face.

"Ohhh! You got me. You..."

"Bitch," I supplied. "Yeah, got you good." I mimed marking up a score. "Listen, Amanda, House rules. No one gets to order you into bed, not even me. Blood, on the other hand..."

"I'm happy with that," she said. "The sooner the better."

"No argument from me. As soon as it's quieter."

She paused, considering what she was about to say.

"You know, I'm happier than I ever imagined I could be in this situation," she said. "I understand that it's dangerous in Denver and I've no fighting experience, so I'm not much use to you in that way. I *do* have other skills you need."

"Like?"

She cleared her throat, seeming unsure how I would take what she had to say. "My job back in Detroit... well, I was... I *am* a psychoanalyst. I can be useful. I can probably help you with that warped sense of humor you're struggling with, for instance."

"Bitch!"

We laughed and she marked her score on our imaginary board.

"But seriously," she said. "I think Tove and Tamanny could use someone to talk to who isn't quite so scary."

She smiled to soften it, but she was right. Whether I was scary or not, I sensed both the girls would find her much easier to talk to than me.

And Kath, I thought. *But one little step at a time.*

"You're on."

We linked arms and returned to the party in the main living room.

But despite the face I put on, I couldn't shake the feeling that events had started to slide out of control. Those crows hadn't been there yesterday.

What had changed?

Tullah had stopped hiding and started to make a run for home.

Wherever it was she'd been hiding, it had been good enough to defeat the searches of even the Empire of Heaven's elite Adepts. But now she was moving and it would be harder to hide.

So, they knew she was moving. They hadn't found her, but they had the next best thing; they knew where she was heading for and that was almost as good.

And 'they' included the Hecate and her Northern Adept League coven.

Sneaking Tullah past them and back to Kaothos had to be our top priority.

The only good thing about it all was that I wasn't going to get conflicting demands on my time from Athanate and werewolf hierarchies.

On the Athanate side, Skylur was all caught up in whatever urgent situations had taken him so abruptly to New York. Probably high level Emergence issues. Nothing to do with me in the immediate sense.

On the werewolf side, Felix and Cameron were caught up in becoming mated, consolidating their packs into a single entity under their joint leadership and then extending the association of the League of Southern Packs. They'd be far too busy to rattle my cage, and there was no other halfy ritual scheduled.

Which left me, Bian, Diana, our Houses and Haven's ex-Ops 4-10 troops to concentrate on the Adept issues and getting Tullah home.

No need to panic. It's manageable.

Climb a big mountain one step at a time.

Ha!

Chapter 13

The next day, there was still no call from Tullah, and no response from Matt when David messaged him repeatedly.

Yesterday, having a couple of days off had seemed like a gift. Now, waiting until evening to visit Haven and talk to Kaothos was a frustration.

I called Bian several times and got her voicemail.

I tried to put it aside and join in with another pajama and bathrobe morning. Then I got dressed up for lunch, including one of my Christmas presents, a pair of kick-ass combat boots from David and Yelena. They were designed to the general specification of Ops 4-10 combat footwear, except these were handmade by my favorite shoemaker, Werner, just like my cowboy boots. That meant they fit perfectly as soon as I put them on, and felt like I'd worn them for years. I could see them getting a lot of use. And as Yelena pointed out, my cowboy boots weren't the best for some of the action I got involved in.

We made it all the way past lunch before the outside world intruded again.

A call came for Alex. Felix and Cameron wanted him to meet them, and when the alpha pair who commanded the League of Southern Packs asked for your presence, you shrugged and went. So much for the werewolves being too busy to intrude on our vacation, but if it were important, I reasoned, Alex would have known more about it.

Something in my gut didn't like this. Why Alex alone? Why not both of us?

Still, I got the sense that a second day sitting around Manassah wasn't his idea of fun and he wasn't too unhappy to be called away, so I didn't voice my concerns.

At the front door, we shared a lingering kiss that lit the gold fires in his eyes and then he was gone.

I made sure everyone else was otherwise occupied and then I took over the sunroom and interrogated Nick, Flint and Kane on magic.

I wasn't expecting a simple fix, but the more we spoke, the more difficult it sounded to rescue Tullah.

If she needs it. The girl is good. Think positive.

Neither did it seem we could take on the Hecate or the Denver Adept community head to head. What we *might* have on our side was unexpected ways to create workings, like we had by spirit jumping into trees.

"Shamanic Adepts are regarded as outlaws," Kane said. "Our methods are forbidden, which means covens don't use the energy the way we do."

"Because, although the way we use the energy makes us potentially stronger, it makes the results less predictable," Flint took it up.

Kane completed: "Or safe. Get it badly wrong and a shamanic Adept could hurt a lot of people. Do that enough times and people will start to take notice."

"But it also makes us unpredictable."

"Go back to 'stronger'. The new, structured Adept methods with the whole coven..." I prompted.

"Each member works only on one element or thread of a working. One person to weave it all together."

"It can only be used as well as the Weaver who uses it. But each element is simpler, so there's less chance of getting it wrong. The other problem is, the whole is only as strong as the weakest member of the coven."

"That's how we broke Wendy's casting," Flint said.

"The Hecate's *coven*'s casting?" They nodded. The Hecate was the coven's 'weaver', the front woman for a spell that was a joint effort by the rest of the coven, and the Denver community leader was their 'weaver', who used his title as his name.

"What did you actually do to break the casting?" I asked.

"They'd chosen a summer day. I breathed in pollen and kinda shared the sensation with the coven," Kane said. "It was consistent with their working, so they didn't pay attention to what I was doing."

"And one of them has allergies?"

"Yeah. Not that she actually inhaled any pollen, but it totally seemed like she did, to her. It messed with her concentration. They hadn't thought of protecting themselves against that. She sneezed and the whole structure weakened just enough."

"Tricky." I liked the way they'd done that. "But you said the Hecate is strong. Couldn't she have overcome that?"

"She *is* strong, but she limits herself using this process. All she does is design the working and control it. The real power comes from the weave of the coven. Any part fails, even a little, and the whole structure is weaker."

"So how strong is she alone? And what's her spirit guide? Why can't I see?"

"Wendy's *strong*," Kane said, shrugging. "If she didn't play by her own rules which limit her, we wouldn't want to go against her."

"We don't know what her spirit guide is," Flint said, shaking his head. "Feels crazy different, but never got too close, obviously."

"Sometimes you can't see," Nick interrupted. "No matter how close. But it makes me wonder why she hides."

There was an embarrassed silence.

"Okay," I said. "You want to know about the elephant in the room. Ask."

The boys ducked their heads and let Nick speak. "What happened to your spirit guide?"

Even though I'd invited it, the question hurt.

"Plain answer is I don't know." I took a deep breath. "I can tell you about it, and see if you have ideas."

Nick knew most of what had happened in New Mexico when we rescued Diana; he'd been at the ritual just before. But even he didn't know the details of what had happened when Kaothos and I had broken the lock that the Taos Adepts had used to imprison Diana. Flint and Kane knew nothing about any of it.

So I talked through the pain, and the boys became wide-eyed.

Right up to that night, I'd had a wolf spirit guide, Hana. And she hadn't been alone in my head. There'd been Tara, my twin sister, stillborn and yet somehow alive inside me. The one whose wisecracks and simple presence had grounded me as far back as I could remember.

Hana and Tara had been there when I performed the first halfy ritual for a werewolf that was dying because she was unable to change. That was Olivia, and the ritual had been down in Carson Park, on the border between New Mexico and Colorado, with Were armies poised on either side.

It provided the boys with background, so I told them about the halfy ritual—the sacred places, dancing in the firelight, dancing through clouds of smoke, catching glimpses of spirit figures. The confusion. The pain. The blood. The way everything seemed part of the ritual.

Talking about that loosened me up and I managed to continue on into the rescue of Diana and the loss of my spirit guide.

My throat went dry, my voice quiet. My heart raced and my body ached with remembered pain.

The Taos Adepts had been maintaining the spell on Diana. They'd made a circle around her, and stood at their points, feeling secure in the knowledge that the spell had been set up so that physically attacking them would discharge the force of the spell through Diana.

And not just Diana. The spell's power was drawn from the life force of captive children. I'd been told all of them would die if I attacked the Adepts.

I tried to disarm the spell by channeling that power through my body. It felt like every vein caught fire, every bone was broken, every muscle torn. Pain on pain.

Then Kaothos came, blotting out the sky.

She'd broken the spell, and reflected the backlash away from the children and through the Adepts who'd created it. I thought I'd known pain before, but Kaothos blazed through my mind. I felt as if I was falling into the sun, and the whole night was aflame. When I came to my senses, the lock was gone, and Taos Adepts were still standing rigidly in their positions, their heads actually burning, a stench coming off them as the skin of their faces melted.

And my mind had been torn open, allowing madness to flood in. I'd gone rogue.

I needed to prove to myself I could tell this story, even though I could see horror growing on the boys' faces, grimness on Nick's.

I'd killed the leader of the Taos Adepts, Taggart. I'd ripped his throat out and thrown him at Diana's feet like an offering before some bloodthirsty, ancient goddess.

Then I'd chased down and tortured Amaral, the man responsible for the kidnapping of Diana. I kept him alive, in pain, *feeding* on his suffering, as if I was a Basilikos Athanate.

I remembered that unthinking hunger of being rogue. I remembered it in my jaws and belly.

But from the moment Kaothos had burned herself through my mind, there had been no Tara. No twin sister. No Hana. No spirit guide.

Diana and my House had repaired me, brought me back, but I had a hole in my chest that nothing else could fill.

My whispering pattered away into silence.

I blinked and took more note of the looks on Flint and Kane's faces. More than horror at my story.

"What is it?" I asked them.

They exchanged looks in the way that they did.

Flint spoke first. "It's not about going rogue or that stuff. Don't think you're rogue anymore. It's about the rituals and what you and the dragon did when you saved Diana."

"What?"

"You know how myths have a basis in fact?"

"Sometimes," I said.

"Yeah, okay, sometimes. Thing is, there's a sort of understanding that magic takes a lot of forms, and dark magic is dangerous stuff. Evil."

"I think I got that, from what happened to the Taos Adepts." But as I said it, I realized that wasn't exactly what they were talking about. "Wait. You're saying that the halfy rituals are dark magic? Diana's rescue was dark magic?"

It was Kane who answered. "The way you described them, they're all focused on pain and fear and blood. And death—for the rescue, you and the dragon killed the Taos Adepts."

"Like human sacrifices. That's pretty much the definition of dark magic, or blood magic, right there," Flint said.

Blood magic. I felt the echo of their horror through my eukori. It chilled me, radiating cold out from the pit of my stomach, silent freezing fingers reaching, wrapping my heart and lungs.

"That's not the way it was," I said.

Wasn't it? How much did I know about what I was doing? I was insane at the time.

I stopped myself from saying that the Taos Adepts deserved what they got.

Who am I to judge?

That magic hadn't really come from me. I wasn't that powerful. It had come from Kaothos.

Nick hadn't said anything. His head was down.

With a sinking sensation I remembered that Nick had actually spoken to me of his concerns about Kaothos. Down in New Mexico he'd told me that his people feared the Thunderbird, and those that had chosen it as their totem had died out because it was too powerful a spirit.

Too powerful, or too evil?

In my head, echoes of the Hecate's voice mocked me. *Dracul means dragon, and it comes from drac, meaning devil.*

Chapter 14

Kane opened his mouth to say something else, and Nick's head came up quickly.

"Stop," he said, his eyes glinting.

We were all silent for a long minute.

"All very well being self-taught until you teach yourselves ignorance." Nick glared at them. The two younger men sat back, looking embarrassed. "Does *the seed in the heart* not mean anything to you?" Nick went on.

It was obviously a saying from some teaching that they shared, and Kane lowered his head. "Intent," he mumbled.

"Evil intent, evil magic," Nick said. He turned to me. "Yes, your way is dangerous. Your powers seem to come from your anger, fueled by pain, channeled through Blood. This is strong, violent magic. Deceptive magic. It can turn in your hand."

He paused, but neither of the younger Adepts argued the point.

Neither of them openly agreed either.

"It's because of this, the shamanic tradition is wary of these elements," Nick said. "It's also part of the reason why the modern, structured methods were developed, restrictive laws were made and whole covens encouraged to participate in all spells. But the fish can still rot from the head, like the Taos Adepts."

I could see the boys weren't buying into this completely, but Kane had a harder time hiding his opinions than Flint.

Still, they didn't interrupt as the skinwalker spoke on: "If your purpose is evil, and your consideration is focused only on you at the expense of others, then you could describe it as dark magic. If your purpose is to break an evil working and the energy rebounds on the Adepts who created it, then that's not."

"A human sacrifice," Kane responded, as if he'd forgotten I was right here. "A circle of Adepts paralyzed where they stood and being burned alive. The leader's throat torn out."

"The Adepts got hit by the rebound of their own spell," Nick replied. "*Karma*, the Asians say. *Threefold thy acts return to thee*, the old Celts said. Your intentions come back to you."

"No one was being burned," Kane said stubbornly, "until Amber and the dragon got involved."

"Burned? No. Tormented? Yes. The fact that the rebound took the form of fire was probably because that's what Amber visualized as the pain. Her own pain." Nick turned to me. "You didn't actually visualize anyone else being on fire?"

"No," I replied. "And as for 'sacrificing' the leader—he attacked me. I killed him. I didn't have any intention for it to be part of some ritual. But if we've eliminated evil intentions on my part..." They didn't so much nod as drop their eyes, reluctantly. "Why's it so dangerous? And how dangerous?"

If blood magic is the basis of the halfy ritual, what will I do? I can't refuse to help them.

It was Nick who responded. "Look, all magic is addictive, even to Athanate and Were, and they only use it in passing. Much more for Adepts. Magic, pure magic itself, is power. The feeling of summoning and using it is pleasure, and when you add on the pleasure of being powerful, being able to do these things, even the weakest of magic can be addictive. Adepts start off knowing they shouldn't use magic casually. They should only use it when it's essential. Never for themselves. But as they go on, they always find there are more reasons to use it. Reasons become excuses. Then justifications. They start to believe they're okay, because they control it. It doesn't control them. They could stop anytime, but why should they? It's at that point the world begins to look different. Soon, everyone else is wrong, and the use of magic is right."

"That applies to all Adepts then," I said. "Even shamanic. Any type of magic."

Nick nodded.

"It does, but more for dark magic. The darker the magic, the closer between the thought and the deed, the shorter the time between the effort and the reward, the more powerful the magic is. And the more powerful the magic is, the more rewarding it is, and the quicker it drives out doubts."

I laughed, the sound a little shaky. "I can't light a candle with magic of any shade, so I don't think that's what's happening to me. It seems all I can do is channel something for the halfies. That's not for me, and it's essential for the Were."

On the other hand, the ritual *was* some kind of magic. And I *had* broken the lock that the Denver community had put on Tullah's powers. With Kaothos' help. Where did things that seemed natural for Athanate and Were stop, and magic take over?

Kane and Nick argued the point while I fell into thought.

But what about Kaothos?

What about the legends that said an Adept would lose control of the dragon?

Were dragons automatically dark magic?

Kaothos? Evil? *A devil?*

But then I thought back to the Basilikos team that had hidden out in the high plains at Bow Creek Ranch after the last Assembly at Haven. I thought of the layered, Aztec-style mini-pyramid they'd built in the barn. The children they were sacrificing. They were Athanate, not Adepts, but they'd definitely been performing some kind of magic rituals.

That was dark magic. I *felt* it. I couldn't define it, but I knew it.

Not the same as Kaothos. Not at all.

"I'm getting short of time," I said. "There's a lot more here to get back to, but I need to wrap this up now and get out to Haven."

I rubbed my face. So many unknowns. I had to deal with the immediate first.

"So this thing with crows yesterday," I said. "If we assume it's the Denver Adepts, is it just because they've got a problem with me?"

Nick shook his head.

"They've had a problem with you for a while. If they'd tried this before, I'd have noticed it. It's new."

"And it's not the Hecate, you think. So it's either caused by the Hecate's arrival here, or they have the same reason she has—they know Tullah is heading for home?"

He nodded. "The Denver Adepts want that dragon and they think she'll come here at some point. Or you'll lead them to her."

Damn. Three groups of Adepts facing me. The Northern Adept League, who know Kaothos is here with Diana and that Tullah is coming. The Denver community, who only know Kaothos is Tullah's spirit guide and think they'll catch both of them coming home. And the Empire of Heaven, who secretly don't believe Kaothos is dead and are looking for Tullah.

And in the meantime, if Flint and Kane's reactions are anything to go by, all of these Adept communities will regard me as some kind of blood magic witch.

Chapter 15

I left Nick talking to Flint and Kane. Jen wasn't in the living room. I found her in the bedroom, packing her business suits into a case on the bed.

"What's happened?" I said, my heart sinking even further. We were supposed to be enjoying ourselves together. First Alex, and now Jen.

"Skylur happened." Jen's mouth twisted. "He needs me in New York. Business never rests."

"No!"

She sighed and folded a couple of scarves into the case. "I've already complained. Much good it did." She glanced at me hesitantly, looked away. "It gets worse."

"How?"

"Skylur's ordered Yelena to fly me there in the Pilatus. We'll be staying a couple of days."

"He can't do this!" Why was he going back on his word? "You're my wife and kin. She's my Diakon. You're needed here. *And* it breaks his rules."

She came over and hugged me.

"Honey, he makes 'em, he breaks 'em. I'm surprised he's lasted this long."

"What do you mean?"

"You've kinda forgotten, but Yelena's Carpathian. Genuine Carpathian, not just by infusion like you."

I gritted my teeth. I couldn't shout and swear like I wanted to. It wasn't Jen I was angry at.

I tried to speak calmly.

"And Yelena's my House now. House Farrell. Sworn to Panethus. Not Carpathian."

Yelena spoke from behind me: "Yes, but I was born and raised, infused and trained in the domain of Carpathia." She had the suite across the hall, and she'd have heard us talking. "Carpathia closed borders to all outside Athanate long before I was born. No news comes out. Skylur will say I know more about the domain than anyone else he has access to." She shrugged. "He's probably right. I can understand that he wants to find out anything I can tell him."

"He wanted to take her away down in LA," Jen said. "Diana told him to wait until you were more recovered."

"It's only talk. Only a few days, Mistress," Yelena said. She joined us and Jen slipped an arm around her, pulling her into our embrace.

Yelena was putting out pacifics to calm me down.

"Keep them to yourself," I snapped. "I'll be angry until I'm ready to stop."

They laughed, a little humor in a bleak afternoon. An indulgence of my immature reaction.

"I have to finish packing." Yelena pulled away. She kissed my cheek in parting and returned across the hallway.

"And me." Jen returned to her case.

Her voice took on a casual tone which warned me something else was coming. "Skylur's let a lot of things slide while you were in Diana's care."

"Such as?"

"Biting," she said, not meeting my eye. "You. Me."

I sat down on the bed abruptly. She was right, of course. Jen was running Altau Holdings for him. Yes, she was my kin and bound to me, and I was bound by Blood oath to him, but no other Athanate in his position would have someone like Jen, a human, that close to him, with that much control over his House assets, without biting her as well. And he hadn't bitten me, either.

"You think this trip is all about biting you?"

"No, honey. The business is real and it's a good time to get things done that'll be easier if I'm there in New York. It's just I think he'll take the opportunity to ask, and I don't feel I'm in a position to refuse, any more than you would be. He's not singling me out. I'm the only one on his staff he hasn't bitten. It's just the Athanate way." She refolded her scarves, her graceful hands becoming clumsy and her voice tight. "In fact, it's probably not sensible to refuse him anything."

My stomach got that out-of-control dropping elevator sensation.

Blood and sex.

Jen came and knelt in front of me.

"Honey, it's okay. It'll be fine. We haven't got... what was the phrase you used? A suburban, white picket fence kind of marriage. A hybrid vamp, a wolf and a human? It's kinda a given we'll have problems. Problems which we can get over."

I wanted to say it was still unfair, but she was right. We had no neat human borders.

She took my hands and kissed them.

"I know I'm not saying this right, but Alex and I knew we'd have to talk about this soon. It's not as if it's all about me. On one hand, you need more kin, and on the other you're in the same position here, with Bian, as I will be with Skylur."

My mouth opened and closed a couple of times, but again, she was correct. This was House Trang's territory. Bian had every Athanate right over me and my House. My Blood, by Athanate law, and my body, by custom.

And she'd made it clear she was attracted to me. Many times.

"She has sixteen kin at Haven," I said, because I had to say something. "Why would she bother with me?"

Jen snorted, dismissing my argument.

"I'm jealous," she said. "Of course I am. But I got into this with you, knowing what I was getting into. And I've always known that I'd need to separate what I could control from what I couldn't. If I get hung up on things I can't control, it'll eat me away from the inside, and there's no defense against that."

"Well, Bian's one issue. On the other, I have katikia, Jen. I don't need more kin."

Jen gave an elegant time-will-tell shrug. "Maybe. You know, I like Bian. She's been much more understanding than we have a right to expect." She took a deep breath. "I'm not going to be upset about that."

I knew she wasn't telling the complete truth, but I was too shocked and upset to say so.

"I love you," I said instead.

"And I love you too." She kissed me and it was all right for a minute.

Then she chased me out, saying she needed to concentrate on packing. Her eyes were misting.

Yelena's door was open. She had less elaborate requirements for clothes than Jen, and she was finished packing.

"I've told Julie to take you to Haven," she said.

"Thanks," I replied dully. My Diakon was being efficient, but it wasn't what I wanted to talk about. "Jen's just told me I should be getting more kin and be prepared for Bian to make demands."

"I know," Yelena said. "Is hard for both of you. I understand."

"It is hard, but *I* don't understand why it needs to be like this," I said. "I'm Athanate. I enjoy sharing Blood with you. I haven't demanded you to come to my bed. I don't mean you're not attractive. I mean..."

The words seem to twist around inside my head but Yelena understood. She laughed.

She was about to speak when Amanda interrupted us, coming in behind me and looking worried.

"I'm sorry, Amber. I seem to be apologizing for Flint and Kane all the time."

"It's okay." I waved off her apology. "They just accused me of being a blood magic witch performing Satanic rituals. No big deal."

That was spiteful and unnecessary.

"Sorry," she repeated.

"No, Amanda. I'm sorry." I ran fingers through my hair and tried to visualize gathering the stress into my lungs and blowing it out of my body. This little vacation had started so well. "I need them to say things like that, because if they think it, that's the attitude I'll face out there from other Adepts. I need to know that."

"It doesn't excuse them," she said and moved forward awkwardly to give me a hug.

I squeezed her back and we both got a reminder of how much we were looking forward to exchanging Blood. Just not quite now.

"I promise they won't be so crass again." Amanda hurried out, her face warm.

I watched her go, still enjoying the pulse of desire for her Blood.

"Need to scratch that itch before it bites you," Yelena said quietly, straight-faced.

I glared at her.

"Is old Carpathian saying," she protested.

She was trying to make me feel better. I was House Farrell, and she was my Diakon. She was being ordered to leave her new kin behind while she went to New York so my ultimate boss could be sure of her reliability, as if my word was not enough. And that meant, as Mistress of the House, I'd failed her. I should be the one trying to make her feel better.

"Amanda and I will bite each other as soon as it calms down," I said. "And there's nothing else in it."

"Maybe." She grinned briefly and then got serious again, unknowingly echoing Jen. "Is difficult time. Don't waste it on worrying things you can't control. Skylur? He's being an asshole, but he's not here, and he's not going to hurt Jen or me. Bian? How bad is that? Felix and Cameron? All quiet. Empire of Heaven? Far away. You have Adepts in Denver. You can't fight them, so don't fight them. Don't get caught up. Get Tullah back with Kaothos and let *them* handle the Adepts."

"Wise words, Diakon. I'm not sure I can avoid the Hecate."

"The ice bitch wants to speak to Diana, let her speak to Diana." She tilted her head to indicate the rest of the house. "Your Adepts say she's powerful, but not so powerful she could do something to Diana and

Kaothos, I think, yes? Is not your fight. Your job is getting Tullah back. She hasn't called yet?"

"No. I'm getting worried. Matt promised she would call."

After a scatter of calls on Christmas day, the cell phone had been quiet. Right on cue, it pinged and I grabbed it without even checking the number.

"Tullah?"

"No." The voice was calm, precise. It made me wonder what it took to ruffle the Hecate.

"Speak of the devil," I said. I wasn't going to ask how she had my number.

"We were speaking of dragons, actually, last time, and I know she's back in Denver now."

It chilled me that she knew, but I wasn't going to confirm it to her, so I said: "What do you want, Hecate?"

"What I want is to avoid the horrendous mistakes that Diana, you and Tullah are about to make with Kaothos."

"What mistake would that be?"

"Almost anything you do. Even if you do nothing. You're blundering in the dark."

Dark. Dark magic.

I didn't want to even think about that until I'd spoken to Kaothos.

"And you, in contrast, are an expert with dragons. Got a long history with them."

If my sarcasm bit her, it didn't show in her voice, which remained quiet, her wording careful.

"No, we don't have a long history, but what we do have is a sophisticated structure that is designed to avoid mistakes. I dislike analogies, but if you had a live grenade, you wouldn't give it to kids to play catch. You'd give it to someone who understands explosives."

"A dragon is not a grenade."

"I did say I disliked analogies, which often seem designed to encourage argument and ignore the central issue—"

"The central issue being what you do with something as powerful as a dragon spirit guide."

"Yes," she admitted. "You can't use her to power unstable, unpredictable shamanic workings, or even structured workings, if you don't have safeguards in place. You have none of those safeguards and no ability to create them. You have no idea of the power you're trying to control."

"So you want Kaothos. You're like the Empire—you want to take her for yourselves. Do you have someone lined up already who'll take Kaothos? Do you even believe you can persuade her to move?"

I was arguing from a position of weakness here. Kaothos had moved before, from Tullah to Diana. An instinct, I'd been told, something hypnotically attractive about Diana's power, even though Diana wasn't an Adept.

Was it purely instinct?

She certainly hadn't wanted to move from Diana to the Empire's chosen Adept.

Could she choose where to move to? If not, was it going to be possible to get back to Tullah? Was Tullah not strong enough?

Was the Hecate strong enough?

Her voice interrupted my thoughts. "I'd rather discuss all that with Kaothos."

"I don't have her cell phone number handy."

My snark was rewarded with a faint sigh. "Just tell Diana she must allow me access. It's important. More important than anything else. More urgent even than your enemies gathering, about which you seem to be almost willfully ignorant."

What? Enemies?

I'd have to find out what she meant, but for her to tell me now would put me more in her debt.

"What if Kaothos refuses?" I said instead.

"Then we all have a problem. You, me, the whole world, including Kaothos."

The line went dead.

Chapter 16

Would getting Kaothos back to Tullah just cause an even more serious problem?

Ignoring Yelena's good advice, I worried that around in my mind on the way to Haven.

That and the reasons the Hecate might have for lying about it.

Though she hadn't killed me when she could have.

Okay, maybe she just saw me as an easy way to get to Kaothos, and kept me alive for that, but I wasn't sure she needed my help. Couldn't she and her coven fight their way into Haven? Pull the whole place into the spirit world, where there were no firearms and their magic was lethal?

Flint and Kane didn't think she could, but she'd caught them off guard down in RiNo.

If she could just kidnap Kaothos, and hadn't, it was a point in her favor.

But Kaothos a devil? No.

I'd have to hand the decision about what to do with the Hecate over to Diana and Kaothos. I forced my mind away from her and thought about things I might be able to control. Maybe.

Where was Tullah? Why hadn't she called? How far away was she?

None of *that* circular tail-chasing was getting me anywhere either.

Julie drove and said very little. I sensed she wasn't happy about Yelena's situation. It made for an unusually quiet and tense journey, and it was a relief when we turned into the open gates at Haven.

There were ex-Ops 4-10 people everywhere. Some faces I knew. Most of them knew Julie.

Normally, I'd have expected smiles and high fives, but either they had something going on, or we didn't look approachable this evening. It wasn't until we reached the guard on the front door that someone spoke to us.

A message from Bian.

She wanted Julie to go down to the gym to help out assessing some new arrivals. I was instructed to visit the Dark Library, fetch a couple of books that were waiting there and then join Bian and Diana down in Skylur's Lyssae hall.

I'd heard Skylur speak about the Dark Library, but I'd never seen it. Haven was like an iceberg, with most of it hidden below the ground, and I knew both the Lyssae and the Dark Library were only accessible from secret elevators.

Bian's instructions explained how to get there: *End of the ground floor corridor, room on the right, stand on the circular pattern.*

I'd been this way a couple of times, but it was still a little strange when curved glass whispered out from the wall to surround me and then the floor dropped away.

At the bottom, I ended up in a blank passage with featureless walls and dim lighting.

This way to the Dark Library?

No signs. There looked to be a door of some kind at the end. Perhaps it was in there.

I touched the door, and I could feel it begin to open, but the lights in the passageway went out.

Maybe there was a timer on them.

I felt along the wall.

"There is no light switch," a voice from the darkness said.

Crap. Dark Library, as in literally dark.

"How the hell am I supposed to see well enough to pick up a couple of books?"

"Give it time."

The voice was dry and soft, whispery.

"And you are?"

"Ptolymeus."

Old, old Athanate. Centuries old.

Something tickled a memory. Things that I'd seen and heard started to come together like a jigsaw puzzle.

"You dress dramatically," I said. "Black cloak with a hood." I'd seen him walking along a corridor at Haven once—arms outstretched as if *feeling* his way.

The laughter was like paper rustling.

"And Skylur calls you Tolly?"

Ptolymeus—Tolly-may-us—*Tolly*. Skylur had said something about *Tolly's unverifiable assertions*. Tolly was the guardian of Altau's library, their printed knowledge, and their arcane lore.

"You have me," he said. "Tolly. The blind mole in the basement. The poor, abused servant hidden from view."

My eyes were adjusting. My wolf-eyes went deep into the infra-red, and from his body heat, I could make out his form sitting at a table not far from me.

There were steps down, which no human would have been able to see.

And there were books waiting on the table, cooler than the wooden surface of the table itself. I could see them more as an absence of warmth, but their shape was unmistakable.

I went down the steps and walked across carefully to pick up the books.

"These are for me?"

"Yes. Your eyesight is excellent. I would suppose that's the wolf in you."

"Probably. Tell me, why have no light in a library?"

"There are books in here that would fade. In fact, some of them would actually crumble in the light," he said. He made a dismissive waving motion. "And I have no need of it."

"So people have to know what books they need before they come and ask you?"

"It's more the case they have to ask House Altau," he replied. "If he agrees, I merely serve. Some books I can let out, some I have to read down here to the person requesting."

I opened one of the books from the table at random. "You can read this?"

I couldn't even see the writing.

"Of course." One hand stretched out and the fingers skimmed over the surface of the book's page. He spoke, but since he was speaking a language I didn't recognize, I had to take his word for it.

I wanted to ask *how*, but maybe that was a sensitive area.

Instead, I asked: "And this library is... I mean, the scope of it?"

"Everything written that the Athanate people have ever collected, or been interested in, that I have heard about, I have bent my mind to obtaining." His voice was less dry now. "All praise to Altau for sponsoring and protecting this vital work down the ages, without one moment of doubt. Knowledge is power, and only the Carpathians' library at Hutsul could in any way challenge the Dark Library for scope."

He paused and I sensed him stirring in the darkness, beneath his enveloping cloak. "I so want to talk to the librarians in Hutsul, Amber of House Chrysos, the Golden House, the long-lost House of Carpathia."

"It's Amber of House Farrell, sub-House of Altau, recently-found in Denver, Tolly. I have no idea of my welcome in Carpathia, and no plans to find out."

"Perhaps," he said. I got the impression the topic was not closed. "Forgive me. For me, this is my life. Altau desires the power of knowledge. I desire knowledge for its own sake. I will not rest until I have gathered it all, every book."

"Okay." I bit my tongue. I badly wanted to ask him if he had a copy of Twilight, or a download of the internet, but restrained myself. "If I ever have the opportunity to set you up with a session in Hutsul, I will."

"Thank you."

"Meantime, I'll take these to Bian." I turned.

"Tread carefully, House Farrell."

Does he mean not to trip on his steps? Or something else?

I inched my way back to the door. It was ambient temperature, and a lot harder to see than he was.

"Left a bit," he said helpfully. Then: "Give my regards to my cousin."

I opened the door and went out. The lights in the passage came on just enough to make the library behind me seem like the blackness at the bottom of an old, forgotten mine.

"Sure," I said to that darkness. "Who's your cousin?"

"The Lyssae you call Anubis," he replied as the door began to close and the lights gradually brightened in the passage. "He hears all that's said, you know, even in his stillness. And if he could talk back, what he'd say is keep well away from magic, especially dark magic. *Well* away."

Chapter 17

After Skylur's freaky library, the elevator took me back up a level to Skylur's freaky audience hall.

At least there were normal lights this time, instead of the muted neon-blue I'd seen before. And Diana was waiting by the elevator to embrace me.

I was clumsy with the books I carried and dizzy with the feeling that I usually got around Diana: as if gravity tilted toward her. She secured me in her arms and I inhaled lungfuls of her scent; it was like coming home.

"Beloved," she whispered, and kissed my neck. The memory of the pleasure of her fangs in my neck warmed me. And the memory of her words to me in LA—*you are the flower in my desert and the promise of rain*—made me want to lay all my troubles at her feet and let her tell me what to do. It would be so easy.

As if she sensed that, she sighed.

"Alas, for your promised rest with your House over Christmas. I'm sorry."

"I'm just glad you're back," I said, but the deep tension in her body did nothing to dispel my growing sense of unease. I'd been worried for her safety while she was alone, out on the road. A stupid fear really; if she couldn't take care of herself, there was the small matter of having Kaothos with her. But she was here now, as safe as we could make her... and she clearly wasn't feeling relaxed.

The overgrown lizard herself was coiled along one length of the hall, watching me with her lantern eyes and making little sizzling noises of welcome. I didn't know what full-size meant for a shape-shifting dragon spirit guide, but there seemed to be more of her every time.

In the remaining space, they'd brought in partitions and furnishings that made the hall a comfortable apartment, if you ignored the spooky statues of the Lyssae, Skylur's peacock throne and the way the walls ran with water. I got that the water was some kind of focus for a working which hid the Lyssae, and now Kaothos, but I still found it eerie.

Bian and Alice stood in the middle, waiting for me to join them. Alice wasn't in chains, which I saw as a good sign for her. I gave them both one-armed hugs, nearly dropping my armful of books again.

If Bian had been a cat, her tail would have been thrashing, despite the smile she gave me.

There was a table to the side with a collection of old books and scrolls, many of them opened. Some of the alphabets I'd never seen before, and I couldn't read *any* of them. I left the ones Tolly had given me with the rest.

I got us going. "The last message from Matt was that Tullah's on her way, but the Empire's stepping up the search. We can't get hold of her directly and Matt's not responding now. I had another urgent message from the Hecate, just before I left to come here. And to top it all off, the Denver Adept community is staking out Manassah."

Bian's eyes narrowed. "Another message? The Hecate kidnapped you again?"

"No. I get the feeling that now she's demonstrated she can do it, that's enough for the moment. This time, she called me on my cell. Restated that she wants to meet with the lizard herself."

"Why would I want to speak to her, Amber Farrell?" Kaothos said. Unlike her usual trick of speaking in my head, she was making actual noise this time, though I couldn't tell how she did that. Her mouth certainly didn't move.

"She says we're blundering around in the dark without her. More specifically, we can't use unstable, unpredictable shamanic workings, because we don't have safeguards in place. She says we have no idea of the power we're trying to control. I guess she's offering her coven as safeguard. She says this is more important than anything else, and if we don't listen to her, everyone has a problem."

"Some justification for the first part of that assertion," Alice said. "We *are* in the dark. Less so for the last part—her assistance might be anything but helpful."

"And just how does she know so much about Kaothos and Diana?" I threw in the obvious question.

I'd gotten more sensitive about Adepts since I'd last seen Alice; I could easily tell her spirit guide was a fox. I could almost see the fox floating around her head and shoulders as she looked down at her hands in embarrassment.

"My fault," she admitted. "For a long time, I was part of the Northern Adept League. In fact, I was part of what became Hecate Faith Hinton's coven on Long Island in New York. That's the Hecate Skylur has just met."

It seemed there were interesting things happening in New York as well, but I needed to stay focused on here and now.

"When I worked for the Warders, I fed information back to the League," Alice went on. "I was a spy basically. That stopped when I joined Altau, and you could say the process reversed during the journey with Skylur and Diana. I told them everything I knew about the League."

"Doesn't seem to explain anything. What am I missing?"

Alice looked even more embarrassed. "An Adept as experienced as I am, I should have thought more deeply about my dreams," she said. "Waking and sleeping."

"You mean they can listen in?" I shivered at that thought.

"Not to anyone," Alice reassured me, "but they can eavesdrop on my thoughts because of the years they've worked with me. We are attuned, if you like. Anytime I was outside of the protection of the shielding in the van, they had a group from the Long Island coven close enough to 'tune in' to me."

She held her hands up.

"We had to stop for gas, food and comfort breaks, for instance. Security from Adepts was my responsibility and I believed I was the last person who would have provided a weak point. Surely, I thought, given the projections of Skylur, Diana and Kaothos into the realm of energy, they were the ones who needed protecting. Even without that complacency, I should have been more suspicious of the odd little moments of confusion and blankness. I thought I was just tired or wool-gathering. I *am* a very old Adept. Courtesy of consorting with Athanate."

Diana smiled thinly at her, but remained silent.

Alice was unusual for an Adept. Most Adepts didn't consort with the Athanate. Even Adepts who were friendly, like Tullah's parents, Mary and Liu, thought that Athanates somehow sucked the soul out of their kin. So, as I understood it, lacking access to the Athanate bio-agents to keep them young, Adepts tended to die at standard human ages.

Alice was over four hundred years old, if Bian's sarcastic comment about her being thrown off the Mayflower was true.

Can't they replicate the action of Athanate bio-agents with workings of the energy?

I'd have to ask at a more appropriate time. I had an idea that was another Adept superstition, like sucking souls. Maybe longer life meant more opportunity to become corrupted by the power of magic.

"How safe are we here?" I gestured the hall.

"Safe. It's impregnable to workings," she replied.

Cynic that I was, I doubted that, but I had no real knowledge of magic, so instead I asked: "And what about the safety of Haven from a direct assault by Adepts? I'm having nightmares about Adepts able to throw spells like grenades. You know, bang, and people get shot off into the spirit world, or somewhere under the sea."

Alice pursed her lips. "Doesn't generally work like that," she said and sighed. "Adepts avoid physical violence when using the energy. That's not a moral stand. It's simply that it's nearly impossible to fight and maintain the concentration required to work the spell."

Apart from the 'nearly', that sounded good, but she wasn't finished.

"It's easier to do defensive workings, like the coven prepared a spirit world trap down at RiNo for you."

Would have been useful to know before I went there.

Alice spread her hands. "I have to say that attacking is *theoretically* possible. But it all depends on the strength of her spirit guide, the distance involved, the conviction of every single one of her coven what they're doing has to be done, and their discipline."

"And what *is* her spirit guide?" Diana asked.

I shook my head. "Nothing I could see. My new House Adepts haven't been able to see anything either."

Kaothos huffed. She didn't like not knowing what we might be facing.

"So there might be a potential threat from the new, structured magic. What's your take on the shamanic equivalent?" I asked.

Alice grimaced. "That's the great question. Shamanic magic is as strong as the shaman and his or her spirit guide, at the time the working is attempted. It's just unpredictable and erratic. But look at it this way—Athanate record things." She waved at the books on the table. "If there had been examples of Adepts powerful enough to attack whole Athanate Houses, surely it would have happened at some time in the past."

Bian and I exchanged glances. I knew her mind worked like mine on this. Records would depend on whether there were survivors and witnesses.

"Well, it has happened, of course, in one poorly documented instance," Diana said.

Alice bowed her head. "Byzantium. A dragon changes everything," she agreed.

"So Kaothos could make it the best of both worlds for the Northern Adept League?" I said. "The controllability of structured magic combined with the power of a dragon?"

Alice nodded.

"It seems *they* believe that," Kaothos grumbled. "But from the evidence we can see in the Dark Library, it didn't go as planned in Byzantium."

It was Bian's turn to snort. "A huge library full of obscure stuff that could be translated any way you want. The more you collect, the less you know. The short version..." she held up her index finger, "Adepts, especially modern ones, are generally really good at defensive magic. You don't take them on their own turf." A second finger went up. "That doesn't translate to good offensive magic. They probably won't be able to burst in throwing spells around." Third finger. "Kaothos is possibly what would make the difference to that last item." Fourth finger. "Every time in recorded history a dragon spirit guide came along, regardless of what they were doing, things went bad."

"But not necessarily through the fault of the dragon, Bian Hwa Trang," Kaothos hissed.

I stopped them before they got into an argument.

"It doesn't change anything. We have Kaothos here. We don't want the Northern Adept League or Denver communities to take her away. We don't want the Empire of Heaven to find out she's alive. First thing is to get Tullah back and re-linked to Kaothos, but we don't know where Tullah is, and she isn't answering calls. There has to be a way to find her."

Diana and Kaothos kept stubbornly silent.

"Here's another thing," I said. "Everyone is going on about how powerful Kaothos is; just look at the effort being put into hunting her down. They don't seem especially worried about any difficulties in capturing her. Isn't this like hunting a tiger with nothing but a stick?"

"It would be, once the full link between host and dragon has matured," Alice said. "That's why they're hunting so urgently—to get Kaothos while she's far short of her potential."

"And her full potential?"

"We don't know. The Northern Adept League has been researching this. The Hecate may know. Our guess..." Alice shrugged. "Enough to level whole cities. As to your question about Kaothos finding Tullah now, yes, she probably *could* find her, if she came out of hiding in this dungeon. We may soon be at a point where the threat of being discovered by the Empire's Adepts isn't enough to prevent her taking that option."

Diana took a breath to speak and stopped herself.

"Am I missing something?" I asked. "You guys are in the middle of an argument?"

"It's been suggested, so I have made it plain I'm not willing to wield this power," Diana said. "And so, it seems we have to ask you to step up again, Amber. However much we wanted you to have an opportunity to rest, to settle your House, we need you to find Tullah, while Kaothos and I need to remain in hiding."

I sighed. No one promised me life would be fair.

Bian looked pissed.

"I could help, Amber Farrell," Kaothos said. "The problem is, this may be more urgent than we thought. If it is, it's much more urgent."

I looked at them all. "I don't understand what's going on here."

It was Bian who answered: "The books suggest there's a time limit for spirit guides returning to their original hosts. One we're approaching."

"A limit for ordinary spirit guides, not dragons," Kaothos hissed.

"So spirit guides do jump from host to host sometimes?" I asked and Bian nodded. "And if we don't get Tullah back, Kaothos has to stay with Diana?"

"And Diana risks ending up as Lyssae," Alice said. "Spirit guides and elder Athanate do not mix well in the long term."

My gaze went along the walls, where the Lyssae stood, Anubis first among them.

Keep well away from magic, Tolly had suggested.

But I had Hana, until she'd disappeared. It hadn't been a problem.

Apart from me being a blood magic witch, maybe.

Especially dark magic, Tolly had said.

"Okay," I said. I didn't want to get into this with the rest of them. "My urgent task is to find Tullah. That means you guys can concentrate on talking to the Hecate. Maybe she has some ideas."

Bian touched her ear. She was connected into the security system, and I could tell something had come up.

What do you want to bet it's for me?

But I had one other thing I couldn't leave any longer, even if I was scared to hear the answer.

"Can I speak to Kaothos alone for a moment please?"

There was not enough space in Skylur's dungeon for Diana and Alice to move away without being able to overhear anything spoken out aloud, but they were familiar with Kaothos and the capability she had of speaking mind-to-mind.

I went and sat cross-legged on the floor by the dragon's head.

Coiled and laid out along the wall as she was, Kaothos looked uncomfortable now, brooding and angry.

I had two things I wanted to talk about. I guessed the dark magic was the more difficult one, so I started with the issue I thought would be easier.

You know what I'm going to ask, don't you?

Yessss, Amber Farrell, I think I do.

The coils stirred. The huge eye in front of me burned and flickered.

Of all my friends, you would have been the first to know that my spirit guide was gone.

Coils began to slither against each other. She was here in a physical body, not as a projection. The weight of her coils threatened to break things.

I was, she said.

She was hissing now, as if pressure was building up in an old steam locomotive.

Yet you said nothing. Does this mean you know what happened to Hana and Tara?

I do, she said. *I am sorry, Amber Farrell. I am sorry.*

Cold fear collected in my stomach.

Are they gone forever? I asked.

Kaothos twisted and shimmered in distress, the weight of her words in my head seemed tauter. *You said I must not lie to my friends, but you also said I must honor my word.*

It's hard sometimes, I said. *What happened?*

Tullah made me promise. She wants to tell you herself.

This was confusing me. *About what?*

When we were all distracted by the pain of destroying the lock that held Diana, the dragon said, *I moved from Tullah to Diana.*

I remembered:

All the screaming merging into one, endless, wordless song in my head.

White fury in my head. The entire energy of the lock collapsing, burning through me. Kaothos pulling it through herself instead.

Fire in my veins. Me screaming. Kaothos screaming. The whole Taos community of Adepts scattered around the hillside, all of them, screaming. All of us bound into this one, hideous pain.

White. White. White. Burning my eyes.

"I remember," I said aloud, my voice shaky.

Hana was in the same pain, the dragon said. *She was under the same urge as I was to move to a stronger host. Tara was simply caught in the flow.*

My mouth fell open. Of course!

Tullah has them? I asked. *They'll come back when you go back?*

Kaothos twisted more.

If we get Tullah back in time. These books Diana has been reading, they tell her that spirit guides cannot go back if they spend too much time in their new host. It does not apply to me; I can go back. But—

I interrupted her. Surely she wasn't saying...

What happens to Tara and Hana if you go back to Tullah and they can't move?

The dragon began to shimmer and thrash. Her body, so solid a minute ago, was passing through the furniture now.

I do not know, Amber Farrell. I am sorry. Tullah is sorry. We are very afraid.

She twisted once more and vanished. Her presence, so powerful in the room before, was suddenly simply not there.

I spun around. Had it upset her so badly she'd left the protection of the dungeon?

Diana made a calming gesture.

"She's not really gone. She just gets upset easily at the moment," she said. "We really need to find Tullah. I'm afraid that means *you* really need to find Tullah, though we'll do anything we can to help once Kaothos comes back."

Bian touched me on the shoulder.

"Julie's just taken a message from Pia. You're needed urgently back at Manassah. Something's seriously wrong with Scott. And there's also a problem with Tove."

Oh, hell.

Chapter 18

I drove, despite my mind whirling with the news about Tara and Hana. Julie got to hold the cell phones.

We made great time in the Hill Bitch. People saw it coming up in their mirrors like Thor's hammer descending on them and got the hell out of the way.

As I drove, I got the bare details about Scott from Pia on my cell phone's speaker.

He'd woken up fevered and shivering. I knew that was reasonably common in crusis. That didn't worry any of us.

He was talking, but, according to Pia, he was lapsing into incoherence from time to time.

Crusis affected different people in different ways. Talking rubbish wasn't so worrying. It didn't mean he was going rogue.

But what wasn't common was he was getting terrible pains throughout his body. From his description, it was as if his limbs were being twisted, or at times, as if he were getting electric shocks.

Pia was on a simultaneous call to Bian and Diana and they were really worried to hear that he had that kind of pain. It wasn't a common feature of crusis.

I got a sick feeling in my gut. My first infusion was going wrong.

Was I venomous? Would Scott die? Or go rogue? It would be my duty to kill him if he did.

My House. I'm thinking of killing a man I took into my House and infused. My responsibility.

Could Diana do something? Could we move him to Haven?

I could hear voices in the background. Amanda—in tears, trying to hold them back.

"He wants to go outside," Pia said. "Into the garden."

No one else spoke.

My call.

"Let him," I said, ignoring the ice in my chest. "Only the garden, and stay with him, of course. Move the guards to the front of the house."

Because the guards around Manassah were still human. Security was still being provided by my old friend Vic Gayle. Another thing I was going to have to re-evaluate.

"Just keep telling him to keep it together," I said. "I'm nearly home."

Five minutes later the guards saw us and had the gate open in time for us to drive straight in.

I ran down around the house and into the garden, Julie close behind me.

Scott was lying in the shadows beneath the gaunt larch and thick cypress trees that bordered Manassah. Amanda was clutching him to her as if she were trying to shield him from the pain in his body. Pia looked as if she were trying to pull Amanda back. Flint and Kane stood awkwardly, unable to help.

Scott had clearly gotten worse.

"She's locked them together with her eukori," Pia said. "I can't break it."

Scott's back arched and his heels drummed in the dirt.

There wasn't time to ask anybody else for help. All I had was an aching certainty that if Scott died while they were locked together like this, then so would Amanda.

I grabbed her head.

"Amanda!" Her eyes were open, but they looked straight through me. I tried to compel her, and I had no more success than Pia. Her eukori was bright and hard as steel.

In desperation, I reached out with my eukori.

Julie and Pia first. Then Flint and Kane.

I took their strength and slammed back into Amanda's mental defenses. I *tore* her away from Scott, physically and mentally.

Eyes blind with tears, she swung fists wildly at me until Julie caught her wrists.

I ignored that. I pushed the other eukoris aside and linked into Scott, not holding him, simply resting my hand on his chest. He'd torn his clothes as if the touch of them was painful. His bare skin felt feverish. I pushed my senses beyond that and felt the surge of Blood in his veins, the throbbing of his heart, the air rushing into his lungs. The mad scurrying of his thoughts.

And yet he welcomed the pressure of my hand; his thrashing calmed a little.

Why had I put my hand on him like that?

It just felt right.

Was there something going on at an instinctive level between Scott and me? Did I have a special bond with an Athanate that I had created?

Then why didn't this feel like connecting with another Athanate?

Because it didn't feel like that at all.

And yet he *was* becoming Athanate. He had to be. He'd be dead if he wasn't.

"Hurts," Scott groaned.

"I know," I whispered. "I'm sorry."

I could *feel* it. The pain. Muscles cramping. Joints in agony. Skin tearing. The *need* for something without knowing what it was.

I pulled as much as I could bear from him. I could sense him struggling against it.

The pain made it difficult to speak. My mouth felt numb. My jaw wanted to clench, but I forced the words out.

"Our pain," I said. "Share." It came out as a gasp.

"No."

But I was stronger than him. I took more, until it seemed to fill my body. Everything hurt. Everything felt wrong. It hurt so much, I wanted to rip my skin off and scream bloody oaths at the sky.

Stop thinking like that. Pain is an old friend.

I could work with it, and it was somehow familiar.

Even in the heart-squeezing grip of the pain, I shuddered. *Blood magic witch.*

"Stay with me, Scott."

He groaned. "Can't."

"You can and you will." I bowed my head and tried to clear my mind as the urge to scream built and built in my chest.

Think.

There was a reason he'd come outside. He needed... more space? More light?

"Move away," I said over my shoulder. My voice was hoarse.

There was movement behind me. A little of the pressure eased off and Scott responded as if it had been a weight on him.

It's too soon for him to develop that kind of ability in eukori.

I dug deeper in his senses, trying to work out what his body was doing, what it needed.

Cold—he wanted that.

Dark—it'd been too bright in the house.

He'd wanted the sensation of the wind, the sweet pine scent of the trees.

Oh, my God! That's why this pain is so familiar.

Oh, shit!

No time. I have to do what I can.

I took his hand. "You have to trust me, Scott," I told him. "I'm the one who infused you, and your body knows it. Listen to it. Listen to me."

"You're Farrell?" His voice cracked.

I nodded. There was only a little time.

"P... P... Pleased to... meet..." He gave up and his eyes closed as another storm of pain built.

"Don't fight me," I said, and let the pain flow through me while I tried to send back what I knew he needed. He had to sense what I wanted him to sense.

Our hearts surged together, beating so fast I felt lightheaded.

Run!

There was no space here at Manassah, but my memories were vivid. I ran in my mind, through the deep shadows of the trees at Bitter Hooks, and Scott came with me. I forced my memories into him, so his own eyes couldn't see, his body couldn't feel.

See! Through the trees. As free as the wind.

Wrong! Something wrong, I could almost hear his mind was telling him.

No, this is right. This is us. This is how we are.

There. The light. There!

"Run toward the light."

Fear coursed through him, and I cursed my clumsy mental metaphors.

"It's not dying," I said, through gritted teeth. *Closer. Closer.* "It's rebirth. Follow the sound of my call..."

In our shared vision, we burst out of the trees to the clearing around Falcon's Bluff. I let him truly see me, and see himself in my eyes.

"No!"

He stumbles, his body suddenly uncontrollable. He's falling. His joints demand to move in the wrong direction.

No time for anything else. No other way.

"I am your alpha," I snarled. "If you stumble, I will raise you up."

I put all my strength into that, as if I could *will* him to do what he needed to do.

In the gloom beneath the larch and cypress, Scott's body arched in one great spasm. A last tortured sound was torn from his throat, and then he collapsed.

Chapter 19

"I warned you," I said as I pulled myself shakily to my feet.

"Scott?"

Julie let Amanda go and she ran past me, just as Scott managed to get himself under control enough to stagger upright.

He was a handsome man, and he made a handsome wolf too, even if he was a bit unsure about it.

Amanda didn't hesitate or show shock; she knelt and threw her arms around his neck.

Not what I would recommend with a werewolf, especially a brand new werewolf who was also probably suffering from Athanate crusis. Fortunately, Scott just stood there, looking wolf-embarrassed.

It was Pia who broke the silence, with a short laugh. "Well, now we know what happens when you infuse someone. You get hybrids."

I nodded. "I guess so. Of course, he hasn't shown us he's Athanate yet, but I can't see how he'd turn out only werewolf."

How did that make me feel?

When Skylur and Diana first realized I was a hybrid, they'd been astounded. That was nothing to the reaction of most of the Athanate community. I was an anomaly, a *freak*. There had been those in the Assembly who'd wanted me killed. The more rational of them claimed it was because the influence of becoming a Were at the same time as I was working through Athanate crusis meant I was certain to go rogue.

The Were hadn't been much better to start with. I guessed I'd gotten past that with the halfy ritual, but suspected many of them continued to think I was a freak. A useful freak maybe, but still, a freak.

In a strange way, I'd enjoyed being the freak, and now I wasn't the only one.

I felt kinda upset about that.

A couple of more sensible thoughts came to me.

First, would this make Mykayla change her mind?

Second, and more important, I couldn't let Scott out of my sight for a while. I knew from personal experience just how difficult it was becoming Athanate and Were at the same time. There was a risk he'd go rogue, and my enemies, Were and Athanate, would love it if they could say my infusions did that.

I was fairly sure I could keep Scott sane just by keeping him close by, in the same way that Alex had helped me.

"This is a first?" Flint interrupted my thoughts. "A hybrid? I mean by biting."

"As far as we know," I said. "Let's get him inside, out of sight."

Kane gathered Scott's ripped clothes off the ground. "I'll get him my spare tracksuit."

He ruffled Scott's back as he passed, and Scott bared fangs silently. Amanda might be able to take liberties, but the others had better not.

Definitely not letting him out of my sight for the moment.

In the living room, we sat and watched as Scott paced up and down, getting used to his wolf form with its extended senses.

He sneezed at some smell and Amanda laughed nervously.

"When does he change back?" she said.

Scott's head turned and his yellow eyes locked on me. He understood perfectly what was being said, of course.

"When he wants to," I replied.

Werewolves *could* get lost in their wolf form, but that was something that affected older ones, not a cub like Scott. Though, of course, he was a very old cub. How old had Amanda said he was? Two hundred and thirty? He'd been a poet, a contemporary of Shelley and Byron in Georgian England before she'd taken him as her kin.

In any event, my answer seemed to satisfy Scott and he continued walking around the room and sniffing things.

"Or when I tell him to," I added.

I am your alpha and I am the Mistress of your House, Scott.

The side of his lip lifted; that *might* be a sort of wolfy smile rather than a snarl, but I had the feeling until we got through the Athanate crusis and sorted out the werewolf alpha signals, Scott was going to be a handful for me, no matter how nice and polite he was as a man.

A challenge.

I don't back down from werewolf challenges. I can't. I'm an alpha.

Scott needed me to guide him. He couldn't have any idea what he'd gotten into. Even if he *didn't* go rogue, there were paranormal laws he could break that would end up the same way for him.

Kane came back in with the promised tracksuit. Seeing Scott still in wolf form, he grunted and sat down next to Amanda. He and Flint were on either side of her, eyes fixed on the wolf. Scott's lip did that twitching thing again, and I felt the faintest deep rumble of Were dominance display coming from him.

Enough.

I had a second problem tonight, as if a furry, snarling Scott wasn't enough.

"Look, this is weird for all of us," I said, "and you all have questions, but I'm not sure I have the answers. What I need now is to know what's happening with Tove."

Pia looked uncertain. "She said she was bored and wanted to go clubbing."

Amanda nodded, eyes never moving from Scott. "She was getting agitated."

"So what happened?"

"I wasn't sure what to do," Pia said. "I mean, she's not a prisoner here, is she? Anyway, she didn't know where to go and she has no money, so David offered to go with her."

My fault; I'd been too distracted to leave specific instructions about Tove. More truthfully, I hadn't really wanted to think about her. I was beginning to regret offering her a place to stay. Not just because she was going to be difficult to handle, but also for her own sake. It hadn't been safe for people to be too closely associated with us for a while now, and it looked as if it was going to get worse.

So much for the what-ifs and maybes. David's decision to go with her was better than nothing, but I was unhappy with it. The Northern Adept League hadn't actually threatened us yet, and the Denver Adepts only had an issue with me directly, but still, I was *not* having my people out there without backup.

"Do we know where they are?" I asked.

Pia nodded. "The Pool. I think she overheard you talking about it."

The Pool was a club, just south of the Capitol, off Broadway. Its name wasn't actually the Pool, but no one remembered its real name.

I'd been speaking to Jofranka this morning and mentioned I'd heard that the DJs on tonight were Electric Breath. They had been my favorites on the illegal rave circuit, and it seemed they'd gone respectable while my back was turned.

Meanwhile, Pia was right, Tove wasn't a prisoner, and we had no real right to prevent her from doing anything she wanted, however self-destructive that might be.

I wasn't sure she was out to score drugs. In fact, I suspected she wanted to turn herself around. The trouble was, no one had been able to have any meaningful conversation with her about what she really wanted. She'd been reasonably polite: thanked Jen, thanked me, thanked Yelena. Apart from that, *yes* and *no*, mainly, and little or no eye contact.

Nick Grey had seemed to get through but apparently, whatever Were stuff that needed Alex had turned out to need him as well.

So it was down to me. I had to make progress with Tove. And I sensed my time to do that would be very limited soon. Tonight it would have to be—make or break.

"I'm going partying," I said. "With Julie and Keith."

"Not a great idea, Boss," Julie said.

She and Yelena hadn't been happy with some of my decisions about security and safety recently. They had my sympathy on this one, but I wasn't happy with the alternative.

"Probably." I laughed it off and gave her a hug. "And we're taking Scott," I added.

Everyone looked at the wolf. The wolf stared back, lip lifting again.

"Two legs or four?" Pia asked with a small smile.

"Much as I'd love to stroll into the Pool with a huge wolf straining on a leash, I think we'll go on two legs," I said.

I turned to the Adepts. "And one of you two. Who's the better dancer?"

"That'd be me," Kane said.

Flint rolled his eyes but didn't bother arguing.

By the time I looked back at Scott, he was in his human form, looking... not actually sheepish, but a little confused by the carryover of his emotions from his wolf form. Keith nudged the tracksuit aside with his foot disdainfully and led him off to find clothes he could borrow.

"Will he be all right?" Amanda came to me and asked quietly.

"No point whispering; he has wolfy hearing now." I grinned, then got serious. "To partly answer your question... it'll be better for him if he's with me for the moment. I'm sorry I can't give any more assurance than that."

Amanda wasn't happy, but kept silent.

"I know it's difficult," I said. "I'm guessing you still feel he's your kin, your responsibility. But now he's also a werewolf, and I'm his alpha. He's become my responsibility."

"Or a hybrid instead of a werewolf," Julie said. "Even more clearly Amber's responsibility."

I could see Amanda struggling, but in the end she nodded.

She was standing close to me. I took a deep breath, savored the scent of her marque and felt my eyes go black with desire for her Blood.

The pulse in her neck responded. Our Athanate instincts didn't care what else was going on.

But she took off after Keith and Scott, which might have been a good thing.

Julie cleared her throat behind me.

"We can't take weapons into the club, but I think we should put some in the car," she said.

"Good idea."

The others went off to get changed, which left me with Pia.

"You're taking the lead on mentoring Scott?" she asked.

"I think I have to," I said and she nodded.

"Yes. My experience is limited..."

"But?" I prompted.

"When I was in House Altau, we used to interact a lot more with the Denver pack."

"I remember Felix saying something about that," I said.

"Okay. We never had a hybrid, obviously, but we did have new wolves team up with new Athanate, so I got to see how the new wolves act."

Bian and Diana had both said something to me about that as well. Athanate in crusis had an urgent need to bite, all while being subjected to the torrent of heightened senses and unpredictable emotional swings. It was dangerous. Kin had to be trained on how to handle that.

It was similar with new werewolves; violence was part of what made them werewolves. They had to learn to control their violence.

And although Scott had started off with turning wolf, I had to assume he'd have Athanate fangs as well soon. He'd have the problems from both sides.

House Altau and the Denver pack used to have some kind of scheme where both new Were and new Athanate were able to let off steam together.

I was a little slow this evening, but I finally saw where Pia was heading.

"Have I got this straight?" I said. "All those newbies used to get together and screw each other's brains out?"

"Yes," Pia said. "It seemed effective. Just something I thought I should remind you about."

"Yeah. Good call," I said, keeping a blank face over my totally freaked-out mind. I was Athanate, but clearly not quite Athanate enough.

As I pulled on my jacket—actually one of Alex's—my cell pinged.

Jen.

"Hi," she said, making it bright and cheerful. "Just wanted to hear your voice. We're on the ground at Cincinnati. Got some time while they refuel us."

"Hi, Boss." Yelena's voice cut in. "All good?"

I snorted and gave them a rundown of what had happened at Haven and afterwards.

"So now you need to go out to get Tove and David back?" Jen asked.

"I need to get David. Whether Tove comes back is up to her."

"You need to find Tullah and then let her and Kaothos face down the Adepts," Yelena said. "Don't need risks like tonight. Julie or Keith go with you?"

What she really wanted to say was that I shouldn't go out at all.

"Both of them," I said. "It'll be fine, but there's bound to be something you want to share from the wisdom of the Carpathians on this?"

She thought for a moment.

"Yes, Ukrainian proverb, very famous. Woman who licks knives, one day will cut tongue."

Chapter 20

I managed to drive us down to the club without cutting my tongue.

Yelena had a point, I guessed. I was taking too many risks. But every point of decision had worse outcomes than the one I'd chosen.

Which was not to say the decision this evening was safe or easy.

We parked on Lincoln and walked.

The club worked hard on soundproofing, but with our wolfy hearing, the rush of synthesizers over the heavy heartbeat of the music seemed to reach out to us as we approached.

Scott reacted. Ideally, he should have been somewhere quiet and familiar with me and Alex and Amanda, in soothing surroundings, getting used to his wolf. It was just too bad that nothing in Denver was familiar, he'd barely met me, and he'd yet to meet Alex at all.

So, instead of that quiet time, I was taking him into a bright and noisy venue where he was going to be surrounded by a herd of excited prey. Already, mingling with the crowd at the entrance, his heart rate and respiration jumped up a notch.

I couldn't leave him behind. I couldn't leave him in anyone else's care. All I could do was take his hand as we walked in, and the physical contact seemed to help.

"Chill," I said. "We shouldn't be here long. In and out."

He didn't reply, but he seemed okay while we touched.

It was the calm before the storm.

I'd been there before, but none of the others had. As we descended into the basement, the reason for the club's nickname became apparent to them. The theme color was blue, ranging from light swimming pool blue to deep space violet. There were 'windows' on every wall, made to look like stained glass and backlit. There were strobe spotlights on the ceiling and a swirling layer of water-vapor mist above the dancers that made it feel like everyone was dancing in a fog.

Electric Breath were already up and running. They were two goth girls who took turns sharing the DJ work with leading the dancing, and their routine was working well tonight.

And just as we reached the dancefloor, my nose finally worked through all the haze of adrenaline, sweat, drugs, alcohol and perfumes.

There were werewolves in the club.

And they weren't Denver pack.

Scott smelled them a second after I did and I had to grab hold of his arm to keep him in place.

Julie reacted by slipping in front of me, and Keith covered our backs. Kane did something that I felt as the skin-prickling sensation of magic stirring, without knowing what it was. None of them knew what was going on, or what had triggered the response from me and Scott.

"Easy!" I shouted above the music. "Calm down."

Wolf territory didn't apply so strictly at the moment. Wolves from all over the US could be here in Colorado to visit Felix and Cameron out on the ranch at Coykuti. They could be here to meet me for another ritual. There were lots of reasons there might be wolves in the club.

I knew it and it still felt wrong.

Scott didn't know the background; he was stuck at the *my-territory, not-my-pack* stage. His new instincts hadn't yet worked out that if he attacked them, they'd kill him. Easily.

"Bar area." I had to shout again.

The bar was a split level on one side, above the dance floor, and steps to it were right ahead of us.

I managed to get them there without letting go of Scott and without anyone noticing how oddly we were behaving.

If they weren't completely zoned out with the music, the dancing wolves would have noticed us by now, but I hoped they'd register us as part of the Denver pack and not necessarily a threat.

All assuming, of course, that they were here legitimately.

At the bar, it was less frantic than the dance floor. I explained to the rest of them. I sent Keith and Julie to get us drinks. I used Kane to help me frogmarch Scott to the far corner where we got lucky and took over a table as a group left.

Scott understood all the words I'd used, but he was a long way from controlling himself. He was being overwhelmed, so I sat next to him, held his hand, held his eyes and kept speaking to him.

"Just a couple of werewolves. It's not like we're in danger, or we're surrounded by other packs. It's safe. This is our territory. They're visitors."

Over and over, until finally some of that berserk wolf-gold faded from his pupils. He wasn't relaxed, but at least he wasn't on the point of exploding anymore.

By the time I'd achieved that, only Kane was sitting with me.

I looked over at him. "Julie? Keith?"

"Down to the dancefloor. They'll get Tove and David to come up."

"Good."

They'd bought us bottles of my favorite Blue Moon beer. Kane pushed mine over, and after a quick check with me, slid one across to Scott.

I took a long pull. Not a very elegant way of drinking, but it tasted so good and I needed it.

"A couple of werewolves came up to the bar area and looked across at us," Kane said. "Then they left."

I didn't like that.

It wasn't as if werewolves were like the Mafia; I hadn't expected them to come over and pay their respects. But to come up, look, and go away... not good. For no reason I could state, it didn't feel right.

There wasn't time to think any more deeply about it. The rest of the party returned to the bar area, escorting Tove. David, Julie and Keith retreated to the bar. Kane joined them.

Scott made to get up too, but I shook my head. I wanted him right here, sitting down and holding my hand, not tearing someone's face off because they'd stepped on his toe.

Tove slumped down in the seat, her head down, a sheen of sweat on her skin and sparkles of water in her hair from the mist over the dance floor.

Twenty-two years old. Four years out of Minnesota, the first three years in LA waiting tables and hitting the Hollywood auditions. Then Forsyth happened. By the time we met, Tove was working in Van Nuys, charging a hundred bucks a time and calling herself Celeste.

Something resonated, and even if I couldn't help every woman whose life Tanner had blighted, I *could* help Tove. Or that's what I thought at the time. I wasn't so sure now.

In the deep blue lighting, we all probably looked unhealthy. She certainly did. Pasty skin. Circles under the eyes. Her vital signs were about as erratic as Scott's were.

Yelena had warned me Tove was a mess when she'd flown her back. The girl had pulled herself together for Christmas Day, but now the withdrawal symptoms had their claws deep in her.

We could partly fix that, Pia told me. Athanate bio-agents could remove the physical symptoms.

The trouble was, they wouldn't necessarily have any effect on the mental symptoms. *And* I would need her to consent to being bitten while not under compulsion from the aftereffects of drugs in her system: *my* rules for my House, so I'd have to stick to them.

How to get through to her?

She was going to be agitated and irritable and—

"So what's it gonna be?" she asked, her voice waspish and her eyes finally coming up to meet mine. 'We were just worried for you, Tove', or 'you have no right to do this, and don't you appreciate what we're doing'?"

For a moment I was too shocked to react, and Scott exploded onto his feet.

His face was distorted with anger. He was a breath away from turning wolf right there.

"Scott!" I grabbed his arm again and pulled him back.

Tove's mouth was slack and her eyes wide with fear. Even without changing, Scott was reeking of violence.

The others came over from the bar in a hurry, as much to shield us from other eyes as to give Tove and me a little privacy for our chat.

I had to leave her to the others for a minute while I locked eyes with Scott again. I touched him with eukori, but he was such a tornado of emotion it didn't seem to register with him.

"Back down, Scott," I said. "Back down. What would Amanda think of how you're behaving?"

He didn't like being asked that, not one bit, but it got through all that mindless instinct and connected with his brain.

He sat back, burning with frustration, all that churning emotion and nowhere to ground it, but just—*just*—under control.

Which allowed me to turn my attention back to Tove.

Do I really want this?

Now?

I don't back down from challenges.

Under that stubbornness was another thought—*if I can't get through to Tove, will that mean I'll fail with Kath as well?*

Tove had flipped from angry and aggressive to withdrawn and scared. She started to cry.

I pushed her bottle of beer closer to her.

"I'm sorry," she said.

I took another pull of my beer to give myself time to calm down. I'd have preferred a screaming argument with her. With the noise level in the club, no one would have noticed.

"Why?" I asked eventually. "Why are you sorry?"

"Because, everything I do or say, I fuck things up."

Maybe she wanted me to say something comforting like *it's not your fault.*

I shrugged. "Tell me about it."

She had the beer bottle in her hand and began picking at the label like a scab. Tears slowed. David brought her paper napkins from the bar and she blew her nose.

"I'm afraid to talk. I'm afraid to be quiet. I don't know what you want from me. And you do want something." She looked angrily at me, daring me to deny it. "No one gives me something for nothing. I learned that real quick."

"What do you think we want from you?" I said.

She looked around at us, and then she lowered her head again. "You're some kind of sex cult, aren't you?"

I had to laugh, even if it made her flinch.

She went back to angry and defiant.

"I know you're private investigators and company execs and all sorts of shit, but I have eyes, you know, I can see. All that touching and kissing and stuff. No one sleeps alone."

I was still laughing. It wasn't that funny and it wasn't helping the situation, but I couldn't help it.

How screwed up could this situation get?

"It isn't really a sex cult, but you're right, in a way," I said and took another drink from my beer before continuing. "So... think of it as a cult, if you like. Think of it as we want to recruit you."

She looked genuinely puzzled.

She wasn't faking it. I touched on her emotions with eukori and it seemed she didn't understand, but mainly that she was afraid. Her life was miserable, but she'd come to terms with it. Misery had become familiar; she was too scared to let it go. It was as if she'd convinced herself that her misery was what made the pain tolerable.

"Why would you want me?" she said.

I didn't answer right away, because in truth, at that moment, I didn't really want her in my House. There was too much going on, and she was trouble.

And yet, I could still see, under the hard shell of scars, the fresh-faced Minnesota teen who'd run up the steps into the airplane, full of hope and dreams that she'd make her name in Hollywood and show all the people back in her sleepy home town that there really was a whole world out there and a way to grab it.

All she'd shown was sometimes it grabbed you right back.

I didn't owe her personally. But Very Special Agent Ingram of the FBI had put it well in his lazy Texan drawl: *Sometimes I have to ignore the big picture and make it about one person. A representative for the whole. A place holder to take the place of all the others I can't really help with my justice.*

I sighed in frustration.

I couldn't say that to Tove. She wouldn't understand it.

However I dodged it, I *did* owe her, in lieu of all the girls that Forsythe had gone on to rape after he'd raped me and I kept quiet. All the girls I couldn't do anything about. All the wrong I couldn't right.

On the other hand, I didn't want to *make* her accept anything. It was the same argument that Jen and Pia had made about Kath, and they were right: she'd had enough forced on her.

We weren't getting anywhere, and I needed to get Scott out of this environment.

Time for plan B. At the possible cost of breaking my word, I had to shock her into making the first positive move. Or not.

"Look." I pulled out a wad of cash I'd picked up before leaving the house. "Trust is difficult, Tove, and I need that before we can do anything. I need you to make a choice. So, this money is yours. Free. You can do what you want with it. It's enough to pay for the airfare back up north. You could go home. You think your family doesn't want any more to do with you, but I can guarantee you're wrong. It doesn't mean that it'll be easy going back, but I believe you're strong enough, deep down. You know you are."

I took a deep breath. "Or you could blow it on enough drugs to kill yourself. I hope you don't do that, but if it's what you really want, there's nothing I can do to stop you, nothing anyone can do. If that's what you want."

She started crying again.

"Or..." I put the money into her hands, closed her fingers over it and then wrapped mine around them. "Or, you could decide you're going to fix things here in Denver, with our help. That's the hardest path of all, but it's the one that *will* work. The trouble is, I can't prove a thing to you until you trust me, and ask me to help. And mean it."

I was backing her into a corner, which made me a mean bitch, but it had to be done.

I'd gotten through to her; I could tell.

At that moment, Kane's head snapped up and swiveled to look down toward the entrance steps on the other side of the dance floor.

The hairs stood up on the back of my neck.

Adepts. Strong ones.

Chapter 21

I leaped to my feet and looked down into the steaming pit of the dancefloor.

All I could see were shapes moving in the water-vapor mist, lit by the flickering strobes. Then, like the winter breath of buffalos, the fog swelled and rolled at the stairway to the bar. Out of that came three people, climbing the steps.

I knew the one in front. Ken Weaver, the leader of the Denver Adept community. Not the type to hang out in clubs. No, this wasn't a social visit.

"Shit."

Nothing I could do about Scott.

"Julie, Keith, take Tove outside."

"Boss—"

"Do it. Then get back here."

They grabbed a startled Tove and marched her out.

My heart was in my throat as Weaver passed them at the entrance to the bar area.

He looked aside at them, disdain clear on his face, but he didn't make to stop them.

One problem less.

"Scott. I don't think they'll try anything here. Keep it together," I said.

Scott growled, but I could live with that, as long as he didn't lunge across the table.

On my other side, Kane prepared something; it felt like insects skittering across my flesh. A defensive working of some kind?

Would Weaver use magic?

I didn't think they'd try anything here, in full view of the people in the bar. But what if they'd prepared a working to snatch us away into the spirit world? Could Kane stop them?

Weaver's group came to a halt beside our table. He looked briefly at Kane and Scott, then ignored them and sat down opposite me. The other two stood behind him.

He was a big man, heavy shouldered, dark haired. He had piercing blue eyes, the sort of color they called Persian blue, from the antique pottery glaze. They stared at me from under a heavy forehead and thick eyebrows.

He leaked power, so much it made my skin itch. He was strong, and he'd gotten a lot stronger since I last met him.

There was a different tingling sensation of a working from him. Kane tensed up, but all that happened was the noise of the club around us faded away into the background—still there, but not so loud we couldn't talk.

"A rogue Were, an outlaw Adept and a human woman who stinks of addiction," Weaver said. "You keep strange company, Farrell, especially in places packed with humans."

Scott and Kane both 'smiled', but their appearances couldn't have been more different.

"Says the man using magic," I replied. "The woman has left and it's none of your business what my Athanate House does or who's in it, Weaver."

"You're actually claiming these in your House?" His fingers, small for such a big man, flicked to indicate the others.

"Still none of your business. Send any complaints to House Altau."

Weaver might be powerful, but he would have to be all kinds of crazy to contemplate taking Altau on, given Skylur commanded every Athanate in the country.

"Your leader has his own concerns in New York, I hear." Weaver gave a dismissive wave. "It's not important. Where is Tullah Autplumes?"

Not Kaothos? Not 'the dragon'? Tullah...

"Another member of my Athanate House, and another person who's no business of yours."

His eyes narrowed and glinted.

"She is part of my Denver community of Adepts, not your..." He restrained himself. He hadn't been about to say House. He'd probably been about to call it a brothel or something.

I didn't wait for him to finish. "She hasn't been a member of your community since you tried to prevent her from using her spirit guide."

I'd broken that lock down in New Mexico. A good thing I had, too.

Mind you, saying that she was part of my House was half a lie. She wasn't bitten or bound. A good thing that Weaver was no Truth Sensor.

His skills seemed more in the compulsion department.

I could feel the power building up from the three of them, like the threat of a thunderstorm.

I locked my eukori down. It wasn't enough.

The music Electric Breath was playing slowed to a serpent sway; it became cold as a reptile's blood, and it had a need that was insidious, narrow and demanding. It had eyes like a raptor that could see deep into my soul, and a sibilant lizard tongue that spoke of the falling of stars and the death of all dreams.

"HEY! RED! Wanna dance?"

The confused vision of flying snakes emerging from the dark jungle swamps vanished. Sounds returned. Electric Breath were playing van Burren trance music, the bass pumping energy through the floor.

A very drunk, kinda cute guy was leaning over the table, clutching the edge for support. How he'd decided my auburn hair was red under the club's blue lights was one of those mysteries that will never be known, but he'd arrived like a beautiful car-crash into the complex working that Weaver was attempting.

My heart rate sped back up from the doldrums and air rushed into my lungs.

"Another time," I said to my savior and managed to wink at him. "When you can dance without me holding you upright."

My voice sounded raw against the noise that had returned. The boy looked upset, but Julie and Keith returned at that moment. Keith guided the drunk back to the bar. Julie stood behind the Adepts and got *real* close, so close that I could feel them twitching.

She and Keith couldn't have known how Weaver had attacked us, but they sensed what was needed.

Scott looked confused by everything, as if he'd woken up in the middle of an argument.

Kane smiled again.

Did he just use magic to lure that guy to come over and interrupt? I wondered.

Anyway, between the notice we were being paid by the rest of the bar now, and the distraction of Julie's threat, Weaver wouldn't be able to maintain enough focus to make another working.

"Try that again, Weaver," I said, to make sure he understood, "and you'll find out what kind of weapons my team can smuggle into dance clubs."

I suspected Julie had a ceramic blade hidden up her shirtsleeves. Not very long and probably only good for a couple of stabs, but more than enough to kill.

How the hell we would fix that with the police afterwards, I didn't know.

Weaver's face was stiff with anger, but I didn't care; something else was happening now. I looked around, trying to work out where.

"Farrell!"

Weaver tapped on the back of my hand to get my attention back. His touch was like a discharge of static and I only just stopped myself from snatching my hand away. I wasn't going to give him the satisfaction of letting him know he'd startled me.

The air right beside us boiled.

It gave him a scare, but I'd had some warning, and I'd seen it before.

This time I was expecting the white hair and cold blue eyes that stared at me across the table.

"The gang's all here," I muttered.

Her lips thinned.

She liked my jokes. We were nearly best friends.

A couple of people in the bar might have noticed, but it was dark in our corner and the Hecate wasn't only half there, like last time she used this trick. I saw a guy hold up his drink and frown as if wondering how strong it was.

"Hecate," Weaver said stiffly. He obviously hadn't been expecting her to come here, and certainly not by using her aural projection trick.

They weren't working together. I didn't think Weaver even knew that Kaothos had moved to Diana.

If they're not working together, can I use that?

Or have I now got twice the enemies at this table?

"Weaver," the Hecate replied, matching his tone. "Good. As Amber says, we're all here, and it appears we have a common goal. It would be senseless for us to work against each other. Let's talk."

Apparently, her projection power didn't extend to sending a spell to silence the club around us, and I wasn't willing to let Weaver do it again, so he and I had to lean forward to hear each other.

"There is nothing the Athanate can provide except risk," Weaver said.

"Yet they seem to hold the key," the Hecate replied. "However reluctant they may be, we need to persuade them to share."

I didn't rise to that bait, buying some time instead.

"All this getting together. What about the werewolves?" I asked, sweetly, and Scott shifted in his seat again. I was back to holding his hand and willing him to remain calm. I was amazed he had managed it so far.

Weaver was stuck. I could tell he wanted to say that there was no place for animals in whatever plans he was brewing, but he knew I was a hybrid, and I'd seen his nervous glance at Scott.

"What about them?" he said, brushing his hand across his chin. "What part do you think they could play?"

"I think all of us should be in the Assembly, and any issues you have should be brought up there, under rules that are agreed by all."

Weaver's mouth twisted. "The werewolves aren't going to submit to your Athanate lawyers' club."

As he spoke, things changed again.

"I think they will," I said. "If you don't believe me, you could try asking them yourself."

The person I was going to suggest he ask had just come into the club. I hadn't had time to catch his scent, but I knew the feel of him in my eukori.

Zane.

He was the Albuquerque alpha. Both New Mexico alphas, Zane and Cameron, had a reputation for being crazy. People were starting to understand that crazy behavior was a deliberate mask, but in Zane's case, I wasn't sure it was all mask.

Still, his ultimate alpha, Cameron, was now mated to my ultimate alpha, Felix, which meant we were effectively in a sort of super-pack that covered New Mexico and Colorado. Not that it gave me any clue as to why he should turn up here. No problem. I wasn't looking that gift horse in the mouth.

He reached the top of the stairs and I took a moment to enjoy watching him.

He wasn't the sort of alpha who bulked up with weights; instead he was tall, balanced, wiry. He had bronzed skin the color of wild honey. Sharp, proud face. Black hair tightly coiled, glossy in the lights. Slim hips, long legs and an unhurried walk.

That's what every eye in the bar could see, and half of them were watching.

What they couldn't sense was the paranormal.

Zane put out a werewolf aura of violence on a tight rein, delivered with a double helping of dominance. It was a dangerously attractive mix for werewolves and it had gotten much stronger now that Cameron and Felix had united the packs.

The air seemed thinner all of a sudden.

He set my pulse racing, just like he had back down in Albuquerque, when I flirted my way to beating him at poker.

Down girl, dammit.

Weaver turned, and I could tell he knew who it was by the way his muscles tightened across his shoulders.

Zane arrived at our table.

"What a night out," the Albuquerque alpha said. "Were, Athanate and Adept enjoying the Denver scene. I'm sorry I have to break it up."

His voice was rich and full. It was the only thing about him that was false. I knew there was a different voice hiding underneath that studied way of speaking. The real voice would sound like hot, humid nights, sitting on the creaking wooden stoop to catch a breath of wind, the talk slow and the beer warm, sweat glistening on bare skin where the moonlight caught it—

I shook my head.

Why am I mooning over him?

"Amber," he said, and I looked up to meet his eyes, one green, the other brown. "You're called."

I got up, pulling Scott to his feet.

"Hold on," Weaver said, getting up too. "We need to talk. This is vital, for all of us. I'm not having Athanate and Were screw everything up over some petty territorial argument."

"Vital enough for you to try and break into my head?"

"That's interesting," Zane said. "You'll have to explain that to me later—magical violence against the pack. But right now, Amber and I have to go."

"Wait!" Weaver ran his hand across his chin quickly. The man had more tells than Switzerland. "Look, I'm sorry about that earlier. It's only because this is so very important. We need to get Tullah back. She's not safe. And you realize, don't you, if she's not safe, then neither are we."

"I can agree we need Tullah back here," I said, "and she needs to be safe."

"One step at a time, then." Weaver reached into his pocket and froze as Julie moved. I held up a hand to stop her from killing him.

Weaver carefully drew out a business card and handed it to me. "When you've finished, as soon as you've finished, come see me," he said. "Doesn't matter what time."

He made to leave, but Zane stopped him.

"We have a thousand wolves in Colorado and they know you, Weaver. They know your scent. They know every member of your community. They can track you all across the entire country. Don't mess with us."

Weaver pulled away. "I give my word that she won't be harmed or forced in any way other than by the persuasion of reason."

"Then I'll come visit," I said.

He nodded abruptly and the three of them walked quickly toward the exit.

Hecate's projection was standing next to me like a ghost. "Take his word with caution. You know my requirements, Amber."

"And you know mine. Tullah back first."

She sighed.

"That may be a problem, but I promise I will do everything I can to get her back to Denver."

Words were easy, but I could play that game too.

"Okay. I promise I'll pick you up at your apartment tomorrow, and you'll get your opportunity to talk."

She looked suspiciously at me, but I had my game face on.

"A deal, then."

Her image retreated into the shadows and vanished.

At Zane's urging, we hurried out of the club.

"You sure you know what you're doing with those two Adepts?" Zane said.

I shrugged. "Gotta be done. What's the hurry tonight, or did you just come in to rescue me?"

He snorted and didn't answer.

We left the club. There were two cars waiting outside, and a group of werewolves I didn't know. They weren't Albuquerque or Santa Fe—I would have recognized their scent.

"Just you and him," Zane said, pointing at David and then waving us toward the second car.

"What? No. Not unless you explain."

What the hell would the pack want with David?

"Orders." Zane got in my face. "You and David Thaler. Now. We're already late, after having had to come down and find you."

"Not my problem, Zane. And what's more, I'm not going anywhere without Scott."

Tension crackled between us. All my team stepped in and backed me up. Zane's werewolf escort came up on their toes.

Shit! What the hell is going on?

I was still holding Scott's hand, afraid if he lost that personal contact with me his instincts would take over.

Zane looked at us and exhaled slowly. "The cub can come, at your own risk, but I warn you, a meet is no place for him. The Adept too. Not your House kin."

I had to reluctantly admit that Julie and Keith were clearly another matter entirely. Yes, part of my House, kin to my Diakon, but not actually paranormal. Not likely to be welcome at a werewolf meet.

They were going to argue, but I shook my head.

Zane couldn't force me go with him, not here, in sight of people, but he *was* speaking with the authority of the alphas.

"Yelena's going to fry me when she finds out," Julie hissed.

"Going to fry me too," I said back. David, Scott and I squeezed into the back seat of the second car. Zane and Kane went into the first and we took off, leaving a pissed Julie and Keith behind.

Chapter 22

The driver and his buddy refused to answer my questions: *alpha's orders*. The only other things they would say was they were from the Tucson pack and that the biggest werewolf meet ever was going on.

And Alex hadn't even known about it, let alone me.

Not a good sign.

And meanwhile, now we were out of the claustrophobia and adrenaline overload that had been the club, I could sense the Call of the packs. Scott felt it too, and it wasn't helping.

His breathing and heartrate hadn't come down since we'd first arrived at the club. He was sweating, even in the cold. Under the circumstances, I'd say he was holding it together well, but that would count for nothing in the meet.

"You hearing me, Scott?"

He nodded.

I pushed him back against the seat, tried to get him to relax.

"You're doing great, but it's going to get harder," I said.

"Tell me."

"We're going to a meet. Lots of different packs in one place."

"I understand," he said. "It'll feel all wrong. The same way it did at the club. The same way those jerks in the front feel wrong."

I snorted and bit my lip.

"Yeah, like that, but a thousand times worse."

"What do I have to do?"

"Don't get into a fight. These werewolves will be on edge. They'll push and snarl instinctively, testing you out. But if it gets to a fight, they'll all be experienced at fighting. You're not. They'll kill you."

He took that in, didn't like it.

"What do I do?" he snapped. "Look at the floor? Lie on my back?"

His lips stretched as if he were trying to snarl.

"No. That would be almost as bad. Push back. Snarl. But if it goes beyond that, I'll handle it. Or David will."

He thought about that for a minute, frowning. "Why?"

"Because you're in my House, and it's what we do for each other. At least until you learn enough about werewolf rules to survive."

He grunted. "They have rules? Werewolves have rules?"

I laughed. I couldn't help it. He smiled.

I felt the Tucson Were in the front turn and look at the pair of us. I could read that look—*Crazy Denver pack. Must have caught it from New Mexico.*

I sobered quickly. "Yeah. Your instincts are already learning them. All you need is a bit more time."

His mouth twisted at that, but he didn't say anything more.

By that time we were headed through Aurora on Colfax and I knew where we were going: the Denver pack owned a huge fertilizer factory out this way. It was close enough to the city while still far enough from the encroaching housing projects to remain isolated and secure.

It was where they processed dead bodies to keep the deaths hidden from the police.

What the freaking hell is going on?

My gut tightened.

Had something happened to Alex? Was he in trouble?

Or was it me? Was I the one in trouble?

Either way, why the hell hadn't I been told?

In the same way I had arrived here last time, the nearer we got to the factory, the more the Were and Athanate fight-or-flight hormones kicked in, until I was stretched and taut as a violin string.

Desperate to sense Alex, I reached ahead with eukori, using David to boost me, but there was simply too much going on, too many auras and emotions swirling around. There were packs, *lots* of packs, in the factory. We went around to the back. There were ranks of trucks parked outside. And a couple of buses.

Again, why the hell hadn't I been told?

We parked at the end of the a row, and I stepped out.

I could hear live music. The sound of a foot-stomping tune from inside carried clearly in the night.

I dragged in lungfuls of air that was full of a scent which flowed like crude oil leaking out of the factory. That scent carried a torrent of emotions—excitement, arousal, rippling with dark streaks of fear and anger.

And a flood of Were dominance. I reckoned at least a couple of dozen alphas were bottled up in that big building—out of their territories, out of their familiar zones, and damn near out of their minds.

Blood too. That tide of scents swirling around me carried blood with it, and death.

Someone had died inside that factory this evening.

Scott smelled it too. He was standing stock still, with his eyes closed. From a distance, I'd have thought he was relaxed, but he'd developed an impressive sub-audible werewolf warning growl. He knew in his mind the truth about the danger he was in, but his body hadn't learned it yet.

I took his hand and squeezed until he looked at me.

"I can't leave you outside."

"I understand."

"Stay close. Keep *thinking* about what you're doing. Don't just react."

With David on the other side of Scott, we walked down to the end, where there was a small door and a couple of guards illuminated by a bright yard light.

Kane joined us there. Zane hadn't waited—he was already inside.

"Ready?" I asked.

Of course he wasn't, but Scott nodded, and in we went.

We stood, dazed, as our eyes adjusted.

What light there was came from the middle of the depot, where they'd made a tall bonfire out of wooden pallets. This was the old loading bay area of the factory—big enough for a dozen eighteen-wheelers to back in side by side, and the walls were corrugated iron so I guessed the fire risk wasn't high.

Not good enough for werewolves, so they'd lined up a bunch of workbenches near the bonfire and men and women were dancing on top, some juggling flaming sticks, tossing them from one to the other. One shirtless woman did her own thing, and damn, she was good at it: throwing the burning sticks high, catching them and drawing with fire across her bare belly and breasts, all while her hips circled smoothly to the beat of the music. If the benches didn't catch on fire, some of the werewolves watching would.

The music came from a group down the end who'd brought guitars and drums. They stood in a cleared space and made good enough music that most of the crowd were dancing.

Some had started to shed their clothes.

Well, it was hot, between the metabolism of pumped-up werewolves and the bonfire.

The ratio of male to female werewolves was about three to one. In packs, that was normal—a lot of female werewolves had a couple of lovers. Here at a meet, it was asking for fights, especially as most of the alphas weren't in this section. No one was fighting yet, so I decided whoever organized it so the werewolves blew off steam by dancing might be a genius.

Maybe.

As long as we kept away from the main crowd in the middle, I was thinking it wasn't going to be as bad as it might have been for Scott, until I realized not all of them were focused on the dancing.

Three young werewolves on the edge of the crowd had turned and were watching us.

In the light from the flames, I could barely see the detail of their faces. Their scents were mingled with a hundred others. They could have been anyone, and the same went for us.

They snarled at Scott and David. One of them reached out to grab my hand and tugged. Maybe it was his idea of an invitation to dance.

Scott snarled back at them.

Oh, my God.

My new cub had a *real* snarl. More than that, his face flickered, part-changing—something that only mature werewolves were supposed to be able to do.

My hand was let go, quickly, and the youngsters were saved any further embarrassment by a swirl of newcomers who came in and flowed between us. We got some token snarls from them, but more show than anything.

We backed up until we were against the wall, well out of the way.

"My, what big teeth you have, grandpa," Kane murmured to Scott.

Scott was trying hard not to smirk. I think he'd been as surprised as we had.

"Great party," David said. "Much better than the club."

I didn't agree. The three youngsters had probably done us more good than harm, but I was picking up other stares from across the room. One or two noses were wrinkled at the scent of Athanate.

It was a shock. I supposed it was too much to expect the halfy ritual to have bought all the Athanate some goodwill, but if those noses could smell Athanate, they should have been able to work out who it was.

Maybe the Southern League had expanded so quickly, there were wolves out there who genuinely didn't know about me.

Or... maybe they knew something about tonight I didn't.

I was saved any further wondering when I recognized a group of faces who were making their way to us.

"Billie! Great to see you," I called out.

Billie and the Belles were the only all-female pack in the Los Angeles area. After an initial misunderstanding one evening back in LA, when we'd unknowingly invaded their territory, we'd gotten along well.

Maybe they could tell me what was happening here.

But Billie wasn't smiling.

She threw her arms around me in a hug and spoke in my ear.

"Let go of the cub," she said. "We'll look after him and your friends."

The Belles had surrounded David, Kane and Scott. Scott's hand slipped out of mine.

Billie grabbed my head before I could turn and protest. She gave me a little shake. Her face was tight with anger, but not aimed at me.

"Focus on yourself," she said. "Don't worry about them."

"But—"

I didn't get time to finish. Zane was back and Billie allowed herself to be pushed aside.

The man had never developed any regard for personal space. He was all over me—pushing me back against the wall, hands on my ass, my hips. I hadn't minded back down in New Mexico when I'd been flirting with him, but things were different here and now. On top of that, all the bullshit surrounding this meeting was getting to me. I was *angry*.

I lined him up for a knee in the balls.

His whisper was sharp as a pin in my ear and so quiet no one else could hear.

"Amber, not much time. Listen."

I held back the knee for the moment and let go with the mouth.

"You listen! You practically arrest me—"

"What part of *not much time* are you too stupid to understand?" he growled. "There are people watching and I'm not supposed to be talking to you, so in addition to you *listening* to me, we're going to have to put on a show."

He kissed me.

Not a polite kiss. A searing, lip-bruising kiss, a hungry kiss, the sort of kiss that sent flames down my body, made my insides loose and my legs weak. I put my hands up to push him away and felt the heat of his skin all the way through his shirt, the hard edges of his belly muscles, the tension of desire in his body.

Felt it. Loved it.

I didn't push, but he broke away. Not far. Barely enough to talk.

"Damn, woman, kissing you like kissing a branding iron." His voice was raw, his vocal cords all torn, his speech pattern ripped right back down to that desert peon he'd been.

He kissed my neck. My head went back, offering my throat. My hands pulled his shirt open, clawed at his taut flesh.

Only for show.

Who're you kidding?

He certainly wasn't doing this for show. He'd gotten his body between my legs and I had some hard evidence pressed against my belly about what he wanted to do to me.

Breathe! Breathe!

Heaving in lungfuls of air only made it worse. His scent was thick with crazy wolf desire, like tires screaming on hot tar, like the wind whipping my face, like that moment when you stomp on the brake and *nothing happens*.

His hand bunched in my hair, tugged. The muscles of his back flexed as he ground himself against me, then suddenly he was swearing coarsely in Spanish and shuddering with reluctance as he pulled back.

"Mierda! *Mierda! Stop!*" he grunted hoarsely, lips at my ear, voice like a crow. "Oh, shit, woman! *Bruja!* Make me fucking crazy. Got to listen. All this gathering packs into the League. Brought too much *pinche política* with it. Couldn't speak at the club. Not supposed to talk to you. Not supposed to show favor. Don't know who to trust in the new packs."

"What?" I couldn't stop my hands from sliding over his sweaty back, underneath his shirt. I was dizzy. Eyes closed. If he let go, I'd collapse on the dirt floor.

What the hell was going on? It was like my body wouldn't obey me when I told it to stop.

"Yeah. Too much talk, not enough fangs and blood," he said. "Then all of a sudden, challenges."

Breath caught in my throat.

"Who?"

"The El Paso alphas are challenging Alex."

"*What?* What the hell is happening, Zane?"

We were too close to look into his eyes. I got my hands back between us to push, but they'd developed a mind of their own, too interested in the sensation of his flesh.

What's wrong with me? Something in the beer at the club?

I felt like I'd been roofied.

Zane was still talking, short sentences like he hadn't got enough air either. "Cameron and Felix been trying to handle it. Saying you're a special case. You're the one who runs the rituals. But El Paso say you can't be an alpha. You're just part of the Deauville pack. They should take over the pack."

"Hold on. Slow down." My mind was spinning. "El Paso *alphas*? A pair? And they're saying I'm *not* an alpha, so they're going to challenge Alex alone, without me? I stand aside?"

"That's what Cameron wants." He hurried on. "The pack can't refuse a challenge. Alex can't take them both. They're old alphas." He shook his head as if to clear it. "I've seen them fight. Your man may be good, but he can't take both. Cameron's trying to give Alex a chance. Make it one on one. That means you gotta keep out of it."

"No! I'm co-alpha. I can't ignore the challenge either."

"This is a wolf fight, Amber. Leadership fight for the pack. Four-footed. You haven't done any of that. Listen to me: you're dead if you go to your wolf and mix it with them. Cameron's trying to keep you alive."

Alive.

And maybe Alex dead. And I'd be in the El Paso pack.

Or I could fight and we might both be dead. Then every halfy who couldn't change would be condemned to death as well.

What's worse?

The questions didn't seem to make sense. I couldn't think about them.

What's wrong with me?

Whatever it was, it wasn't being helped by the Call that was forming among the packs here tonight. Every pack used their Call to catch the members up into some important pack activity. Usually hunting. But tonight, the merged Call of every wolf here was an insidious mix of excitement and lust—and not just lust for blood.

It seemed to pour down on us from every side, thick as molasses, sweet as sin.

My mind and body were racing off in different directions. *Danger, Alex, fight, death* pulsed through me, but against that was an overwhelming tide of lust.

I wasn't the only one. The meet was getting out of hand. A few guys were shouting at each other and looked ready to fight. Some couples were finding dark corners.

I didn't know what Felix and Cameron had planned for this meet, but they were on the brink of losing it.

All I could think of...

The overhead lights came crashing on, flooding the whole space in a burning, arc-bright light.

Chapter 23

"*Mierda!*"

Zane recovered first. He grabbed my arm and pulled me toward the end of the building, to the cleared area where the band had been playing.

"But Scott and—"

"The bitches will keep them safe," he said. "Trust them."

"Scott's a hybrid. He's not ready. He could do anything."

"Not if they stop him, and they can. Forget about them for the moment."

We were at the edge of the area. The band had been playing acoustic instruments, so had simply walked away, leaving it empty except for sand on the floor, put there to soak up the blood.

That got through to me. The daze of lust ebbed and let the anger have free rein, as Felix and Cameron appeared at a door in the front. They led a group of werewolf alphas out.

Alex!

My heart leaped.

He grimaced at me, then shook his head as I made to go to him.

Zane gripped my arm, hard enough to bruise.

"Wait," he hissed.

Felix was in his usual dressed-down style—a pair of dark jeans and a crisp white shirt. His deep-set eyes were shadowed in the harsh lighting and his mouth was tight. Angry as he looked, the Denver pack alpha was radiating dominance. So was Cameron, by his side. She wore red pants and a pale blue top that could have been sashaying down the catwalk in Milan, but her expression would have frozen the fashionistas into their seats.

When I'd last seen them, Felix and Cameron had been snarling and spitting at each other like a pair of male lions challenging to lead the pride. Despite appearances, Zane had assured me that they were a done deal from that moment, and as good as mated.

Looked like he'd been right. I could practically see the bond between them. I could taste their dominance, which had always been high, boosted by being mated.

Hell, does that ever change things in the werewolf world.

But is that part of the reason for their behavior tonight?

They all lined up and Felix nodded at a couple of the alphas, who stepped forward.

"Most of y'all know me by now," the man said, "I'm Caleb Oaken, co-alpha of the El Paso pack with my wife Victoria."

He was tall and lean, broad across the shoulders, with a powerful body. His eyes were sharkskin gray, his hair was the color of straw, and he showed the tan of a man who spent a lot of time outside.

His wife was dark, a couple of inches taller than me, with the eyes of a hunter and the body of an athlete.

She spoke, and although her voice was soft, it carried. "We've run that pack in El Paso for over a hundred years, and that's a hundred *good* years, friends. We've grown the pack. We've led 'em, cared for 'em, kept 'em hidden from humans, and been considerate neighbors to the packs around our territory."

She paused. The silence was broken only by the crackle of bonfire flames until she spoke again.

"Now we understand the changes that are coming our way. We know we can't keep hidden forever, so we all need a plan for that. This Southern League's a good first step, which is why we agreed to become part of it, pretty much as soon as we got asked."

Her husband took over again.

"But we ain't some come-lately pack gonna be along for the ride. We're fixing to be part of the steering and less of the paddling, if you get my drift. And that there seems to be a problem.

"Now, I have no real problem with the fine people I find in the Southern League, on their own account. But what I do have a problem with, is where they're at. As my wife said, we're hundred year alphas. That's given us perspective, and that there perspective is necessary for the League. Alphas who ain't been alphas for more'n a handful of months are sitting high, when for the good of y'all, we need experience at the top."

There was a stirring in the werewolves, an agreement.

All it did for me was to ramp up the anger. They were just a pair of opportunists looking for an easy way up the hierarchy of the League.

"It's because of that, we challenged the Deauville pack," Victoria said. Her eyes swept across the gathering until they found mine, and locked. "They ain't minded to step down, as is their right, which is why we're come to this impasse. We're challenging, for their pack and position, as is our right."

The El Paso alphas stepped back and Felix looked across at Alex, who shook his head. He wasn't going to step down—*couldn't* step down and wasn't interested in talking about it.

There was movement around Zane and me. Pack Deauville gathering. Nick and Olivia. Even Ursula and Ricky, though both of them were officially still lieutenants in Felix's main Denver pack.

Beside them, Rita, Zane's lieutenant in Albuquerque, there to support him.

Cameron cleared her throat, not meeting my eye.

"Despite talks, it seems this can't be resolved amicably, and that poses a problem for Felix and me. We're not willing to risk the loss of the woman who you all know runs the halfy rituals as well as being co-alpha of Deauville. But we can't forbid challenges. So, it's our decision that this challenge can go forward on the basis of a single combat between Alexander Deauville and Caleb Oaken."

The anger that had been steadily building in my head finally exploded.

"No!" I shouted.

I tore Zane's restraining hand off and stepped forward.

Cameron held up a hand. "Amber, you can't—"

"No, Cameron, *you* can't. You can't demote me without even talking to me first. This isn't the Confederation, where they appoint alphas they want in the sub-packs. I'm co-alpha of pack Deauville. We accept the challenge, El Paso. For pack and position. To the death."

Shock passed through the building.

Some of them yelled out in support, caught up in my anger because it *felt* right, it felt more werewolf than El Paso's smooth argument.

There was shock on the faces of the alphas as well. All of them, especially El Paso.

It only made me more angry.

"All of you." I pointed at the alphas and then swung around to take in everyone. "We're not animals, and these rules aren't written down anywhere outside of our werewolf instincts and habits, which we don't have to follow. We don't have to do it this way. But hey, here we are. Great. If you're stupid enough to keep working this way, then you're going to have to be stupid enough to take the potential consequences. Even if that means the packs shrink again."

I could feel the fury that my outburst had caused, not least from Felix and Cameron.

Tough.

Alex was by my side, as angry as I was.

"Hell, Amber, what have you done?"

"Yeah. Way to go, eh? Piss them all off."

Poor choice of response. His eyes went all wolf-gold.

"This is deadly serious."

"I'm sorry. I know it's serious. But we're supposed to be co-alphas. Whatever happens has to happen to both of us, or Pack Deauville has all been a lie."

He flinched, and the shock shaded his eyes back to green.

"No!" The word was ripped from him. "They persuaded me..." He dropped his eyes. "I'm sorry. I shouldn't have agreed to this. I couldn't face the thought of losing you. Can't. Maybe we can back down. We don't need to be in this hierarchy."

"No, we can't back down, Alex. You know in your gut, we can't." I grabbed his head and shook it like Billie had earlier with me. "Time to focus. No time left. We fight. We can do it. What tactics do you think we need?"

Alex closed his eyes for a moment. His heartrate inched down from its peak.

"Same as before. I have to take him," he said finally, indicating Caleb Oaken with a nod. "But it'll take everything I've got. I need you to keep that bitch off me, and she's no powder puff."

"Sounds like a plan."

"We *had* a plan. Stupid plan that seemed to make sense politically. I'm sorry." His eyes flicked to where Felix and Cameron stood glaring. "Now we have a couple of problems, including them—"

"One problem at a time," I cut across him. "We fight El Paso. You kill him. Forget about her. Even if I don't have experience fighting as a wolf, I have some tricks she won't have seen."

It was a bluff, for his sake. I wasn't sure if he actually believed me, but there was no time left: Caleb and Victoria had already stripped.

Out of their clothes, they looked even stronger.

An eye-twisting moment later they were in wolf form. Black, gray and white. Big. Fangs like knives. They stretched and shook, looking like a couple of athletes limbering up, unconcerned about the coming confrontation.

Alex and I shed our clothes.

In a bad situation, I had to go for the simplest strategy—banking on Alex killing Caleb before Victoria could kill me, or get past me to help Caleb against Alex.

I knew my defensive role wouldn't sit well with me once I was in my wolf. On four feet, I'd want to attack, and I didn't have enough experience on my side for that. What did I have? Probably more strength and speed than my opponent was expecting. But the boost I could have had—from the fighting instincts of Hana, my spirit guide—that was missing.

Eukori? I reached out and touched my House: cold, focused determination from Alex, absolute belief from David, agitation from Scott. Uncertainty from Kane. Maybe he was wondering if he could get away with helping me. But eukori would be difficult to use in a fight, and there'd be no way I could compel Victoria not to attack.

I touched on the El Paso alphas. A sense of confidence. Eagerness. Bloodlust.

Maybe eukori would give me something like a warning of their intentions.

I was grasping at straws.

Alex changed to wolf.

I stood a few moments more, running my hand over Alex's back and deliberately smiling at the El Paso wolves, waiting for that pre-combat focus to snap in while I reviewed what little I did know about actual werewolf fighting.

I'd fought Noble and won, but he hadn't been an experienced fighter, relying instead on his sheer size and strength.

I'd seen Rita kill, and that had been about the speed and ferocity of her attack. Not what my role was today, and anyway, she was a cougar. Different beast entirely.

For a second, something almost surfaced about Noble, but my world was narrowing to a single, sharp point and the watchers were getting impatient.

I changed.

Damn.

My wolf felt unfamiliar to me. Not enough time spent on four legs.

I was bigger than before. More dominance. Something to do with the growth of the League. Not important—not enough to make the El Paso back down.

Threat. Need to kill.

I pulled myself back, reining in the wolf instincts. Alex and I would die if I went into an attack frenzy. I had to control myself, control my anger till I needed it.

From what Alex had told me, the real business of werewolf fights, like a lot of other types of fights, was done at the start, when the opponents sized each other up.

The El Paso wolves split and started to circle us in opposite directions.

It began.

Chapter 24

Alex and I moved to the center of the fight area. He turned to follow Caleb, and I tracked Victoria.

My wolf didn't care that the El Paso were more experienced.

Kill. Threat to pack. Kill!

I was salivating. I lowered my body a little.

As they completed the half circle, they crossed each other, Victoria in front of Caleb. To keep tracking her, I moved in front of Alex.

Victoria lunged.

Feint!

I snapped and snarled at her, but she came nowhere near me.

I knew my response was clumsy, and her feint had been elegant, a clever test of my speed.

Her lips came back off her teeth and her nose wrinkled. She was laughing at us.

Harsh sounds. Excitement. Shouting.

I blocked out the noise of the crowd. Victoria was everything.

Kill!

At the full circle, Caleb took the inside track. I passed in front of Alex again.

Caleb lunged at me.

No time! Huge. Fast.

His fangs tore at me. Both Alex and I tried to bite him, but he was gone as quickly as he came.

Up close he was really huge. Almost as big as Noble had been, but *fast*. Hell!

And I had blood on my shoulder.

Victoria's nose wrinkled again, and as my anger spiked, she charged me.

She was even quicker than Caleb.

Fangs high, claws raking, then her head dipped and shot in.

Raked my wound.

Pain!

My jaws closed on air again.

Kill!

No chance to kill her. Not important. Had to keep focus. Didn't matter how many times she bit me—all I had to do was keep her off Alex.

Breath shaking with blood lust. Legs weak with the need to kill her, the need to feel her throat in my jaws.

I was whining in frustration as she kept circling and I had to follow her.

She sees my blood. Sees the pain.

It excited her. I could see the growing confidence in the way she circled us.

She knew I was fast. I knew she was faster. Even the boost from my Athanate blood didn't match a hundred-year-old werewolf.

She still needs to kill me. All I need is to keep her out.

My bleeding had stopped. That was one thing Athanate were very good at.

Pain I didn't care about. Pain was an old friend. Anger, too.

I reached with eukori, tasted the El Paso alphas' excitement, their certainty, their fevered, almost sexual eagerness for a double kill, but my eukori told me nothing helpful about their fight strategy.

I really needed Hana. My spirit guide would have read Victoria's wolf down at the level of instinct and given me warning of when to move, the same way she'd read Noble's wolf. Completely inexperienced as I had been in that fight, she'd gauged Noble's movements well enough for me to respond as if I were used to fighting. Well enough that I'd gotten a grip on his throat, even though his enormous size had allowed him to throw me off.

But no Hana today. Why did my thoughts keep going back to the fight with Noble? What was it about that fight that could help me today?

Alex's flank brushed mine. I got a sensation of tension building. That was all the warning I got.

Alex moving. Fast!

Crabbing in a circle around us, seeing how overmatched I was by Victoria, Caleb had gotten overconfident. He was too close to us and his weight was all wrong. First mistake.

Alex had been watching for that the whole time.

Despite all his experience, when Alex attacked, Caleb tried to move back to give himself time to regain his balance. Second, fatal mistake.

Alex had come in low and he launched himself up with all the power in his hind legs. Caleb was much bigger than Alex, but his weight was out of place and he wasn't so big he could absorb the shock of the attack. He was thrown backwards and immediately Alex was at his throat.

Victoria charged me.

Come on, bitch.

I tensed for the impact, but she didn't go for my throat or body. She side-stepped at the last moment, slamming her rock-hard shoulder into me and then she was past, aimed like an arrow for Alex's unprotected back.

No!

I rolled, came up, claws scrabbling for purchase on the slippery sawdust floor.

The front of the throat is the most vulnerable part and Alex was turned away from her, but her teeth in the back of his neck would slow him, distract him, hamper him, when he needed all his concentration, agility and balance to keep Caleb down.

I'd failed him.

I'd failed both of us.

I leaped. She'd gotten her teeth in Alex, but exposed the back of her own neck to me.

My jaws closed, my fangs pierced her flesh.

Kill.

But the same lack of quick vulnerability protected both her and Alex. A back-of-the-neck kill is slow work unless you're *much* bigger. Meanwhile, Alex was carrying the weight of two struggling wolves.

Victoria had known. For all the thrill, she'd made a stone cold assessment. She allowed me to bite her, knowing I couldn't kill her in the time it took for Caleb to get free. And once Caleb was free, Alex couldn't fight him with Victoria on his back, let alone both of us. Alex was going to die.

And then I would.

Because I wasn't big enough. My jaws were gaped too wide on the back of her neck, and like that, they weren't powerful enough.

I needed jaws the size and strength of Noble's.

Shocking memories seized me.

Noble, testing his strength by biting through human thigh bones. Biting clean through.

Noble, crouched over his living victim, leeching her mass from her to make himself bigger, a working that fed on her terror and pain.

Dark magic. Blood magic. Evil.

No!

I couldn't do that. I couldn't use blood magic.

And because I couldn't do that, Alex would die.

I didn't have the power and I didn't know how to use blood magic.

I bit down as hard as I could. I twisted and turned to try and make Victoria panic and let go. She didn't, but the shifting weight on his back loosened Alex's grip.

Caleb got free.

No time.

No choices left.

I'll damn myself, but I won't let Alex die.

I couldn't do it alone.

In panic, I reached out with eukori to Kane. It wasn't the usual gentle flow. It was hard, like lightning bolts crossing, with explosions wherever my eukori touched his aura.

Sheer horror from Kane as he understood what I was trying to do.

Time slowed. The world around me shifted. Became fluid. The ground simmered like boiling water and the infinite sky wheeled above us all to a different clock.

Kane was bound to me, however he struggled against it. I reached and *pulled* raw power from him, *through* him. Dark power. Power in the earth. A power waiting to be called.

Pain and blood and screaming.

My throat and jaws burned, swelled.

An explosion of pain. My body. Other bodies. Cracking.

Shouting.

Victoria was getting weaker and I was getting stronger. The muscle mass at the back of her neck protecting her was shriveling and my jaw was swelling.

She's screaming. She can feel what's happening and she's screaming.

Fear. Feed on it. Makes me stronger. Kill!

I tore the shuddering wolf bitch off Alex's back and shook her like a rag. Blood sprayed everywhere. I felt the spine break and break again. Felt her absolute terror as her body snapped and her mind sank into the darkness.

I didn't leave it there. I bit and ripped again. Bit through her throat. Destroyed her neck. Her head rolled away, smeared with red.

Caleb froze. He'd been on the point of leaping at Alex. Now he was unable to look away from his wife's body, even when Alex's jaws closed on his throat.

Alex didn't need my help with him.

I turned away. I stayed in wolf form to stalk along the line of watchers, a growl swelling in my chest. Some had supported the El Paso alphas; they backed away from me. Others cheered, but no one touched me, painted as I was with blood and gore.

Have a good look. I am death. You wanted this. You cheered for it.

Alex's big wolf joined me, but he walked on the outside, between me and the crowd. I knew what he wanted, but I wasn't ready, even if he was my alpha. He had to nudge and nip until I turned in toward the center where the two bodies lay.

The berserker exultation paled, draining strength from my limbs and coloring the anger with the first breath of sorrow. However we'd come to this, however much their deaths were their own fault, those bodies were two people who'd lived a hundred years. They'd loved each other. Their pack—now *our* pack—had probably loved them.

But I wasn't going to forget they'd killed others. I wasn't going to forget their sick anticipation of killing us.

I didn't want to change back to human. The sorrow would be worse. I knew the nausea would come, and along with it, the same horror I could still feel echoing from Kane. Not only that I'd killed Victoria by biting her head off, but that I'd used blood magic to do it, *and* I'd torn the power through Kane himself while trapping him so that he'd felt it.

I'd done it without being taught. It was natural for me. *Blood magic was natural for me.* Not the magic that Tullah had tried to show me—something more raw, more powerful. Something evil. Flint and Kane had been right about the rituals. They were blood magic. My magic was dark, and I'd come into my own, without Hana as a spirit guide, without any guide. And there was no going back.

Cameron and Felix were waiting. They were pissed I'd challenged their plan and risked myself. The whole place picked up on it. They were seething.

Alex growled and changed back to human.

I needed to be with him to confront Felix and Cameron, but I needed to do other things first.

I stopped in front of Kane and changed.

Chapter 25

"Kane," I said. It came out hoarse, and it felt like my throat had rusted. I didn't know what else to say, so I tried: "I'm sorry."

"Sorry?"

Billie and Scott were stood next to him. Alex behind me. Of course they didn't know what had happened, but all of them reacted to his obvious anger with me by growling at him.

He stiffened at the menace. His eyes were wide with shock and his face sweaty.

I waved everyone back, and I pulled Kane closer, accidentally smearing blood all over him.

"Yes, I'm sorry. It goes against everything I should do as House Farrell. It wasn't planned, and I was desperate. I had no idea it would happen like that."

"That was dark magic, and you used me."

"Yes, I know. But think what the alternative was."

His face hardened.

"There's always a good reason for the first time."

"We have to talk later. This circus here isn't finished."

I motioned Billie back and asked her to look after him. She looked sideways at the Adept, but just nodded.

"We did it," Alex said. "You did it."

I turned to him. His eyes were all green again.

"Yes. But you don't understand. I pulled magic through Kane and—"

"I don't care," he said. "You're my wife, my co-alpha, and you've done the impossible." He stared intently at me. "I'm sorry I doubted you. It won't happen again."

He hugged me, making even more of a bloody mess of both of us.

"I—" I began.

"Keep it to yourself; there's no time now," he said. "We've got to take control of our pack."

Our pack.

Werewolf rules: the El Paso wolves had to individually submit to the pair that'd just killed their former alphas. Or they could challenge us.

Alex and I had no time to clean up, and that was part of it as well. Let no one forget what results from a challenge. It wasn't only El Paso blood either. Changing back had re-opened wounds we'd received in the fight.

Alex had his chest and belly raked with multiple parallel slices from Caleb's claws. I had rips in my shoulder.

Each of the pack that was present passed in front of us. They gave their names and their position in the pack. They confirmed their loyalty to the pack and to us as their alphas. Then we had to part-change back to wolf while they stretched their necks out and held that pose. We closed our jaws on those vulnerable throats. Leaked Caleb and Victoria's blood over them.

Many of them were scared, and with good reason. Taking over a pack this way, we were allowed to kill any we didn't want. All it would take would be to close our jaws.

Some of them were dominant wolves, but none had the strength to match Alex and me together. They were all dazed. Half of them hated us, but werewolves in a pack whose alphas were killed in a challenge had limited options. No one wanted to be an outcast, especially when the League was collecting packs into its loose structure. A pack, even a new pack with new alphas, felt better.

The whole El Paso pack numbered over three hundred. Like Athanate, werewolves generally try to merge into their human communities, so most members had been made to stay at home this time. Forty-five of them had been brought to support their alphas and each one of them swore loyalty and put their lives into our jaws.

Alex didn't have an issue with taking any of them on, and I wasn't about to kill anyone else tonight, if I could help it. I liked maybe a half-dozen of them and hoped they would reciprocate when things settled down. I could start with a small group and win the others over later.

I *didn't* like four or five of them, and that concerned me. Only time would tell.

Our pack.

Even distracted as I was, I could feel the boost of my dominance simply from being acknowledged as the alpha of a larger pack.

The last El Paso werewolf returned to the crowd. The bodies of the former alphas had been cleared away and somewhere in the building they were being converted to fertilizer.

We weren't finished.

Felix and Cameron wanted their turn. They wanted us to re-pledge our loyalty to them.

It was clear to me that something had happened while we'd been accepting our new pack members.

Alex, still burning adrenaline from the fight, didn't like submitting to them at all. He'd been angry at the start, and winning hadn't made him feel better. The day's negotiations to avoid this fight had obviously been rough for him. But though we'd grown in dominance, Felix and Cameron were co-alphas of the whole League. I guessed there might be alphas out there who could challenge them, but we couldn't.

We swallowed our anger, said our piece and stretched our necks.

I saw Cameron's fangs close on Alex's neck. It was as much as I could do to hold still. She wasn't my favorite bitch at the moment. Much the same opinion she held of me, I guessed.

Felix's jaws closed on my throat. He wasn't at all concerned by the gore.

I shivered, feeling his dominance ramping up.

This was no touch and go on our throats. Their jaws held us, and both of them were growling aggressively.

I felt my body tense. Fought it to relax. Didn't push back against that dominance display.

Not enough.

The jaws didn't slack off.

The crowd stirred, aware there was something going on.

One or both of us would die in the next few seconds. We were too dominant. We were a challenge to Felix and Cameron just by existing. If only one of us died, the survivor would be less dominant. Less of a challenge.

And they needed me for the rituals.

I couldn't stop my eukori reaching for Alex. Locking onto him. He knew.

If they killed him, they killed both of us.

I'm sorry, Jen. I love you. Sorry, everyone at home. And Bian, Tullah, Diana, Skylur. Sorry.

I should have done things differently, but I couldn't. I just couldn't.

I'd know I was about to die before. Many times.

I'd known it tonight.

I'd known it back in the jungles of South America, the place where I'd started down this path, where I'd been bitten by a rogue Athanate, the last survivor of the crazy House Chrysos, the lost House of Carpathia.

Blocking out the nighttime stars in front of me is the darkness of Hacha Del Diablo, the Devil's Axe, a soaring leftover of volcanic rock. I'm slumped against a tree at its base. I touch my neck and know I'm going to die. My arterial blood is pulsing sluggishly over my hand, black as oil in the darkness. My team is waiting for me, wherever it is you go when you die.

I still have his severed head at my feet, the creature that killed my team. The creature I killed, and who killed me.

There's blood everywhere. His. Mine. All over my face, down my chest...

"Amber."

One hand in mine. The other touching my cheek. His face close to mine. Concerned.

Alex brought me back gently.

I blinked.

Felix and Cameron were standing in front of us, addressing the crowd.

"...so there will be changes, brought on by what has happened here tonight." Felix was talking, his voice low and hard. "Cameron and I will take over the task of bringing new packs into the League. That means we will be needed wherever there is a new pack to persuade. We'll take some with us, for strength and to show how wide the League can be, but we'll travel light."

Cameron, her voice all smooth and late-night radio next to Felix's growl: "So we'll be leaving our packs in place. And since we're co-alphas, they are essentially one pack and will behave as such. A challenge to any part of that pack is a challenge to the whole pack. To us."

She stopped and eyed the silent crowd.

"One pack," she repeated. "New Mexico and Colorado combined."

Felix took over. "Given the distances between Santa Fe and Denver, we're leaving lieutenants in charge locally. In Colorado, we appoint Alexander Deauville."

"And in New Mexico," Cameron said, "We appoint Zane Quivira."

"The new pack will need to coordinate in defense," Felix said. "This area of the Rockies is where the attention of the Confederation is focused. They've tried before and we bloodied them. They *will* attack again, somehow, somewhere. They must be defeated, which may take all the efforts of the New Mexico-Colorado pack. And to ensure the two parts of the pack work seamlessly and without friction to achieve that end, we appoint Amber Farrell as liaison between Zane and Alexander."

Oh, shit.

Chapter 26

While I was dealing with that bombshell, there was more.

The entire El Paso pack was to be moved to Colorado as soon as possible. Alex would be responsible for setting them up with jobs and accommodation, using the resources of the Denver pack as a base. Integrating them into the human and Were communities.

At the same time as he settled the turbulence inevitable in the bloody takeover of a pack.

A logistical and emotional nightmare.

To make it worse, Cameron and Felix wanted Nick Grey and Ursula Tennyson, our two skinwalkers, to accompany them and help break down misconceptions and show how welcoming the League was.

They weren't accepting any argument from me either.

Ursula, strictly speaking, was Felix's pack, and she wasn't going to argue with him. How she squared that absence from work with her full time job as a veterinarian, I wasn't sure.

Nick wasn't willing to let Ursula go alone, so I'd lost that argument before I'd even started.

Hardly surprising I wasn't in a polite mood when Rita appeared at my elbow with my clothes and a towel, suggesting I should take the opportunity to clean myself up a bit. I snarled.

The were-cougar let my anger flow over her without so much as a ripple. She led me off into a wet room in the depths of the building.

After being stark naked in front of everybody for the last half hour, it was too late for me to complain about modesty when David came with us.

He wanted to help with healing my shoulder wounds.

"What about Scott?" I asked. "David, you can't leave him alone out there."

"The Belles seem to have him in hand," Rita deadpanned, and David smiled.

Rita's green eyes gave nothing away, but I knew she was curious about what had happened. She knew about size and power in a fight. She knew about the difficulty I should have had biting the back of Victoria's neck.

"And Kane?" He was just as much of a worry to me, after what I'd done.

"He's okay," David said. "The fight seemed to upset him."

He was watching me closely.

Great. Both of them suspected more had happened in the fight than had been apparent.

"Come," Rita said quietly, testing the warmth of the water coming out of the hose. "You did this for me once before. Allow us to do it for you."

"Thanks," I muttered.

The water sluiced off me and made a red spiral down the sunken drain. It occurred to me that the wet room hadn't so much been put here for the comfort of the workers, as for exactly this task—getting rid of evidence. How many challenges and deaths had this place seen? I shook my head in frustration. No point in dwelling on it now. I was going to have nightmares about this night's work without making them worse.

Rita sponged my back. And front. Ran fingers through my hair as she rinsed it. All business.

When the evidence of the fight was all flushed down the drain, David licked my wounds, the unripe berry smell of healing aniatropics stinging my nose.

It was standard Athanate assistance. I'd done it for the wounds that Rita had received after the fight in Albuquerque she'd mentioned. It felt a little strange to be the one being helped, but David was my House and it was comforting.

While he did that, Rita stood behind me and dried my hair with the towel.

It wasn't that their help was unwelcome. Absolutely not. It was... intimate, and I didn't want to reawaken the craziness that had exploded with Zane before the fight.

What had that been about? Other than the obvious?

Rita cleared her throat, uncharacteristically hesitant about what she was about to say. "Cameron suggested we should leave someone here in Denver with you to compensate for taking Nick and Ursula."

Cameron could damn well kiss my butt at the moment.

I needed Nick.

I needed him to help me repair things with Kane, to help me find out what this power was and how I could either use it safely or not use it at all. And the trouble with not having Nick, was there was no one else in the packs quite like the skinwalker. For one thing, no one with the knowledge of magic and the grounded common sense Nick had. 'Replacement' or not, I was still pissed at Cameron and Felix for taking him.

Maybe I could talk to Alice about tonight. She was the oldest Adept I knew about. She had to know something about this kind of magic. And then it was just a matter of whether I could understand what her response was.

Rita spoke again, quietly. "I volunteered. If it's okay with you."

I twisted around. "What? Seriously? Of course it's okay."

She wasn't Nick, but adding a cool, lethal were-cougar to my House?

I got a throb of Athanate fangs, but I pushed it away. She meant a temporary position. She wasn't volunteering to be in my House. Not offering her throat and her Blood.

"It would be me and Lynch," she said, still not meeting my eye. "He's decided I'm his alpha."

Lynch was the only other were-cougar I knew. He'd been a halfy who'd showed up uninvited at the ritual I held in Bitter Hooks. Nick had been the only one who wasn't surprised when Lynch had turned into a cougar. Lynch hadn't had a pack, and it was excellent news that Rita would take him under her wing. Paw. Whatever.

And despite the offhand way she said it, Rita was pleased as well.

"Good. And once we've got my current problems out of the way, you can help teach me how to fight on four legs."

I nearly bit my tongue as soon as the words slipped out.

Rita looked up. "Not sure you need it, but I'll gladly teach you what I do anyway."

We came back out to find the majority of werewolves had left.

Lynch was waiting for Rita, his face questioning her and clearing as he saw the answer in her expression.

The Belles were still there, looking after Scott, and he looked okay.

But Kane was toe-to-toe with Alex, and I could feel the tension off them from across the width of the old loading bay area.

I ran.

Alex looked like an extra from a horror film. He'd cleaned his face, and dressed, but he hadn't visited the wet room and there was El Paso blood smeared over his clothes and hands. Even without that, whereas Kane wasn't a small man, he didn't have that focused killing-machine look that Alex had tonight.

"Ease off, guys," I said quickly. "This is my fault."

"Your fault we're still alive," Alex growled, his eyes not leaving Kane.

"Yes, but it's the way I did it."

"You pulled magic through him," Alex said. "I get that. Not great."

"Dark magic."

Alex's eyes narrowed and he turned to look at me with worry in his eyes.

"This is mine to handle," I said. "Please."

"I did say I wouldn't doubt you again." Alex stepped back and took a breath. Some of that deadly focus seemed to slip away from him.

He looked back at Kane. "She risked her life twice for me tonight. That might not mean much to you now, but you'll realize she'd do it for anyone in her House, without a moment's hesitation."

That registered with Kane—made him blink.

"Alexander!" Felix was calling him from the door.

"I have to settle our new pack," Alex said. "You're still wanted here."

Then he leaned over me. "I love you."

We kissed.

I got chills. And I also got stomach churn at the thought of the effect Zane had had on me before the fight.

All down to the Call? *No. Something wrong.*

Not going to happen again, but *now* I had to work as liaison between him and Alex.

Felix came back inside and I heard Cameron calling me.

"We still need to talk, but are you okay for the moment?" I asked Kane.

He nodded. His face all closed and guarded.

Felix waved me to follow and I had to leave it for later.

Cameron was waiting for me with another alpha, one I didn't know. Another alpha who wasn't happy with me, from the look on his face.

I sighed.

At least this one was more restrained about it. If my performance earlier hadn't been enough for him to remember his manners, then maybe it was Cameron's comment about any challenge being a challenge to her and Felix.

"Amber," Cameron said, by way of explanation. "Explain what you instructed Benjamin Stillman to do immediately after the ritual at Bitter Hooks."

Oh, crap.

I'd forgotten to discuss that with Felix or Cameron.

"I told Ben to collect every name and contact number of every halfy and make sure that they all had each other's information," I said, rubbing a hand across my face. It'd been a long day and it looked like getting even longer.

Ben Stillman was a cub from the large Cimmaron pack, neighbors to both Felix and Cameron. I'd saved Ben from Zane down in Albuquerque and, in return, Ben had been eager to help me with the rituals. I thought his confidence in me, a confidence he enthusiastically communicated to the halfies, had been one of the reasons the Bitter Hooks ritual had worked so well.

"Why?" Cameron asked.

I huffed. "It was just so they could talk to each other. Maybe, in the future, help with other newbies in their packs who have difficulty changing the first time."

"Not undermining pack authority?"

"No," I said, though I'd known at the time that some alphas would see it like that.

"Have you instructed him to go beyond that?"

I frowned. "No."

"Anything to say, David Thaler?"

David gave an embarrassed cough behind me. "I helped Ben," he admitted.

Someone had brought out a laptop and set it up on a table. I had no idea where this was going until David connected to the internet and went through a security and password system.

PACKCHAT said the banner across the top of the screen.

Oh, hell.

"Keeping track of people's contact details would have been a full time job," David said. "Ben asked me for a solution, and I suggested it would be easier to make them update their details themselves. Once you have that, well, it's only a couple of steps until you have a sort of social media for werewolves. We made it very secure, of course."

"And very popular," murmured Cameron, taking control of the cursor and making an idle loop around a number at the side of the screen recording the people online. Nothing in comparison to human social media, but many more werewolves used Packchat than had actually attended the rituals.

She clicked and scrolled until she found a female werewolf's profile page.

The girl had posted a human profile picture of herself about to change to wolf. I knew she was about to change to wolf because she was stark naked, on all fours.

There was a tagline underneath: *Can you catch me? It's worth it.*

Some posts below suggested, colorfully, what might happen.

Cameron clicked again and found something very similar with a young male. *Want me to go all alpha on you?*

David blushed. "There aren't any moderators, so we don't actually censor the pictures or the messages they post. It's a bit of a free-for-all, I'm afraid. I didn't anticipate what would happen. I accept it's my fault."

Werewolves. Free-for-all. I could imagine what was going on, and a lot of it between neighboring packs. No wonder this alpha's nose was out of joint.

David and I were in such deep shit.

Felix started laughing.

Everyone turned to look at him.

"You're worried about stuff like this when humanity is about to find out that werewolves exist?" He snorted. "If we survive that, and I really mean *if,* then there'll be werewolves on human social media making indecent proposals to each other, and to humans as well. Nothing we'll be able to do about it."

Cameron nodded her agreement and the angry alpha who'd complained shrunk a little.

"David, make sure there's a facility for all alphas to get access and monitor their pack members," Felix said, "but otherwise leave it as it is."

He draped an arm around the angry alpha. "Come, Ernesto, we're done here tonight. Let's go and have a drink."

That was *so* not the grim Denver alpha I'd known. Mating with Cameron had uncovered some old people skills in Felix I hadn't thought existed.

Everyone stirred and started to head for the doors.

"I have my truck," Rita said. "I can drive you home."

"Your home too, at the moment," I said. "Yes, please, but not straight there. Gotta go see Weaver. David, call Julie and Keith. Get them to meet us there."

I really didn't want to see him tonight, but we had a time limit to get Tullah back and besides, every day she was out there, I got the sense it was getting more dangerous.

Kane was waiting for us, not looking happy, but not saying anything either.

I retrieved Scott from the Belles, which involved a lot of hugs and kisses and congratulations on my fight. They'd been behind me all the way, which helped me feel better about it.

Scott got hugs and kisses, too. Seems they enjoyed having him *in hand,* as Rita had put it.

As we climbed into Rita's midnight-blue Dodge, I asked Scott how he was.

"Okay." He frowned, his face a picture of seriousness. "Apart from a sudden, intense desire to visit LA for some reason."

I laughed. I needed that kind of humor on this dark night.

"Yeah, I bet."

Chapter 27

Weaver lived in the small town of Erie, halfway to Longmont, and it was the middle of the night. Whatever he'd said about *doesn't matter what time,* I didn't want us to drive so far out of our way to find him asleep, so I called ahead.

"Hello?" a man's voice said. Not Weaver—an older man and a cautious opening.

I went for polite. "Sorry to call so late. It's Amber Farrell. I was told to visit as soon as I was ready. Can I talk to Weaver, please?"

"Of course, Ms. Farrell. One moment please."

Polite seemed to be the mode of the evening now.

"Thank you for calling," Weaver's rumbling voice said almost immediately. "Are you on your way?"

"We are," I replied, stressing the *we*. "Just so there's no misunderstanding, the werewolf business I was called away for was a challenge. I've just finished killing the challenger and I'm in no mood for bullshit tonight. Tullah and her family need to be back in Denver, safely. We take it from there."

"Understood. I apologize again for earlier tonight. And again, I'd like to reiterate it's because I'm very worried for Tullah. I agree the most important thing is to get her here safely. As you say, let's take it from there."

He couldn't have been more reasonable if he'd tried.

I told him I'd see him in half an hour, and Rita headed north on I25.

I was shotgun and Kane was in the back, squeezed in with David, Lynch and Scott.

They'd picked up he had a problem with me, and their instinctive reaction was to give that attitude right back to him. That's what a pack or a House was all about. It wasn't comfortable for Kane in the back.

And, as much as I appreciated the support, it wasn't right.

In a crazy way, this was the same sort of problem I was in with Kath. With the backing of my House, I could get into Kath's head and fix her regardless of what she thought about it. For all the good intentions, that would be like violating her all over again. I needed her to want help, to ask for help.

I could fix Kane too. Whether he wanted it or not, I was House Farrell and he was part of my House by Amanda's oath to me. But there was no point in asking Pia to draw up a House constitution that limited what could be done to members of my House if I was going to be the one to disregard it. I wanted Amanda and her kin in my House. I wanted them to be in the position that their first, instinctive reaction would be to support me whatever and whenever. But the tricky part was I wanted them to want that without any force on my part.

"Ease off, guys," I said for the second time that night. "Kane has a legitimate reason for being angry with me." I took a calming breath. "I'm going to explain, but this is a House secret. Understood?"

Cautious nods.

"I was only able to defeat Victoria by pulling magic through Kane to increase the power of my bite."

I was looking into the back, but I could feel Rita's close attention and understanding. She'd known something was wrong.

"Wasn't just magic," Kane said.

"No. Absolutely right. Just as background for the rest of you, Flint and Kane have been concerned about the magic I use for the halfy rituals, for example. Concerned that it sounds like dark magic to them. And although I had no real idea what I was reaching for tonight, what arrived seems to fit the description of blood magic or dark magic."

It was quiet for several moments in the car until Scott spoke: "What are the implications of it being dark magic?"

"Powerful," I said. "Maybe easier to use. But also addictive."

"It turns the purpose it's used for," Kane said. "Might start out with the best intentions, but that much power, of that type... it ends in evil."

"Nick doesn't agree," I pointed out.

"But now, thanks to Were political problems, we aren't going to have Nick with us," David said, looking for the right way out. "But we do have two Adepts who could help ensure that it doesn't turn to evil. Which is important because those halfies depend on that ritual."

"A ritual that makes more monsters like tonight?"

Kane was angry enough he wasn't thinking through what he said.

Scott's lip twisted into a silent snarl.

"Sorry," Kane muttered.

"I can understand you don't have a very good impression of the Were community from that meeting," I said. "Just the same way anyone might get a bad impression from the wrong meeting of Adepts."

Half of me wanted to leave it there and let him mull it over. I had a feeling he'd be okay once he'd had time to think it through, but I needed to be sure about him now. I needed him to watch my back while I met with Weaver.

"I shouldn't have done that," I said. "If there was any other way, I wouldn't have. But, under certain circumstances, I'd do it again."

"What circumstances?"

I shifted in my seat and frowned. "I can't give you a list, but lethal threat to any member of my House, including you and me. Same with people associated with me. Threat to Emergence. Danger to a large number of people. That sort of thing. It would be a long list, but all of it on the basis there would be no other way."

"This Emergence thing is just politics."

"It's not, Kane. It really isn't. It's part of why we're in this situation now, where you can't be part of House Lloyd without also being part of the whole Athanate community in the US." I took a breath. "I know you and Flint think you're good enough that you can take Amanda and go undercover. You can't. It just isn't an option."

I saw the defiance in his eyes.

"Really," I said. "But I promise you this: if we can't work out a way for you to be part of my House, I'll release Amanda from her oath and put you on a flight to Ireland myself."

Defiance changed to surprise. Scott growled.

"I don't want to do that," I said. And I didn't. Just saying it had felt like cutting my own flesh. "I want you in my House. I want you to help me with magic. I want you to help me be a liaision between Were and Athanate, and maybe Adepts too. I will let you go if you can't. But tonight, I need you to have my back when we visit Weaver. To keep a lookout for any magical tricks. You good for that?"

"Yes," he said quietly.

"Talk to each other," I said to them all. "Explain about Emergence. Explain about dark magic. Let's be all in the same House, at least for tonight."

I hoped I'd done enough for Kane, without upsetting Scott, who would be in a terrible position if House Lloyd left. He was Amanda's kin, but he was my cub.

He'd calmed down since the club. He still looked wild, but under the circumstances, I thought he'd done very well. However, I doubted that we were out of the danger zone with him. Providing I got the chance, I was going to have to keep him by my side for a while, however inconvenient that was.

Julie called David back on his cell, and confirmed she and Keith were ahead of us. Twenty-five minutes later, we saw them standing next to the Hill Bitch, parked near Weaver's house, waiting for us.

They grabbed me in a three-way hug before I could speak. My team could sense something of the night's events even without being told.

"What the hell happened?" Keith growled.

"Werewolf challenge," I said leaning into the warmth of their embrace, inhaling their Yelena/House Farrell scents and feeling better.

"Shit," muttered Julie.

I didn't want to talk about it. "They came in second."

"Bian's been calling," Keith said, touching the comms device in his left ear. "They have some emergency going. Confederation werewolves spotted in Denver."

"She's spoken to Felix?"

Keith nodded.

I started to ask what Bian was doing tracking werewolves, but it wasn't important right now.

"You have some weapons in the Bitch?"

"Yup."

Julie handed me my HK Mk 23 in a clip holster, which I checked and then hung from my belt.

"Weaver's given his word, but I want us to be carrying and I want it to be obvious."

They nodded and Julie slung an MP5 across her chest. Keith shrugged on a bandolier with assorted flash bombs and grenades.

David looked in the back of the Hill Bitch and came away with a Sig that he'd trained on.

Scott raised his eyebrows. I shook my head. Until he and Lynch were checked out with weapons, I didn't want them shooting near me.

Kane folded his arms. He wasn't interested in that kind of weapon. Fine by me as long as I got warning if Weaver pulled some magical trick like trying to move us to the spirit world.

Given just a second, I would ensure it would be the last trick he pulled.

But how would I get that warning?

I couldn't watch Kane and ignore signs that Weaver might be giving.

My eukori would give me a clue, but did I want to use it? How would Kane react if I had to connect to him through eukori again?

With my attention turned to it, I could feel that dark power I used to kill Victoria, right now; I could sense it seething in the cold night.

Blood magic.

What the hell? Why had I been able to access it? Could I ever use my eukori again without pulling some of it in?

The memory of that power burn made me go weak. I didn't understand anything about it. How I'd called it. How I controlled it.

Were Flint and Kane right? That it would turn to evil and I couldn't trust it.

Maybe.

And yet, to have it on tap? To use it for things that needed to be done?

The hairs on the back of my neck stood up, and it wasn't because there was any spell forming near me. I was hearing the sweet siren call of power deep inside me.

I could have used it to defeat Felix and Cameron.

Crazy. *Not* what I wanted. I shivered and tried to put it out of my mind.

So... no eukori at this meeting. For warnings, I was going to have to rely on reading Weaver's expression and body language.

Just like all those poker games, back in Ops 4-10.

Concentrate, I said to myself as we walked up to Weaver's house.

I didn't know what to expect. It was at the end of a road and surrounded by trees and fences. On the outside, it was a sober, two-story brick mansion. Upper floor rooms had half-moon balconies outside, protected by old-fashioned white balustrades. I guessed the place must have seven or eight bedrooms, at least. There were probably great views of the Front Range during the day.

The lights were on downstairs, and an elderly Adept was waiting to let us in.

He blanched at the sight of all of us standing on the doorstep, half of us armed, but made no comment, instead waving us to come inside.

We followed him across a hallway, into a living room.

The house was a strange mixture of neo-classical and Americana. The ceilings were vaulted. Rooms were lit by chandeliers. Doorways to passages were arched between slender Greek-style columns, painted bronze. In contrast the living room had a monstrous ranch-house fireplace with a railroad tie set into stonework, serving as a wooden mantel. A scatter of old Western furniture seemed out of place standing on domino-tiled floors. The walls were covered in panoramic artwork depicting gold-rush mining scenes.

It smelled strongly of spicy cooking, barbequed meat, beer and wine, but apart from the Adept guiding us, the house might as well have been empty.

Through an archway, I glimpsed a kitchen built around a glossy, granite-topped central work area that looked like it had been ripped out of a spaceship. Presumably the source of the cooking smells.

It was silent now, as if everyone had cleaned up and stepped outside a few moments before.

Spooky.

But I got none of the skin sensations that indicated anyone was using magic. A quick glance at Kane and he shook his head. Nothing he could sense either.

We might be walking straight into a magical ambush, but I was still too unsure to reach out with eukori.

A few steps ahead of us, down a hallway, the Adept knocked quietly on a wide door and then opened it.

Weaver waited inside.

Chapter 28

Julie, Scott, Kane and Rita followed me in. Lynch, Keith and David stood outside the door.

The room appeared to be Weaver's study, and it was dominated by an old oak desk in the middle. Where the walls weren't lined with books, there were more works of art, this time bronze relief panoramas—again depicting old mining scenes.

Weaver rose to his feet, ignored the display of our weapons and called for more chairs. He was acting like a completely different person from the man at the club.

"Bourbon?" he offered, holding up a bottle of Woodford Reserve from a table beside the desk.

I took a glass. The others shook their heads.

The elderly Adept delivered some stacked chairs and slipped out again.

Everyone except Rita sat down. The were-cougar leaned against the wall and became eerily still, green eyes fastened on Weaver as he sat back behind his desk and sipped his bourbon.

"Can we start again?" he asked.

I nodded.

I didn't trust Weaver, but I'd let him make his case. Maybe he *could* help to find Tullah. Then it was a matter of getting Kaothos back with Tullah and letting *them* sort out the local Adept community.

I hadn't thought he was dangerous the first time we met, back in the fall, before I'd really gotten a grip on the paranormal world. It was past time to re-assess. This man ran the Denver Adept community. That alone meant I needed to be careful.

He was a big man, six-six or thereabouts, with dark brown eyes, heavy shoulders and curly hair the color of old copper coins. He wore jeans, a black shirt and glossy Chelsea boots. A formal leather jacket was draped over the back of his chair.

I went straight to the point. "So, how do we find Tullah?" I said.

He looked down at his drink and scratched his chin before replying.

"First, who is *we*?"

"My House and House Trang."

"Not the Hecate?"

From his tone now, and the earlier meeting at the club, it was obvious they weren't working together. And I was betting he wasn't as well informed as Gwen—he didn't know that Tullah and Kaothos were temporarily separated.

Something to keep quiet about.

"No," I replied to his question. "I hardly know the Hecate, and since she was previously out to kill people who are now members of my House, I'm wary of working with her. On the other hand, if she can help, why not use her?"

He grunted and leaned back in his chair. "She's not to be trusted."

"Hey, all of you want Tullah for your own purposes," I said. "What I want at the moment is to see her back safely. Someone or something is obviously preventing that. Help me find her and then we talk to *her* about who *she* wants to work with."

He ran a hand through his hair.

"I am willing to work with you on that basis. You won't find the Hecate so accommodating. Whatever she says, she wants the dragon above all else. You and everyone else, including Tullah, are secondary to securing that."

He was *really* worried about me working with Gwendolyn. Why? What did he think I had that would make a difference to her?

Puzzling.

I *had* believed the Hecate thought I was important only because I could get her access to talk to Kaothos and Diana. But Weaver didn't even seem to know Kaothos was at Haven. He thought Kaothos was hiding with Tullah. So why would *he* think the Hecate wanted to work with me?

I put that aside. I didn't trust him enough to ask.

"You claim Tullah's wellbeing is important to you, but it was you who put a lock on her to stop her using her magic."

He nodded. "I did. It was for her own safety. Did you think she was really in control down in Carson Park, when the dragon got loose? It turned out well enough, but that was dumb luck."

Did he have a point? I sipped my bourbon and thought about it. If she'd been in control, maybe Kaothos wouldn't have ended up in Diana.

"There's an undercurrent to your comment. The Athanate are always quick to condemn the Adepts for tough choices we have to make," he went on. "You don't like the way we protect the paranormal community by removing those that cannot or will not abide by rules, despite your own methods."

His gaze turned to Kane and I was reminded that Gwendolyn had said something similar about 'rogue' Adepts.

"Tullah never broke any rules, as far as I'm aware," I said. "Right up to the point where you put the lock on her."

He stroked his chin. "Actually she broke several, not least of which was not informing us about the nature of her spirit guide." He raised his hands. "That's in the past, and not important any more. My point is, the rest of the paranormal community make their own difficult decisions without appreciating ours."

He waved a finger at Scott.

"For instance, your new werewolf is calmer now, but he was on the point of berserker rage in the club earlier tonight. If you had the ability to put a temporary lock on him, one that would have prevented the wolf emerging, or the anger exploding, no doubt you would have used it. Instead you had to make him accompany you, despite the danger and inconvenience, so that you could take action if he slipped any closer towards going rogue."

Scott's lips pulled back. Not quite a snarl, but close.

However, Weaver's comments—like the Hecate's—appeared so sensible and logical, I felt I couldn't argue. But they still tasted *wrong*. I couldn't tell if he was lying, but I thought, like me, he was half-saying things so he wouldn't seem to be lying.

I changed tack.

"Let's talk about mutual enemies then. What's preventing Tullah from coming back to Denver? Or more importantly, who?"

He spread his hands in a gesture of uncertainty. "Possibly the Empire? They've had Adepts in the country, as you know. And however Altau managed to persuade them to leave, that's not to say some haven't come sneaking back. Or it could be the Hecate's doing, distracting us here while her Adepts are hunting."

"Okay." I heard what he said, but I didn't agree; I still didn't trust him any more than I had when I came in. "What about how we get her back? Why come to me? What do you think I can do that you can't?"

"Ah. Well, you see, you're the key to it, for four reasons." He ticked things off on his fingers. "You're from the paranormal community, so there are no security issues involved in working with you. You have some ability with the energy yourself, which will help. Tullah's a close friend and you're motivated to find her. And you're close friends with her parents as well."

"From what you're hinting, there's some kind of location magic that involves me and my friendship with Tullah?" I raised an eyebrow at Kane, but he remained expressionless. "A stronger version of things like eukori and the werewolves' Call?"

"Yes," Weaver said, leaning forward. "It's a structured working that is too complex and dangerous for shamanic magic. Using you as a focus, the community working together will enable us to project your awareness, a sense of you, like a beam of light in the darkness and tune it to Tullah, so others can't listen in. She'll recognize your aura and respond, although it may take a few attempts."

Flint and Kane had managed to find where the Northern Adept League were in RiNo, so I didn't entirely buy this was too complex for shamanic magic. But I wasn't about to tell him that. It did sound like it was the next level of complexity.

"Can Tullah and I talk while using this? Or is it just a sense of my aura that she receives?"

He shook his head. "No talking. When she responds, you'll be able to sense a direction." His hands swept across the desk to illustrate his words. "Then we move to one side and try again. Another reading..." He drew lines with his fingers. "And where the readings meet, there's where she must be, trapped somehow."

"I understand. But you're claiming I'm the key. There are people in the Denver Adept community that have known Tullah their whole lives, who she must know as well as she knows me, if not better."

He looked embarrassed. "She no longer trusts the community." He rocked back in his chair and sighed. "This is all due to the lock and that was entirely my doing, but as I explained, I was only trying to do the responsible thing."

"I don't think it's just about the lock, Weaver. You led a revolt against her mother to take over the Denver community."

"No. I acted absolutely within the rules laid down by the community," he said. "In the event of the use of lethal force by magic without prior license, any community member has all offices suspended for an enquiry. We're all signed up for that. I just happened to be next most senior."

I huffed. He had an answer to everything.

"Okay. So, your community working with me sends out a signal," I said. "But we don't get one back unless Tullah wants it. Have I got that part right?"

"Exactly."

"And Tullah can tell it's not just me, but it's me working with you?"

"Yeah. She'll know it's us."

Both Kane and Rita stirred for the first time since Weaver had started talking.

When Rita stopped moving, she had such an uncanny stillness, you almost forgot she was there. Kane hadn't so much as blinked even when Weaver made his comments about being outside of the Adept law. If they both moved like that, it was telling me Weaver's last statement wasn't the same level of truth or ambiguity as the other things he'd been saying.

Interesting.

I would have to come back to that, but while he was talking freely, I wanted more from his perspective without him understanding why I wanted it.

If I was going to be a cog in the Denver community's working, I'd have to lower my barriers, and as soon as I did, they'd know what kind of magic I used. They'd know the halfy ritual was based on Blood magic. I was scared they'd sense that I'd used Blood magic to win the El Paso challenge if I let them in my head.

I was surprised Weaver hadn't sensed it in my aura already. Or maybe he thought it was all because I'd come straight from killing my challenger, and nothing to do with the *way* I'd killed her.

Would they still work with me when they knew about the Blood magic? Or would they be horrified like Flint and Kane?

The silence had stretched on too long. Weaver was holding out for a yes.

"So, your community is okay working with an Athanate like me?" I said instead. "You know, the same evil Athanate you say steal souls?"

Weaver grimaced.

"That's old shamanic superstitious language coming through, from Adepts who've adopted the new methods after starting from shamanic."

It had been. Tullah's mother, Mary, had used those words: that the price of Athanate long life was the souls of the people who gave their Blood.

"Suppose you put it in your modern words then," I said.

Weaver leaned back and reached for the bookshelf behind him for a slim, old volume.

Discourse on Free Will and Determinism, the title said.

I raised an eyebrow.

"Modern words," Weaver said with a small smile, "for a discussion that's been engaging some of the finest minds for hundreds or even thousands of years. This is Erasmus and Luther exchanging letters in the 16th century."

He pushed it to one side.

"They put it all into Christian religious terms. Erasmus said humanity had the choice of good or evil, and therefore must have free will. Luther said we are either bound to the will of God, or Satan. And although neither of those two came down and said it in so many words, others have equated the free will they talked about with the soul."

"Athanate feed on the Blood of their kin, not their souls," I said.

"Indeed, that's the accurate, observable reality, and I'm not trying to forge a metaphysical connection between Blood and soul. But tell me, what free will do kin have? Not individuals, you understand, but as a whole. How many decide they no longer want to be kin? How many would fight against what their Athanate masters wish? Over time, how many simply accept it?"

"And that's *soul*?"

"I'm trying not to use concepts that can only lead to discussing subjective definitions of intangibles. The core problem is that the Adept community believe the Athanate, intentionally or otherwise, take the free will of their Blood donors from them." He held up his hands. "It's an item for much later discussion. To answer your original question, yes, we will work with you on this overwhelmingly important issue, and then, at our leisure, we can debate together how Athanate might progress without infringing the free will of their donors."

I took a deep breath. Damn, but he and the Hecate had awkward arguments that were difficult to counter. Still, Jen and I had talked about this, and I wasn't buying his kin-as-slaves view. But at least I'd opened the talk up enough for my next question.

"This beam of awareness working you say you'll do, it's got to be powerful. Does that mean it's dark magic?"

Weaver blinked and his mouth turned down. "We dislike all the old descriptions like soul and dark magic. There is the energy and it's used in workings. It's harder or easier. Everything else is a human construction of perceptions overlaid on it."

My turn to blink, and I noticed Kane stirred again. My little Adept didn't like that summary from Weaver.

But *I* liked the sound of it. Magic is neutral. Everything else is up to the person or people using it. Including addictiveness, evil, soul stealing and the rest. Just human perceptions trying to make sense of what was happening, using real, tangible terms that we could understand and communicate.

Except it didn't *feel* like that. The power I'd felt and pulled through Kane, that didn't feel like some objective, neutral power; it felt like something that wanted to be used, something with intent. Something that would whisper to me in the quiet, and if I gave it any leeway, would never release an inch of it.

"That's been interesting, thanks," I said. "I did promise I would talk to the Hecate tomorrow... well, later today now. But I think we can say we're reaching an understanding about getting Tullah back."

Weaver was about to object, probably about the idea of my talking to the Hecate, so I finished my drink and stood.

To give him his due, he saw us politely to the door and offered a hand to shake. It would have been rude to refuse, but I regretted it immediately, getting another static shock like I had in the club when he'd touched my hand.

What was it with this guy? Did he have polyester underpants or something?

He hadn't really given me enough reason to dislike him, but I couldn't wait to get out.

Chapter 29

We left, and Kane was barely outside the house before he was complaining that Weaver had deliberately dodged the question about blood magic.

"He's probably going to sacrifice a goat, or something gross," he muttered. "That man is dark as shit."

"You didn't believe what he said about Tullah being able to know who's calling?" I asked.

"No."

"What about the rest of what he said?"

Kane shrugged. "I'm not a Truth Sensor. He didn't seem to be lying, but I don't think he told the truth either. I think he's a frigging genius at saying things he could halfway justify, and hiding what he doesn't want to talk about."

He might not like how I'd used him, but outside of magic definitions, Kane and I agreed on things. And yet there was the nagging feeling I was slipping toward making the wrong decision about Weaver—working on my gut, when I should be thinking it through.

Kane wasn't quite finished. "I don't trust him and I don't think we should do anything that involves him. If he and his community can do this working, then so can Flint and I."

"Except they know what they're doing," I pointed out. Weaver was the head of an Adept community. They had to know more about these things than a pair of renegades.

"So *they* say," Kane retorted. "Even if they do, how do *you* know what they're doing?"

Both Rita and Scott picked up on the tension again.

Rita gave Kane a long, cool look that should have made him more afraid than it did.

I *could* shut him down. Whatever he and Amanda finally decided, at the moment, I was Mistress of his House and he was out of line.

Scott didn't know what to do. The conflict upset him at a level he hadn't experienced before. I was his alpha, but both he and Kane were also Amanda's kin, so part of Scott's instinct was to defend him, just as another part was to defend me.

He didn't know how to handle it and that was making him angry.

His heartrate surged. I took his hand again, willed him to stay calm.

Then all of us were distracted by Keith waving urgently at us, listening to something on the comms device in his ear.

"Trouble," he said. "Some of the El Paso pack aren't happy with you, and it seems they have friends in the Confederation. There are a couple of trucks heading this way."

"Who's telling us?"

"Bian."

What's she doing monitoring werewolves? And how?

Not important at the moment.

Keith offered me his comms.

Eww. That earbud had been in his ear.

I put it in anyway.

"Bian? A couple of trucks?"

I listened to her brief rundown.

"That doesn't sound like the Confederation," I said. "They go for overwhelming superiority. And as for El Paso, no way it's the pack members who were at the factory; Alex and I would have known."

"Of course you would have known if they weren't sincere, Round-eye. Alex is here at Haven with your new pack. They've told him Caleb and Victoria weren't sure Felix would play straight on getting you to the factory, or honoring the challenge, so they had a team in Denver ready to track you down and pick you up. That's the team after you."

Huh? Two things: Alex at Haven? And El Paso's challenge was about me as well as position in the new super-pack?

No time to question those as Bian went on. "Seems like El Paso were also hedging their bets by talking to some of the Wyoming werewolves. *Might* not be Confederation. Long story short, you have two trucks with eight or nine werewolves converging on your spot, and they aren't going to invite you to a dance."

"How the hell do they know where I am?"

"They had a drone on you. Lost you on the interstate, then picked up your parked truck from the infrared signature."

"Okay." Bian was obviously hacking their cell phones. That was more indication this wasn't a well-planned attack.

Planned or not, it wouldn't make any difference if we died because of it.

I looked at Julie and Keith and the canvas bags in the back of the Hill Bitch. "We got enough to handle this?"

They nodded.

It worried me to have to ask Keith. He wasn't fully fit: he still had a slight limp from being shot in LA, despite the very best of Athanate care from Yelena. But even so, three people trained by Ops 4-10, with backup, against a team of werewolves who had probably never worked or trained together?

Unless they had something extraordinary I didn't know about, it was no match.

"Hold on, Round-eye, you don't need to do this," Bian was protesting.

"Can't take this back into town," I said.

"You could go back into Weaver's house and wait. I've sent an Ops 4-10 team and a cleanup crew. They'll be with you in about twenty minutes."

I laughed. "No way. Firstly, I'm *not* going to be obligated to Weaver and secondly, that sort of backing down would be a very bad move in front of my new pack."

She knew me well enough to accept that.

And my thinking was good. Especially about the pack. Why had it seemed, just for a moment, such a sensible idea to go back and get Weaver's help?

Put that shit aside and concentrate.

Old Ops 4-10 training took over.

Five minutes later we'd split our resources between the Hill Bitch and Rita's Dodge. We were heading back out of Erie as if we suspected nothing.

There were headlights in the night behind us.

"Take a right here," I said. I was using Julie's comms unit now and speaking to Keith, who was driving the Hill Bitch.

We turned south, avoiding the Erie Parkway's wide open road that would have taken us straight back to I25.

I looked up at the sky, but I couldn't see anything of course.

"A strong Adept could pull that drone down," I said to Kane.

Could I? Could I reach up with the dark power and haul it right out of the sky?

Would I even need to go through Kane?

I was starting to think I wouldn't. Something had happened to me earlier. Something had changed. The safety had come off.

"I could," Kane said. "But it's easier to jam it."

He closed his eyes and my skin prickled as he did a casting.

I left him to it, ignoring the tingling in my hands that wanted to show I could do it quicker, better.

"Keith, we're going to take the left turn coming up now, the dirt road, and accelerate hard. I want a lot of dust."

"Affirm," Keith said.

Seconds later, the Hill Bitch suddenly swerved and shot off down the county road, dust billowing in our headlights.

"Go," I said to Rita, and she took off in pursuit, her smile thin and her eyes bright. My were-cougar was enjoying this far too much.

"Lights off," I said.

Bian swore quietly in my ear. "They're about three seconds behind you, Round-eye."

"You can do a handbrake turn in the middle of the road, Rita?"

She laughed.

"One second. On my command. Keith, lights off and get back here."

Tricky, as I couldn't see the Hill Bitch and I didn't know how close we were. "Rita... *now.*"

The Dodge slewed and spun around to point back the way we'd come.

"Out," I said to David and Kane.

Three little seconds. Nothing but the dust we'd kicked up, already thinning.

Two. The lights of the trucks chasing. The Hill Bitch came alongside us.

"Full beam, and get out," I yelled, jumping clear.

I was relying on self-preservation and werewolf-sharp reaction times, and I wasn't disappointed.

The lights dipped as the front truck slammed on his brakes. Then they swerved. And the following truck hit the leading one as it also slammed on brakes that didn't work so well on dirt. Didn't hit hard, but enough to shove them both into the side.

Nice of them not to hit my trucks.

Julie fired her MP5 and the front truck's screen shattered and fell inwards.

I put eight quick rounds through the side windows and doors of the second truck.

Keith hurled a flashbomb into the lead truck. Rita threw hers through the windows I'd just broken. Not lethal, but anyone alive in those trucks was going to be deaf and blind.

A guy jumped out of the back. Shotgun lifting. Looking wildly around. I fired again. Tap, tap. Tap. He fell backwards.

Spring the magazine. Replace. Chamber. Back searching for targets. All one continuous movement.

The flashbombs went off. We were protected by being outside, but I was still seeing stars for a few moments.

A door opened. David fired the Sig. A body slid down onto the gravel and stayed there.

No return fire. And none going to come now.

Julie and Keith coordinated evacuating the front truck.

David, Rita and I worked on the back one. Less smoothly, but the two of them would have done well in Ops 4-10.

Nine attackers.

Four dead bodies.

Four wounded. One probably not going to make it.

And one cub, wet pants, temporarily blind and deaf, but otherwise miraculously unhurt.

Standing back from us, I could sense Kane was upset. And Scott was shocked—partly by the violence, partly by his wolf reaction to it.

I put them out of mind and focused on the task in hand.

By the time Bian's Ops 4-10 team and the clean-up crew had arrived ten minutes later, we'd tended to the wounded and loaded the dead into one truck.

I got a salute and a well done from the Ops 4-10 team leader. I remembered her from my time.

"Did they make you Sergeant before it all went away, Annie?"

"They did, ma'am."

I laughed. "Don't *ma'am* me. I'm just another civilian now."

"If you say so, ma'am." Her lip twitched, but then her expression changed as she looked over at the prisoners. Went bleak as a storm clouds rolling off the Rockies.

"Not tonight, Annie," I muttered and went to stand over them.

I nudged the cub with my foot. "On your feet."

He scrambled up, heart racing and the stench of fear on his breath.

I sniffed.

"You're not El Paso. What's your pack?"

"Shut up, boy. We're dead anyways." One of the wounded.

I pointed the Mk 23 at the one who'd spoken. That close, the barrel looks like a freaking cannon. He got the message and shut up.

Without the support of his pack, the cub answered. "Black Hills, ma'am."

Black Hills and Thunder Basin, to give them their full name. Not a Confederation pack, last I heard, out there on the Wyoming-South Dakota border. Just big enough, just far away enough from the Confederation to not be worth the trouble. But close enough to want to be friendly.

And the Confederation, frustrated in its attempt to drive down the Rockies through Colorado, might be looking east across the plains.

Black Hills trying to buy a guarantee of independence?

"You drive?" I asked.

"Yes, ma'am."

"Well, kid, I suggest you load the living into the back of this truck and then drive all night. You could make the Black Hills in time for a late breakfast with your alpha. And when you do, you tell him to call me, *if* he has the balls, so he can explain what the hell he thinks he's doing."

I gestured and he bent down to help the first one to his feet. The boy moved slowly, as if he was expecting me to shoot him in the back as soon as he turned away.

I gave him some room and turned my attention to the last two sitting propped against the truck.

They were El Paso, and they hadn't missed me saying 'the living' got to leave.

"There is no El Paso pack anymore," I said. "The pack that was El Paso now belongs to me and my co-alpha, by right of challenge. You two are outcast. Try your luck with Black Hills or the Confederation if you want, but if I ever see you back in Colorado, you'll join the others as fertilizer. Now get out of here."

They got.

Annie had organized the second truck with its load of dead werewolves to return to the fertilizer factory. The clean-up crew were spraying chemicals over the road to destroy the blood spilled during the ambush and aftermath.

We were done here, but I lingered for a second or two longer while Rita got in Kane's face a little way off from where the headlights were shining through the steam of our breath.

"Yeah, five living," he was saying, not realizing I could hear him. "What about the four dead to add to the total for the night?"

"You're being an asshole, Kane. They'd have killed us to take her. Your magic any good at stopping bullets?"

"We could have done it another way."

"Yeah, and you could be dead. This way worked fine. You know, by werewolf law she should have killed the survivors. She's probably going to have to persuade Felix and Cameron not to go scorched earth on the Black Hills pack now, and if she succeeds it'll be because none of us were hurt. Thanks to her way of doing it. You draw your own clear lines for yourself, but don't try it on other people in the real world. Especially the werewolf world."

Kane backed off, blinking. Knew a bit about magic, but not so much about werewolves.

I raised my voice. "Time to go home."

Not only did I have a job to rebuild bridges with Kane about the type of magic that seemed natural to me, I was going to have educate him with some of the more brutal aspects of the paranormal communities. At least for the second, I'd expect the rest of the House to help.

Flint and Kane on their own could probably have lived their entire lives without overstepping the personal boundaries they laid down. The way they lived, if they ever felt they'd come to the close attention of too many humans, they could just move on and disappear. But history had shown the paranormal communities that their way didn't work for bigger, complex groups.

We split up between the trucks. I went with Rita. Kane opted to go in the Hill Bitch. I shrugged. It wouldn't have been ideal to talk to him in the car but it was his loss; much as I loved the Hill Bitch, Rita's Dodge had heating.

Chapter 30

We got back to Manassah at around 4 a.m., both trucks together.

Amanda and Pia were waiting up for us, and I guess it was obvious to them Kane and I had a problem. I could see them stiffen up right away.

I ignored it and pointed Scott at the master bedroom. "You're sleeping in there until you're stable," I said. "Go take a shower. Towels in the bathroom. Spare bathrobe, comforter and pillows in the closet. You get the couch."

His lip thinned, but he'd gotten enough control not to snarl at his alpha for being bossed like that.

I ran a hand through my hair tiredly. The scent of Scott sleeping in the bedroom was going to drive Alex crazy when he got back. As if I didn't have enough trouble in that area with Zane; someone was bound to tell Alex what had happened just before the fight.

I still didn't know what to make of that. It gave me an odd, uncomfortable feeling, like looking back on something I'd done when I was drunk. It was embarrassing. Unfamiliar.

That's not me.

Kane walking away without speaking brought me swiftly back to my more immediate problems.

I held up a hand to indicate I needed to speak to Amanda, and then briefly introduced the others.

"This is Rita. Lynch. Pia. Amanda." I pointed at them. I wasn't up to lengthy explanations tonight. "Rita and Lynch are staying with us for a while."

Pia and David exchanged a silent message in a look, and it was David who took Rita and Lynch off next door to find spare bedrooms. Being the gentleman he was, he even offered to carry her backpack. The sound of Rita's laughter as they left only made the silence in the hallway deeper.

"Amanda, I've apologised to Kane..."

"What happened?"

"I'll explain it all later, but I pulled magic through him. Dark magic. I really don't want to lose you, but I'm not sure I can tell him what he wants to hear from me. I can't tell him I won't ever do it again. Please, go talk to him, then come talk to me."

She hurried after Kane, looking worried.

"Want to talk about it to us, boss?" Pia lead me into the living room and fixed me a rum.

Julie and Keith settled silently into the smaller sofa and waited.

I didn't know where to start.

"Tove came back," Pia said when I didn't immediately speak. "She was jumpy, but I think you've gotten through to her. She seems to be getting to that point where she realizes what a mess she's in, and that we're probably the best chance she has. She's asleep now."

"She gave back the money, too," Keith said. "It's in the safe."

There was another one of those waiting gaps in the conversation.

"David told us what happened at the werewolf meeting," Julie said, turning her head to look at the side of the house where Kane had gone to Amanda's suite. "But there was obviously more going on under the surface. Why don't you start from when you left us outside the club?"

Fair request.

I didn't want to, but this was my House. I owed them the truth, and so I started speaking about why Zane had come and collected us for the meeting out at the fertilizer factory.

I hadn't gotten far, no more than the background behind the challenge from El Paso, when Amanda came back in, with Flint and Kane.

My heart was in my throat at the sight of Amanda's face, pale with anger.

Was using Kane to channel Blood magic enough to break the Athanate oath she'd given for her House? Had I lost them already?

She sat stiffly beside me. Flint and Kane sat cross-legged on the floor.

"I have sworn my oath," she said, not meeting my eye. "I need to hear what happened, from your perspective."

Shit.

One more interruption: Rita and David.

Rita took a chair, David went and stood behind me to massage my neck. Until his thumbs pressed into the muscles, I hadn't realized how tense I had become.

Flint was quiet, but his face wasn't as closed as Kane's.

I started again. Went back over the situation with the Southern League—the need to allow some of the old traditions to remain while such a fundamental change was made to the independence of packs. How the challenge from El Paso fell into this gray area. The way Felix and Cameron had felt they needed to protect me. The bending of the rules to exclude me from the fight. My explanation that I'd thought it would have done more damage.

I went on to the explosion of emotion I'd felt when I heard Cameron's work-around, my instinctive refusal to allow it, then followed by the cold reality; Alex in single combat against Caleb had probably been better odds than both of us against both of them, because Victoria outclassed me fighting as a wolf and would leave him to face both of them.

"And you couldn't fight in human form?" Amanda asked. "Wouldn't you have been better that way?"

Rita answered for me. "Not when it's a formal challenge, with lives and packs at stake. Then you have to fight as a wolf." She held up a hand to stop me continuing. "Maybe it's just detail, but you were acting strangely before the fight."

My stomach sank. I had to explain that as well? To my House?

But she was right. I had to explain *because* they were my House. Even Rita.

"This is not for discussion outside the House," I said, and held Rita's level gaze until she nodded.

"While Cameron and Felix were still arguing in the back of the factory, Zane got the Belles to cover for him and he came to warn me what was going on. To warn me not to get involved in the challenge."

"That went well. What a surprise." Keith said, with a lopsided smile. Trying to lighten it up. Julie jabbed him in the ribs.

"Yeah. Anyway, I guess Cameron sent him, but he wasn't supposed to be telling me anything and he was worried the El Paso pack or their friends might be watching. So he had to pretend to be coming on to me..."

I felt the color creeping up my face.

"I'm not... I don't know what happened. When Rita says acting strangely, I guess she means I was about to get mounted on the wall."

"He was—" Pia started.

"No. He wasn't forcing me," I said. My face was hot now. "I came on to him."

"Coming on wasn't one-sided, from what I could see," Rita said quietly. "Not that I'd expect anything else from him."

"It's not what I'd expect from *me*." I looked at the ceiling rather than catch anyone's eye. "I thought for a moment someone must have slipped me something in my beer at the club, but..." I shrugged, "I'd have burned that out of my system by that time."

"Not necessarily," Amanda said. "But I don't think we need to go any further into this. You were acting out of character. Does that mean it also affected your decision to fight, and what happened in the fight?"

"No." I struggled with putting it into words. "If Zane had come on to me, say, a year ago? Hey, he's too sexy for his own damn good, but I *am* attracted to him. Deciding to fight had nothing to do with feeling strange. Feeling strange was all about making out with him only days after..."

I held up my left hand with the twin rings that Jen had got for us. No, we weren't married, but we *were* committed to each other.

Whatever that means.

Jen saying she understood about Bian.

That she'd talked to Alex about it. That he would be okay.

But Zane? Oh, no. Whole different ball game for Alex.

Aloud I said. "It was almost like it was happening to someone else. Like I didn't care. Like I had no inhibitions about anything. Nothing to do with the fight."

I closed my eyes.

The fight.

Sitting there in the luxurious comfort of the living room at Manassah, it should have been difficult to think back and capture that exact horror and fascination of the formless power lurking in the darkness beneath me. The terror of it. Knowing it had been waiting there for me to *reach* in this urgent way. Knowing it was a sort of a trap. Something that I couldn't undo. Knowing my desperation was all part of the trap.

It wasn't difficult to capture it at all. It was burned into my mind, and while I stumbled putting it into words, Pia's eukori slipped effortlessly in. Then David. Amanda. Sweeping in Julie and Keith and Rita. Flint. Finally, Kane.

They all became witness to the bone-deep shock of it all, seen up close through my eyes.

Alex unbalanced by our combined weight on his back and the fangs in his neck.

Caleb poised to kill him.

Knowing Alex would die.

Accepting the trap because I couldn't let him die.

Sucking that power through Kane, without knowing how or why.

Terror and fascination.

The horror knowing what I was doing to both Kane and Victoria.

Kane's feelings, shocked and sharp and deep as knife wounds.

The memories of the pain exploding through my body as the magic worked. Anger. Fear. *Dark* sensations and emotions. *Feeding* on them, growing stronger. The obscenity of it—using Victoria's own terror as part of what made me able to kill her.

Her despair.

The violent need as I killed her.

Then afterwards, the sickness at it all. The nausea at what I'd done.

Tears gathered in my eyes.

Amanda knelt and gathered Kane into her arms. Flint hugged them both clumsily.

David kept massaging my neck. Pia moved to press her body against mine.

As if the physical contact could drain some of the pain bubbling up in both of us.

It did help.

My House.

"What's done is done," Pia said.

David shook his head. "Frankly, rather this than the alternative."

Amanda turned to me, her eyes troubled, but steady.

"You still have my oath," she said.

She turned to look at Flint.

He nodded without hesitation.

Kane: his acceptance was slow, but it wasn't grudging. He'd seen what happened through my eyes. He wasn't happy about it, but I could feel his aura through my eukori.

"We'll talk to Kaothos and Alice tomorrow." Pia kissed my cheek and rested her head against my shoulder. "They'll know what this is and how we all deal with it."

Their pressure on my eukori started to feel uncomfortable. I eased them out, and they accepted my need for privacy.

It wasn't quite that.

The thought of Kaothos and Alice poking around in my eukori unsettled me. As if... as if whatever it was, this brooding darkness, it was mine. For me to handle. Alone.

Chapter 31

I asked Julie to describe her impressions of the visit to Weaver and the attempted ambush afterwards, saying I'd add anything I felt she missed.

As I'd known she would, Julie made a good, neutral summary. None of us *liked* Weaver, but none of us had enough reason to not work with him, if it meant getting Tullah back.

"He's our best bet," I said.

That discussion slowed. The others thought we shouldn't make a final decision without a better grasp of what the Hecate might offer as well, and it seemed clear we couldn't work with both. Julie was adamant that just because Weaver said she wasn't to be trusted, wasn't enough reason to refuse to speak with her.

"Apart from kidnapping Amber..."

I had to laugh at that. *Yeah, apart from kidnapping me. And spying on Alice.*

"Apart from that," Julie continued, unfazed, "she's been reasonably polite, and all she says she wants to do is meet the dragon. I say we go at least that far with her."

That was on the list for 'tomorrow', which was now today. Late as it was, no one showed any sign of moving. I had the feeling they were waiting for me go to bed, but I was slumped back on the sofa and it seemed a long way up.

"She's also part of the Northern Adept League, which has a large community in New York, so we need to progress carefully and keep Skylur in the loop. I'll relay that through Bian," Pia said, closing off that topic and moving to what we were going to do with Tove.

The girl had made a good decision, and a brave one; she'd come back to us for help. But Amanda was quick to say Tove might not yet have reached the point where we could really help her.

"She's may be in that really difficult stage, where she thinks she might need help, but doesn't want it; where she believes she's in control and can handle her need for drugs. If we push her too quickly, it could make her turn inwards, characterize the addiction as part of herself, and try to handle it alone."

"Of course we could ignore that softly, softly approach and just bite her," Keith said. "The Athanate bio-agents would eliminate any physical dependency or need for drugs, won't they?"

I knew my former boyfriend and he wasn't really suggesting this. He wanted the arguments laid out while Kane was sitting there listening. He wanted Kane to see how we worked.

He wanted an argument and he got one. Yes, the bio-agents would eradicate the addiction, and Athanate relergic abilities could erase the memory of being bitten, but the memory of her life as an addict was too much. Erasing that much memory would probably not be possible, and in any event, it would damage Tove's mental health.

More than that: as with Kath, it was immoral to force a solution on Tove.

I closed my eyes and let them talk, turned my attention inwards. No one moved, but they all seemed to drift away from me. I looked inwards, to find it was waiting.

I could fix Tove. And Kath. No memory blurring. No bio-agents. No damage. They'd be healthy and happy. I could make sure of that.

Why not use this? Just because of questions about morals?

All it would take...

To reach down and use that power.

Huge power.

I opened my eyes in shock.

Couldn't the others sense it? The whole physical house seemed to be holding its breath. The power I'd felt during the fight was *there.* Right there. Seething all around us.

No. They can't feel it.

Because it's not there. It's here. Inside of me.

It's part of me. Always has been.

I got up off the sofa, fast enough that it caught their attention.

"Sorry," I said. "You guys talk. I'm going to bed."

The group broke up with yawns and tired hugs all around.

"Yeah, good idea."

"Big day tomorrow."

"Ha! Today, you mean."

"'Night."

I left the good-nights behind quickly. I needed a shower. I needed to scrub myself clean. I probably still had traces of Victoria's blood in my hair, touching my scalp, and the thought of that made me shudder.

When the last of the blood was gone, maybe I'd have gotten rid of these disturbing sensations of this power urging me to use it. The feeling of it.

Maybe.

Scott had managed to make it through the shower and toweling himself dry before his tiredness had taken over. He was sprawled stark naked on the bed, dead asleep. So much for him sleeping on the couch.

I snorted and left him there. My shower was more important than shifting him. Or ogling his body, however pleasant.

I turned the jets and steam on full. For a few minutes I was blissfully alone, hidden from the world as I scrubbed any last remaining traces of the fight from my body.

Alone with my thoughts.

What if Diana hadn't completely cured me down in LA?

What if this was my madness coming back?

No. The power was *real*. It had leeched body mass from Victoria and added it to my wolf jaws. An average adult wolf might have a jaw force measured at about 400 pounds per square inch. A werewolf would be bigger and stronger, but not strong enough for the bites I'd made. The strength in my jaw had built and built, relentlessly. What had it reached? 1000 PSI? Higher? That was hyena territory.

A whisper of a voice reached me. Tolly, sitting in the darkness telling me what his cousin, the Lyssae we called Anubis, would say about magic: *keep well away from magic, especially dark magic.*

And we called him Anubis because, although he was Athanate, he'd part changed like a werewolf, and had a dog-like face. What if that wasn't a dog, but a hyena face?

What if using dark magic like that would make me end up a Lyssae?

Tired as I was, that kind of leap almost seemed to make sense to me.

Crazy! Stop it.

Yes. And that was why Adepts sometimes killed crazy people, because part of being able to use the energy was sheer belief, and some crazy people had more of that belief than people who weren't crazy.

It didn't feel crazy, this power. It felt scary. I liked scary. I'd made my living in Ops 4-10 throwing myself out of the back of aircraft, at night, with nothing but a rubbery suit and a too-small parachute to carry me down safely. I *liked* danger and thrills and adrenaline.

I couldn't stop thinking about the power.

All I really could do was admit to myself, hidden in the steam with my mental shields up, that the power was exhilarating as a nighttime parachute jump.

Even more.

I wanted to use it again.

Why shouldn't I?

I'd be in control. I'd use it for the right reasons.

The circling thoughts eventually died down and I got out of the shower, feeling clean and exhausted. I might actually be able to sleep once I cooled down.

The whole bathroom was steamed up, so no glimpses of me in the mirror. Nothing to send my mind off down another track, wondering what had happened to Tara.

I walked out into the bedroom, naked but for the towel I was using to dry my hair.

And sensed someone else in the room.

Chapter 32

"A soft-boiled Amber. All hot and pink and wet. Cute."

I had to laugh. "What are you doing here, Bian?"

"Skylur's orders."

"Our lord and master instructed you to enter my bedroom in the early hours of the morning?"

"Well, not exactly, but I have some latitude in how I carry out my instructions, Round-eye."

I snorted. So much for falling asleep.

I *had* gotten sleepy, otherwise I'd have noticed her arrival much earlier. But it seems I'd juggled one hot potato until it was cool, only to have another tossed at me.

Just what was my local Athanate boss doing that required her to visit me at a time she'd legitimately expect me to be in bed?

Blood. Or possibly body and Blood.

I got goosebumps and my neck muscles went all loose in anticipation.

Carefully avoiding Scott sprawled on the side, I sat at the end of the bed and continued toweling my hair. I was still naked. I guessed putting on a bathrobe wasn't going to achieve very much at this point.

"Let's get this lump into the bed first," Bian said. "I'll pick him up and you sort out the sheets."

Scott was in one of the deep sleeps that characterize Athanate in crusis and Were in transition. We could probably have tossed him on the floor without waking him, but I guessed the bed was big enough, so we might as well put him in it.

She lifted him and I pulled the sheets back, allowing her to arrange him neatly.

Then she took the sheets from me, but paused before covering him.

"Pretty," she said. "Your new sub-House knows how to pick them."

She angled her head as she looked up and down his body critically. "I love them like this. All limp and vulnerable. It's so cute."

I laughed. "You're just being rude, Pussy-cat. Leave the poor boy alone."

She smiled and tucked him in.

Since she didn't seem in a hurry to jump me, I put my bathrobe on and we curled up side by side on the semi-circular sofa in the bay window.

I could never be absolutely sure which Bian I was dealing with. She could switch from serious to playful to predatory in the space of three breaths. So far tonight, I'd gotten the playful. I searched her face for clues and found she also looked tired to the point of exhaustion. And worried.

For me?

"Congratulations on winning the challenge and dealing with the ambush," she said quietly.

"Uh. So, what does Skylur think of it all?" I knew *those* orders—she had to report to Skylur anything of significance in Denver, day or night.

"He's worried, and when he's worried, he changes things. I think he's satisfied that Felix and Cameron have now put in place protections for you from the werewolf side—"

"He called them directly?"

Shit. In the middle of the night. I was going to leave it till the morning. Morning as in when the sun was up.

"Yes."

I chewed on that. I was supposed to be syndesmon, the ambassador, between the Were and the Athanate. He wasn't supposed to talk to them on significant issues without me being briefed and giving an opinion, or even being present. I guessed if I challenged it, he'd hide behind the argument that the conversation was about me personally, rather than about Athanate-Were relations.

I'd have to let it pass.

Bian had waited, letting me think it through. She resumed. "Security is a growing concern. I've started a couple of processes. Hear me out."

"Okay." Duly warned, I settled back, crossed my arms and pinched my tongue between my teeth.

"I've just called Victor Gayle about the security for Manassah."

I grunted.

Vic had been getting twitchy about the number of people from his security and investigation agency he was committing to guarding a house which, as far as the personnel could see, wasn't under threat. Vic himself had some idea that there were threats, but without bringing him and the whole security team into the paranormal secret world, we couldn't brief them thoroughly. And as Vic had pointed out, badly briefed security is only one step above no security, let alone the danger his unsuspecting people were facing.

Again, Bian waited before continuing. "So they're now being phased out to go back to normal security and investigation work, and in their place, Skylur's assigned some of our Ops 4-10 troops."

"Neat solution," I said. Ops 4-10 veterans knew about the paranormal and had volunteered to join. "But they were supposed to be spread all over the country to provide security for all Athanate Houses."

"They still will, but you come first."

"I'm flattered."

"Good," she said. "I've also been talking to Alex."

My heart skipped a beat. Alex had gone to Haven. Why?

"About what?"

"Your new, very large and unwieldy pack. Whatever did you think?" She fluttered eyelids.

I ignored the teasing. "What exactly about the pack?"

"What to do with them. Haven is now Hotel Werewolf. Skylur's ordered that Alex gets whatever he needs. Place for the pack to stay, jobs, transport. All for asking."

Alex hadn't even had time to call me about it. Looking at it soberly, on the one hand, that was a lot of good news about our pack. On the other...

"What's the cost for all of this?"

"How did you become such a cynical woman, Amber?"

She hooked an arm around me and pulled me into a brief kiss and cuddle.

"Relax," she said. "Despite appearances, Skylur regards you as a vital cog in his Emergence plans. 'You' includes your kin and your House, and your relationship with the werewolves, so that includes your pack as well. He needs that relationship to be secure and stable, not distracted by the logistics of your new pack. The same thinking applies to establishing a relationship with the Adepts. Any help he can provide toward getting Tullah and Kaothos back together is all wrapped up in that. No obligations on your part, other than to keep doing what you're doing. As long as you achieve complete success of course."

I snorted.

But... the Athanate and Were worlds were looking out for me. That part felt good.

Whatever fine words Skylur had used, they weren't really able to help with the Adepts. That part came down to me. Responsibility and danger all twisted together.

"Now, as for me," Bian said, her voice going all smoky, "I might have a couple of favors I want to ask, in due course. But for now..."

"Yeah?"

Her voice changed to brisk and businesslike. "I'd like to sleep here, and I'd like to use Jen's conference call system in the morning, in..." she glanced at her watch with a sigh, "a little over five hours' time."

When she said 'here', I knew she meant in the bed in this room.

"Sure. Mi casa and so on." I made my voice as nonchalant as I could. "What's so important about the conference call?"

"Orders from Skylur. Every major House." She got up, yawned and stretched. "He's picked a new Diakon and wants to introduce them."

"Huh? Oh. Yeah." My tired mind caught up: Skylur had burned through his Diakons recently. Bian had been his Diakon, replacing Naryn originally, then Naryn had come back, then Tarez briefly had filled that role down in Los Angeles. But all three of them were now set up in key locations—LA, Boston and Denver. They couldn't be spared.

Skylur would need a Diakon, and he'd need one in New York, full time.

For a moment, I panicked. *Yelena!*

But no. That wouldn't go down well with the Panethus Houses. Although Yelena had only been in Basilikos Houses as a spy, there was the minor matter that she was Carpathian originally. Not a good political move for Skylur to steal her as his Diakon.

No. He'd play it safe. Someone to keep the Panethus party happy.

"Go to bed, Round-eye." Bian disappeared into the bathroom and I heard the shower start up a minute later.

I switched the lights off, shucked the bathrobe and slipped under the sheets on the opposite side from Scott.

Incredibly, I was almost asleep when Bian returned, warm, naked, and smelling of my shampoo and Jen's minty toothpaste. Naturally, she decided she wanted the middle of the bed and climbed in all over me.

By the end of that, I was most definitely not asleep, but all she did was curl up alongside me.

I kissed her forehead.

Deep breath.

"What do you want me to do, Pussy-cat?"

"Hmm?" Her voice was blurry. Then she switched to Vietnamese, which really threw me for a second. "I'm sleepy. Tell me a bedtime story, sister," she said.

Not what I was expecting.

Strangely enough, it was something that was easy for me. When I'd learned Vietnamese in the army, one technique our tutor used to fix the sounds of the language in our heads was to make us recite simple children's stories from memory.

I cleared my throat and began.

"A long time ago, a beautiful princess lived in a great city, a wondrous city, a city whose temples overlooked the bay where the Mother of Waters met the endless shining sea..."

"I love this one," Bian murmured.

"Every day as the sun dipped and the cool breezes began to waft inshore, the princess would walk barefoot on the soft sands and listen to the tales that the Mother of Waters brought all the way from the distant cloudy mountains, the strange land where it was always cold and the wind blew night and day. Where the people sewed their prayers into flags and hung them out, so the wind snapped and flapped the flags and lifted their words right up to the ears of the gods."

"Mmmm."

I barely got past the introduction of the fierce red dragon that lived at the top of those distant mountains, and Bian was so deeply asleep, she rivaled Scott.

Me, I was wide awake.

Chapter 33

Bundled back into my bathrobe, I padded barefoot into the dark living room, which was lit only by the glow from the embers in the fireplace. I was unable to decide whether I was frustrated, relieved or amused by Bian's simply falling asleep after I'd wound myself up to be a good little Athanate subordinate for her.

Not so much winding up needed really.

It wasn't worth trying to go to sleep now, and I might as well use the time to think through what had happened over the course of this night. But I wasn't so self-absorbed I didn't register there was someone else in the living room.

"Thought you might have trouble sleeping." Amanda's voice spoke softly.

"You too?"

"Mmm."

I fixed myself a rum and joined her on the sofa in front of the fire, where she sat, all tucked in and wrapped in a large fleece blanket.

We touched glasses. She was drinking one of Jen's favorite brandies. The aroma mingled well with her scent and the wood smoke from the fire.

"How's Kane?" I said.

"Upset, but not so angry now."

"I'm sorry to put your House under strain. It's not something I planned."

"I know that." She sipped her drink. "Flint has helped a lot. He's calmer about it."

"Yeah, he would be. It must have been a hell of a shock for Kane when I pulled that power through him."

"Hmm. Flint reminded him about that aural projection you all did. There wasn't anything dark about that."

Hearts not beating. Limbs not moving. Seeping slowly into the frozen ground. Cold as eternity. Cold as the stars in the night sky. Cold as death.

I shivered. Projecting my senses into trees was *not* going to become my favorite pastime.

And it wasn't the same as pulling that dark power—not at all.

I got up and put another log on the fire.

Amanda had unraveled her blanket and held it open when I turned back to the sofa. We wriggled closer and tugged the blanket until we were cocooned together.

It was little things which kept catching me off guard: the speed with which Amanda had become part of my House; the way sharing warmth felt so natural, as if we'd been doing it for ages; the way her marque had become familiar.

My fangs pulsed, reminding me there was some unfinished Athanate business there. *Familiar* wasn't good enough.

I sipped my rum, concentrating on the smoky taste, then reached out to place the glass on the side table so I could snuggle lower into the blanket and pull my arms inside.

"I suspect..." Amanda started and frowned.

"Yeah?"

"Like Nick said, that what they use isn't so different. It's all on the same spectrum. I think that may be what disturbs Kane so much—the thought that he might be using magic that comes close to what he says disgusts him."

I shook my head. "I can't judge. They have more relevant experience."

She shrugged. "Anyway, they finally got off that and changed to discussing whether they can do the direction-finding spell that Weaver mentioned."

"And?"

"They think they can, if they use your power boost, like they did for the aural projection." She smiled. "And then they got very quiet and thoughtful. I decided to leave them to it."

"If they can work with me, I'd rather work with them than Weaver. I know I'm not being fair to him. He's the head of the local community and only doing what he has to, but..."

"Well, I think you're being excessively fair to him, from what Kane told me. Anyway, we should talk about direction finding with Flint and Kane tomorrow."

We listened to the fire crackling as the log burned. Watched the light dance. It was comfortable. Relaxing.

"Am I crazy, doc?" The joke question slipped out before I could catch it.

She laughed.

"Sorry," I said immediately. "I'm not being serious. It's probably the question you dread being asked as a psychiatrist."

"You mean in the middle of the night, wrapped in a blanket, drinking in front of the fire, and being asked by someone I haven't even done an assessment session with?"

"Yeah. Something like that."

I leaned my head on her shoulder, ready to fall back into companionable silence.

"Don't be sorry," she said. "What makes it different is you're the Mistress of my House. You get to ask me whatever you want, whenever you want."

I chuckled.

"So what specifically made you ask that question?"

Oh. She was taking me seriously.

There had been shrinks assigned to the unit back in my Ops 4-10 days. I'd steered clear of them as much as possible, but if they'd run cozy sessions like this...

"I can't even convince some people that I had the spirit of my dead twin sister in my head. Now I'm pulling on some dark power and I can't tell if it's something inside me or outside, evil or just powerful, and whether I want it or not. I don't know."

"Well, all Adepts seem to have spirit guides. That doesn't make you any crazier than the rest of them."

I laughed. "Fair enough. That still doesn't explain Tara. But anyway, the thing is, I went rogue down in New Mexico. I *was* crazy. And afterwards, Tara and Hana were gone."

She huffed. "So let me get this straight. You're trying to fit in a theory that you've always been a bit crazy and you got more crazy. Then they had to fix you, and that cured you of hearing voices. And, by the way, all Adepts are a bit crazy. That about right?"

It sounded dumb when she said it out loud, but I could only nod. That kinda summed it up.

"But you're still an Adept. If it was craziness that made you an Adept and you're still an Adept, why haven't you re-created the voices in your head?"

"I don't know. You're the shrink."

Her turn to laugh again.

"I'm only a human shrink," she said. "Let me see. Hmmm. By human standards, of course you're wildly insane; you believe in vampires and werewolves and witches. But by paranormal standards..." Her hand emerged from the blanket and waggled uncertainly. "I *think* you're in the normal distribution for sanity, sort of, for what it's worth."

"You think? For what it's worth?" I started giggling and that set her off too. "Ringing endorsement or what?"

"I can't tell my Mistress she's insane. If you're insane, that would mean your whole House is insane, and that Scott will go insane, and I can't handle all that. I can't make myself believe it because I don't want it to be possible. Which is not exactly a sane thing for a psychiatrist to say."

We were skipping along that strange boundary between serious and silly, like old friends. It felt good.

She reached out to take another sip from her brandy, and went serious again.

"Something *has* happened to you tonight," she said. "You haven't gone crazy, before you ask, but we can all sense it, even me. Still, that's all for tomorrow, and Pia made me promise you should get *some* sleep."

"She left you here to watch for me?"

"Guilty as charged, your Honor."

She wriggled around beneath the blanket until she was facing me rather than the fire and our arms slipped easily around each other.

"If you can't sleep..." she murmured and lifted her chin to expose her throat.

This was *not* going to send me to sleep.

I felt the gentle pressure of her eukori and welcomed it in. I could feel her eagerness, the way her neck felt loose, the deep thrill of anticipation, the ache in her jaw, all overlaying the exact same sensations in me.

I burrowed down with my face against the warmth of her neck and let her marque softly fill my lungs. The tensions of the day evaporated, pushed out by desire.

Goosebumps. All over. Our hearts thumping against each other's ribs. Gentle movement against me. Her breath on my ear. Pleasure pumping into our bodies with each heartbeat.

I ran my tongue over her neck, lingering, searching out the urgent pulse beneath her skin.

Here. Here. Here. It called to me.

One second my jaw was throbbing in time; the next, my fangs had manifested and sunk into her neck

She gasped, held me tightly.

I *pulled*, and the pleasure burned through me like lava, lighting up the sensitive taryma, the network of channels that took her Blood from my fangs down to the Athanate glands at the base of my throat.

Yesss. Mine. Mine!

Mistress of the House. I was supposed to be calm. The perfume coming off her skin filled my nose and the need to absorb it into my marque, to make it *mine*, was flooding my head.

She didn't struggle. Her eukori told her what I felt, the mounting pleasure, the overwhelming *need* that woke even the wolf inside me. And yet she relaxed into it. She fed from my enjoyment. Her hand came up to stroke my hair.

Such bliss.

Every muscle in my body felt alive and yet loose.

So warm, so comfortable.

My fangs disappeared and I licked the wounds on her neck clumsily.

So tired suddenly.

I tilted my head back.

Her turn.

My racing heart slowed. Down. Down. Right down.

Strange.

"I... " I couldn't form the words. It was getting dark, so I couldn't see.

"Sorry," she whispered as I slumped. "A little trick of the Blood."

Chapter 34

"Breakfast!"

I woke like a cartoon character, all staring eyes and levitating off the bed.

Luckily, Bian and Scott were standing well back. Good thing. They had trays of food. Eggs. Bacon. Toast. Waffles. Honey. Coffee. Valuable stuff. Not to be knocked to the floor.

Heaven.

Wait one moment.

How did I get here?

Amanda knocked me out. Some kind of trick with pacifics in her Blood.

Under instruction from Pia, I'd bet. The pair of them working together.

I growled, but my stomach told me breakfast was more important. They would have to wait until afterwards.

And I had to admit, I did feel much better, even if I'd only slept a few hours.

Even though some of that time was filled with the most detailed erotic dreams.

Of Scott.

I *hoped* they were dreams.

Just as Bian put the tray on top of me, my memory engaged fully and reality hit.

"I'm supposed to be meeting the Hecate!"

"Not just yet," Bian said, holding down the tray so I couldn't get up.

"What do you mean?"

"I talked it through with Pia earlier and I put in a holding call to the Hecate."

"What? Why?"

"Pia said you shouldn't be woken too early after you'd finally been encouraged to go to sleep. I agreed with her."

"*Encouraged to go to sleep*. Is that what you call it?" I didn't bother mentioning that her climbing into bed with me hadn't exactly been encouraging me to sleep either.

"Neat trick of Amanda's. I'll have to get her to show me how."

"Get in line. And guess who I'm going to practice it on?"

Bian laughed. She and Scott sat cross-legged on the bed as I started eating.

"There's been a call from Felix and Cameron, as well," Bian said. "We told them you'd call back when you were ready."

I winced. That wasn't as bad as Yelena's way of dealing with Felix's calls, but my alphas wouldn't expect to be told to wait because I was asleep.

"They're *very* interested to hear about Scott," Bian went on. "I think they'll ask little Scotty to go pay them a visit soon."

"Little Scotty sitting right here," Scott said with one of his twisted smiles. "Reporting that werewolf ears work well."

Bian grinned at him.

I looked at the pair of them and blinked. Scott was all loosened up. The hair-trigger tension in his body from yesterday was gone.

Oh, hell.

"Have you two been introduced?" I asked carefully.

"We're well beyond that, Round-eye," Bian said. "We've slept together, remember. In your bed."

'Slept' my ass. That *hadn't* been an erotic dream.

My brain connected up the dots. Pia, last night, saying that House Altau and the Denver pack used to have an agreement: Were cubs and new Athanate in crusis getting together to blow off newbie steam without anyone getting hurt. Hot sex as therapy. *It seemed effective*, she'd said.

And who'd been Diakon at Altau then? Who'd been the liaison with the pack? Who'd organized those orgies?

Bian Hwa Trang.

Sometime in the morning, my sleeping brain had been linked to Bian's eukori while she screwed the new-Were madness out of Scott.

Which, it could have been argued, was the responsibility of his alpha. Me.

I cleared my throat and caught her eye.

As I expected, butter wouldn't have melted in her mouth.

"Thanks," I muttered.

She was looking out for me. Again.

Time to get back in gear. I put aside a burst of irrational anger directed at the Hecate.

"When do you start your video conference, and how long do you think it'll be?" I asked Bian.

"About ten minutes, and I'm hoping it'll be brief. Say finished in an hour."

"Okay. Scott, would you go and ask Pia to invite the Hecate to come here, please?"

Scott nodded and slipped off the bed.

Bian raised her eyebrows.

"The Hecate wants to talk to Diana and Kaothos. Even though she knows where Haven is, there's no way I'm taking her there. No way you'd let me take her there. So..."

"You'll use Jen's conference call system to let them talk. From here, where you have security."

"I don't think the security will be needed."

"And I'm here," Bian said. "What's she like?"

"Eerie. Scary," I replied. "You think you're in control and then you find she can come along and yank you into some weird version of the spirit world, where she can do anything. Yeah. Scary."

"Hmm. She can do that when she's prepared. Like down in RiNo. She got ready and then lured you there."

"I understand," I said. "You're thinking she's somehow made me invite her here."

"Did cross my mind."

"If she was going to do that, she'd have made us invite her to Haven."

"Unless she can't manage to compel me, you and Diana at the same time. In which case, her thinking might go, why not come here and grab some hostages."

"Some she'd already grabbed before."

"And me. But knowing I'd be here..." Bian trailed away, looking thoughtful. "Really could make you paranoid, this stuff."

I had to smile at that.

"Anyway," Bian said. "Let's proceed on the basis she's just coming here with good intentions. I've alerted our Ops 4-10 troops. If something goes wrong for us, something far worse will go wrong for the Northern League."

I shivered. Bian was nothing if not well prepared.

I needed to start thinking about the Hecate's visit, but first I should take the opportunity to talk to Bian about something else entirely.

I glanced across the room. The bedroom door was closed.

"So, ummm, last night," I said.

Bian looked at me, still all wide-eyed innocence. "Yes?"

I sighed, and tried to get her on the defensive. "You and Scott—"

"Oh, yes. *Very* enjoyable. We didn't disturb you, did we?"

"No. But..."

"Why did I jump him, instead of leaving it you?"

"Yes."

"For a start, he really wanted it and he really needed it. Cubs are like that. For another, I like him, and it's done him a world of good."

"I can see that."

"And you were asleep."

"You woke me earlier, after your shower."

She laughed. "When I got here, the only thing on your mind was going to sleep. As it turned out, that was what was on my mind as well. It's been too hectic at Haven. And you tell a mean bedtime story."

She wasn't lying, and she wasn't telling the complete truth either. She'd been worried about me. She'd come to see if I was all right.

She crawled up the bed and sat beside me.

"Tu casa es mi casa, Round-eye," she said and switched to Athanate. "So ykos mo ykos ei. Your House is my House. Your responsibilities are my responsibilities. So Scott is my responsibility, too."

"Fair enough. But with that responsibility comes rights."

"And you were expecting me to exercise them with you." She rested her head on my shoulder. "Your Blood is mine, sister. Your body is mine. But you've made a constitution for your House about exercising those rights. And I find that's mine too."

A constitution that said no one in my House would need to share Blood or body without their permission, freely given.

"It was never meant to apply to people outside of my House. It's not meant to apply to you."

"Then I choose to let it apply."

Her words fell, soft as feathers, heavy as thunder, and I realized how much I loved this woman. I'd loved her from the time I'd first met her.

She'd made me scared. Angry. Happy. Frustrated. Horny. *Alive.*

I had pushed her away. Denied myself and her.

And I couldn't deny it any longer.

It didn't make any difference to the way I loved Alex and Jen. But I wanted it to make a difference to Bian.

"When it gets hectic at Haven..."

I swallowed. My throat felt dry. She waited.

"Why don't you come stay here?"

"We could have a pajama party? With Jen and Alex? I love pajama parties. But wait. You don't have pajamas."

She was impossible. Or maybe, the refusal to be serious was hiding that vulnerable part I'd seen such brief glimpses of before.

"Do so," I played along.

"No." She shook her head. "You may have stolen some of Alex's, but you don't use them except to wander around the house, so they don't count. And Alex never wears pajamas in bed either. But I have a solution! I own a business making silk PJs. They'll be a present to you. So what will we do, get in a pizza and beer and chill?"

"No. We'll probably cook our own dinner and eat it in bed. With champagne."

"Hmm. Sounds naughty."

"It might be. We have rules in this house for eating in bed," I warned her. I picked up a crispy slice of bacon and held it out. "For example, only finger food, and you're not allowed to feed yourself."

She nibbled the bacon delicately out of my fingers.

"And you're not allowed to lick your own fingers."

I waggled my fingers. Moving deliberately, and without breaking eye contact, she licked them clean.

I tingled all the way down into my belly.

"I think I'm looking forward to this pajama party," she purred. "Meantime, I have a video conference to attend, and you need to get ready to say hi to the Hecate." She looked me up and down. The sheets had slipped a little as I'd sat there.

Oh, what a shame.

She licked her lips.

"I assume you're going to get dressed to meet her? Or do you think you'd be more distracting like that?"

Chapter 35

Forty minutes later, the Hecate and one of her coven arrived at the front door.

I'd only had time to talk to Pia and Julie about the Hecate's visit and arrange for Diana to be expecting the call—there had been no time for any discussion about knocking me out last night. No time for anything else.

Amanda stood nervously to the side.

And Tove! Damn.

I'd forgotten all about her, and I couldn't explicitly warn the Hecate not to speak in front of her about the paranormal world. I felt a surge of anger. At myself, for being disorganized. At Tove, just for being there. At the Hecate. At everything.

Where did that come from? What's gotten in to me?

No time for that.

I would have to take whatever steps were necessary with Tove later. That was my Athanate responsibility.

The Hecate stepped inside first. She was in her customary inappropriate clothing for winter—thin black clothes and a leather duster. She'd gone back to the white hair and frozen blue eyes.

Cold air from outside blew in with her, dropping the temperature and making me shiver.

That cold blue gaze swept across the hall and everyone inside.

A threat assessment, or I was a pink banana.

Have I just made a really dumb mistake?

Too late now.

I cleared my throat.

"Hecate, welcome. May I introduce these members of my House. Julie Anderson. Pia Shirazi. Flint and Kane you know already. I believe you've also met Amanda Lloyd. And this is Tove Johansen, a visiting friend from Clearbrook, up in Minnesota. This is Hecate Gwendolyn Enkil...ay."

"Enkeliekki. Hecate of the Northern Adept League. I'm pleased to meet you all." She stepped to one side, allowing me to see her colleague for the first time. "This is my colleague, Gabrielle Desmarais, from Quebec."

"Hi!" Gabrielle said with a wave at everyone.

She was wearing gray snowboarding pants, riding low on her hips and a size too big for her, the ends scrunched over her no-nonsense work-boots. Her chunky maroon hoodie was similarly loose. The grunge snowboarder effect was completed by a black neck warmer which she'd used to tie up her flaming red hair in a ponytail, right on the top of her head. I had to bite my lip to keep from smiling; that hairstyle somehow made me think of a firecracker going off.

Completely different. She and the Hecate might have come from different planets.

"Hello," I replied. "I'm Amber."

"Yeah, I know!" She stuck out her hand to shake. "Rad place you got!"

Our hands touched and gray eyes widened abruptly as she registered something from the contact.

Yes. Beneath that noisy exuberance was an intelligent, curious young woman.

And a witch. A powerful one.

I had to remember that, too. My instinct was to like Gabrielle, but I couldn't trust my instincts at the moment. Even if they were good people, these two weren't necessarily on my side.

I felt lightheaded. Something about allies. I had to keep in mind that I should be evaluating others and not basing it on instinctively liking them.

I needed to call Weaver as soon as this was over.

He'd be a better bet. Why was I talking to the Hecate at all?

Whatever mistakes had happened, Weaver and the Denver community would be better for Tullah than the Hecate and her northern coven.

I had to get Tullah back here in Denver. Soon. Tullah. Whichever way it took.

I blinked.

Concentrate! Focus!

I was under intense scrutiny by the Hecate. She was crowding me so much that I sensed Julie tensing up.

I got chills.

Something's wrong. Something bad just happened.

"We need an urgent, private talk with you," the Hecate said, her voice even more clipped than usual. "Right now."

"What a coincidence," Bian called out, coming down the stairs. "So do I."

"Your video conference..." I said.

"Finished."

The one word was delivered with bite.

Wow. Something had really twisted her tail. Or someone.

"This is *really* urgent," the Hecate said. She and Gabrielle exchanged looks.

Something very, very wrong here.

Sinking feeling in my stomach. Legs weak.

Bian looked coolly at her. "Well, we might as well have our private conversation in Jen's study then."

She turned back.

"You two," the Hecate said, pointing at Flint and Kane. "Come."

She followed Bian. I reminded myself again how much she moved like a predator. Like Rita did when her cougar surfaced. That killing focus.

Gabrielle trotted to catch up. Flint and Kane waited for me to nod, then they went.

Julie stepped forward. We had discussed how to handle security and she was supposed to be with me at all times while the Hecate was here, but I had Bian for the moment.

Julie wasn't taking no, and she was staring at me.

She knew something was wrong.

I went up the stairs and felt dizzy.

Jen's study with all the conferencing equipment was a few steps down the corridor. Somehow I got inside.

"Tell me what happened last night," the Hecate demanded, before I'd even closed the door. "Every detail. Especially—"

A surge of adrenaline seemed to clear my head.

"If this is about my aura being polluted because I pulled some power of dubious origin for a shapeshifting trick," I said, "my House has already dealt with that, and I consider the matter is internal."

"It's not about that." She sat down abruptly at Jen's conference table. "Sit here." She indicated the seat next to her.

I didn't see Bian move, and I hadn't even registered she had a knife, but before anyone could twitch, it was at the Hecate's throat.

"Bian, no!" I didn't dare make any sudden moves. Gabrielle had frozen. As had my two Adepts.

Julie had her Sig out.

"Let's slow down a bit," I said carefully.

"What a good idea," Bian replied. "Starting with you, Enkeliekki. Why do you *so* suddenly, *so* urgently need to talk to Amber *all alone*?"

"Hardly alone, is it?" The Hecate stared ahead, inhumanly motionless. She hadn't flinched, for all that her heart was racing. "I'm going to take a wild guess you're House Trang. Your reputation precedes you."

"How nice. So you'll know I'm not bluffing then. If you like your head balanced prettily on your neck, I suggest you answer my question. What's so suddenly urgent?"

I felt the prickle of a working, but it died away before I could call out a warning. I couldn't even tell who'd started to cast.

The Hecate sighed.

"As you wish. Someone has invested hidden workings in Amber," she replied. "Cast a spell over her, if you prefer the old terminology. It has the same form of subtle workings that most Adepts would not even be able to sense. Gabrielle and I can because we've seen this recently. It's intended to attack below the level of awareness. Unfortunately, in Amber's case, it's even more complicated. These workings are feeding off something powerful. And they're accelerating."

Chapter 36

The shouting stopped relatively quickly after the Hecate's bombshell.

I sat at the conference table feeling oddly disconnected, like I'd been pumped full of drugs or something. Yes, the last day had been weird, but my life was like that sometimes. I couldn't sense anything eating away at me.

Could I?

Except...

Nothing like being told something's wrong with you, for you to start thinking there's something wrong. That incident with Zane last night? Pulling that power during the fight? The dark magic itself? The bursts of anger and adrenaline this morning?

Flint and Kane looked as if they were becoming convinced. Apparently, they'd thought the oddness they'd seen in my aura had something to do with using blood magic.

Too out of it to join the discussion, I went on autopilot. While they were arguing about what constituted blood magic, I managed to connect the video conferencing system to Haven, and a few seconds later, Alice appeared on screen.

"No, not yet," the Hecate said, looking up at the interruption. "We have to nullify that working first, Amber. We can talk later."

"What working?" Alice leaned forward. "What's going on?"

Diana appeared on the screen, and a second later, Kaothos, in the shape of a lizard.

"Can I have a moment's quiet, please?" I said.

Everyone subsided.

"Thank you." I pointed as I made introductions. "Diana Ionache, Alice Emerson, Kaothos. This is the Hecate of the Northern Adept League, Gwendolyn Enkeliekki, and her colleague Gabrielle Desmarais." My voice sounded strange in my ears. Blurred. "The original purpose of this call was for me to pass the whole problem of communicating between the League and the Assembly on to wiser heads—"

"Our primary request was to talk to the dragon," Gwendolyn interrupted, her eyes fixed on the screen.

I ignored her, ignored the flaring irrational anger, concentrated only on speaking slowly and clearly. "All of which has just been derailed because apparently someone has hit me with a secret working that only the

Northern Adept League is trained to spot, and it has to be fixed right now for some reason."

"Why is the League so familiar with this working?" Bian asked.

Her knife was back in whatever hidden sheath it came from, but the suspicion wasn't.

"We've been seeing it in Adepts from the Denver community." It was Gabrielle who spoke. Her voice was much quieter now. "All of them had workings like this. It's so good at hiding itself, none of them realized it. Part of the disguise is achieved because the working moves so slowly. But Amber's is more complex and faster. *Much* faster."

My body was flooded with adrenaline. My legs felt so weak I slumped back down in a chair. Sounds began to fade into each other.

"Who made it? What does it do?" Diana.

"The questions should be the other way around," the Hecate. "If we know what it does, as a whole, then we would know who made it."

Those icy blue eyes drew mine to them. "What does it do?" she said. "From what I can sense, it's a twisted bundle of compulsions, each wound tightly around the other. We recognize them from the Denver community Adepts we've tracked down. These workings attack the inhibitory systems of the brain. The problem is..."

Adrenaline never made me feel like this before.

Something was really wrong.

...trapdoor spell...

...doesn't like being discovered...

...she's losing consciousness...

...don't touch her...

Why was I looking at the ceiling? Why was it so dark?

Shouting.

Bian wouldn't let the Hecate near me. Flint arguing. Diana's shouts came from the conferencing speakers.

It feels like I'm drowning. Like those old nightmares while I was in crusis.

I'm terrified.

I can fight anything in front of me. Anything I can see.

But I can't fight what I can't see or touch or feel.

Everything seemed to be rushing past me in a flicker of movements. Every flicker was another thing happening to me. I had to slow down.

Slow down.

Flint.

I could feel his aura. *The Raven*. Urging me. Pulling me downward.

This way.

My eukori opened, mingled with his aura. The Coyote joined us. No holding back. No hesitation.

Sinking together into a darkness described only by textures.

Great sacred shapes holding us within their stillness.

No heartbeat. No breath. No movement.

Yet I could sense it wasn't enough.

In some other place, my hand reached out into the gathering darkness, past Bian.

I was beyond other options.

I could feel the Hecate take my hand. I needed to speak a word. It was difficult. Something else wanted me to be silent, wanted to crush the air from my lungs, but the word needed to come out. It was a word that jumbled itself in my head. It hung there, like rocks in the silent earth, like the deepness of roots, the solidity of tree trunks.

"Trust," I breathed finally, forcing the word out into the world.

Bian stood back.

For a second it seemed I could *see* the Hecate, *really* see her. Not just physically, but a greater shape, a terrifying phantom form that seemed more solid than her body, surrounding her, holding her up with huge shadowy wings that enfolded me in them.

A shape holding a strange, flaming torch that blazed in the darkness so fiercely it blinded me.

Chapter 37

It'd been too dark to see, and now it was too bright.

It was important. I had to be able to see clearly.

Sweat was pouring off me. I was panting in the thin air. My heart labored and my limbs felt like jelly.

The wind froze the sweat on my forehead and brought to me the distant calls, harsh as screaming crows, from lower down the mountain paths.

I tripped, fell. One hand to break the fall, the other to protect the M-14 rifle.

Shit!

Voices behind were too close. I had to buy time for the extraction.

Rested the rifle on a handy rock and squinted back down the way I'd come.

Why the hell was it so bright?

And who was that sitting beside me in the flare of sunlight?

Not to mention, why was I back here?

I'm in Denver now.

"What's happening?" I said.

"First, you're going to be okay."

Gabrielle, by her voice. Standard rehearsed words, not her usual way of speaking at all.

I knew the routine. Patient in shock. Reassure them first. Next thing...

"I'm here to help you, and we're—"

"Cut the crap, Gabrielle. What's happening?"

"You're under attack from a malicious working. We need you to fight back, but your brain doesn't have the right references. You need something more physical, and the concept of a tree didn't work well, so I sort of made a suggestion and your memory came up with this."

Fight. Okay. Understand that.

I eased up, caught a glimpse of movement back down the track and squeezed off a shot.

Ducked.

Listened to the *wheep* of bullets fired back. Overhead, but far too close. Still, the pursuit had slowed down.

"Shit, you used to do this for a living?" Gabrielle asked.

"Yeah."

I came up at a different point, picked something that didn't look right and fired again.

There was a scream, quickly stopped.

More firing at my position. Three, maybe four people firing. That probably meant two or three sneaking forward while they kept my head down. Bad odds.

"You know, I think I preferred being a tree," I said.

"We could visualize the working as a fungus eating its way into you. Or insects burrowing. The trouble is visualizing how you fight that."

I snorted.

Up, pick target, shoot, drop back.

Miss. Eyesight still a bit blurred.

"Where's the Hecate?" I said.

"Gwen's on the other side, unpicking the working."

I laughed out loud.

"I'm here and she gets to visualize sewing?"

"The working has no obvious physical manifestation, but that's the way she visualizes it. Like a sort of series of links with knots that weaves in and out of your aura."

Up. Shoot. Drop.

Immediately popped up in a different place.

One of them had stood up to shoot at where I had been. Dumb mistake.

He made no sound as he collapsed. Lucky hit, 7.62 round right through the head. A scream from one of his friends. An order, harsh and abrupt. Then silence.

"I can die here, can't I?"

"Yes," she said simply.

"What about you?"

"I'm not physically interacting with your spirit world, but I'm linked by aura."

"That means it's dangerous for you? And the Hecate?"

"Possibly. Much less than for you."

"Thank you anyway." I put my head up, saw nothing and dropped back again in one movement. No shots, no sound.

Meant the creepers were creeping up on me.

Pretty much the way it played out when this actually happened. What was it? Five years ago?

"Julie warned me not to tell you what to do, but I have to say, it doesn't feel like it's working well enough at the moment."

"Everyone's a critic," I muttered. I hurled a stone at where I guessed most of them were, and managed to time it so I looked just as it bounced off a rock.

One head raised to see what made the noise. One round that way and two more on either side for effect.

Cursing and then silence again.

"Any genuine help you can give me?" I stopped. "Sorry, I didn't mean that to sound so bitchy."

"Don't blame you one bit. You're one tough bitch." I could hear the smile in her voice.

There was no shortage of rocks to hide behind, so I ran up the track, darting erratically from cover to cover, until my lungs were burning again.

Then I found a good spot and rested the light M-14 pointing down the track. I pulled my dusty brown keffiyeh up over my head until only my eyes were showing, and draped the tail over the rifle barrel. Hardly good camouflage, but the best I could manage in a hurry.

Gabrielle had come with me. I was annoyed that she'd had to put no effort in while I was trembling and panting.

"Talk to me quietly," I said. "Tell me what happened."

"Okay, here's how it went," she said. "You got invested with a multi-part working, sometime between when we took you on a little spirit walk down in RiNo and this morning. It's still this morning, by the way. Just. The working had a trap which activated when we discovered it. Would have killed you if you hadn't acted. You're still a bit dazed and confused, but it looks like you *are* going to be okay, all other things being equal."

She gave me an opportunity to react, but I guessed it'd be quicker if I let her speak. I watched the dusty track. I didn't understand how fighting old memories here manifested as useful assistance in the real world, but I understood I had to fight. I understood *all other things being equal* meant not dying here.

"I had to pull your aura out of the trees, into a spirit world, but your body's been kinda frozen at the point you did the dive with your two Adepts, and that's reflected in your aura. That's why your eyes were adjusted to darkness when you woke up here."

I could hear things she *wasn't* saying, but I stayed quiet.

"The other side, back in the study, you're still unconscious. That was a real smart move, projecting your aura into the trees. They tell me you're untrained, but I swear, I've never seen someone spirit jump so quickly. And you kept enough awareness that side to say you trusted Gwen. Those were the two moves that saved your life."

"The working was supposed to kill me?"

"Not obviously. *That* kind of working, Flint and Kane would have seen." She moved. I could now see the shapes of her features and the hair pulled up on her head. My sight was coming back, as she'd said it would.

"It's difficult to describe without getting into Northern Adept League jargon, but here's the short form. Think of it as starting with multiple, unrelated workings. The first, a very careful working with a specific design to—"

"That was the stuff the Hecate said about inhibitory systems?" I interrupted. "Perhaps you can turn that into words a dazed and confused bitch can understand."

She laughed and moved to sit beside me.

"Yeah. Inhibitions. Imagine whatever you wanted to do or say, you went right ahead, immediately. Didn't give it a second thought."

"Got that bit. You wouldn't want me out in society."

"Especially if you're a powerful paranormal. Now, some of those inhibitions which stop you acting like that might be intrinsic, and some the result of conditioning. Am I using words that are simple enough for you, in your dazed and confused state?"

"Y'know, if I could spare enough attention to hit you, I would."

"Good. You're getting better; Gwen's making progress. So, you have this structure of inhibitions, and the first working was eroding it, a bit at a time."

There was a movement on the trail, like the flap of clothing. It *was* only clothing—a keffiyeh tied to the barrel of a Kalashnikov probably. A test to see if I'd shoot at it.

I let my breath trickle out slowly.

Focus.

A man dashed across a bare patch. Another.

I shot the third before he was halfway across.

Two more showed over the top of their cover and I shot one of them.

Turned and raced up another fifty yards.

Settled down to wait again.

"Go back a bit," I said to Gabrielle. "The Hecate... *Gwen...* said you recognized the working because you found Denver community Adepts with it. You mean wandering around with their inhibitions damaged. They were doing what? Zapping people who cut them off on the highway?"

"Yes and no. Yes, we found them like that. No, because the inhibitions were being replaced by compulsions to obey commands."

"This has to be an attack on the Denver community," I said. "Obey who? And why me as well?"

Gabrielle shook her head. "There were no handy little labels to tell us, and the whole thing was subtle enough that the Adepts themselves didn't realize it. But who do you think?"

She moved closer. I could make out enough to see she was watching me intently.

Despite everything, my brain seemed to be operating.

"You're suggesting this was Weaver?"

"Could be." Her tone was very careful. Very casual. As if she didn't want to push me.

"No," I said. "No. Can't be."

"Still got its hooks in you, hasn't it? It's really good. Very clever. If it'd been a full-on compulsion you'd probably have noticed, and Flint and Kane certainly would."

I was shaking my head, but I couldn't deny it was the obvious conclusion. Why would I *want* to deny it? Had Weaver behaved in a way that would make me want to trust him? Or the reverse?

What if it was exactly the other way around? What if all this was the result of the Hecate...

"Someone said something about a trapdoor?"

"That's the really evil part. Again, Flint and Kane would have spotted a spell obviously designed to kill you. Instead there were these subtle spells doing hidden things, right up until they were discovered. At which point they merged and transformed into a lethal working. You got dizzy and ten minutes later you would have been dead of a brain aneurysm."

So... not the Hecate. Probably. If she'd wanted me dead, she could have killed me in the spirit world. And it would hardly be a help to getting Kaothos to trust her if I died. But what if she'd just wanted me to do what she told me?

What if this is all a double bluff?

Think!

Weaver: he had threatened me in the club. He and the other two from the Denver community had been trying to force me to say where Tullah was. Kane had distracted them, and their working fell apart before they could finish. He'd been smart enough not to try it again with us alerted.

Then he'd tried to play Mr. Nice Guy.

And just before Gwen had joined us by projecting her aura into the club, he'd touched me on the back of the hand, as if he'd been trying to catch my attention. I'd got a static shock from his touch.

Again, when we'd been leaving his house and he'd put out his hand to shake.

No. This is ridiculous. Paranoia.

Or was it like Bian said? Paranoia might be what kept me alive.

"What does Bian think?" I asked Gabrielle, while I tried to churn through the convoluted reasoning of who'd done this to me.

"She hasn't killed us yet."

I laughed again, silently this time.

A rock way down the track seemed to shimmer. No way that was heat haze at this temperature. One of them was trying the same trick I was using—disguising his head and rifle with his keffiyeh. Except I was watching him and he was looking for me.

Small target. Difficult shot.

Let all my breath out. There were tiny movements; his barrel was following the track upwards as he searched for a clue to where I was hiding.

Breathe in. Smooth. Slow. Pressure on the trigger growing.

He was nearly looking at my hiding place.

The M-14 kicked, as if it had a mind of its own, and the shot was something separate from the rest of me.

I could see his head snap back and the Kalashnikov jerked, pointed downward, went off.

Something was unraveling, like a thread, inside my mind. As if the Hecate had cut the last anchor point that had kept me going back time and again to defend Weaver.

Nothing moved on the track.

"He touched me in the club," I said. "Just before the Hecate spirit-walked in to join us. He touched me on the back of the hand. It felt like a static shock."

"Very slick," Gabrielle said. "Never heard of it done like that before. A little distraction while he invests the working into you."

"And again, at his house."

"He wouldn't need to do it twice. What had changed?"

Smart question.

"I'd just told him I was going to talk to you today."

"That's why this working is so much more powerful. He boosted it and made it rapidly lethal if Gwen happened to discover it. Which she did."

It felt strange to be talking about this like it was some classroom theory. This was a working that was trying to kill me right now.

"Shouldn't Kane have noticed it? It was right in front of him."

"No. Not unless he was actually watching for it. These workings are really cunning. They look harmless, unless it gets looked at—then suddenly, it's deadly."

"I didn't think you could do things like that," I said. "Certainly not someone like Weaver. He wasn't even leader of the Denver community, and yet he's some kind of ninja spell-master? And anyway, this wasn't the sort of thing the Denver community did, was it?"

I couldn't reconcile my image of Tullah's mother, Mary, who'd been leader of the community, with this description of malignant spells and lethal traps.

Meantime, I needed to remember: I could die here. The track down the mountain was too quiet. If they were moving, and I couldn't see them, it could mean they knew exactly where I was. They could be trying to flank me.

"That's exactly the way we're thinking," Gabrielle said, as if it were only some puzzle she was attempting. "If there had been this level of mastery down in Denver, we'd have heard of it. We think... well, that's a part of what we came to talk to you about."

She shut up suddenly. I had the sense she'd said more than she'd intended.

My gut tightened.

Danger. Multiple sources. Back in Denver. And here. Close. Very close.

In that Ops 4-10 operation that lent its appearance to this spirit world scenario, the guys chasing me up the mountain had known about the extraction. That's what they'd been trying to stop, and they'd known I was holding them up.

Here, in the spirit world, I sensed the attack was about to change. As if that last thread that the Hecate had cut had caused an unexpected effect elsewhere.

A trap within a trap.

My eukori reached out, and the dark power was there, just as it had been at the Were challenge. The same sense of strength rolling off it in waves. The same promise: learn to use this power and all your problems end.

Another trap.

I could see it with eyes that were open somewhere else. I could see it was connected to the same working that was attacking me. That's why Weaver's working had become so powerful, so quick. It was using my own strength against me.

Turn that strength back on it.

My whole aura reached for it.

Death or life. Mine.

Linked to me through her aura, Gabrielle gasped as pain flooded through me.

I did what instinct drove me to. I couldn't achieve it alone, but I could use Gabrielle's knowledge like I'd used Kane's.

"Gabrielle. I've got an idea. I'm sorry—"

"Go! Quick!"

I reached through her, all the way back to Manassah in the physical world and I *pulled.*

In front of me here, four men, widely separated, broke cover barely thirty yards away and started sprinting toward me. Screaming and shooting. They couldn't aim a rifle for shit while they were running, but among four magazines of thirty rounds, they might still have a bullet with my name on it. *Would have,* if they got close enough.

I shot the one on my right, moved in one, squeezed, missed.

Too much attention on what I was trying to do with the power.

Not enough time!

A bullet whipped past my ear.

Then I felt a shift, like the earth itself punched me.

The third guy was pointing at me. I could see the perfect circle of the barrel. See his finger pulling the trigger again. I was dead.

And then there was a clatter of rapid shots.

Julie and Keith, pulled here into Gabrielle's spirit world, just as I had been. Reacting on instinct. Saving my life.

One down. Two down. I got the last one.

As he died, his Kalashnikov slid out of his grip. It landed in the dust by my feet.

"Done," whispered Gabrielle. "Shit! Talk about a close thing."

And the mountains turned to mist.

Chapter 38

I came around to the sound of Diana and Kaothos repeatedly asking for me while tense arguments raged in the background.

Bian was cradling my head and half my House loomed anxiously over me.

I sat up and flapped a hand at the camera so those at Haven could see I was all right.

The conversation going on was tangled. The Hecate's patient removal of the workings had triggered the last trap and nearly killed me. That was true, but without her, the workings would have killed me anyway, or made me crazy. And *nearly killed* didn't count, as far as I was concerned. Besides, the Hecate and Gabrielle hadn't been trying to kill me. Those workings had.

Threaded through that discussion, they were trying to understand how the workings actually operated. Workings which leeched the victim's own energy to power themselves were sophisticated, but a fairly common model, apparently. The domino effect, feeding the energy from any working that was stopped onto the next, *that* was highly unusual and complex. It was that sort of secondary, anti-tamper style trap that had come closest to killing me at the end.

Gabrielle explained the theory of how Weaver had invested the workings in me by a simple touch, which led to the question of how Weaver had gotten so powerful. Alice couldn't believe it was him, but there seemed to be no other candidates.

Then there was the part where Gwen gave her opinion that some of the damage to my inhibitory systems was older; it had to date from before Weaver. She claimed Weaver's workings had attached themselves to structures that had been harmed before and insufficiently repaired.

That went down well with Diana and Alice.

"This is getting ridiculous. You can't make adaptive workings like that," Alice insisted. "You started off talking of workings so cleverly structured that they respond to threats. Then you're claiming Adepts in the Denver community have been invested with these without realizing it, so not only incredibly complex and powerful, but able to be cast without the victim even being aware."

"Maybe you've never seen this level of skill out here, in the Rockies," Gabrielle snapped back.

"But we *have* seen it before," I said, slapping the table to get their attention.

It worked. They went quiet. It was uncomfortable to have the Hecate's ice-cold stare directed back at me. For a moment I sensed the shimmering vastness of a figure around her. Then it was gone. No one else seemed to notice anything.

Had that been her spirit guide? What was it?

I'd already sensed Gabrielle's spirit guide without really thinking about it: a red hawk. But her leader's? Apart from these glimpses I *thought* I caught, nothing.

I shook my head to clear it.

"We saw workings like this," I said. "Back in the fall, at the last Assembly we held in Haven."

Alice and Bian got it. They'd been there. They immediately knew what I was talking about.

"Explain," the Hecate said.

"Two Athanate had workings invested in them, forcing them to betray us. As soon as they were discovered, the workings switched purpose. They didn't kill the victims, though."

"What did they do?" Gabrielle asked.

"Erased their minds," I answered with a shudder. I could remember, far too clearly, the awful, utter blankness on the faces of Marlon Pruitt and Judicator Philippe Remy.

"We didn't know enough about Remy's movements before the Assembly," Bian said quietly. "But we could account for almost all of Marlon's time for months back. It was what confused us—we thought there wasn't enough time to put him under such a strong compulsion, which is what we decided it was."

"Very similar in outcome," the Hecate said. "I admit, I think it would be too much of a coincidence for these two scenarios, the Assembly and the Denver community, *not* to be related."

"So who do we think was responsible for Pruitt and Remy?" I asked. "If Weaver had been involved back then, Mary would have known."

Tullah's mother was still leader of the Denver community at that stage, and she'd been sharp enough to have known what was going on in the magical community.

"What about Matlal?" Pia suggested.

"That doesn't make sense," Bian said. "Matlal tried mind games on Amber in the Assembly and she kicked his ass. No way he was a master Adept, capable of this kind of powerful working."

There was a sudden silence in the study.

"He tried an Athanate compulsion and failed? That's why Basilikos threw him out as their leader?" The Hecate's voice was sharp. "Because it was so extraordinary that a young Athanate could beat him."

We might as well have put out a tasty bone for a well-trained dog; Gabrielle was practically quivering.

"What if the extraordinary thing wasn't his weakness?" she said and paused before going on: "What if it was Amber's strength?"

Bian pursed her lips. "More likely it was Matlal's Diakon, Vega Martine, who gave him the appearance of strength. Now, *she* could be a master Adept, but she wasn't in the Assembly, so she couldn't help him."

I remembered Vega Martine with a chill.

Yes, I'd agreed she had to be the power behind Matlal, but if she'd had this kind of strength with magic back at the time of the Assembly, my gut feeling was she'd have used it somehow, and she hadn't.

Gabrielle wasn't listening to Bian; she was focused on me.

"What if that contest with Matlal was the first time she used her hidden powers?"

I shook my head. "It's not like that. I can't do anything by myself. I have no real ability. I need to use other people's skills."

"I don't believe that, but think back, Amber." The Hecate stood and leaned forward over the table. "What do you remember about beating Matlal?"

Bian tensed, but the Hecate made no other move, and my flesh wasn't creeping, so she *probably* wasn't doing anything magical.

"Pain," I said. "Anger. His attack was a direct Athanate mental attack. He was strong and he was angry. It's like being hit in the head by an icepick."

I closed my eyes and let my memories of that day come flooding back: Jen kidnapped and tortured. Crashing in through the warehouse doors to rescue her. Jen killing Hoben, but being so badly wounded she almost died. And yet we'd still had to rush to the Assembly, get past the Lyssae and then endure the unending political attacks on me and my House, from both Panethus and Basilikos. And at the end of it all, the final insult, Matlal's mental attack.

Bian had been holding me back the whole Assembly. I'd been so angry most of the time, I'd wanted to kill people right there, and Matlal broke something in me, and gave me an excuse to fight back with everything I had.

Which was a buried anger, anger so violent and formless it made my whole body burn.

I was speaking without being aware of it and stumbled before finishing: "I just took all that anger and pain, and I pushed it back through the channel he opened into my head. He collapsed and I thought that meant he wasn't the strong one. That it had to be Vega Martine."

"He 'broke something' in you," the Hecate said with heavy emphasis. "And then you reached down and found a well of emotions like pain and anger that you thought must be your own. You didn't need to manipulate it, Amber. You didn't need skill. Once he'd opened that channel, all you needed to do was fire it back down at him."

"If it was the same shit that you pulled through me, I'm surprised you didn't snuff him out with it," Gabrielle said. "He's gotta be strong to have survived."

Diana brought us to a halt then and made us go through, step by step, what had happened over the last few days. The kidnapping to get our attention, the spirit jump into the trees, the crows used as spies, the meeting down at the club, the werewolf challenge from El Paso, how I'd killed Victoria, the visit to Weaver's house out in Erie.

Slowly pieces were being put together.

As far as Diana and Alice were concerned, they'd known for some time that I carried a family curse. I had to backtrack for the Hecate and Gabrielle.

It'd been Tullah's mother, Mary, who first told me, although she'd been vague. She'd said I had a working hidden deep inside me and that it might be for good or evil, blessing or curse. I hadn't really believed it, even when I'd had dreams where my grandmother, Speaks-to-Wolves, had called me *cursed and blessed*.

Then Alex had compiled a chart of our branch of the Farrells since arriving in America. Every single firstborn had died, either in birth or infancy. I'd lived because my twin, Tara, had been delivered moments before me.

So cursed, clearly. Not blessed.

I'd put it all aside: as an Athanate, I couldn't have children. The curse would not be passed on.

But what if this power I'd been using came from the curse? What if it was like Weaver's workings, and capable of adapting to circumstances? What if it decided my generation hadn't paid enough of a price? What if—

"Amber?"

I blinked. Zoning out was not a good thing to be doing today.

"It makes a kind of sense if the power is actually from the curse," I said. "I don't understand how, but it *is* dark magic, isn't it?"

The Hecate disagreed. "There is no dark magic, or all magic is dark. All power carries its own potential evil, and the stronger the power, the stronger the potential."

"But it *is* dark," I said. "This power—it's all about hate and anger and pain."

"I'll give you that, but the negative associations of 'dark magic' come about because darker emotions are easier to arouse and harder to control in a positive way."

"So you're saying Amber could use anger as a resource for a working that produces a good outcome?" Flint said.

"Yes."

"But it's easier to align an outcome with the emotional power of the working," Kane said. "It's easier to kill someone if the power you're working with is based on hate."

"Easier, yes. I don't want to get into semantics about what a 'good' outcome might be, viewed from opposite sides of a conflict," the Hecate said and waved the arguments away. "All magic can be used for evil. All magic can be destructive. All magic can be addictive. The greater the power, the greater the potential."

She sat back down and continued:

"All of this is extremely dangerous for Amber; she's untrained and she's been damaged. At any other time, I would recommend rest and healing, but we don't have that time. Weaver wanted to use Amber to find Tullah because they're close, but he *can* use others in the Denver community, and he will. He'll be looking for Tullah right now. If he catches her, and finds the dragon's not with her, he'll use her as bait, physical or magical. He will make Tullah Kaothos' weakness."

She stopped, and there was silence for a minute.

"Tell me, Hecate," Diana's voice sounded flat coming from the speakers. "Are you committed to restoring Kaothos to Tullah?"

"Yes," she replied without hesitation. "They belong together. Any other arrangement weakens their power."

"And after that?"

"We can talk about how we proceed," she said smoothly. "I agree with you and House Altau that Emergence is coming. As timely and clever as Skylur's human-facing policies are, there are things the Athanate are not doing, or are not fully aware of, matters we've touched on today. Things that are as important as Emergence. The Assembly *needs* to work with the Northern Adept League."

Another long silence.

"Bian, bring the Hecate to Haven," Diana said.

"Diana—"

"I'm aware this breaches Skylur's security orders. He's not here. Do it on my authority. Bring Amber and her Adepts as well."

I took a break while Bian grudgingly argued the details with the Hecate.

Chapter 39

I went to the downstairs study.

Just a couple of months ago, this had been where my private investigator business had been based; where Jofranka, Tullah and I had worked.

I sat at my desk for the first time since Tullah had kidnapped me and taken me off to New Mexico. It felt strange. Smaller. Like visiting somewhere I'd played as a child. Yet I could clearly remember thinking how complicated my life had gotten back then.

There was no business left; it had been transferred to Victor Gayle's security firm, so the top of the desk was clear except for my photos and mementoes.

Dad and me. Top and me. And Tara's plaque.

I picked the plaque up. It was dusty. I hadn't taken it with me to New Mexico. That was hardly my fault, since I'd left unexpectedly. But I hadn't asked for it to be sent to California while I was there. Because Tara was gone. Hana was gone. And this plaque would have been a brutal reminder of that.

Now I knew where they were.

I took a tissue from a drawer and gently wiped the dust off.

It was a very plain plaque. Jet black granite, a little larger than my hand, glossy once it was clean. Cursive letters in the bottom right-hand corner, in a style I'd imagined my sister would have used for writing, spelled out her name. *Tara Farrell.*

Before the battle at Carson Park, any reflective surface used to be good for talking to my twin sister. Any mirror or shiny surface like the plaque, I could look into it, see my reflection, and know that's what Tara would have looked like. And I'd talk to her, just like anyone with a twin sister would. She'd talk back.

How crazy am I?

The lights in the room were off and the blinds were closed. I could see myself only as a shadow on the surface of the plaque.

Me. My shadow. Not Tara.

I knew Tara was some special part of me, and we were supposed to be together. Chatima, the powerful shaman down in New Mexico had told me as much. She'd spoken to Tara and Hana. She'd called Tara *Sky-fallen*. She'd given me the necklace; Tara and Hana had helped me understand the messages woven into its structure. The same messages that had unlocked the ritual and saved the lives of hundreds of Were.

Our ritual? Our magic?

What had Tara said?

We're not the flame. We're the wick.

As if we didn't actually do magic—we were simply a channel for magic to happen. Or a catalyst.

And that was fine.

But now, whether I could manipulate it or not, there was this power I had access to. *My* power. *Dangerous* power. A curse I'd somehow found a way to tap into. A Celtic curse on my family? Why? Who was behind it? I didn't know, but as for using it, I was the woman who licked knives, as Yelena said.

The talk upstairs had been about inhibitions and compulsions and psychological structures.

I'd probably always had some slightly odd mental structures. What had happened at school, and afterwards in the army, had damaged them. I'd always been a risk-taker, adrenaline junkie, and someone who operated on gut instincts. Then in short order I'd become Athanate, werewolf and some sort of Adept. And rogue.

Now it had been all topped off by Weaver's working attacking me.

Which the power of the curse had helped me defeat.

I had to acknowledge that using this power was dangerous. I could feel it already—the little scratching beneath the surface of my mind, telling me that I could use it to do this and that. I could fix things. It would be so much easier if I accepted it. Learned to use it.

For all the Hecate's calming theories, I knew Kane's view was closer to the truth for me. I couldn't use this power for good. It was too focused on negative emotions and too strong. In the end it would overwhelm me. Not its fault, not my fault, just the way things were.

Tolly's warning: *stay away from magic.*

Shadows seemed to stir on the surface of the plaque. I tried to focus on what lay behind the shadows, the sounds and images that would help me. All I could see were more shadows, and hear my own voice murmuring and echoing words.

I am lost; I have no guide but myself.

I am none of the things they think I might be.

I am the sum all I've ever done, all I ever will do, and all that has been done to me, or ever will be done to me.

I blinked. There was a choice and yet there was no choice at all.

Tullah, Tara and Hana. Getting them back was all one task now. And it was urgent. Kaothos might be able to move back to Tullah, but Alice's research suggested Tara and Hana wouldn't be able to move back to me.

I needed them back, whatever the cost.

If I had Tara and Hana back, if I was whole, I might stand a chance against the insidious power of the curse. And yet to get them back, going up against the powerful Denver community using weapons I didn't understand and with allies I barely knew, I might need to use that same power. Which would mean it would get a hold on me.

How would it end?

I could easily die without even finding Tullah. Or the power could overwhelm me. What then? Become like the Lyssae? Was that the real threat behind Tolly's warning?

Enough. My fangs stirred. I bit my thumb and pressed it to the edge of the plaque.

I was going to find Tullah and Tara and Hana. I would use whatever I could. Even the power, the curse, whatever its threat was. On this, I gave my blood oath.

Before that, in whatever little time left before Bian and the Hecate reached an understanding on security issues, I had people to call.

Chapter 40

Alex first. He was in El Paso, taking the loyalty oaths of the rest of our new pack. *Our* pack. I should be there. I could imagine the questions they were asking about me. The whispered comments when Alex was out of hearing.

She's not a real alpha they'd be saying. *Can't be mated with Alex. Did you hear about the way she was behaving at that club in Denver? And later at the factory with that alpha from Albuquerque?*

Cast-iron certainty: there would be problems from what had happened last night.

None of which I said to Alex. I downplayed what happened after he left the factory. It was bad enough I wasn't down there with him; it'd be a disaster if he stopped to return here because of me.

I had to tell him about the El Paso renegades, and how I'd run them out of Colorado. It would have been a whole lot neater if I'd gotten their names at the time, but Alex approved anyway.

His growl over the cell phone reached down into me and I let him talk on for the pleasure of hearing his voice.

He had a lot to say about his complex task down in Texas. He couldn't just uproot the entire El Paso pack overnight. Like any pack, the members were embedded into the human society around them. There were houses owned, contracts for employment or business, obligations, friends and families outside of the pack. All of which needed careful management to disentangle.

Then, as he sent them north, the new arrivals in Colorado would need organizing on this side as well. Skylur had offered support, and Bian was happy having them temporarily in Haven, but they'd need jobs and places to live, and they'd need them quickly. Someone had to push the right buttons at the right time.

All of which was exactly the sort of thing I should be arranging, as the Denver-based part of the alpha team.

"That's what I need to do then," I said.

He was quiet for a moment. "It sounds like you've got your work cut out already."

"I have, but this is *our* pack. I can't be down there with you now, so I have to fix that as much as I can, *where* I can. That's here, in Denver."

"Our pack." His voice was quiet. "Still hits me when you say it. But it is our pack."

"You know how I feel, because it's the same thing you feel. Leave this end to me."

"You sure?" His voice slowed. "I was thinking of asking Zane for some help."

"I'm sure." My heart skipped a beat. Despite the fact that they'd be cooperating under orders from Felix and Cameron, for Alex to come right out and ask for Zane's help like that was... awkward, in an alpha sense. Whether they wanted it or not, there would be dominance issues coming from such an appeal.

And I didn't want Zane up *here* before I'd had a chance to talk to Alex face to face about last night. *That* had dominance issues that made the other pale in comparison.

Naturally, we could ask Felix for help. There were still lots of members of the Denver pack in Colorado. That was the sensible option, but neither of us was suggesting that. In werewolf terms, it was even worse—like admitting to our alpha we couldn't handle the task. That we didn't deserve to be alphas of a big pack.

That was why Alex was thinking Zane was the better choice of two bad ones.

"Leave Zane out of it," I said, more confidently than I felt. "I'll find a way to handle the pack in Denver. Don't know what I'm gonna do yet, and I may not give them exactly what they want, but they'll get what they need."

He growled again, and this time I could hear the undertones. He was pleased I was going to manage the Denver end of the transfer, that we'd sort this out ourselves.

He didn't ask for details, fortunately, because I didn't have any.

And he was missing me already. I got that undertone too, raising the hairs on my arms and making me shift pleasurably on my chair.

Down girl.

"I'm visiting Haven today," I said. "I'll take it as an opportunity to talk to the ones that are there already."

"Okay. There's only a handful there. I'll send you a list by text. They're mainly youngsters."

"I understand." I could sense in my gut the sort of decision he'd had to make about who to take back to El Paso with him. He'd have taken any of Caleb and Victoria's lieutenants, any senior werewolves and any who needed to get back to El Paso for employment or business reasons. Regardless, it would leave the ones staying in Colorado feeling a bit abandoned and rootless.

I'd have to fix that.

"All of them know you're the boss," he was going on to say. "I'll be up in a couple of weeks with the second batch, and I can't promise the same of them. They'll have given me their loyalty, but..."

"Yeah, I'll have to bite a few of those necks, alpha style," I said. "Got it. How long until they're all here?"

"They'll be trickling up for months," he said. "I could probably leave them with a lieutenant to sort them out in a month's time, but Felix and Cameron need a replacement pack in El Paso. I'm going to have to be around at least some of the time to help with that."

"Have they chosen a pack?"

"Not yet. By the way, you *are* going to call them, aren't you? I've already had one snarly text."

"I'm on it," I said. "You spoken to Jen?"

He growled: "You know that woman is stealing my company from under me."

I laughed. "Yeah. And? You spoken to her?"

"I got three whole minutes between two meetings."

"Good. And she's not stealing your company. She's getting her people to run it while you're in El Paso."

He chuckled. "Yeah. That's what she said."

"She's got your back, hotshot. *We*'ve got your back."

"And I got yours."

It felt good to hear him say it, and I wasn't done talking to my husband, so the polite knock on the door was not a welcome interruption.

"Yes?" My voice came out as a snarl. "The door's open."

Rita came in with that cougar-prowl way of walking. She was dressed to go out.

"Apologies for interrupting," she said. "Bian will be down soon to take you to Haven anyway."

The sound of Alex's laughter came from the cell. "We'll finish another time," he said. "Love you."

He ended the call.

"Bian could have interrupted me herself," I said to Rita. "What's up?"

What crisis now?

"Tove asked if the two of us could go out shopping," Rita said, and shrugged. "I don't think you'll need me at Haven, and it'll get Tove out of your hair for a while. Keep her from brooding. It's a fair request, too. She's wearing other people's cast-offs. I wanted to check with you."

I laughed.

Big crises and little ones all together. All the time.

"She'll need some money," I pointed out, and went to the safe where I kept cash. "You know she's not aware of us?"

"She's aware," Rita said. "Just doesn't know the details."

"And she's a recovering addict. I'd like her to keep recovering."

"Yeah, I got that. No sneaky little side-trips to pick up some gear."

"Okay." I started counting out some bills. "Why do you think she picked you to go shopping with? Just out of curiosity."

"We're both outsiders."

I frowned and stopped counting. "You're not an outsider."

"Well, less than her, I guess, but I only got here last night." She shrugged and then folded her arms. "She said she liked my clothes."

She was embarrassed that Tove had complimented her style? I added a couple more big bills. Dressing like Rita was a whole level more expensive than dressing like me.

"Then she has good taste," I said. "Next to Jen, I think you're the most elegantly dressed woman I know."

"Thanks, Boss."

Now she was embarrassed and pleased. I liked the 'boss' too.

I wasn't quite finished. "Take Lynch."

"Shopping with the girls?" She grinned. "Okay, but he won't thank you."

"Take one of the guards as well. Lynch can treat it as training for how to provide security." I sighed. "As much as I love that you've come here, you need to understand that being around House Farrell isn't going to be safe. You're going to need to be aware of threats all the time."

"Exciting," she said, her eyes all cougar green as she scooped up the cash. "Thanks for this. Can I check, I was right to bring this to you?"

"Yes. Certainly while you're settling in, keep checking with Yelena or me until we tell you otherwise."

She nodded and left.

I sighed again. *Yelena*. I missed my Diakon. I needed her back. Just knowing she was around and might disapprove served as a brake on my crazier ideas. Or some of them.

And she also kept the small stuff away from me, like Rita asking if it was okay to take Tove out shopping.

How on earth did Bian manage without a Diakon?

I shook my head and called Felix. This one was going to be a whole lot less fun than talking to Alex.

Chapter 41

"Amber."

A growl, but not much like Alex's. An annoyed growl from the co-alpha of the Southern League.

This conversation was going to be like a fight, and if we were fighting, I'd want him on the back foot, so I got straight in.

"Felix, hello. I have a suggestion, as syndesmon between Athanate and Were, that I'd like you and Cameron to consider."

There was a change to the quality of sound as his cell phone went to speaker, and it was Cameron who replied. "We're listening."

Yes, pissed off Felix and pissed off Cameron. Because I couldn't answer their call quickly enough. Wonderful.

"The full Assembly isn't going to meet again for a long time," I said. "My recommendation is you use that time to negotiate with Skylur. Representation agreements will still need the whole Assembly to ratify, but you could arrive at that meeting with half the battle over."

"We can't sit in New York and talk," Felix said. "We're too busy putting the League together."

"Exactly, so you need someone to do it for you."

"You?" I'd managed to surprise Cameron. She knew what I thought of politics.

"Not me," I said. "I have a good relationship with Skylur, but he needs me here in Denver, and so do my new pack."

Putting pack before politics got a quieter, almost approving growl.

"Who then?" Felix said.

"The Heights."

There was a deep silence following my suggestion. The four big LA packs used the style of calling their alpha by the pack's name. The Heights pack reached all the way into East LA and then extended out west and south, taking in half of the Cleveland National Forest. Like all the LA packs, open space for them to run was at a premium, and they were a pack that was more urban based than those in the Rockies for example. The pack members might or might not want to move to New York, but it wouldn't be because of the urban nature of the territory.

And their alpha, the Heights himself, was an oddity among all the alphas I'd met. He was a political animal. When the idea of werewolf representation in the Assembly had first come up, he'd been practically salivating about getting involved.

"Interesting." That's all Cameron had to say on it. The lack of argument was eloquent. I'd put good money on the pair of them seeing the Heights' political nature as an irritation, or possibly even a potential threat. Especially if he were left out there on the West Coast and not wrapped up in a job that would keep him busy.

I didn't leave them enough time to get on the front foot. "I also think that you should take the opportunity to grant the Heights' territory to the Belles."

Put like that, it got exactly the reaction I expected.

"No!" Felix snarled. "That's crazy! She's a competent alpha, but it's a tiny pack. She has, what, twenty members? We'd be setting her up for a challenge. A series of challenges. It could destabilize the whole region."

"Maybe," I said, because that was *way* more diplomatic with your boss than saying *you're wrong*. "Work with me a while on this."

No audible response, so I went on.

"Can't leave that territory empty, right? *That* would destabilize things. Billie's survived in the middle of LA, squeezed between four large, aggressive, male-oriented packs, and the Belles are all female. Tell me how she isn't able to handle it. What's more, if you word it carefully and make it an acceptable option, some of the Heights pack might prefer to stay there, even under a new, female leader. Which is also fine for both sides. Heights won't need that big a pack in Manhattan."

Felix laughed. "Damn! That's some 'careful wording' you're talking about," he said.

"Or Athanate mind-voodoo," Cameron said. "Can she do that shit to us over the phone?"

"I think she just has." I could hear Felix's twisted smile.

"All right," Cameron said, meaning not *all right* at all, not yet. "We'll take it into consideration. Did Altau put you up to this?"

"No. All my own scheming," I said.

"Anything else you want to suggest?" Her voice was low, and less amused than Felix's. "A new pack for El Paso, maybe?"

Which was an absolute trap. She was handing me rope to hang myself with. I knew I should shut my mouth, but I found myself saying: "Not an area I'm knowledgeable about, alpha, but I think the Albuquerque alpha should be involved in that discussion. Whoever you put in there will be his neighbor; Albuquerque's only 250 miles up the road."

I'd said it mainly as an idea to make sure Zane kept out of my hair for a while, but as I was speaking, I pictured the geography of that corner of

New Mexico and Texas, and a real idea hit me. A way to get Alex back quicker and Zane too distracted to come hassle me.

"Why not make El Paso a sub-pack of Albuquerque?" I found myself saying. "I'll bet you've always had sub-packs out in Gila and Mescalero. Move one of them down the road. Save a lot of time and effort."

"Been talking to Zane, have you?" The growl had gotten silkier. More dangerous by the minute.

"No, ma'am," I said, heartrate inching up.

I couldn't leave it there. I'd gotten in this deep; I had to talk my way out of it now. "I thought about it. You all had New Mexico stitched up tight as a wet boot, and yet there's this big claw of Texas sticking right into it, with El Paso on the tip. And there's all that good werewolf territory in New Mexico around there: White Sands, Gila, Lincoln, Brokeoff Mountains, Desert Peaks. There's no way you were going to let a big pack like El Paso come sniffing around that. I'm betting you had sub-packs in Gila and Mescalero just to keep an eye on them."

A moment of quiet, then Cameron responded, "I'm betting I'll have my jaws around your throat next time we meet, Amber."

A warning threat: more show than substance.

And a thrill: I'd been right, and they *did* have sub-packs there.

All I could say, of course, was: "Yes, ma'am."

While she was still talking to me, even threateningly, she wouldn't be ripping my throat out.

I hoped.

And maybe I really had given them something that would keep Zane busy at the far end of New Mexico and out of my pants.

Felix cleared his throat and changed the subject. "How is Scott doing?"

"More wolf than vamp at the moment," I said, "but I sense the vamp is coming. He's less volatile than he was yesterday. No problems changing form."

"So quick," Felix muttered. "Like they say your vamp crusis would be quick. Anything else of note about his change?"

"He's got an attitude on him when he's four-legged. As a cub... I mean, as Athanate kin he's two hundred years old, but as a wolf, he's brand new, and you expect him to be a bit uncertain. Nope. He's not dominant enough to take me, but he's like a burr under my damned saddle."

"Shocking," Cameron said, all soft voice and sickly-sweet sympathy as she took her revenge. "Imagine that, getting grief from a subordinate wolf."

"Ma'am."

I didn't mind cringing a little for her. This conversation had also given me a new idea for Scott I'd have to come back to later.

"I'm not sure how he'll be regarded by other packs," Felix was saying. "As a hybrid I mean. You personally, you get a grudging pass from some of these new packs on the basis of the halfy ritual. He won't have that."

Cameron took over. "We're throwing a lot of new and uncomfortable ideas at a very conservative population of Were down here, Amber. I don't want any more challenges or excuses for fights. We're going to need to see how they react to Scott under controlled circumstances."

"Bring him to the next ritual," Felix suggested. "If they associate him closely enough with you and the ritual, he might gain some of your protection."

"Good idea," Cameron said.

"When?" I asked.

"A couple of weeks maybe. We'll have to start organizing."

"Can I make one last suggestion?" I said.

Cameron was ominously silent, but I could still hear the smile in Felix's voice. "You'll make it anyway, so I'll say go ahead."

"I come down to you, with Scott, rather than you all come back up here. Maybe get Alex and some of my new pack down there too."

That was assuming I hadn't been killed, or killed myself in the meantime, but I wasn't going to say that.

"Nick Gray should be able to find a suitable place, if you give him a day or so to look," I added.

"Now *that* is an excellent suggestion," Felix said. "Okay. We'll be in Louisiana somewhere. Ben will organize details through PackChat and cell phones."

Bian put her head in the room.

"Time to go," she said loudly enough for them to hear.

"We'll talk again, when you have time," Cameron said. "And if you don't find time, we *will* talk when you come down here."

Oooh. Snarly boss.

The line went dead.

We divided ourselves into several cars. I was in Bian's car, with Julie and Scott.

Scott hadn't expected to be needed out at Haven, but he was polite in his two-legged form and came without arguments.

Traveling together gave me a chance to test him out and see how stable he was. We talked: general chat about what he had been doing in House Lloyd, and what he thought he might be useful for now.

I was no werewolf expert, and there *were* no hybrid experts, but I though he was going to be able to handle the challenge I would give him later.

While we were talking, I tried to call Jen, but she wasn't picking up.

Then, just as we pulled into Haven, there was a text message from her.

Yelena's on her way home, it said. *I'm fine. Busy! Call me in an hour or two. Love you.*

Chapter 42

"You're not serious!"

Alice was unhappy with my proposal and I could tell I was going to have a battle with Bian and Diana, too.

Six of us were in the magically protected dungeon, deep beneath Haven, sitting stiffly around a plain wooden table: Diana, Alice, Bian, me, Gabrielle and Gwen.

Even if I still found her scary, she got to be 'Gwen' rather than 'the Hecate' for saving my life.

To Gwen's frustration, Kaothos remained silent and invisible, but I could feel her there.

And the Lyssae as always, standing against the walls. I couldn't stop myself from looking down at the far end to meet the glazed eye of the dog-faced Anubis.

I could hear the whisper of blind Tolly's voice, speaking about his cousin, as if it reached out to me all the way from the Dark Library: *He hears all that's said, you know, even in his stillness. And if he could talk back, what he'd say is keep well away from magic, especially dark magic. Well away.*

I took a deep breath.

Calm.

"I am serious," I said. "You all can stop me, if it's a mistake, but let me make my case first."

Everyone waited and I spoke each sentence with a pause to get nods of agreement:

"The most important thing is to get Tullah back. To do that, we need to know where to find her. To find her, we need to do one of these difficult aura projections. The best person to do it for Tullah is me. We need to do it as soon as possible, because Weaver will be using the Denver community Adepts to do the same thing."

"That kind of working is dangerous, especially for you," Alice interrupted.

"It's most dangerous because I haven't had any experience of doing it. I'm not suggesting I can become an expert. What I'm saying is we should have a trial run over a shorter distance, helped by the experts we *do* have here. Checking Weaver's house is an obvious choice for that. We need to do it anyway, but I don't want to send a team of guards there who could run into some kind of magical trap, given what we've seen Weaver can do."

"The traps could be laid for whichever way we go there, including a projection of your aura," Gwen said. "Although I back up what you're saying, we're still rushing into this."

"And delaying will produce what benefit?" I shot back at her. "How long before you can train me as an Adept to your level, given I haven't even got a spirit guide now?"

"Got you there, Gwen," Gabrielle said.

I guess she'd forgiven me for pulling power through her. Or maybe she hadn't. My paranoia raised its head. What if she knew it was too difficult and wanted me to fail?

Out of sight, under the table, I balled my fists. We needed to make progress more than I needed to indulge my suspicions.

"We can spend time getting to know each other afterwards," I said. "Let's go up and try this projection right now."

There was no point in doing it from here in the dungeon. The same workings that protected Kaothos from being found by Empire, prevented any magic from getting out. Diana and Kaothos would have to stay down here. The rest of us would have to go back upstairs, where we could team up with Flint and Kane, who were waiting in the main living room.

I got a reluctant agreement and we left in pairs, using the small secret elevator to the ground floor.

After collecting my two rogue Adepts, Bian guided us to an empty room on the top floor, all the while quizzing Gwen about the spirit walk.

"In fact, Gabrielle is the expert on projecting auras," Gwen said. "She'll be the one who runs this."

Gabrielle took over smoothly.

"There isn't one simple spirit world," Gabrielle said. "It's like it has layers. You can skim the outer layer. That's what Amber is suggesting."

"This isn't like the spirit world when you kidnapped Amber?"

"Captured her attention. No, that was deeper." She started bouncing around the room as if unable to contain all the energy in her body. "Okay, so layers. The top layer is what you call spirit walks, visions, dreaming world, stuff like that. That's what we're doing here with Amber, spirit walking. All of us stay here in this room and project our auras with Amber to just skim the spirit world."

"And that's safe?" Bian pressed her.

"For something close and quick, it's safe. Much safer than the next level," she said.

"But there's always danger when you open your aura," Alice interrupted. "Same sort of thing when you try opening a channel to attack someone with eukori."

"Like we were discussing about Matlal earlier?"

"Yes. He opened the channel to attack Amber, and she attacked back, even though she probably couldn't have opened that channel herself."

My eukori was much stronger than they realized, thanks to my Carpathian heritage. Some time, I was going to have to explain that to them. For the present, I stayed silent and listened.

"And what about the direction-finding kind of spirit walk? The kind we'll need to locate Tullah?"

"Different kind of thing," Gabrielle said. "You can't spread yourself that thinly, that far, that long, across the spirit world in a simple spirit walk. You'd screw up your head or run out of power. You need the next level down, the type of working we call a substantiation. That's what we did down in RiNo, and to do that, at least one of you actually physically enters the spirit world. Whole different set of issues."

"This exercise now only needs a spirit walk," Gwen said. "It gives us an opportunity to all work together instead of against each other. We'll be there in aura with Amber to keep her safe."

"To keep us all safe," Kane said.

Bian subsided, unconvinced but unable to mount any informed arguments.

Gabrielle touched my arm. Now the zany, hyperactive woman changed into someone more calm and professional.

"We're going to put you into an environment where you feel comfortable and in control," she said, "and then visualize a path to Weaver's house. I'll kinda pick your aura up and it'll be like we're flying. It'll be fun."

I nodded and hid a smile. I had ideas about fun that I probably shouldn't share with this young woman.

She pulled a straight-backed chair into the center of the room and tapped it.

"Sit here, and let's get started."

A little shiver skated across my skin—half anticipation, half the feeling of the magic building: Gwen and Gabrielle on one side, Flint and Kane on the other.

Very different magics.

"I saw how you interacted with Gwen's substantiation of the spirit world," Gabrielle said. "We won't go into that depth with an aura projection, but I think we can work with your imagery."

"You need to explain all your jargon to me."

"Some time," she replied, "when I haven't had a fire lit under my butt."

I had to grin, at the same time as feeling a little embarrassed that I'd suspected her of wanting to set me up to fail.

She walked behind me and her hands dropped on my shoulders, pulled me back into the chair.

"Relax," she said. "I just meant we're going to go with all that neat Native American feel. We'll start by breathing deeply."

I was still too tense. Her fingers dug expertly into my shoulder and neck muscles until I'd relaxed enough for her.

After a minute she began humming quietly, in a rhythm like the one Nick Gray, the skinwalker, had used for the rituals. It was simple, classic Native American—HEY-ya, hey-ya, hey-ya, HEY-ya, hey-ya, hey-ya. Her foot tapped it out against the wooden floor.

Flint sat cross-legged on the floor, next to a coffee table he'd pulled closer to me. He began to brush the top of the table with one hand and slap in time with the palm of the other. Kane also hummed, moving around the room, so it felt as if his sound came and went, weaving itself with the others. They all blended together into a soothing, hypnotic sound.

The room was very warm, reminding me of the heat of bonfires when we'd done the ritual at Bitter Hooks. Gwen drew the curtains closed, making it dark.

I could sense Gwen, even when she was behind me, like she had a sort of gravity to her, pulling at me. She was *strong*.

"Shut your eyes," Gabrielle whispered.

I did. I was so relaxed by now, I was finding it difficult to stay upright. It wasn't that I felt heavy. Quite the opposite. I was light as a feather.

Gabrielle worked my hair in a loose braid, out of the way, then her fingers traced patterns on my eyelids, across my cheeks, over and over, barely touching.

My body pulsed to the rhythm that Flint and Kane made. The whole room did. I could feel the walls move in and out in time, like a heart beating.

Gabrielle had gotten some paint from somewhere. I could feel it, slightly oily on my skin. She was drawing war paint on my face. Streaks of black fanning out from the bridge of my nose across my cheeks, my forehead, my eyelids, until it became a solid band.

Crazy.

I began to float. There was no room, no sensation, no rhythm that wasn't part of me.

"Open." A whisper, lost in the chant. Like the wind's murmur, high in the cold mountain passes. A wind that brought scents of distant meadows and a warmer, gentler place.

"Open."

I strained forward, sensing a path through the darkness that lay across my eyes.

It was as if I had to fight against a weight to raise my eyelids. Then they suddenly flew open and the world came rushing back at me.

"Shit!" Someone swore.

Chapter 43

All Haven is a dream of ancient black veils that stir in a spirit wind. It's populated by ghosts. Ghosts that drift through the translucent corridors and rooms, each one a little blood-red ember, like the scatterings of a dying fire. My heart does not beat now. My limbs are cold, bent and reaching for a sun that does not warm.

...can't do it like this...

...spirit jumped into the trees again...

...have to bring her back...

I can hear them. I pay no attention.

The tree spirit is just a first step outside.

I breathe in, a great rush of air, that lifts me up and shoots me outwards, dragging them with me, like ants on an eagle's back.

I can see. All the way past Golden, across the Boulder turnpike, to Erie, and Weaver's house.

I can reach...

"Slowly!"

That was a voice I couldn't ignore like the others. That was my House calling to me.

Kane and Flint. Working together. It was their skill I was using, boosted with the League's power. *Not* the way Gwen and Gabrielle planned it. I laughed madly. Score one for the wild talent.

Calm.

I was impatient, but I let them catch up before I reached out. I hoped it wasn't my real body, but it felt like it was. It felt like I'd just stepped out of a thick fog onto one of the patios at Weaver's house.

This is not a real body.

I would be a ghost to anyone in the house, and they would be to me, but the house was empty of life. I could see right through it. None of the embers that showed living people to my tree-spirit senses.

I reached out to the window, but my hand passed through and I felt the others calling me back.

"Whoa," Flint said. "Let's check a little first."

"Yes, please," Gwen said.

Gabrielle was swearing colorfully under her breath.

They all sounded as if they were talking just behind me, but I turned around and there were no other ghostly images there. Back facing the house, I could make out a hazy image of me in the patio window reflection. A ghost of a ghost, dressed in buckskin and a bead necklace, with war paint covering half my face.

Cool.

In my projected aura, I didn't feel Flint's magic; I saw it. His working to check the house floated like thin smoke from a wood fire, spread itself out against the window and then seeped in.

Inside, it began to turn black in some places.

"Booby traps," Kane said. "Physical. Explosives triggered by opening the window, I think."

Not that I'd have actually opened a window. I was a ghost. But a good thing we hadn't sent anyone to physically check.

"And traps on the doors," Flint added. "Also, alarms. Motion sensors and so on."

"Neat work, Flint," Gabrielle said. She seemed to have gotten over having her projection torn out of her hands.

Gwen did something and I watched shimmering black snakes slip through the walls of the house. They followed Flint's smoke magic, then overtook it and spread out into every room.

There was an electric spark, like a major short-circuit, and one of the snakes disappeared.

"A trap designed for a spirit walker," Gwen said.

Good thing they made me wait.

Another spark, that seemed to catch several snakes, and then nothing. The snakes drifted away and Flint's smoke began to dissipate.

"There's no one alive inside," Gwen said finally. "No traps left for spirit walkers."

"Alive?" I asked, hearing something in her voice.

"There's a dead body inside," Gwen said. "In the living room."

"Weaver?"

"We should be so lucky. More likely the old guy from last night," Kane said. "To provide fuel for the spirit traps."

Even my aura projection could feel the chill that gave my body, back in Haven.

"We can go see," Flint said. "It's difficult to be sure, but I think that's all the traps and sensors marked out, and the magical traps sprung. You need to be aware, your projection is a working that touches the real world, okay? It can cause sound, change the temperature, even possibly even nudge something. A normal explosion won't hurt you but..."

"You don't want emergency services coming into the house because we set an alarm off or there's a report of an explosion," Kane finished.

I could feel the power stir beneath me. I could make sure there was nothing left for them to find. No traps. No building.

Locked together like this, they could all feel what I was feeling and probably guess what I was thinking. No one spoke.

"Okay," I said. "Warn me if any alarms are about to go off."

Weaver and the Denver Adepts weren't here, but I needed experience in this kind of magic, and I guessed this was a relatively safe way of gaining it.

I drifted in through the glass of the windows, passing through my own image with a shudder. Given what I was doing, it was strange to find that affected me, but it was really spooky.

Gabrielle murmured inaudibly.

I made my way to the living room. The body was the elderly Adept who'd greeted us at the door last night. He was lying on his back, arms and legs spread out, throat slashed open.

"It's entirely possible Weaver knows that his magical traps have been sprung," Gwen said. "We shouldn't stay long, in case there's something else lurking."

I nodded. I could tell she felt the motion, understood it.

There wasn't a great deal I could do; looking from this aura projection was like looking at an underwater scene. Everything waved slowly, pushed by currents I could half-sense.

Still, nothing seemed to have changed from my visit last night other than Weaver had killed one of his community just to set a trap on the chance that we would spirit walk into this house.

There was the same unused fireplace. The furniture. The Gold Rush artwork. The chandeliers.

The place had felt empty before, and in the eerie, drifting shapes around me, it felt even emptier.

I went down the corridor to Weaver's study.

Some of the books were missing—there were gaps in the shelves that hadn't been there. Everything else was the same, down to the bourbon bottle on the side table, and the glasses we'd left on his desk.

I turned around, too quickly, and the image of the house I was seeing lurched and swayed to catch up. The artwork in the rest of the house was paintings; here in the study it was three-dimensional reliefs and my vision swaying somehow gave the illusion of life to the depiction of mining scenes. They moved. My heart stuttered. For a second it was as if the men and mules in the artwork were real, trapped in there...

"Enough," Gwen said.

A flutter of panic, of things sliding away from me.

"Temperature rising!" Kane.

"Back. Now." That was Gabrielle.

But I couldn't feel Gabrielle and Gwen.

There was a pressure on me, like I'd dived into deep water. Darkness. Silence.

I'm somewhere outside, far from the smells and sounds of cities, in twilight, with the weight and fragrance of pine trees surrounding me and the incredible splendour of the Milky Way wheeling overhead.

Coyote and Raven stand there, watching me.

We're close. Linked by aura, just as if I were using eukori.

Raven bound to Coyote, and Coyote to Raven. Raven bound to me.

Coyote and me...

Kane is guarded.

"Swear you'll never use that power like that again."

I hear him in my mind.

"I can't," I reply in the same way. "The world isn't like that."

They're not happy.

I sighed. "You know, I had this sort of conversation with Skylur about the limits of what he'd do. Came down to it, basically anything, if it delivers Emergence rather than the alternative. He'd sacrifice himself and his whole House, me included."

Neither of them said anything.

"That's what I'm signed up for. Now, I'm not the main cog in the machine, and I don't expect to be able to tell whether something I do would have a significant effect on the whole of Emergence. I will do what Skylur tells me to, even if that includes using dark magic. Which sucks, because you've got to trust me, trusting someone else's call."

There weren't any happier. With auras meshed like this, there wasn't any way I could lie and they knew it.

"Best I can say is I'd never use it for personal gain or for something trivial. But give me the same kind of situation, where I have to pull that magic through you to save Alex or any other member of my House, and I'd do it. No question."

"Your House means us? You'd pull magic to save one of us?" Flint asks.

"Yes, of course. And the reverse. That's the way my House is."

Coyote blinks.

Better, but not quite there yet.

"I get the idea we're going to need to use whatever we have to get Tullah back," I say. "Including everything you might be able to do, or I might be able to do through you. I'll be there for you. I need to know you'll be there for me."

Coyote and Raven look at each other.

I felt them slipping away, but I couldn't go back yet. Something else called me, even as I felt them pulling me back to Haven.

Something stronger. Something further away. Something...

Dark.

The cold, deep earth is all around me. Not the cold of Denver. Not the same... taste of rock. A place with wetness in the soil, filling my tree-spirit senses, filling my mouth, my nose, my eyes. Soaking into my roots.

My roots. A great mass of tangling roots, like worms, deep, reaching into the darkness, stretching, feeding.

Feeding on the rot of old deaths and decaying bodies. Gaining from it. Power.

Power coming up through my body like lava rising in a volcano.

I must scream, but all I can do is rise up from the dread, swell out and sense...

A graveyard. My branches sway in the night sky above a graveyard.

Moonlight etches the lines of an ancient church, its walls rising up as if to escape the horror in the earth. Every stone is covered in lichen, the plant grasping at the building, holding it, clawing at it, whispering the promise of ages: that every wall will fall, every stone will be brought down, all will return to the earth where the dead lie patient...

A pressure is building in my chest, threatening to tear it open.

I must scream.

I could feel Gabrielle's hands gripping my physical shoulders again. Pulling me. The wood of the chair I was sitting in pressed against my back. The room in Haven mingled with Weaver's study and the ancient churchyard. Color crept in at the edges, pushed out the ghosts.

Faces were moving around me. Mouths. Words.

Back.

A staggering rush. Air blasting in my lungs. Blood pumping. Everything fast and slow at the same time.

I jerked in the chair as if I'd fallen into it, a gasp of shock ripped from my dry throat as fragments of the nightmare images scuttled away like bugs in daylight, to be replaced by the ice-cold blue of Gwen's stare right in my face.

"Frigging awesome!" Gabrielle said, apparently oblivious to the strange deviations in my return from the spirit walk.

Chapter 44

There was no war paint on my face. I was wearing a sweater, jeans and boots. My hair *had* been braided by Gabrielle as she soothed me into the right state of mind for a spirit walk, that much was real and physical. The rest was part of the interpretation I had made of it. Or...

Bian's face was very close, pushing Gwen aside. She was speaking to me. It took a moment before I could understand what she said. I seemed to be hearing through a kind of filter that changed her words into gibberish.

"I'm okay," I said, with a mouth that felt full of cotton wool. "Just disoriented."

I squeezed her hand, and let her help me to a sofa.

Words flowed over me. Nothing about speaking with Coyote and Raven. Nothing about a graveyard. Nothing about a church in the moonlight.

Flint and Kane wouldn't want to speak in front of the others. Fair enough.

The other...

That church. Not to share with anyone. Mine. Only I was there. Only I saw that church.

It was already fading, like dreams in the daylight. Yet I didn't want to share it with them.

In the meantime, someone really smart had requested that coffee be brought to us, and I managed to lift a mug without spilling any.

"I would guess Weaver left within minutes of you." Gwen was speaking to me, but it was Bian who answered.

"As far as we know, Weaver thinks Kaothos is with Tullah. If he boosted his spell to kill Amber and left booby traps all over his house, I think it means he's given up on any plans of using Amber as a way to get to Kaothos, and any plans that he might have had to cooperate with the Northern Adept League."

"Which means wherever he's gone, he's looking for Tullah," Gwen said. "He's going to his backup plan, to search with magic, but using someone from the Denver community instead of Amber."

"Will it work?" Bian asked.

"Yes," Gabrielle said. "It might be slower than with Amber, but it will work."

"And if we don't get there first, what can he do, once he finds Tullah, and realizes she doesn't have Kaothos?"

"Use her as bait," Gwen said. "That's what you'd call dark magic and it would require a lot of power, but it could be done. It would need the whole Denver community, somewhere safe and well away from us, to stop us interfering."

Gabrielle looked as sick as I felt, but Bian pushed on: "Using Tullah as bait isn't going to make Kaothos happy. What do you think Weaver could achieve with the dragon after doing something like that?"

We were all watching Gwen. She took her time answering.

"I suspect, whichever way he achieved it, his only intention has ever been to get hold of Kaothos. Which I think means he has a plan to bind the dragon. I don't know how. There would be an order of magnitude more power required than we've talked about so far. But if he succeeds, what can he achieve with a captive dragon?" She sighed and proceeded with visible reluctance. "Spirit guides are raw power. It's the host that constructs the purpose and function of a spell, which means the workings are limited, to an extent, by what the host believes can be done, and how they think the power might need to work to achieve it. The last time the world had a dragon spirit guide, military technology was at a level of armor and arrows, swords and spears, slingshots and maybe a bit of naptha or gunpowder. At that time, a host might accidentally have found a way to invoke lightning if there were the right type of clouds around, or a way to make the wind blow or mist to form." She paused and let us see where her line of thought was headed. "Now we have the knowledge of atomic structures, light and electricity, the physical laws that govern the universe. It's not as if the host and dragon are going to achieve this power without long effort and application, but in the end, I can't imagine what the potential limitations might be."

All of us sat in stunned silence for a minute. That's what the prize was.

"No wonder the Empire was so committed to finding Kaothos," Bian said eventually, and because I knew her, I sensed what her next words would be. "So what do the Northern Adept League think they're going to do with a dragon?"

"Get Tullah back here. Get Kaothos back where she belongs. Then protect and guide," Gwen said.

Well, there was a whole week of argument as to what 'guide' meant when the rubber met the road, but Gabrielle moved quickly to redirect us.

"Let's go through what we saw again in case we missed something," she suggested. "Memories from spirit walking fade quickly, just like substantiations do."

"Explain jargon, soon as we're done," I said.

Gabrielle glanced at Gwen, who nodded.

Forcing myself to speak in whole sentences, I walked them through everything I thought or heard or saw, right up until we left Weaver's house and I went *somewhere* else alone.

I couldn't recall any smell or taste or touch from the house. Talking about it took longer than the spirit walk had, and there was nothing new to add: Weaver had been there. He'd left quickly, taking some books, killing his colleague and leaving behind traps.

He was a powerful enemy that we'd underestimated, but at least we had a true idea of what we were facing now.

And Gabrielle had been right about my memories of the spirit walk—already they seemed faded, more unreal, more dream-like. Even the last part—the terror of being held in the earth, feeding on the decay of bodies.

All the others kept on speaking.

"That's the way of the spirit world," Gabrielle said. "Spirit jumping and spirit walking are projections of the aura into the surface level of spirit world." She held her hands up and rubbed them together. "This world and the spirit world touch at the surface all the time. They influence each other, but they don't actually mix a lot. Still, a projection into the spirit world, that has an effect. Think of it like putting your hand into a mountain stream. The water gets all turbulent around your hand and your hand gets cold. Take it out and the water goes back to flowing like it did before. Your hand gets warm again."

"You aren't fully *in* the spirit world," Flint said. "Your body stays right where it was, but your aura is there and it can be damaged, and you'd bring that damage back."

"But RiNo was different," I said. "We were *there*."

"Yes. That's the next level," Gabrielle said. "The first level of substantiation. But they're related; I was afraid when I lost control of the projection we were trying today, that you'd end up creating a substantiation."

She started pacing.

"That jargon," I reminded her.

"The spirit world is *different*. It's *flexible*. It's none of the things we think it is."

I shivered at that phrase and Bian looked worried again. She touched me briefly on the arm.

I gave her a smile and straightened up.

Mustn't zone out.

Mustn't see things that aren't there.

There wasn't any way that Gabrielle could know that phrase was close to the one Speaks-to-Wolves had used to me: *You are none of the things they will think you are.*

And maybe I'd imagined the whole churchyard scene.

Gabrielle didn't notice my reaction, and Gwen took over.

"For this aura projection, you created an interpretation based on the spirit jump you did with the trees, Amber. You got sensations of a difference in the passing of time, which led to the way you saw buildings as impermanent structures, and which then translated into that sort of ghostly, translucent image. Like a dream. In the same way, you might start a dream from a single, imagined point and then justify and interpret everything you experience afterwards, based on that single point."

"For a substantiation, you need a convincing interpretation, a set of convincing rules, like a backdrop that will run itself for a while." Gabrielle took it up again, so enthusiastic she couldn't let Gwen tell it all. "It's difficult to make it dream-like if you have a group because our dreams are so different. And even if you have a consistent substantiation, pulling other people into it makes it vulnerable. If we'd made the sky green when we kidnapped you in RiNo, we'd have had to fight against your belief the sky couldn't be green. So we made it so much like the real world, or what it might have been, that you accepted it. As it was, you unconsciously sensed it was a spirit world and changed the way you looked to fall in with the way you think about the spirit world."

A Denver area empty of people and in a different season? Turning to my Native American side had seemed obvious to me.

"But you actually move your whole mind and body into a substantiation, and unless you can construct a set of rules that redefine physics, physical laws still apply," Gabrielle was saying.

I'd missed something.

"You said firearms wouldn't work," I pointed out. "They work on physical laws."

"Yes, that's more complex—"

A knock on the door interrupted us. It was Julie.

"Diana would really like an update," she said.

"Yes, we should go back." Bian got up quickly and guided us back to the library which held the elevator down to Skylur's dungeon.

The elevator took a maximum of three people at a time.

I pushed the others forward, until there were only Bian and me left, and I took her arm.

"We need to talk," I said.

Bian didn't meet my eyes.

"You're worried," I said, straight out.

"Watching a spirit walk is scarier than I thought," she said.

"I wasn't talking about that, and you know it."

Dealing with a Bian problem, I took a Bian solution and ran with it. I grabbed her and pinned her up against the wall.

She'd been Athanate a lot longer than I had; she was stronger than me. Still, body mass and height counted for something. She struggled a little. Until she saw I was enjoying it.

"You're worried," I repeated.

Now I got the full-eye glare. "I won't hold you to your word."

"'Come to a pajama party' is a phrase, not a word."

"Smart ass."

"Let me get this straight..." Keeping the pressure on, I shifted my body against her. I enjoyed that too. "You think the only reason you got the invite was because my inhibitions had been damaged by Weaver's spell?"

"It's a reasonable analysis, isn't it?"

"It's a guess and it's wrong."

On top of the pounding heart and growing heat in my body, I was putting out Athanate pheromones by the bucket, and still wasn't getting through, so I kissed her. Hard.

Her awkward stiffness melted away. Lips softened and parted. Hands came up to hold my head and her legs lifted to wrap around my hips.

The elevator whispered back up and she broke the kiss with a sigh and a small, relieved, cat-got-the-cream smile for me.

"They can wait," I growled. "That was only one issue I wanted to discuss."

"Consider me convinced by your argument on that issue," she purred, kissing my neck. "On the other hand, we do have to go down, and Diana can probably smell your pheromones all the way from the dungeon. She's going to know exactly why we're late."

I laughed at her phrasing. "So? My inhibitions are damaged. Who's going to blame me?"

"Can't argue it both ways, Amber. Come on."

Her eyes warned me she meant it, so I let her down. Hand in hand, we went and stood on the elevator platform. The clear doors slid out to surround us.

I put my lips against her ear. Whether or not anyone was watching and listening, I was well aware Skylur had recording devices all over Haven. Just because I couldn't see one in this elevator didn't mean there wasn't one. "The other issue was: what twisted your tail so much in your conversation with Skylur's new Diakon this morning. Don't like him?"

"Her," she corrected me. She kissed me again briefly and then her teeth nibbled deliciously at my earlobe. "You're right," she whispered, voice going all business again. "We do need to talk, you and me. I don't trust your Hecate, for one thing. Maybe that's because I had a bad start to the day. Or I should say *we* had a bad start to the day. We're going to have orders from Skylur, and I just know they're not going to be easy. We'll need plans and backups and options. There are a *lot* of issues coming out of New York, but the biggest one for me is who he's chosen for his Diakon."

"Not jealous, are you?"

"No. The reason I'm angry is his new Diakon isn't Panethus. She's frigging Basilikos."

Chapter 45

I was so stunned by Bian's news I kept losing the thread of the conversation when we were all seated down in the dungeon again.

A *Basilikos* Diakon for House Altau?

What the hell was Skylur doing?

We had to speak about it, but not in front of the Northern Adept League.

And I had to concentrate. Gabrielle was talking about the spirit world again.

"...the kind of direction sensing we need to do to find Tullah is a whole leap more complex than spirit walking to Erie. It'll need substantiation, and careful planning. It'll need all the colleagues we brought with us to Denver, and we'll need time to prepare. Even if Weaver's already trying the same thing, we can't skip the preparation."

"How long?" Diana asked.

"We would be ready tomorrow night," Gwen replied.

"That's a long time. Does Weaver need as much time to prepare?"

"Yes, but he might have started earlier. Just as we might have started earlier, if we'd had this conversation yesterday," she said pointedly.

"Why can't you use the substantiation you had before?" Bian asked. "The one you used to kidnap Amber?"

"They don't... persist. It isn't there anymore."

Both Bian and I caught that hesitation, but Bian was quicker to ask. "You mean the spirit world just returns to the way it was, like you were talking about upstairs?"

Alice cleared her throat. "That's for spirit walks, and no, she doesn't mean that exactly. What actually happens to substantiations is much stranger than that and more dangerous. Stronger substantiations consume weaker ones."

Bian and I spoke at the same time.

"Stronger?"

"Consume?"

"Stronger means more consistent, or better constructed," Alice said. "Or even larger. And yes, consume, as in the stronger absorbs the weaker substantiation, including everything in it, and grows as a result."

She ignored the glare she was getting from Gabrielle and pursed her lips. "It might serve you well to think of the spirit world as a sea," she went on thoughtfully. "Firstly, that it's full of predators that get more dangerous the deeper you go. Secondly, that you can start to attract those predators simply by stepping carelessly into it."

Gwen cut her off. "That's part of the reason why we need to prepare carefully. The risks are manageable with the right preparation. No matter how important it is to find Tullah, we achieve nothing if our substantiation fails."

The Northern Adept League might be working with us for the moment, but it seemed to me there was a reluctance to share some of their arcane knowledge.

"It's also evident from the simple spirit walk we did upstairs that Amber is... headstrong to use for the focal point," Gwen went on. "In a quick, easy spirit walk that doesn't matter too much, but the kind of search we're talking about might take hours, or days. People will get tired and make mistakes. That's the sort of thing that can attract other, predatory substantiations."

"You imply these substantiations can somehow be aware of each other?" Diana picked up on that detail. "So could Weaver be able to use a substantiation to spy on ours, and to attack us?"

Gabrielle let Gwen answer. "It's possible, yes."

"Right. Let's be positive and assume we avoid Weaver during our search, because it would be difficult for him to predict where we're searching," Bian said. "What if Weaver's substantiation lurks around Denver, because that's where we have to bring Tullah back to?"

Gwen frowned. "*Around Denver* doesn't mean exactly the same thing in the spirit world. He could lie in wait for us, yes, but that would mean he wasn't searching. I'm not sure he'd do that. What's more, you're implying we'd use the substantiation to bring Tullah back."

Gwen shook her head.

"We wouldn't advise trying that. How to explain? We want a substantiation that's quick and mobile and doesn't attract attention. If we make it robust enough to pick up Tullah, let alone her parents and any others she's with, that makes it much bigger, more noticeable, slower. What I'm advising is to find her and then go pick her up in that van you used to get here from California."

"Which can be shielded," Alice said, and nodded agreement.

Kane shook his head. "Depends on where she is. There are snowstorms over the Rockies again. Roads will be closed."

"Even if they're not closed... driving a van through snow..." Flint left it hanging.

"There aren't really any other options," Gabrielle said.

But the look on Flint's face was clearly *so you say.*

"Anyway, maybe we'll find her driving up I25," Gabrielle said brightly.

No one replied to her attempt to lighten it all up. Tullah had to be hiding and she was hiding well. The Empire's Adepts had been looking for her, and they hadn't found her. Weaver had probably been looking already, and he hadn't found her. I didn't think she was on the highway.

"It's not getting any less urgent, as we sit here," Diana pointed out.

It wasn't, and I felt the ability to come up with a better solution was being held back because we didn't really trust each other.

I sensed Gwen's frustration building that Kaothos wouldn't speak to her, tempered only by our common understanding that the most urgent thing at the moment was to get Tullah back.

It was like a playground seesaw: Gwen was still hiding her spirit animal. Kaothos hadn't revealed herself. They didn't want to tell us too much about the spirit world. Flint and Kane thought they knew things the Northern Adept League weren't saying.

Neither side willing to play nice.

And down at the end of the dungeon, the lips on Anubis' dog-face seemed to be drawn a little tighter, as if he were watching me and snarling.

Keep away from magic.

As if we had any alternative. We couldn't find Tullah any other way.

Gwen brought it to a close. "If we're agreed this is how we're going to search, it means we should start preparing as soon as possible, and we'll contact you if we come up with a better plan."

There were nods around the table.

Maybe Gwen sensed the same thing about trust, because she went on, "Before we go, I should say something else. I hinted to you this was not only about the dragon, but also about your enemies."

"We know Basilikos hasn't been defeated," I said.

"I understand, but it's not really old Basilikos or the new Hidden Path party that I'm talking about," Gwen said. "It's the individuals themselves."

"Matlal," I said, since his name had come up today. "Vega Martine." As I said it, I remembered others who connected to those names: Mirela Tucek, who'd disguised herself and her troop of Carpathian ninjas as nuns in the Convent of Saint Vasilica outside Taos, and who'd been the one to free Matlal; Colonel Peterson and the survivors of Ops 4-16, the evil shadow equivalent of Ops 4-10. "Tucek and Peterson," I concluded. "We know they're still alive."

"Yes, and from today, maybe you should re-evaluate how dangerous they are. They were working with that psychopath Noble. They were behind the collapse of House Romero in Albuquerque. They were behind the corruption of the Taos Adept community, which gave Amaral the means to capture Diana. They were one of the clients of Forsythe's sick trade in children. And those are only the schemes we know about."

"Yes, but what are you suggesting we do? Matlal is in Mexico."

"I'm suggesting that country boundaries mean nothing to him, and if they mean anything to you, you're giving him an advantage which he will continue to exploit. Amber, I understand the concern that the majority of Ops 4-10 operations were illegal because they took place in secret, in countries the United States wasn't at war with, but did you not get the job done? Are you not capable of doing the same, more secretly now?"

Ops 4-10 *had* gotten those sorts of jobs done. House Altau had enough Ops 4-10 and Athanate and Were allies that we *probably* could do something similar. But what if it went wrong?

"I can't give you any insight into what Matlal's plans are," Gwen broke into my thoughts. "But I hope I've made you rethink the level of threat posed by him and his allies, down in the Yucatan."

"You know where he is?"

"Not exactly, but I can tell you someone with significant levels of power is experimenting with the spirit world down there, and *we*," she laid heavy emphasis on the word, "are going to have to do something about it."

She sat back, and there was a finality about the comments. She'd given us information without asking for anything back. We'd have to come up with an equivalent.

Diana stood up. "We must let you go and prepare. We'll see you back here at Haven with the rest of your colleagues tomorrow evening."

We were still awkward with each other. Hands were shaken. Tight smiles exchanged.

Gwen's eyes lingered a second, and I wondered if she was going to ask me if something happened at the end of the spirit walk that I hadn't shared with them.

Or I could share it, and show I trusted her.

Then the moment passed.

Alice escorted Gwen into the elevator, and next trip Bian went up with Gabrielle.

Chapter 46

"What the hell does Skylur think he's doing?"

Not how I should be talking about the head of Panethus to his oldest friend, but I'd bottled this up throughout the conversation with the Northern Adept League and it had to come out. No matter how close Skylur and Diana were.

Diana walked around the table and lifted me into an embrace before replying.

"I don't know, Amber, but I trust him absolutely. Whatever persuaded him to take this decision will be for the benefit of Emergence. I know that in my heart."

I breathed in her soothing marque and let it fill my senses. I wouldn't say my fears disappeared, but with Diana holding me, the situation didn't feel so bad. Our hearts automatically fell into rhythm.

"The first conference this morning was only a brief broadcast to every Panethus House," Diana said. "Bian is scheduled for a one-to-one conversation with Skylur soon. I'm sure he will reveal more of what's behind this move."

"It's such a shock, hearing it..." I couldn't quite give voice to the feelings I'd had at the news.

It didn't matter: Diana sensed it.

"You felt betrayed," she said. "Understandable, but you should not. You must remember, here in Colorado, we have been given a position of the ultimate trust. We know what really happened at the end of the Assembly in Los Angeles. Skylur trusted you with that knowledge, which could bring down our hopes of an orderly Emergence. You owe him your trust in return."

The elevator whispered back: Tolly had joined us.

He was dressed as I'd seen him before: black robe and cowl.

As he walked from the elevator platform he spread his arms wide. I'd seen that before as well. It was his equivalent of a white cane, I guessed.

Except he seemed to have eyes on his fingertips.

I blinked.

No eyes. Normal hands.

Diana released me to greet him, and I returned to the table, next to Flint.

"Am I likely to have visual side effects after a spirit walk?" I asked him quietly.

"You seeing things?" he asked.

"Hmm."

He waggled his hand. "Most people do after a long one. It wears off, unless you do spirit walks all the time. Then your mind gets used to interpreting stuff differently."

Tolly had shown me he could read with his fingertips and so I hallucinated eyes there.

Great. Have to check the evidence of my own eyes. And too much makes it worse.

"Thanks," I said.

Was that church and graveyard a hallucination? The tree? All just something stirred up in my mind?

I didn't have long to think about it; in another couple of minutes the rest returned and we were all back at the table, except Diana. She didn't sit. She paced.

"Weaver is out there, probably hunting for Tullah already," she said. "She's well hidden, so he might not be able to find her quickly, but *we* need to, because we may be reaching a limit for the time Tullah and Kaothos can be apart without damage. We can't risk that."

We all felt Kaothos stir, but she said nothing.

Diana turned. At that end of her circuit, Anubis was in a line behind her from my point of view. I couldn't stop my gaze from slipping past her to the Lyssae. His eyes gleamed in the shadows and his jaws moved as if he were speaking.

I blinked again.

I needed to get a grip on this hallucinating.

"The *obvious* way to find Tullah is this more involved spirit walk that the Hecate is suggesting," Diana said. "So... do we trust her?"

"I worry that it seems *too* obvious." Bian looked dour. She turned to Tolly. "You've been listening in. What do you think about the Hecate?"

"What she's said seems to be truthful," Tolly said. "I'm wondering about what she hasn't said."

He gestured at our Adepts: Alice, Flint and Kane.

"Never met another Adept whose spirit guide I couldn't even guess at," Kane said, clearly uncomfortable, but not willing to come out and say it. "Doesn't necessarily mean anything, but I'm having trouble trusting her."

"She has that rep, up in the north," Flint said. "That her guide doesn't show. I was sure I'd be able to see, when I met her up close. Can't. Makes me itchy."

"Not that we ever intended meeting her up close." Kane shuffled some more in his seat.

"She didn't reveal her spirit guide, but neither did Kaothos manifest visibly," I pointed out. "I got the impression we were both waiting for the other to make a show of trust, and that was why she told us about Matlal."

I felt Kaothos stir around us again, but she still said nothing and remained hidden.

Bian huffed. "But exactly what did she tell us? Matlal's alive. Vega Martine is alive. Peterson and Tucek are alive and they're all in Mexico. We know all that."

"And we're still not doing anything about it. She's saying there's an urgency—that they're getting stronger."

My opinion wasn't winning them over. Everyone else was still suspicious of the Northern Adept League.

When they'd saved my life, I'd lost that suspicion.

Is that a good thing? Can I trust myself?

Given I'm hallucinating eyes on fingers and Anubis talking to me?

"If they're hiding things from us, are they truly important things?" Flint asked.

"They're being coy about the dangers of substantiations in the spirit world," Alice said. "The longer you search, the deeper you go in the spirit world, the more dangerous it gets."

"But they know *you* know that, and that you'll tell us," I argued. "I think it might be ingrained reluctance to discuss that level of Adept knowledge."

No one answered. We'd hit a stalemate, and Bian moved us smoothly in another direction.

"Do you believe what she said about Kaothos?"

"Or what?" I said. "Do you think she's helping us to create some kind of advantage in the Assembly?"

Diana answered. "She specifically said to me she has no personal interest in the Assembly, and that the Hecate in New York, Faith Hinton, would be talking to Skylur and probably taking any official position within the Assembly."

"And the Hecate's only interest is in protecting and guiding. Even if the dragon's power is as frightening as she said it is."

"I didn't feel any lies when she spoke."

Finally, Kaothos manifested and spoke. "The Hecate seems truthful to me," she said. "I need Tullah back. A delay of a day is too long, but I cannot see any other way around waiting for them. I also wonder what the League wants beyond guiding me."

She faded out of sight again.

Bian and Diana went back and started arguing the presumed politics of the Northern Adept League and how it might affect the Assembly.

I was sitting between Flint and Alice. Flint was muttering to Kane, completely uninterested in the politics. Alice was half listening.

It was too good an opportunity to miss. I needed some answers and yet I didn't want to discuss the details of what had happened at the end of the spirit walk. It felt like it was mine, and that if I talked about it they'd use it to say I needed to rest. Or that it was too dangerous, and they'd find some way of preventing me from using the power.

My oath wouldn't let me rest. Tullah, Tara, Hana. Whatever the cost.

I closed down my eukori and held my pulse steady.

Chapter 47

"Alice, do trees have some kind of special meaning for Adepts?"

"Hmm?" She turned to me. "Trees? Yes, of course, especially in the older Celtic traditions, for instance."

She tilted her head to the side, looking strangely just like Flint when he was channeling his Raven. "You're wondering why you spirit-jump to trees?"

I shrugged. "It works. I'm not concerned so much as interested."

"Ah, well. There's the whole thing about trees connecting worlds, which would have an attraction for you, I suppose. You know: roots deep in the secrets of the earth, trunk on the ground and leaves in the sky. Even more fundamental to the Norse, naturally. All of those myths and metaphors inevitably seep into Adept thinking."

"Why fundamental to the Norse? And what parts have Adepts adopted into their thinking?"

"Well, *fundamental* because in Norse magical traditions, the sacred tree Yggdrasil is the structure of the whole cosmos. Literally fundamental. All creatures are bound to live within Yggdrasil, from the great wyrms of power that coil around the tangle of the roots, up to the angels, the sky gods and goddesses, who hold their courts in its loftiest branches. Bound until the end of the world, when the great wolf Fenrir is unchained. Fenrir will kill the gods and goddesses, while his pack eat the light. Then the roots of Yggdrasil will let loose the earth into the endless dark where the wyrms will consume it, and all that moves upon it."

While I shuddered at the startling imagery her voice made in my head, she snorted. "A wonderful image of human destiny and entropy," she said. "What is tangled becomes untangled and simple and pure, but in doing so, it loses its substance, its grip on life."

I'd *felt* that, and the images flooded back like shattered pieces of remembered dreams. The tangled roots. The deep secrets. The power. The conflict. The emptiness of simplicity.

"Is that an Adept belief?" I asked, forcing myself to speak normally.

"Entropy, yes." She smiled. "Fenrir and his pack, only as a fanciful allegory. Yggdrasil, on the other hand..."

"Yes?"

"There is something about the image," she said, her eyes taking a faraway look. "About the connection of the deep, dark powers to the lofty objectives. About controlling the balance. Anyway, to answer your question, many Adept communities and covens, especially in the Old World, visualize their communities exactly in this way, as a sort of tree. The old ones call it the soultree. Other think of it as a great wheel and so on."

It was chilling. I'd taken a detour on the way back from the spirit walk to Erie. I'd spirit jumped into a tree, in a graveyard. Not any old tree or any old graveyard. My gut was telling me that this tree was somehow the spiritual soul of an Adept community, a soultree.

And my gut was also telling me that this was connected with the dark power I had started to use. The same power that fed the family's curse.

It was also telling me that it wasn't anywhere around here. The age of the church, the gravestones. This churchyard was on the other side of the Atlantic. Ireland, if I had to guess.

Which meant I could spirit jump a *long* way, regardless of what the Adepts said, and I'd visited the Adept community that was the origin of the curse on my family.

"All the paranormal communities do a similar thing, if you think about it," Alice continued. She was really thinking aloud. "It's more than the need for a totem, or an image of what they are or want to be, or a group memory of everything they've been. It's like a reservoir of power that they can call on. It's what pulls them back to the core. The werewolves have the song of their pack that binds them together. The Athanate have the marque of their House. The Adepts have the soultree, or their equivalent."

"It pulls them back to the core? That sounds like soultrees can think and act independently."

"Eh?" She finally stopped listening to Diana and Bian and turned back to me. "I suppose it does sound like that, but I'm not sure that's really it. Are you *especially* interested?"

I was. I needed to understand the nature of the soultree, and how it was linked with the curse on my family and the Adepts who created that curse. But I'd alerted her, and I didn't want others to know this. Yet.

Alice was expecting some kind of response and looking a little puzzled that I was so slow today, so I distracted her with a change of topic.

"You've been open with information," I said. "Why do I get the feeling the Northern Adept League don't approve?"

Alice laughed quietly.

"Oh, I am an abomination to the Hecate and the rest of the League. My mission was to be their eyes and ears within the Athanate world. It was understood I was flirting with damnation, and as far as they're concerned, I fell."

Bian rapped on the table.

"We're running out of time," she said. "I have a teleconference with Skylur in ten minutes, and we'll have even more to discuss after that. What do we think about the League's offer to help?"

Everyone seemed reluctant, so I leaped in.

"If we trust the Northern Adept League enough to have them visit here, then I'm guessing we trust them enough to go ahead with their search," I said.

"Okay." Bian was looking at the Adepts. "Which leaves us a day to come up with a better idea..."

Alice lifted her hands, palm up. "I have no better ideas."

Kane and Flint exchanged glances.

"He won't have it," Kane muttered.

Of course everyone at the table heard, as Kane knew they would.

"*Who* won't have *what*?" Bian asked.

Flint squinted and scratched his ear. "Mr. Tolly here says his library has everything about the paranormal—"

"Everything that involves the Athanate," Kane interrupted. "He won't have stuff about medicine wheels and ghost dances and spirit walks."

Tolly sighed, entirely aware they were trying to play him. "The Dark Library contains books about those topics. What specifically are you thinking of?"

Flint stared intently at him while Kane answered: "Anything by a guy named Oronhiateka?"

Tolly went still.

For a moment, I thought it was a reaction to the name, but the stillness was his way of thinking. I'd heard of people who did memory tricks by putting themselves into a light trance and visualizing themselves physically passing through their memories. Tolly seemed to be demonstrating it.

We waited a minute in silence before he spoke. "Yes. It's not that old, naturally. About a hundred years, but it's still waiting for processing because it's not fundamentally about the Athanate. It appears to be in a code. All I can say is the name of the volume itself."

"Songs of the Long Walker," suggested Kane.

"Indeed."

"We'd like a look," Flint said. "It's possible that it's not really code—"

"It's his own writing style—" Kane interrupted.

"Which we know about."

"And this may have some relevance?" Diana's brow arched elegantly.

"An old guy we met once said Oronhiateka could spirit walk from one side of the country to the other," Kane said.

"Not that we're experts in the League's substantiation, but even they admitted spirit walking is safer than using a substantiation."

"And one of the major reasons for spirit walking is to go looking for something. Or someone. Which is exactly what we want to do," Kane finished.

I could see Bian liked the idea of not relying on the League.

"On the other hand, other people told us that Oronhiateka was crazy." Flint shrugged. "So maybe we'll fall back on the League's way of finding Tullah anyway. Just an idea."

"An idea. Good." Diana rose. "Tolly, take them and retrieve the book. Bian, your call with Skylur, but first, I think you said that Amber has a problem with her cubs."

My cubs. I had a to do double take on that before my brain clicked. The young werewolves from the El Paso pack that Alex had left behind here at Haven.

Yup. My cubs.

Bian nodded and got up. "They were fine when Alex was here, but you need to talk to them now. I'll show you where they are."

I followed.

I'd already had meeting with them on my list of priorities while I was here at Haven. I'd even sent Yelena a text message for when she landed, to pick up Rita and Tove from their shopping trip and bring them here. Rita was an experienced pack member, and I probably needed her insight with my new pack.

I guessed it made no big difference if I started off with the cubs now, rather than later.

It was still intensely irritating that they'd caused a problem big enough to have come to Diana's attention *and* distracted me from the important business of the day, which was finding Tullah.

I was *not* happy with them.

Chapter 48

"They're in the billiard room," Bian said as the elevator brought us to the ground floor. "West corridor, room at the very end in front of you. I have to tell you, I'm not much impressed. The Ops 4-10 guys and gals were keen to meet with some werewolves, but I don't think they are now."

"What's happened?"

She grimaced. "Nothing in particular. Not yet. It was good when Alex was here, but the ones he left behind are like a bunch of immature teenagers. Big, bad attitude with nothing to back it up. Sitting around expecting to be waited on. I need it fixed before there's a problem."

"It will be fixed," I promised her, through gritted teeth. "Have Rita sent to join me when she arrives, please."

My pack. My cubs.

Yeah. About to meet my temper.

We came out of the room where the secret elevator was hidden and I put my head into the main living room. Scott had his nose in a book.

"Scott, you're with me."

Amenable as ever in two-footed form, he stood and followed me out into Haven's central hallway and down the west corridor.

"This is an incredible place," he said, his voice rich with his enthusiasm. "There are books of poetry in the living room written by poets I've never even heard of. Athanate folk, I guess. *Excellent* poetry. It's wonderful."

"Unfortunately, not what we're about today," I said shortly. "This is pack business. Don't get involved until I tell you to."

I could hear the cubs from the other end of the corridor; there was music playing and loud arguments. No one even turned when I opened the door to the billiard room and my temper began to edge into the danger zone.

There were three girls and nine guys.

Two of the guys were at the billiard table, arguing over the rules, and not far short of a fight.

The rest of them were sitting or lying around on sofas like so much discarded laundry. They were all drinking beer.

The music was coming from a stereo. I stalked across and turned it off.

That got their attention.

"Hey, I like that song." The idiot who said that hadn't even turned around.

One of the others noticed who I was all right. "Shit. It's—"

"No more music while you're here at Haven," I said. "No more beer. And when I come into a room, you will shut up and stand immediately."

I said it quietly. There was no need to shout for werewolves, even a bunch of idiots like this.

I was already zeroed in on the main problem. The guy who complained about my turning the music off. He still hadn't even looked around.

"We're not in the army," he said.

Oh, man, if there was a prize for surly...

In two steps, I reached the sofa and grabbed the back of his sweatshirt, ripping it as I lifted him like the dumb cub he was. I dropped him onto the floor.

"I said stand."

Everyone got up, Mr. Surly quickest of all. Anger was burning right through that beer and lighting his face up like a tomato.

"You're right," I said. "You're not in the army. It's far worse than that. You haven't figured it out yet, but you're in my pack."

"Alex is the alpha," one of the billiard players said. He was still holding his cue.

"That's *Mr. Deauville* to you when you're talking to me, and *sir* to his face."

"He said to call him—"

"I don't care what he said. He's in El Paso. I'm here. You have to deal with me, and I say he made a mistake with you. You're in the pack, but you are *not* pack members yet. You're an ill-disciplined rabble with too little to do and no brains." I glared at them. "I don't know if I want you in my pack."

There were glances from the others to Mr. Surly. He was more dominant than them, and he'd been practicing on this impressionable group. The others were looking to him for an indication of how to react. He was the stereotypical alpha—big, handsome, full of muscles and sex. Bloated with his own opinion of himself.

I'd put him in a spot and he decided he couldn't back down. He took a swing at me.

Good. I'd gotten tired of talking.

I swayed back, grabbed his wrist and let the weight of his punch pull me around. I jerked his arm straight, slammed my fist into the back of his elbow and swept his legs out. He fell face down. I twisted his arm and shoved my boot into his armpit.

"Hurts, doesn't it?" I said. "And you can't move or I'll dislocate your shoulder. That'll hurt even—"

One of his girlfriends came at me.

No time for this shit.

I dislocated Mr. Surly's shoulder and punched his girlfriend in the face, knocking her onto her back.

He was screaming from pain. She might have wanted to, but she had no breath, not when my knee landed in her stomach.

I got up quickly. I was out of range when she vomited her beer all over the floor.

The rest stood where they were, shocked into immobility, apart from the billiard player. He put the cue down in a hurry.

It was rougher than the army, but the process felt like a comfortable old coat I hadn't worn in a while, and it worked just as well on werewolf cubs as it had on recruits.

Next phase. Give orders.

"Which of you knows how to put a shoulder back?"

One of the smaller guys made a dazed movement with his hand.

"You! And you!" I pointed to him and the nearest girl. "Put his shoulder back."

They moved forwards as if I were compelling them, their mouths open but silent.

"I can't hear you," I said.

"Yes," they muttered.

"That's *yes, ma'am* to you."

"Yes, ma'am."

"Better. You two," I picked another pair at random. "Go get supplies now and clean up this mess on the floor."

They fled.

"The rest of you, go stand against the wall."

I let my dominance off the leash. Werewolf manners would keep it at a minimum around pack members, but these idiots didn't get that courtesy.

I kept it up while the shoulder was painfully put back in place, the mess was cleaned and those involved joined the rest of them against the wall. Mr. Surly was cradling his arm and, werewolf or not, it was going to hurt for a while.

"You have disgraced your pack," I said very quietly and began to stalk up and down the shivering line.

"I'm within my rights to kill you." I had stopped in front of the two who'd attacked me and glared at them. They couldn't meet my eyes, so I moved on. "As for the rest, I should expel you from the pack. It would save me a lot of grief and you a lot of pain."

They were silent and scared.

"It's taken you a day to go from members of the El Paso pack to rabble. That must be some kind of record. Did you feel your new co-alpha had been cruel, leaving you behind? Poor little cubs. That meant you weren't important. And that if you were second-rate, the co-alpha in Denver must be too."

Twitches. Faces flushed. Shame.

Stupid thought processes, but groups do that sometimes. Now they were realizing it.

Time for the stick and the carrot.

"Let me tell you how it's going to be, and then I'll tell you why you *might* become pack members, *if* you pull yourselves together."

"If you want to get into this pack, this is your daily routine from now on until I say otherwise: you will get up at 05:00, and you will have fifteen minutes to make yourself, your bed and any belongings you have here ready for inspection. You will be told the standards you will be held to, and inspected by people who know every trick in the book. Trust me, you will not want to fail those inspections. You will then have an hour of training before breakfast, and training will continue throughout the day, punctuated by meals. To start with, this training will be mainly in hand to hand combat techniques for you to use on two legs. It will be delivered by people who are better at it than you'll ever be. And it will hurt."

Utter silence. A dawning realization began to drain the color from their faces.

"As you progress, there will be instruction in four-legged fighting techniques. There will also be training in whatever I think would make you a valuable member of this pack. You get no choice and no options on what you get taught."

A couple of them were standing a little straighter with a hint of a positive reaction. I noted them.

"During the day, you'll have no access to anything not essential for your training. That'll change after dinner, when you'll be allowed computers and cell phones. You can chose to use that time to complain to someone you think will show the slightest sympathy, but the purpose of providing you with those facilities is for you to plan the arrival and integration of the former El Paso pack. If you create good plans that I approve of, you'll be given budget and authority to implement them. It'll be your responsibility, your success, or your failure, and the pack will know it."

There were a few *I'll show her* expressions, which were exactly what I was looking for, and I felt a whole lot better about them than when I'd started this speech.

"The best of you might get a chance to become trainers yourselves, because every single wolf in my pack will pass this basic training, or will not be in my pack."

I scanned the line up and down. Just because a few of them looked as if they might be up to it wasn't a reason to give them any uncertainty about the downside.

"Lights will go out at 21:30 and you will fall asleep immediately. If you do not fall asleep, then the regime for the next day will ensure you do on the following night, whether you want to or not."

Now for the bigger stick.

"This will be entirely voluntary. If at any time during this training you elect to leave this pack, your request will be honored and you will be escorted out of Southern League territory. You will never come back. There *is* no way back. There *is* no third alternative."

And finally the biggest.

"I will inspect each of you personally a week from now, or at any time your trainers think you would benefit from an inspection by me. There are three outcomes that could happen from that session. You will return to training and redouble your efforts, you will become outcast, or you will die."

I'd need to talk to them again, but that was enough for now.

"Have I made myself perfectly clear?"

Nods. Mumbles.

Not good enough.

"I can't hear you."

"Yes," from all of them.

I sighed. "You will address me as alpha, or ma'am. Now, I said I wanted to hear you. *Do you understand?"*

"Yes, ma'am."

"Better." I waved Scott forward. "This is Scott. He is one of your lieutenants while your training is going on. You'll be seeing a lot of each other."

I rocked on my heels like Top would have done. "You'll start right now by changing and taking a run around the estate with Scott while I organize instructors for your formal training."

This was a huge gamble, but I had one of my gut feelings about Scott.

He was self-conscious as he shucked his clothes, but as soon as he changed, that lip curl came back. He was a mild-mannered man on two legs and a dominant, aggressive wolf on four. I just hoped he was smart enough to keep it to dominance displays and didn't try fighting anyone at the moment. He was going to have to be trained in the arts of fighting as a wolf. Just as I would.

The cubs shifted shape and I could see by their wolf body language they were accepting me as alpha now, even Mr. Surly. They were less sure about Scott.

That was okay, because I had one last little surprise to spring on them, and I could sense her approaching now.

The door opened behind me and Rita came in.

"Your other lieutenant, Rita."

The cubs obviously recognized her. Every single one of them crouched a little lower.

They knew her, and Rita scared the crap out of them.

I made myself a mental note: I had to find out what had gone on in the borderlands between El Paso and the New Mexico pack's territories.

Meanwhile, my little plan was getting better and better.

"Like a run?" I asked her. "This mangy crew needs work."

She showed the same smile I saw on Skylur occasionally: small and cold and brief as winter sun.

"Tove and Yelena are in the main living room," she said as she stripped.

I called Bian on the cell.

"Wolves are going to be running in the yard for a while. Please don't shoot them. And I need to talk to the Colonel about an Ops 4-10 training regime for them."

She snickered.

"That didn't take you long, did it? Hold on, I'll put you through."

While I waited, I opened the French doors at the end. There was a snow-filled patio with a beautiful view of the Rockies.

The cougar stepped past me, almost daintily, and then looked back at the cubs as if one of them was lunch.

I waved them out, and they came obediently, if reluctantly, keeping as much distance between them and Rita as they could. Scott lowered his head and snapped at the heels of a couple of lingerers, including the limping Mr. Surly. I could almost see the human grin on Scott's face. He was enjoying this far too much.

Then they took off, dark shapes racing through the snow, chased by Scott and Rita.

"Amber?" Colonel Laine's voice came on the cell phone. "I hear you're chasing wolves through the yard."

"Scott and Rita are. I need your help. The thing is, I want to make my pack a whole new kind of pack, starting with these cubs. They don't realize it, but they're in a dangerous place here in Colorado, and we're in a war. I need to put them through an accelerated, basic Ops 4-10 training, starting as soon as they get back from their run and keeping on going until everyone's been through."

I described the plan forming in my head.

"Can do," he said. "Need something to keep the troops interested. I'll send Annie to start things off and I'll get a couple of other sergeants to brainstorm a schedule."

He signed off, leaving me wondering who else I needed to talk to about this scheme.

Alex. He'd need to know what was happening here.

Felix and Cameron. Well, they wanted me to talk to them. Now I had something to say. I didn't *think* they'd bite my head off for this. In fact, they'd probably want the whole Denver and New Mexico super-pack to go through the training.

In which case, we'd need somewhere even bigger than Haven.

And, if the New Mexico packs were involved, I'd need to talk to Zane.

Oh, joy.

It seemed, having plotted to have him distracted in one direction, that I'd managed to find a way to reverse that.

Chapter 49

No response from Alex's cell, so I texted him the bare details and put off talking to our alphas until I'd spoken to him.

Jen's cell still wasn't being answered, so I walked back down to the main living room, wondering what I might need to say to Tove if she'd looked out the window and seen wolves running through the snowy gardens.

That'd have to wait. Yelena was there, slipping off the couch and into my embrace with that slinky dancer's grace.

"Missed you," I whispered. "Everything okay?"

"Of course. Put out tongue," she ordered.

I knew what was coming, but I played along and she pretended to examine it.

"Hmm. Still licking knives."

I laughed. "Guilty. Where's Tove?"

"Trying on her new clothes. She wants to show you."

"She wants my approval?"

Yelena grinned. "Not what she said, but I think yes." She shrugged. "You paid for them."

I sobered. I hadn't expected that from Tove. She was more difficult to read than I thought.

We sat down to wait.

"So... what happened in New York?" I said.

"Lot of talk. Strange. It seemed like little stuff, but they said I knew more than I thought I did. Said it was useful information on the Domain. I think because they hear nothing for so long, anything is something."

"They were friendly about it?"

"Yes. No problem."

"And Skylur?"

I would have been able to tell if she'd been bitten, but I wanted to make sure.

"Very busy man," she said. She knew what I was asking. "Too busy even for Jen."

"I thought the idea was he needed to have business meetings with Jen."

"She's with business team. They're too busy to care whether she's been bound by Skylur or not. I went to see her when they finished talking to me. She's fine. Really. She gave me orders to come home."

I smiled. High as she was in my House, Jen couldn't really order Yelena back here and everyone knew it. But Yelena would have had to be sure that Jen was under no threat to have left her. That made me feel happier.

"Did you meet Skylur's new Diakon?" I asked.

"No. Saw her and Skylur together, but I didn't speak to her." She frowned. "She's old Athanate. Roman. Two thousand years I think. Very tough. Basilikos, but I think not Basilikos like Matlal."

Both of us felt Bian approaching.

"A good summary, Diakon Vylkove," Bian said. "Basilikos, but not like Matlal."

She'd completed her teleconference with Skylur while I'd spoken to the cubs, so there was a clear limit on how much could have been said.

"But why?" I said. Why pick a Basilikos as Diakon? Skylur must be talking to every Panethus House in the world, persuading them he hadn't lost his mind.

I didn't need to voice the full question.

"What he said was that Emergence is coming too quickly. If he had longer, he might try to persuade Basilikos Houses to change their ways. If humans weren't so alert, he might try to eradicate the worst of Basilikos. But it is what it is, and his alternative is to try for a new, expanded party that splits Basilikos and takes in the more acceptable of them. Isolate and marginalize the extremists."

Skylur was famously persuasive, but he hadn't gotten through to Bian on this point.

"I can, almost, see his logic. From a pragmatic viewpoint," Bian went on. "Diakon Flavia had been running the New York Athanate right under the noses of the Warders for over a century, and in all that time, it's been a refuge, like Ireland is now."

"Yes, refuge. Which means mix of diazoun Houses that follow Panethus and Basilikos creeds," Yelena said. "I heard something else strange about Flavia: she's not the only ruler of this little association. She shares the role with a Panethus House."

"And they just get along together?" I asked, stunned.

"Yes. But not just that. The Panethus co-ruler, House di Firenze. He was her Blood slave. Her toru. She freed him when she infused him."

It made no sense to me. Basilikos did not free their slaves, any more than they would make them Athanate. Or co-ruler of a little association hiding out under the very noses of the Warders.

Had I been guilty of a knee-jerk response when I'd heard about his new Diakon? Was there something clever in Skylur's decision? Had he seen something in the Long Island Athanate that he thought would work in the wider world?

I believed it—*wanted to believe it*—enough to wait and see.

And yet, Bian was still angry about something. Her eyes were starting to vamp out to black.

"What else?" I asked her.

She grimaced. "Diakon Flavia doesn't know the real reason behind Colorado becoming a closed Athanate community. Skylur's used her to tell everyone else that it's because we're testing out the effects of your infusion."

"Let me guess. She wants results."

"Lots of them. Now. And she's really unhappy with Haven being used as a temporary stop-off by your new pack. *Unacceptable risk*, she calls it."

"This is crap," I said. "On the infusion, we've hardly had time to observe how Scott has reacted. On the pack, it was Skylur himself who gave permission."

That got a slightly twisted smile from her.

"Not our best argument on Scott," she said. "I've *evaluated* him, and he seemed fine. You trust him enough to put him in charge of training your cubs."

She was right. Not an argument I could have used against Diakon Flavia.

Strangely enough, getting me angry was calming Bian down.

"Look," she said. "Skylur's trusting us to give her something. I understand that Tullah is the priority for reasons Flavia doesn't even know about. But if we go ahead with Mykayla today, I can spin that enough to give us a couple of days."

"Two days! We can't even start looking for Tullah until tomorrow."

I was getting too worked up. I could feel Yelena's eukori touch me, supporting me, but trying to calm me as well.

"Then your House has to step up," Bian went on relentlessly. "Yelena, Pia, Amanda. Even David. We need to know if your infusion is also passed on to others. We have a lot of volunteers from Ops 4-10."

"Once you've infused Mykayla, you could concentrate on finding Tullah while we handle the rest of it," Yelena said.

"I can't just abandon Mykayla after infusing her," I said. "And we don't have enough Mentors anyway."

"I'm making that point," Bian said. "Along with an argument that we need to train new Mentors if the crusis is different. I'm hoping we'll be able to get a couple of recruits, even if everybody is stretched thinly."

I sighed and buried my face in my hands. I couldn't be angry at Bian and Yelena. Skylur and his new Diakon were too far away for my anger at them to be satisfying.

"What else?" I asked. "Tove? Tamanny?"

"I've made the case that Tamanny's too young, and they accepted it. You'll have to come up with some arrangement that keeps her out of the way. Tove... you need to bind her or I'll need to cloud her memories and send her back home."

As she said that, I sensed Tove herself was coming down the corridor, eager to show me her latest purchases.

I felt sick. The last thing she needed right now was this kind of pressure.

Before she could get to us, Flint and Kane burst out of the room two doors down, the one with the secret elevator that connected to the dungeon and the Dark Library.

"Boss, we can do it," Flint called out. He came around the corner waving an old book.

"We don't need the Northern Adept League," Kane said, cannoning into him. "Don't need to wait. Don't need to do anything but spirit walk to find Tullah."

"Sort of," Flint amended. "With... err... a little tweak, here and there."

Chapter 50

"So, all we need is a sweat lodge and a good dose of mescaline," I said after they'd outlined the ritual that a madman had written down in some coded language. A language that my two Adepts claimed to be able to understand. More or less.

"Well, there's a sauna in the house somewhere." Flint refused to give up.

Bian snorted. "One right next to the gym." She was watching us with the sort of fascination people have for the sight of a car sliding down an icy hill.

"It's night, it's snowing and we're sitting fifteen miles as the crow flies outside of Denver, and we don't have peyote," I said. "We're about seven hundred miles north of the Chihuahua Desert, where the stuff grows. It takes—"

"I can score you some mesc."

I had forgotten all about Tove. She was standing in the doorway as if unsure whether to come in.

"Take me an hour or less downtown," she said quietly.

Her head was hanging down and she was finding the toes of her new shoes fascinating.

"Yes!" Kane said triumphantly.

"Hold it."

This was all wrong, and yet I could feel my oath surge in me, just as Kane's enthusiasm had reignited when she'd spoken.

As Bian had reminded me, I needed to talk to Tove, and there was no time to put it off.

We needed privacy. I remembered there were chairs in the room with the elevator. I guided Tove in there and closed the door behind us.

"You sure?" I asked as we sat. "Not just you can do it, but you want to do it?"

She nodded, not meeting my eyes.

"You learn," she said, meaning when you're an addict. "You can spot the clues. It won't take more than a couple of questions to find who deals in mesc."

She looked up and back down hurriedly. "I don't want the drugs." I could see her jaw working for several seconds. "I want to be free of them. But you guys need them for this crazy stuff."

"Crazy is right." I sighed. "You'll need to take someone with you. And you'll need to change. You look like a million dollars at the moment."

That got a fleeting smile, a genuinely pleased one, and a quiet "Thanks."

"So, you've probably got some ideas forming of what we really are. Still thinking we're a sex cult?"

"You're some kind of witches?" she said hesitantly. "Like for real?"

"Right idea. For some of us, anyway."

"That scary woman at the house this morning. You called her Hecate. I *know* she's a witch. I mean, just look at her. Hecate's a witch name, too."

I grinned, but I decided against outing the Northern Adept League just yet.

"It *is* for real," I said. "And we have to come to a decision about what you want to do. It's a big commitment to join us."

She nodded. Her heart rate was climbing, and her hands started their nervous butterfly movements.

"You remember what I said in the club? I can't really tell you what we are until you trust me, absolutely, and mean it when you ask me to help."

I pulled her to her feet and wrapped her carefully in a hug, alert to any holding back on her part.

"You go get us some peyote. It'll take over an hour to get you downtown and back. Just about enough time for you to think it over one last time. If you come back and say the word, I'll tell you what's involved in joining us."

"I always mess things up," she whispered. "What if I get too scared at the last minute? What if I go downtown and see things and I just want..."

"I'm already sure you don't want the drugs, Tove. Scared, I can handle. They always used to tell me in the army, if I *wasn't* scared I hadn't understood how dangerous it was." I pulled away from her and waited till she looked up. "If you don't want to join us, that's okay. We'll get you back to your parents and what's happened here in Denver will all fade into a sort of dream."

"You can do that?"

I nodded and she shivered.

"Can Rita come downtown with me?" she asked. "I don't know why, but she makes me feel safe."

I smiled at that. "You *are* safe with her. Of course Rita can take you. She'll need to change her clothes too. You can advise her on what to wear to blend in."

I took her back to the main living room, just as Rita returned.

"The cubs are being put through some late-night exercises by Annie," she said. "Scott's with them."

I explained briefly about needing to escort Tove to buy drugs. Rita's face betrayed not the slightest question about why I suddenly needed mescaline, but the corner of her mouth lifted a little when I explained they'd have to wear scruffy clothes to pass as addicts.

They left.

I tried calling Jen and still got no answer. There were texts waiting.

Zane: *Call me.*

Nope.

Mom: *Call. It's Kath. It's urgent.*

I closed my eyes and ran a trembling hand through my hair. Right now, my oath was singing in my Blood: Tullah. Tara. Hana. It didn't matter how much I wanted to try and get back on track with my family, I couldn't go and do it now. I'd do whatever I could, when I could, but I couldn't go back into Denver now. I was going to be needed here, when Tove got back.

I couldn't even call, because then I'd have to explain why I couldn't come.

I had to do *something*.

I called Manassah and asked David if he could help. Mom had actually met him a while back, and he wouldn't be as frightening as Yelena turning up on the doorstep. Or as impatient.

Bian heard it all. She was watching me sympathetically, but she didn't speak about it.

"Diana's offering us dinner in the dungeon," she said after I ended the call with David. "Highly recommended. She's cooked her pot-baked Greek lamb with *kritharaki* pasta. Not to be missed. And it'll pass the time till Tove gets back."

I snorted. "Wouldn't dare miss it. For dessert..."

Bian raised an eyebrow.

"Think you can swing a dinner invitation for Mykayla as well?"

She laughed. "Oh, yes. So, Mykayla gets her wish tonight. One of them."

I tried to join in, but my stomach was beginning to tighten at the thought of infusing Mykayla.

What if it goes wrong?

It was *really* bad timing, but at least Bian would have a first infusion to report tomorrow. It'd show Diakon Flavia that we were moving forward. Or give her a reason why we weren't. My heart stuttered again and my doubts must have shown.

"It'll be fine," Bian said. "Diana and I won't let it go wrong. Let me worry about Flavia."

I hoped my first experience of Skylur's new Diakon wasn't an indication of how our relationship would develop. I'd started off on the wrong foot with his last one, Naryn, and had never managed to repair the damage. It had made things difficult at a difficult time. I could do without that happening again, especially at the moment.

Chapter 51

Dinner was as good as Bian said it would be: succulent lamb and old red wine from the Rhône river in France, a wine that smelled of cedar wood with a taste that made me think of dark apricots dried in the desert sun.

"It's from Grange de Beauvenir, one of the oldest vineyards in Chateauneuf-du-Pape," Diana said. "A wine producer before they actually branded the region with that name, from the time when popes lived just down the river in Avignon. It's a beautiful place. Its cellars are dug right into the bedrock and you can still see some of the old buildings. Of course, it's a modern business now, Château La Nerthe, with an actual chateau. These older wines are one of Skylur's many favorites."

"Hope he doesn't miss them," I said, pouring myself some more, and she laughed.

I didn't have Mykayla for dessert. Instead Diana produced a selection of bite-sized baklava pastries, dripping honey. Bian insisted on feeding me a couple. *For practice*, she insisted, with a sexy little smile.

"That was all delicious, Diana," I said as the last of the baklava disappeared. The others joined in.

"It keeps me occupied down here in the dungeon." She waved away our compliments.

After a dinner that had been noisy with talk across the table, it grew quiet, and I sensed Kaothos stir invisibly around us.

Alice brought coffee to the table, and we changed seats again, as we had at each course.

Now Mykayla was sitting beside me. I could taste her eagerness, and her pulse set my fangs to throbbing in time.

To go along with the coffee, Diana sent a bottle of brandy around the table.

I poured myself a shot, a small one, and passed the bottle on.

The evening was a disorienting mix of the everyday and the paranormal—a dinner with friends, with good food and wine, with pleasant conversation. To be followed by me biting Mykayla's neck and infusing her.

I wasn't ready, but I knew I'd never feel ready, and events were shepherding me onwards.

Yelena and Bian cleared the table, over token protests from the rest of us lazy slackers.

Reaching around me to pick up my brandy glass, Yelena took the time to plant a kiss on my cheek and pat me.

"It will be fine," she whispered, at the same time she stole my cell.

One of the many issues adding to my feeling of uncertainty was worry about Tove, who had taken longer than she'd anticipated. But as I was about to ask Yelena to call and find out what was happening, the guards on the gate messaged Bian that Rita and Tove had arrived back with the drug.

Bian had organized one of her kin with the necessary knowledge to perform a chemical test to ensure the mescaline was pure, so there was yet another delay before we did anything with it.

Sensing the turmoil in my thoughts, Diana looked at me. "What do you wish to do, Amber?"

I took a deep breath. "Please ask them both to come down here."

I squeezed Mykayla's hand, and got back an answering squeeze.

As promised, Tove was going to find out what we were about. From a front row seat.

Rita and Tove stepped out of the elevator a minute later.

They were both still dressed in grunge—torn jeans, sloppy sweatshirts, messed hair, and yet they both looked great. I was surprised they'd passed as addicts, although, of course, Tove still qualified.

Tove was trying to imitate Rita's prowling way of walking. It was making them both laugh, and for a second I got another glimpse of that fresh-faced Minnesota teen. How would things have turned out of she'd never met Forsythe? If luck had given her a role to play in a TV series about fresh-faced Minnesota teens. Or if she'd given up in LA and gone home before anything bad had happened?

Too many what-ifs.

I had to deal with what was here and now.

Tove's laughter cut off as she took in the surroundings. The eerie Lyssae standing along the walls. The group waiting at the table.

I patted the empty seat next to me, on the other side from Mykayla, who'd put a possessive hand on my thigh.

Tove sat down, serious and wide-eyed again. Her heartrate soared. Then Rita chased Yelena away to allow her to sit next to Tove. She took her hand and Tove's heart steadied a little.

Interesting.

"Made up your mind?" I asked, trying to be gentle, but also getting straight to the point.

She nodded jerkily.

"I'm sorry I've been such a problem. I get that there are other things happening, important things, and I'm only in the way." Tears gleamed in her eyes as she raised them briefly to look at me. "You don't need this crap, but I know I need help. I can't have you or Rita there all the time for me. I know I'm not strong enough alone. I saw that tonight. You've seen it. I always mess things up."

"I don't see that at all," I said. "But we can work on that view of yourself as we go. What I need tonight is for you to understand what we are and what our helping you will mean. But I'll start by saying this: you will never really be alone again."

I could have offered her a million dollars for the reaction those words got: eyes wide and a deep-down longing that my half-open eukori had no problem in sensing.

"You thought we were all witches," I said. "Still think that? Rita, for example?"

Rita chuckled and Tove shook her head.

"They're witches," I pointed at Flint and Kane. "And Rita's a were-cougar," I said, and smelled the spike of adrenaline.

Tove turned quickly to Rita. The were-cougar simply smiled. Her eyes went a little more cat green, but she didn't say anything. Tove didn't let go of her hand.

I could see Tove trusted Rita to the extent that, when Rita didn't deny being a shapeshifter, Tove knew it was true.

Heartrate climbing again, she turned back to me.

"And although we don't use that name, people would call me a vampire."

Now the adrenaline really spiked. She knew I wasn't joking.

Her breathing doubled and her lips compressed, but instead of dropping her head again, she looked at me straight in the eyes.

My fangs were already throbbing, and that simple act, of *not* looking away, was what my Athanate needed to see.

Mine.

But first things first. Mykayla.

"You're going to have an unusual introduction, Tove," I said. "If you still want to go ahead after that, you'll learn the rest over the next few weeks, but tonight, right now, you'll see the heart of it."

I pulled Mykayla up and sat her on the table in front of me.

She was grinning and wriggling with excitement.

"This is supposed to be a solemn occasion," I said, and she giggled.

"How do you want me?" she asked, but I was already pushing and twisting her around till she was lying on the table, her head right in front of Tove.

Her T-shirt left her neck bare.

I let my eukori spread out slowly.

Mykayla was a pink rose glow, her whole body alight with anticipation. Tove pale as mist, struggling within herself, puzzled and then shocked at suddenly feeling everything that was going on in our bodies. She mistook the sensations, and her hand flew up to her mouth to check that she hadn't grown a pair of fangs as I had.

Rita was whispering explanations in her ear. I doubted much got through at that moment, but that voice grounded her.

I licked Mykayla's throat, fangs aching with the need to bite. I felt the tiny bumps of old healed bites under my tongue, the thud of her pulse as she arched her back, her ragged breath, her arms around me, urging me on.

Oh, yes.

My eukori slipped the leash and flooded out, touching everyone in the room. A much stronger eukori than a young Athanate should have, thanks to my Carpathian heritage, but I couldn't hide it.

And my fangs pierced Mykayla's neck, found her jugular. I *pulled*. Blood coursed into my taryma, down to the Athanate glands.

Yes!

Mykayla groaned and a sweet oblivion of pleasure beckoned, but Diana was already in my head, gently guiding. Mykayla couldn't have been safer, and there was more to do.

Diana stirred the same mix of sensation and memory that Pia had, when I'd infused Scott, but Diana's was so much richer. Almost too much to bear. And yet it came more easily the second time. Maybe because Mykayla was awake and eager. Her excitement produced flavors I couldn't quite describe. Emotions that seemed to soar away as I reached for them. Sensations in her body far beyond her throat.

Behind it all a deep feeling of sacred growth that came from all the Athanate in the room.

And stunned fascination from Tove.

Too soon, my fangs slipped from Mykayla's neck and I went back to licking her skin to speed the sealing of the blood vessels as she relaxed.

In contrast to Scott's infusion, there were no alarms. Mykayla's body had no violent reaction to my bio-agents.

Relaxed, but still eager. She nuzzled against me and whispered into my ear. "Still interested in the double whammy."

I laughed and gave her a brief kiss. No tongues.

"Loser's kiss," she muttered, but she was still happy, and she didn't complain when Bian lifted her up and away.

Tove had experienced all of it, through eukori. That was an... unconventional way to introduce someone to the Athanate world, and I wondered if it would work for or against.

For me, I'd expected my fangs to be satisfied after biting Mykayla, but the reverse seemed to be true: I was even more eager to bite Tove and welcome her into House Farrell.

Slowly. Slowly.

"That... was wild," she said.

"It's given you an idea of what's involved. Still want to be part of this?"

Linked by eukori, I followed every twitch of her decision, balanced precariously between fascination and fear. There was pressure in front of new friends. The mess of her life she was running away from. The fear of the unknown, because even having experienced it through Mykayla, the thought of being bitten, having fangs right in your jugular, was still terrifying.

But what I focused on was the desire to belong I felt in her. That desire was far stronger than her fear. Fighting against it was like fighting against gravity. It was drawing her to me and it would win.

But I was still surprised when she stood, a bit hesitantly, letting go of Rita's hand and edging her butt up to sit on the table.

There was so much I should be telling her first, about pleasure and binding, about Blood and kin, but my fangs were manifesting again and all I did was take her in my arms and lick her neck.

Her heart was pounding and her lungs heaving. I was too excited to calm her down, but I felt Yelena's eukori slip between us and sync both our bodies with hers.

"No fear," I whispered. "No pain."

Her hands crept up to rest on my back. She closed her eyes and she let her head fall back.

There was no real binding needed here. This girl wanted to belong so fiercely, all I had to do was open the door. And if she could conquer her fears like that, she needed no real help from me to conquer her addiction.

But there was an Athanate way to do it. For the second time in quick succession that night I sank my fangs into a throat and lit up with pleasure like an incandescent light bulb.

Mine.

Chapter 52

Diana had an antique French carriage clock on a side table. It struck twelve shortly after we'd cleared away from the table.

"The witching hour, I believe," Diana replied, her serious face belying her tone. "Kaothos is getting restless for us to find Tullah. Are you up to spirit walking tonight, young Adepts?"

Flint nodded.

The drugs had been tested and were pure. They sat in a small paper packet next to the clock.

"Only one of us needs to use it," Kane said. "Better be me."

"You set bars on fire when you get drunk," Flint said.

"Once. It was an accident, and the experience was valuable. I learned better control from that."

I'd sat down on a sofa with a sleepy Tove still draped around me. Rita lifted her off, just as Kane ended the argument with Flint by walking across to the table and dry-swallowing one of the tablets.

Everyone stood, a little uncertain how this was going to go.

"Leave Tove and Mykayla here with me," Diana said. She turned away, her voice tense. "The rest of you go up and help. Let's see if this spirit walking with drugs works."

Bian had ordered the sauna cleared and ready to be used as a sweat lodge.

It looked wrong: an ordinary sauna. Nothing magical about it.

The heat had been turned down a little because we were planning to be in it a long time.

Bian was telling us it wasn't *that* ordinary—it had been handmade from a mix of woods: spruce and aspen, cedar and hemlock. I put my head in briefly and inhaled, enjoying the mix of scents in a lungful of hot air. Sharp and soft. I liked it.

Bian was laying down some ground rules. She wanted Alice in the sauna to try and follow what my Adepts were going to do by instinct, and Bian herself was going to be with us as well, to stop everything if necessary.

"Okay," I said, when she finished. I shrugged. Time was wasting. "Let's go, people."

Kane was already looking a little unfocused. Having got this far, Flint was now hesitating.

Is he embarrassed?

I laughed, and shed my clothes with the economy of movement that any werewolf develops quickly.

"Come on, boys," I purred. "I don't bite. Much."

Kane giggled and shook his head.

Fair enough. They'd watched me biting Mykayla and Tove on the dinner table for the last hour.

The pair of them started to undress.

Oh, very nice.

Down girl! Behave.

However pleasant the view, it was chilly standing outside, and I'd probably be naked with them the rest of the night, so I slipped into the sauna to wait in the hot dark.

Alice and Bian came in first, and seated themselves opposite me, sweat immediately beading their bare skin. Then Flint and Kane. They sat on either side of me. Close.

"This ritual," Flint muttered. "Oronhiateka said he and his friends were touching."

"It's an orgy?" I asked, and Bian snickered.

It was dark in the sauna, but not so dark my wolfy eyes couldn't make out the details of my two Adepts. *Very* handsome. Also *very* well endowed and... interested.

"He didn't say that..."

"Not explicitly," Kane finished.

His heart rate had picked up, either because of the peyote or sitting naked, pressed against me. Or both of the above. His skin temperature had risen quicker than any of the rest of us. To my wolf vision, he was glowing softly in the dark.

Purely for the purposes of the ritual, of course, I reached my arm around him and pulled him close. He was sweating freely already.

I leaned us both back into Flint's embrace. Long powerful arms wrapped us all together.

I found their bodies were hard in all the right places.

And now I was having trouble with my own heart rate.

Concentrate.

We'd spoken over dinner, and I understood what my Adepts thought they knew about this crazy Native American's claim to be able to spirit walk across the whole continent. Oronhiateka said that anyone could spirit walk as far as they believed they could. All the mescaline did, according to him, was lift the barrier the mind imposed. Flint and Kane had suggested that only one person needed to actually take the drug. The others supporting the spirit walk could seek better if they didn't use it. However, we were going to be linked, aura to eukori, so this was going to be a helluva experience, one way or the other.

I knew I could spirit walk a long, long way, at least sometimes. I'd visited the graveyard with its soultree looming over it and I was sure it was in Ireland. But I could reach that far because of the power of the curse, and it only seemed to pull me one way. The soultree was rooted, for want of a better description. I couldn't search for Tullah if I couldn't even get out of a graveyard on the wrong side of the Atlantic.

My oath stirred in my Blood. *Enough delay.*

I reached out with eukori.

Neither of my Adepts held back. That was good and bad. Squashing our slippery, sweaty bodies together was having a predictable effect. It was like falling into a whirlwind of emotions and remembered sensations. Memories of them making love to Amanda chased feelings of raging lust.

My own imagination added to all that hot, slippery, sweaty stuff and embarrassed them even more.

Sweet.

But Tullah. Tara. Hana.

I had an oath.

"Listen, boys," I murmured to them, "I'd be disappointed if you *didn't* have a reaction to me, under the circumstances. Maybe we'll explore that with Amanda sometime, hmmm? But not tonight. We have a job, even if one of us is stoned."

Kane caught a glimpse of my image of him as a glowing man in my mind, and all three of us were suddenly seeing the walls of the sauna covered in radiant, naked men, climbing up the wooden slats.

His aura, under the influence of the mescaline, was strong and difficult to channel in the right direction.

This was nothing like the way Gabrielle approached a spirit walk. She was all about a calm and orderly progression. I got that this was shamanic, and almost the complete opposite of the Northern Adept League's structured method, but couldn't there be something we could use to help control things?

Flint fell back on shamanic rituals. He tapped out a rhythm on Kane's shoulder. Kane took it up, his hand clumsily trying to keep the beat on the wooden planks of the seat, ending up slow and fast, like he was playing drunken jazz.

The climbing men disappeared. In their place, I got the image of a lizard in the desert at nightfall, soft belly sliding along hot rocks, trying to absorb the last remnants of the sun's warmth in the chill of the night.

I was caught in the sensation of soft bellies and hot rocks.

And the sweaty body in my arms. My own body's reactions.

Kane's vivid hallucinations were pulling Flint and me back from the spirit walk.

How the hell was this supposed to work?

I tried concentrating on an image with no lizard. Just a sunset in the desert. Something old, from my days training in the army. I recalled my throat being dry, my body exhausted, but I'd been unable to stop watching as the sun went violent red, spilling across the horizon like an explosion in the clouds. The sky above it was burning yellow shading to indigo, then depthless black behind me.

What if the image of the desert is a clue? Is Tullah still hiding in the Arizona desert?

No. It was false. Random images bouncing between our heads. We had get past those and start *seeing* things. True things.

But forcing Kane away from the desert went too far in the wrong direction.

The sky melted and became gray stone. Stone that was encrusted with lichen. The church in Ireland, as I'd seen it last time. Its windows were black, like shadowed eyes, waiting. The graveyard lay silent around us. There was the soultree. Its branches spread through the night air. Its roots spread through the earth. Air and earth. Power pulsing up through the soles of our feet, swelling our lungs with every breath, our hearts with every beat. Calling to us.

Speaking without words.

Ash?

Something about ash.

Evil. This is evil.

Kane was speaking out loud and we were hearing echoes in our head.

Somewhere else, I knew Bian stirred, and I redoubled my efforts to pull away from this place. I needed to search for Tullah. We had to get back to that.

There was the beat of a raven's wings above me. Flint, lifting us out of the swamp of images that held us down in one place.

Then Kane started singing. Half a song, half a howl. Something that circled around and around hypnotically. I held his face against my throat, tried to hear only the sounds he made. And I finally managed to sync our hearts. Slow them.

For one moment, we were united, straining to return to where we needed to search. We hung in the sky, looking down on Haven.

Tullah floated in front of me, head down, dressed for summer. Lines, light as gossamer, ran over her skin, marking the edges of dragon scales. Not Tullah. Kaothos. She raised her head and her eyes were like lamps.

Look for Tara. For Tara. Tara.

Then as quickly as she'd come, she was gone, and my spirit was freed. I was rising. Soaring into the night sky, high above Colorado, so that the air rushed from my lungs in a scream.

Rising so high.

I can see the Rockies, and the land beyond to the west and north. High plains to the east. Deserts to the south. I can see the clouds in the valleys and the snow hiding the harsh lines of the mountains. I can see the stars and the sky. I can see the clusters of light where people huddle in the dark. I can see the great claw marks of rivers. Canyons. Arroyos. Lakes and streams. Cold and clear.

I can hear dogs howling in the cities below as they sense me.

Werewolves in the hills stop and test the air as I rush overhead.

Singing.

"Amber." Flint's voice was harsh. "You're making a hell of a noise in the spirit world."

He's right. I'm not the freaking queen of the night.

I stopped. Stopped searching, stopped flying. I floated and listened to the night instead.

Tara.

I made the drumbeat of our hearts sing her name.

Ta-ra. Ta-ra. Ta-ra.

If I find Tara, I'll find Tullah.

If this spirit seeking worked on connections between people, it would be *easier* to hunt for Tara. As strong as my connection with Tullah was, it couldn't compare to the connection with my twin sister's spirit.

The whisper of the night winds, rising.

West. Not south. On a line coming from Arizona.

The feel of the gathering storm. Coils of power writhing around me like sweaty arms. The night was swollen with the promise of power, like thunderstorms coming together.

Exhilarating. We were drunk on the power.

Kane howled at the sky and as the howl died away, he was Coyote. A glowing Coyote with eyes like fields of stars. A huge Coyote, big as a horse. Flint and I clung to his back as he took off like a greased hog at the county fair.

Time seemed both slow and fast. I watched lightning crawl like sun-lazy lizards over the bare bones of the Rockies; I saw waves of people come and go, seeking out the precious metals in the cold and lonely places. Bands played as railways were laid triumphantly and then the tracks rusted away into silence. Towns bloomed like fractal patterns behind my eyelids. Some vanished back into the brooding grasslands, others grew hungry and swollen around the knots of rails and roads, swallowing people into their darkness.

Blink and those people were gone. Ghosts. I was looking for ghosts in the high lonely places.

Not gone, not lost, not long ago, as the spirit walks.

There is someone out there, in the night. Someone in the great blank spaces between the huddled lights. Someone hearing me and answering.

The stars were gone and the night sky above was a black mirror. I looked and saw my twin sister. Sleeping. In a dark building. Cold. Caught in a dream.

Then stars shone through again and there was nothing of her presence but a whisper: *Amber?*

There's an aching in my chest. An unbearable loss. It's the void left by my Tara and my spirit guide, and it's the hunger to get them back. My arms are reaching for where I saw her, but distance is difficult to judge, skimming the spirit world like this.

I fell, screaming. Unbalanced Flint and Kane. We crashed to the ground in an explosion of snow. We weren't *there*, but we were bridging the physical and spirit worlds so much, our auras had the impact of a meteorite.

I was dizzy, clumsy. Partly because Kane was in that state from the drugs. Partly because seeing Tara had rocked me to my core.

I could hear our fall echoing in the spirit world. I could see clouds swirling, and things that weren't clouds. If Weaver was watching and listening in the middle of the night, we'd sent a signal out.

We had to get moving. Find Tara and stop before we attracted his attention here.

All it takes to fly again is belief.

But we'd come so far. I couldn't.

The power of the curse stirred beneath me. I could fly again. All I needed to do was let that power flow through me. So easy.

But Kane shuddered and it was the coyote who started us flying again, galloping madly through the air with us on his back once more.

He wanted to head south, but I pulled him more to the west.

There was something from my glimpse of Tara. Not even as much as an image. More like a word that sat just out of my grasp, refusing to be named. It was familiar as a shape in my mouth, as a reaction in my heart to the word, but the letters refused to settle on my tongue.

A cold building.

Surrounded by ice.

Kane slowed. We began to drift, lost in my confusion. Without an objective, our spirit walk had no impetus and we were pushed by the rising spirit winds.

Why would you surround a building with ice?

That wasn't quite right.

Ice. Frozen water. A building completely encased in frozen water. Snow, not ice.

Adepts used water as a medium for workings. Skylur's dungeon had water running down the walls, not because water was magical in itself but because of the symbolism. Adepts could imagine water imbued with magic and that made creating the working easier.

If Alice could shield the interior of a van, Tullah could hide in the same way.

But hidden by her working, she'd evaded the Empire's best Adepts. How was *I* going to be able to find her?

By *not* looking for her. I was looking for my twin sister, and *that* connection was stronger than her working.

I hoped.

I tried listening again. Pointed Kane southwest.

Where would she find a building covered in snow?

Anywhere in the mountains at the moment.

Which one would be safe?

A disused vacation home? Too risky. It had to be somewhere people wouldn't go in winter.

I looked down at the land beneath us. There were huge swathes of darkness between the lights of towns.

In one of those swathes.

An old ranch? Here?

We had flown into the Rockies. We were above the tree line. The Continental Divide, the country's spine, squirmed and slithered beneath us.

How far south were we?

I could see we were past the distinctive barbed hook of Uncompahgre Peak. We were in the heart of the San Juan range, south of Telluride.

Dad had brought me out here to hike. We'd done the trails. If Tara was hiding down there and if Tullah had taken Tara's advice about where to hide... it would be the same advice I'd have given.

So where would *I* hide?

A flurry of memories surfaced. Dad and I had gone walking in the summer. Thin cold air, eagles soaring, snow still clinging in patches above the tree line. Fields of boulders. Blue lakes and rushing creeks.

Abandoned mines.

We'd gone down a mine which had been kept open as a tourist attraction.

We'd visited ghost towns.

Ghost towns.

There were towns that had sprung up like mushrooms in the 1880s when people had been lured out here with the tales of gold and silver. They'd found their metals, but this was a harsh, high land with dozens of 14,000-foot peaks, and there wasn't enough wealth of minerals to justify the difficulties in the long term. The towns had died.

But not all the buildings were gone.

Where had Dad and I looked?

Names passed before my eyes: Howardsville, Buffalo Boy, Old Hundred, Highland Mary. Although the chance of those being visited in the winter was remote, some of them were too close to jeep tracks.

But there were others. Some whose names had been forgotten. Some just a derelict mill on a creek. Off the tracks.

I tried to visualize the pattern of them in the land below, overlaid with the Continental Divide Trail.

The three of us sank lower.

The snow made it difficult to see the way the land rose and fell. Smaller lakes and trails and entire ghost towns were hidden.

Yes. Somewhere up in the San Juan, off the main trails, you could stay invisible until the spring thaws, provided you had supplies.

Find an abandoned building, covered in snow and ice. Seal off part of it. Make a working to shield yourself. Become a ghost.

Tara and Tullah were here. Not far away.

The raven croaked in my ear. "We're making a lot of disturbance in the spirit world. We can't keep doing this. Others are sensing us already."

"Nearly there," I said.

But where? It was no good saying *somewhere in the San Juan*. We could come back here physically and spend the rest of the winter without finding them.

Yet Flint was right. My spirit eyes could see the majestic, stately sweep of snowstorms brushing the tops of the mountains and tumbling softly into the valleys. But overlaid on that was another movement: a deepness of the night, a twisting and swirling that had nothing to do with winds or the shape of the ground.

It came from every direction. Creeping along the spine of the Rockies, rushing over the foothills. Probing and darting. Spirit snake tongues testing the airs. Blind monsters seeking us out. Trying to catch us by feeling their way through the high ranges.

Just a few moments more.

"Amber! We have to go!"

I felt Flint pulling us back.

So close.

Tara is here.

I have to find her. My oath binds me.

I reached. Without Flint. Without Kane. I reached for the darkness inside me with the word it had given me.

Ash.

I called and it came.

There was a huge flash of lightning that tore us apart, tore the whole sky in two, and seared the image of the ground into my eyes.

And then I was falling, screaming, my body on fire.

Chapter 53

"I know where they are."

I'd been hauled out of the sauna when Bian decided that the spirit walk was over, based on the screaming.

Fair enough.

The flames had been an illusion, gone as quickly as they had arrived with the flash of lightning, and I should have laid there quietly while everyone else got over it.

I couldn't. I knew where Tullah was. Our enemies were hunting for her and we had to get out there and pick her up before anyone else did. I'd got an indication of where she was, despite her magical concealment, so I had to assume others could too, especially as we'd led them to the area.

"I know where they are," I repeated.

Alice was giving me the kind of look that says *of course you do, dear.*

After they'd gotten us out of the sauna, we'd been taken back down to the dungeon and laid out on the carpet.

It was quiet and cool. The room didn't move and there weren't glowing figures crawling up the walls. Although Kaothos remained unseen, I could sense her urgent presence.

Diana was worried, and that made me feel bad, but I couldn't stop.

"We need to call the Hecate," I said. "Her Adepts need to prepare a substantiation big enough to get to the San Juan and bring Tullah and the others back here."

Yelena was listening to me. She had my cell. She nodded and left to go upstairs and call Gwen.

Bian wasn't convinced.

"If all you know is she's hiding in the San Juan, the last thing we want to do is call attention to the area. Weaver's watching."

"More than watching," Flint said. "He's looking, and now he knows where to look."

"And she's well hidden, so he'll take a long time to find her," I said. "He can't look all the time. We'll have to sneak past."

"The League are the experts, but I think that might be difficult with a substantiation. And anyway, we'd have to look around too. Even if you're right and she's in the area, we don't know where she is exactly," Flint said.

"I do."

"How can you, if she's so well hidden?" Alice countered. "The Empire's best Adepts looked and they couldn't find her."

"Because she didn't want them to find her, and they had the whole continent to search."

"Amber, you don't even know that she's in the San Juan. Most of this spirit walk was no more than a drug-induced trip." Alice raised her hands as if appealing to the others. "Glowing men, lizards, old churchyards, seeing yourself in the sky?"

I felt Ash stir within me, whispering I could do it all without them. Or I could *make* them believe. The power seethed quietly inside me.

I shivered.

"I know it looked that way," I said. I spoke slowly, desperate to make myself clearer. "That image in the sky was my twin sister, Tara. She's there, with Tullah. That's the whole thing. Tullah *wants* to be found, but only by me, while she's hidden from everyone else. So she asked Tara where she should hide. Don't you see? Tara would have given the same answer I would. She would have known that. We have to go back and get them. I know where they are, because I know where Tara would have said to hide."

"Hush," Alice said, one hand stroking my hair. "You tried. No one could do more. You tried, but it didn't work. Your spirits traveled a tremendous distance, but you couldn't focus on the search with the effect of the drug flooding through your auras. Certainly not after everything that's happened to you. Goodness, Amber! You're still recovering from Weaver's attack on your mind, let alone taking your first spirit walk with the Northern Adept League."

"What if it's like the Hecate said after you got back from Erie?" Bian said. "Your brain takes clues and builds it all up into something you feel is consistent, but Weaver's house isn't translucent as a veil. In the same way, did you see Tara because you wanted to?"

She shrugged. "And you all say there were other spirit walkers attracted to the area. But how do we know it wasn't you all sharing drug-induced paranoia?"

Over her shoulder, Anubis was whispering in the shadows. *Keep well away from magic.*

Kaothos stirred, but she didn't speak, to my hearing.

"It could be drug-induced paranoia," I said, pushing Alice back and getting up. "Or it could be Weaver. We can't take the risk."

"No one is getting into the San Juan in a hurry," Bian said. "There have been snowstorms all night down the length of the Rockies."

On a clear day, you could make it down to San Juan from Denver in six or seven hours. I-70 would get you to Grand Junction. Even with snow, they'd have cleared that by morning. But the highway south after that...

Or you could go south on I-25, keeping out of the high passes, then head east. That'd take eight or nine hours. On a clear day.

But *every* way, in the middle of winter, with fresh snow on the mountain roads, it'd take much longer. Even in the Hill Bitch.

Too long. We need the Northern Adept League's magic. We need to go there using magic.

The elevator returned. Yelena was back, her face as blank and bleak as I'd ever seen it.

"Yelena! What's wrong?"

"No answer from Hecate," she said. "The others there say Hecate is missing. Few minutes ago, walked out of the apartment and disappeared. Spoke to no one."

There was a shocked silence, broken by Alice. "Weaver's taken her," she said.

"I don't know," Bian said. "I thought she was stronger than Weaver. What if they've been working together all the time?"

Working with Weaver didn't make sense to me, any more than Weaver being strong enough to take her by surprise. But that was all overshadowed. Without the Hecate, there wouldn't be a magical way to spirit Tullah out of the San Juan and back to safety in Denver.

Maybe she'd come back. Maybe she'd help. But we couldn't count on it. We were going to have to set out to do it the hard way, snow or not.

How?

I'd lay a bet that Ops 4-10 would have some kind of off-road vehicles.

All I needed to do was convince the others.

"It's no coincidence," I said. "The moment we find Tullah, the Hecate goes missing. One way or the other, this means that others know and they're looking for her down in San Juan."

"We haven't actually agreed you've found her," Alice said.

Diana stopped us.

"Kaothos says we must try to get Tullah back. *She* believes Amber."

Chapter 54

It was still hours to dawn. The Colonel wasn't at Haven; he was sleeping soundly at Manassah.

I called him on the secure landline. He was immediately alert as I explained the situation.

It turned out he had what was probably needed: he'd managed to 'acquire' a couple of ATVs developed for the US in the Middle East. The things looked like they'd escaped from a Mad Max film, but if they could handle sand, they were probably good to go on snow.

Even with them, by the time we got into the San Juan, it would be dark again, but that couldn't be helped.

He started to wrap up and hesitated.

"You know, there's a helicopter, if you can find a pilot. What about Victor?"

"I'd thought about Vic right away, but he wouldn't fly into the Rockies in this weather," I said. "And Jen's helicopter isn't designed for this kind of thing."

I didn't know any other helicopter pilots. And certainly none that were borderline insane.

"No. I mean Ops 4-10 has a helicopter," the colonel said. "It's an evaluation model from the ARH program. The Arapaho. It's stored in the barn, down in the lower field behind Haven."

I knew of the ARH program and the helicopter. Back in 2005, the US Army had put out a tender for a new Armed Reconnaissance Helicopter. The Arapaho didn't make the cut, but it'd impressed someone on the Ops 4-10 review team. It seemed, in the usual style of Ops 4-10, we got our prototype before the DoD closed the project down.

From what I remembered, it was rugged, had long range fuel tanks fitted, and it could carry six in addition to the crew.

But who'd fly it into the Rockies today?

Victor Gayle was my go-to pilot, but his insanity had limits.

"No pilot," I said.

Flint cleared his throat behind me. "There is."

"You?"

He shook his head and nodded to where Kane was still sprawled. "Get him down off the peyote, and he can fly us. He's the best."

Kane grinned and waved. He hadn't managed to get dressed yet.

"You do know that the storms haven't actually cleared the Rockies?" Bian said. "You'd be flying right into them."

Flint pursed his mouth.

"Kane does a kind of spirit walk when he flies. He can sense things like air currents and obstructions."

"And that works all the time?"

Flint cleared his throat again. "Most of the time."

"We walked away from every single landing," Kane called out. "Every single one."

I'd heard enough. The oath flared in my Blood. Whatever it took, I'd get them back.

"Colonel, please ask your team to prep the Arapaho," I said. "Put Annie in charge of the ATVs and send them out as backup, but I'm going to try flying with Kane and Flint, as soon as Kane's ready."

"One hour for the ATV team to get going," Colonel Laine said. "Two hours for the helicopter prep, and an hour after that for your pilot to get basic familiarity."

I hated the delay, but he was talking sense. The helicopter would still be hours quicker than the ATVs. It was about 200 miles down to the San Juan in a straight line, and we'd fly that in ninety minutes.

Weather permitting.

Seeing where you were going was only one major issue. Controlling the aircraft was another matter entirely. An *unfamiliar* aircraft. An hour wasn't nearly enough.

Getting back would take us longer, because we'd need to refuel. I could anticipate trouble finding an airfield willing to provide fuel on a day when helicopters shouldn't be flying. But we'd have Tullah back with us. And Tara. And Hana.

"Diana can nullify the remnants of the drug," Bian said cautiously.

"Gonna get bitten by the dungeon queen," Kane crooned.

Diana's face was pale and taut. "I can remove the chemicals," she said. "The mental effects will last longer, and there's no quick fix for them. All three of you are going to remain affected."

She hadn't said no. I focused on that and started work.

There was a computer with internet access in the dungeon. I pulled up maps of the San Juan and located the place that was still burned into my retinas by the lightning flash.

"There," I said, pointing to a distinctive string of three small lakes that had taken my dad and me a day to get up to and hike around. "There's the remains of an old ore-processing mill on the creek running out of the lowest one. That's where she'll be hiding."

I ignored the skeptical glances.

"Yelena and I will go in the Arapaho. That'll leave us four spaces for Tullah and anyone else with her."

"If there are more than that?"

"Annie and Ops 4-10 can bring them back. Once we've got Tullah, Weaver will be chasing us, not them."

"Can we send Alice with the Ops 4-10 team?" Bian asked. "To give them some magical backup."

"Good idea."

Alice shrugged and accepted.

"That's as much as can be done by you," Diana said. She turned to Yelena. "These two are yours." She indicated Flint and me. "I want them to rest for three hours."

Yelena nodded.

Bian shepherded us into the elevator. Her bedroom was on the top floor and, as described to me before, her bed was covered in black silk and the size of half a football field.

Not how I expected to come here for the first time.

Bian knew exactly what I was thinking, and almost smiled. She waited, arms folded, until Flint and I were snuggled on either side of Yelena and mainlining her pacifics before she would leave.

Thoughts chased each other around my head as I sank into sleep.

Diana was acting strangely. Was it going to be too late to get Kaothos back to Tullah?

Could Kane really fly a helicopter in a storm, or were we going to end up stuck on a hillside somewhere, waiting for rescue while everything else went to hell?

Ash? The Irish soultree. Was that power I could use?

Power from a curse. A curse that had reached all the way from Ireland and killed every first-born child of great-grandfather Padraig Farrell's family. If that wasn't evil, I didn't know what was.

But my Blood oath didn't care.

I'd use whatever I could, and face the consequences.

Chapter 55

For a supposed 'light reconnaissance' helicopter, the Arapaho was huge and noisy. The racket it was making, it was a good thing that Altau owned all the houses up on this ridge.

The helicopter had been painted matte black. The Gatling gun and the missile launch tubes had been removed, leaving a body that tried hard to be sleek. The effect was ruined by two ugly bulges: the overhead one that had been needed to accommodate the thousand horses of engine, and the forward pointing pod of the sensor suite.

There was no time to appreciate its looks, and anyway, my view of helicopters was they were ugly and useful in about equal amounts. Yelena and I got on board, stowed gear and strapped in. I was carrying a standard Ops 4-10 recon pack. Yelena had a cut-down version of it, picking the weapons she was most familiar with.

There were headsets, but the chatter of pilot to ATC was missing. We weren't going to try talking to anyone until we needed fuel.

We lurched off the ground. The tail swung around jerkily. The nose dipped. We started to chase our shadow westwards, picking up speed as the ground fell away.

The cabin had been stripped to essentials. Yelena and I were sitting on a frame bolted to the floor and we were looking right over Kane's shoulder.

He wasn't giggling, so I guess he'd had the peyote removed from his Blood.

I had a TacNet node connected to my headset, so I was getting updates from the colonel about Annie's progress along the roads. Atmospherics were making the connection poor, and I knew I'd lose it in the mountains, but it was good to hear.

Annie had chosen the southern route and I-25 was clear so far. She was making good progress as Kane flew us between Mount Evans and Mount Logan.

The view was spectacular. Tourists would pay for this trip, at least until we got to the part where the turbulence had the helicopter heaving and twisting.

I picked out 285 beneath us, the highway heading up past Bitter Hooks and Kenosha Pass.

It'd been clear air so far, but the clouds were boiling up against the mountains.

The helicopter fell like a fairground ride.

"Should not go down like this," Yelena ground out between clenched teeth.

"Not normally," I said, remembering lots of flights in Ops 4-10 that had been as bad. "We hit a patch of sinking air."

"Huh?"

Flint turned around in his seat. "It's clear just ahead. Look over to the right at the ridge."

We looked. The clouds were like a sea behind the ridge, spilling over and falling like a waterfall ten miles wide.

"That's what the air is doing too," he said. "That's why it's dangerous to get close to the leeward side of a mountain. Doesn't matter how strong your engine is, if the air is sinking faster than you can climb."

Yelena swallowed and looked out the other side as the Arapaho clawed itself out of the sinking air and bobbled upward.

There was only a blur of static on the TacNet; I'd lost contact with the colonel. I switched it off.

We turned southwest and flew back into cloud. Nothing around us but white.

There was a GPS map in the center of the console. From that, I could see Kane was heading for the Monarch Pass, at 'only' 11,000 feet. With a 13,000-foot peak upwind of it.

I could see him settle himself into the seat and smelled the sweat beading on his face.

Fear was good. Fear meant he knew how dangerous this was.

I wanted to touch him with eukori, help him, but I didn't dare disturb his concentration.

The instruments were all computerized. I didn't have the spinning dial of an altimeter to tell me we were falling steadily, but I could see the column on the display.

Flint started calling numbers in a steady voice.

He was changing the display on his side of the cockpit, and suddenly I saw he was looking at a synthetic vision image of the ground below us. I could see a road and I knew he was guiding us to land on it if we couldn't maintain our height. Better than landing a helicopter in a tree, or on the side of a hill.

Flint's voice slowed.

Stopped.

The image of the road on the display got smaller. The altitude started to spin the other way and my ears popped. We were through the pass and the ground was getting further away. The helicopter was flying smoothly.

"Damn," whispered Kane.

I took a few deep breaths. Terrain here was lower by three or four thousand feet. We'd lose that and more as we climbed into the San Juan. The area we were heading for was south of an escarpment where there were half a dozen 13,000-foot peaks, and even the lakes themselves were at an altitude of 12,000 feet.

It would be thin air, churning like a washing machine. The last place we should be flying in a helicopter. The San Juan was an unforgiving place at the best of times. In winter, in bad weather...

Too late to go back, even if my oath had let me.

The clouds grew sparse as we climbed and flew southwest. The ground was hidden; it was like looking at a sea of milk, pierced at regular intervals by dark rock. It had a stark beauty that was almost hypnotic.

Apart from his spirit walk senses, I could tell that Kane was using as little magic as he could to keep us as hidden as possible from Adept eyes. He was relying more on look-down radar and terrain systems. Certainly whenever we flew into the cloud and lost all visual references.

I watched the electronic instruments.

Then suddenly, we were circling.

"Down there," Flint said. He pointed at the map. "We can't go all the way to the lowest one. Kane thinks that'll be too close to the curl from the escarpment. We're aiming for the smallest lake, the one at the top. It's small enough it should be completely frozen over and we can land on it."

I gave him a thumbs-up. No point landing anywhere other than the flat surface of a lake. He could hover, but he'd use a lot of fuel and it'd be a nightmare getting Tullah and the others back up into the helicopter.

We sank down into the milk.

The cloud was a layer. It was clear beneath it, about 500 feet above the top of the ground, with the lakes lower than that. The depth of snow made it nearly impossible to make anything out. I could only 'see' where the string of lakes and creeks were because I knew they were the lowest points between the steep sides of the valley.

If the old mill was still there, at the creek leading out of the last, biggest lake, it was the lump in the snow.

Kane turned the helicopter sharply and we swooped down right where the smallest lake was supposed to be, and then the helicopter's nose lifted sharply.

Oh, shit!

I grabbed my seat and waited for the crash that didn't come.

Instead, the downdraft of the rotor had half-cleared the surface of the lake, revealing it was about fifteen yards wide and maybe thirty long. Kane rocked the helicopter back and forth, and then held it right over the center to wait out the blizzard of powder that was being kicked up.

Hurry up. Put it down, I wanted to yell, but I wanted to be able to fly home even more.

He lowered us an inch at a time.

The last of the snow cleared off the ice and I couldn't wait. I grabbed my gear and slid the door open. The ice looked good. I leaped down and it was like landing on concrete.

Yelena crunched down beside me.

As we scurried to the edge, the helicopter's skids came to rest on the ice. It creaked, but it held.

Great job.

Now it was our turn.

Chapter 56

Kane's part had been all about skill. Our contribution was all about brute strength and stamina.

The small lake was the highest of the chain. We had to make our way down to the lowest, through soft, powdery snow that came up to our chests.

We couldn't just wade through it, because the more you pushed into it, the more packed it became, until it was a solid wall. So we had a choice: every step we had to sweep the bulk of it aside, or we needed to pack it down so we could walk on it.

Snowshoes would have been a great idea. We had none.

It got worse when we finally made it to the second lake. The shallowest snow was in the middle, but I could feel the ice groaning through the snow. We were forced to make our way along the edge.

Every step was a struggle. We found the best way was to pull a foot out of the snow, kick it forward and down, pack some snow underneath until it would take our weight and then switch to the other foot. Every step.

It was exhausting, even for Athanate.

Flint had joined us, and we took turns leading.

Somewhere near the end of the second lake, where it would flow into a stream that ran into the third, we stopped to rest.

From there, we could look down to the third lake and the creek beyond it.

There was no visible movement from the lump I believed to be the mill.

Did that mean Tullah wasn't here?

What would I have done, if I'd been hiding in the mill and had heard a helicopter?

I'd have come out, but that didn't mean Tullah would.

My wolf eyes couldn't see any sign of warmth. Yelena had an IR scope on her MP5, and she was checking for the same thing without any luck.

"You sure, Boss?" she said.

"Sure? No. But she could have some kind of working that hides the heat."

Despite my words, I was starting to think we'd come all this way for a ghost.

"I'll lead for a while," Flint said and began to squeeze past.

He stopped, mid-step, and raised his head.

I listened. Apart from the wind, our panting and the thudding of our hearts, there didn't seem to be anything.

Wrong sense.

I felt it then. A shiver. The slightest touch of magic.

"Tullah's magic leaking?" I said.

Flint looked worried. "No. Lots of Adepts. Structured. Complex working. Not far away. Come on, we'd better hurry."

He started attacking the snow in front of us, desperately packing it down to force a way through. It was even deeper here than on the second lake. Again, we had to take a curved route to keep away from the weak ice in the middle.

"Can you use a working on this?" I said. "Freeze the snow so we can walk on top?"

"Yes," he panted. "But if they're hunting for magic, they'll sense that right away."

Stupid question.

He was right. The use of magic would be exactly what they were looking for.

A third of the way across the lake, Yelena took over from Flint, while I longed for a flame thrower.

All the time, the skin-tingling sense of magic was growing.

We were no more than a hundred yards from the mill, but we couldn't move any faster.

Yelena found a section where the snow was shallower in the lee of the steep valley slope. It wasn't exactly straight, but it was quicker, and as we rose, I could see down to where I thought the mill was.

Still nothing moved there.

Beyond the mill, to the right, I had a clear view north all the way to the ragged escarpment, about a half-mile away as the crow flies.

The wind was picking up and cloud flowed in silky white banners, over the high ridges of the escarpment and down towards us. It was eerily beautiful and frightening at the same time.

It seemed to be funneled at the midpoint of the range. The cloud grew quicker there. It swelled up and the streamers it put out didn't remind me of banners so much as reaching arms.

Flint stumbled and stopped.

"That's not normal cloud," he said. "That's the physical effect of a substantiation. A huge one."

Yelena redoubled her efforts, but it was as if we were moving in slow motion while the substantiation cloud swelled and began to pour over the escarpment.

"They know where we are," Flint said. "No point hiding anymore. I'm going to use a working."

He hauled Yelena back and knelt to thrust his hands into the snow.

There was a crackling noise like tiny firecrackers going off. The snow in a direct line to the mill shrunk and sank down, creating a path which took on the sheen of ice.

"Go," Flint said, still kneeling.

Yelena leaped over him, up onto the path.

It was ice, and the first thing she did was fall over as her feet slid out.

There was suddenly a heat signature from the buried mill. Someone was digging their way out.

I followed Yelena, slipping as she had.

The cloud no longer looked anything like a cloud. It was a swirling mass. A dark growth on the front formed and then shot upwards. It arced down toward us, trailing cloud in its wake like a rocket. When it hit to my right, at the top of the side of the valley, the snow exploded outwards. For a moment I thought it was some kind of magical mortar bomb, but as the wind began to whip the cloud of snow away, I could see the outline of a man, crouched down and aiming something at Yelena.

"Yelena!" I shouted. "On your right! Rifle!"

She looked, lost her footing and slipped.

There was a sharp crack.

I had no idea where the round went, but as long as it hadn't hit Yelena, it was good.

I pulled my MP5 into my shoulder, sighted. Uphill, only about eighty yards. Too short to bother adjusting for wind.

He was moving... turning...

Focus.

I squeezed the trigger.

Hit him high. Good enough. He spun around and fell backward.

"Left side!" Yelena yelled.

She pointed up at the opposite side of the valley. Another of the magical paratroopers had appeared there. He was smarter, hiding behind rocks and shooting at me.

We had no cover, no place to hide, other than burrowing into the snow.

I steadied myself and lined him up.

Three quick shots. I didn't have enough of him to aim for, but I got close enough to make him duck out of sight.

I slipped and slithered down after Yelena while he was hiding.

In the seconds I had looked away, the cloud-thing had come so damned *close*. It seemed to fill half the sky.

It threw out another man with a rifle, back on the right side of the valley. He didn't start shooting immediately, but in a moment we'd be caught in the crossfire with no cover.

"One each," Yelena shouted, firing her MP5 up at the one on the left.

I fired where I thought the one on the right would stick his head up.

Flint arrived, sliding on his belly.

"Can you shoot?"

"Tried once. Missed a barn from the inside," he said.

I looked at the cloud. *Too close*. Another minute and it'd be at the mill.

No other choice.

I thrust the MP5 into his hands. "Point it up there and pull the trigger anytime something moves," I said.

I started to run as fast as I could on the slippery path.

If that cloud reached the mill with Tullah still inside, I'd lose her.

There was a movement ahead.

"Amber! Amber, help!"

It was Tullah. She came up out of the snow like a drowning swimmer.

Flint's ice bridge hadn't reached all the way, and there was no time.

No time.

I slipped and fell.

She disappeared into the snow. It was even deeper around the old mill.

I got up and ran again.

There were shots from behind me. A round went *wheep* past my head. Another.

No time.

The cloud loomed over the mill. Swallowed it.

Tullah clawed her way out of the snow and onto the ice path. She started to run, legs pumping, arms flailing to stay balanced, and her black hair whipping like a flag behind her.

The cloud billowed around both of us. I couldn't even see the icy path beneath my feet.

Sweat froze instantly on my forehead.

"Amber!"

I couldn't see her.

"Tullah! Keep moving. Here! To my voice."

The inside of the cloud stung like ice in a blizzard. There were shapes moving inside it. Shadows. I stumbled, slipped, righted myself.

"Tullah!" I screamed.

Nothing. Darker and darker. No light. No sound, not even the wind. Nothing but pain.

I could feel the cloud now, as a creature. Feel the strength in it. The taste of many minds, merging into a great machine. A machine which rolled forwards, crushing, unstoppable, uncaring.

Too strong.

Weaver. I could sense him in the fog. I lashed out, but there was nothing to hit, nothing to grab.

The world went pale again, turned upside down. I saw a flash of sky, immediately blotted out. The fog around me flared and flickered with lightning. My skin crawled with the feeling of magic.

It wasn't one substantiation any more.

Two? Three?

Fighting. They clashed and I was caught in the center.

A rescue?

The original substantiation, Weaver's, was stronger, better prepared, but unwilling to fight. I could feel the changes inside, the sense of withdrawal.

A moment's hesitation.

That's all it had taken for Flint and Kane to break the Hecate's substantiation back in Denver. But they knew what they were doing.

What could I do?

My strength was my anger. Speaks-to-wolves had told me that. It was all I had.

Don't think of the physical world. Don't lash out. This isn't a place for strength of body, but strength of purpose, focus...

The darkness stirred within me.

Ash.

I'd defeated Matlal because he'd built a channel, a way of touching me with eukori, and I'd been able to direct my anger back down that channel. These substantiations... were they the same?

I sensed targets in the roiling fog around me.

Lightning burst overhead. I caught a searing image of all of us, swimming in the fog.

Weaver. Tullah. Tara...

Tara! Hana!

Gwen!

An Adept. From the Empire of Heaven. I recognized him from the Assembly in LA.

Another. Wrapped in a bloody skin, wearing a horrifying golden Aztec mask. From Matlal.

The power inside me could not be stopped now. It was bursting out.

It was as much as I could do to hold it back from Tullah, from Hana and Tara. And from Gwen.

I screamed as it flowed through me.

Lit them up.

Broke them apart.

One last explosion of pain and I was thrown backwards. I was a hundred feet in the air, above the snowy lakes hidden in the San Juan. I had a moment to grasp how utterly I'd been defeated before all the substantiations snapped away and fled, thrashing like snakes.

Taking Tullah and Tara and Hana.

Weaver had them.

I'd been betrayed. Doubly betrayed. The Hecate hadn't arrived like the cavalry to rescue me. In that last instant, as I'd fought Weaver with the power I hadn't wanted to use, the power that could have dissolved his substantiation around him, she'd protected him.

Tullah was beyond my reach, and Tara and Hana were gone too.

And then I fell, down, down to the deep, cold embrace of the powdery snow.

Chapter 57

"I'm fine."

Lie.

The dungeon was quiet: it had the choking stillness of a funeral after I finished my summary of what had happened in the San Juan.

After Tullah had been taken, Flint had dug me out of the twelve-foot snowdrift I'd fallen into and Yelena had captured the Adepts that Weaver had abandoned.

There'd been nothing else at the mill. No sign of anyone but Tullah.

The substantiations had all disappeared. The clouds in the sky were just clouds.

Kane had flown into Telluride and persuaded them to refuel the helicopter.

Then he'd returned to take us and the captives back to Denver by the safer southern route. The long way back. That gave me too much time to think.

I'd barely spoken till I got back to Haven and met the others in the dungeon.

"The Northern Adept League betrayed us," I said to break the silence. "Maybe not the whole League was in on it, but certainly the Hecate. She was there. When I saw her in the substantiations, I thought she'd come to try and rescue me, but she was there with Weaver. She protected him. I saw it."

I spoke the words, and yet I still couldn't believe it.

I'd *trusted* her.

"And now we have not just Weaver to worry about, but the Empire and Matlal," Alice said.

"We had them to worry about without this," Diana responded. "They don't *know* what we were doing, but Weaver has Tullah. That's what we have to focus on first."

"I don't understand how you attacked the substantiations," Bian said.

"This power, or curse, or whatever it is." I frowned and tried to remember exactly what I'd done. "In the spirit world, you're connected. Not quite like I was connected to Matlal when he attacked me in the Assembly, but something like that. I just channeled it through the connection."

If I were doing it again, I'd do it differently. I'd focus on one at a time. I'd weakened the effect by trying too much. I should have killed Weaver.

But I hadn't. Now he had Tullah.

He'd been trying to find her because he thought she still hosted Kaothos, but he'd have realized that mistake as soon as she broke cover.

Maybe he thought he could use threats against Tullah to force us to hand Kaothos over.

I felt sick to my stomach. We couldn't do that. Not even for Tullah.

Surely, he realized that. Yet he'd gone ahead, at some risk, and taken her.

So he must know she was a way of getting Kaothos, that there was a way of using the link between Tullah and her dragon.

"Now Weaver has them all," I said. "Tullah, Hana and Tara."

"You need Hana and Tara back," Kaothos said. "In the same way I need to return to Tullah."

"We find where he's got Tullah, and we go there and get her back," I said. "I don't know how yet, but it's all we can do. I found her once using Flint and Kane. I can find her again."

"Except now, Weaver's got her and he'll know exactly what he's got," Bian said. "He'll be expecting an attack."

Kaothos hissed unhappily. "Finding her in the way you did would open a connection again. He would be waiting. He would use that connection to trace back to here."

"Are we running scared?"

It was Alice who responded. "However it's happened, Weaver's much stronger than we thought originally. And..."

"And now, he's got the Hecate on his side."

I said the words and felt the turmoil inside me.

Bian stood away from the table, putting her hand to the ear where her tiny comm system sat.

"Are you sure?" she said, and then a moment later: "Alone?"

"Amber." She turned back. "There's someone to see you at the gate."

I frowned. "Who?"

"The Hecate's little friend, Gabrielle."

Chapter 58

Bian wasn't about to let her into the building, and I needed to get out of the dungeon for a while.

Still, I took my time walking to the gate. *Let her sweat.*

I'd grabbed Alex's borrowed ski jacket on the way out and wrapped myself into it. Too long, too wide, but it smelled like him. I'd take that small comfort, today. I didn't know what I was feeling: anger, pain, guilt. Confusion. All mixed up. All looking for some outlet. All urging me to do something. And the sick feeling that I knew the wrong response would make things worse.

Learn more first, I told myself.

In the late afternoon gloom, Gabrielle was standing next to a cheap rental car, dressed in her snowboarder grunge, red hair hidden under a ski cap. A couple of the guards were watching her. There were no guns aimed at her, yet, but she was sensibly keeping her hands in sight and her mouth shut.

She looked pale, and there was a determined frown creasing her forehead.

I slipped through the gate and stood in front of her, waiting.

"The others have left Denver," she blurted out. "They wanted to go home to wait for instructions. They don't know what's happening."

They don't know. Interesting way of putting it.

"What do *you* think's happening, Gabrielle?"

"I don't know exactly." She blinked. Her lips pressed together briefly, as if the words had to be forced out. "But I know she wouldn't betray you."

I looked at her. She looked right back, so I let the anger surface and the Athanate dominance come through. I got that narrow, sharp sight which told me my eyes had vamped out.

Gabrielle wasn't Athanate, but her aura was sensitive enough to pick up Athanate signals, and she knew enough about Athanate to understand she was in danger.

But she didn't take a backwards step.

"You mean *you* don't believe she would betray me," I said.

She swallowed to ease a dry throat and her voice came out hoarse but steady.

"You don't believe she would either."

I let the words fall. Didn't show I'd even heard them.

She still didn't back down; neither did she weaken the effect of her words by saying anything else.

Impressive.

I'd already respected her on the basis that she'd obviously taken a senior position in a powerful community of Adepts while still very young.

But is that all there is to it?

I let a whole minute pass in our staring match before I spoke.

"I think we should take a stroll." I reached back and pulled my hoodie out to keep the wind off my neck, zipped up the jacket, put my hands in the pockets.

One of the guards moved forward as if to accompany us.

"Alone."

"Ma'am." He stepped back. One of Bian's kin. He'd call her as soon as my back was turned. Bian hadn't been happy for me to come out and talk to Gabrielle alone. I wasn't sure why I insisted in the first place. It felt right.

Learn more. With Bian out here, Gabrielle might stop talking.

We had five minutes before Bian came out, I guessed.

I took Gabrielle's elbow to guide her down the road, and we'd walked fifty yards before I spoke again.

"That's quite a statement—that I don't believe she betrayed me."

"But I'm right, aren't I? You *don't* believe she's betrayed you."

"You're not right. You're not wrong. I'm at the point where I can't decide. The thing is, I know what I saw. I'm wondering what you *think* you know happened."

"I don't know."

"You don't know, but you're still convinced she didn't betray us?"

"I said 'you'. I meant you alone. Yes. I'm convinced."

Absolute, utter belief in her voice.

I changed tack slightly. "There's a difference between betraying me and betraying everyone else?" I waved at Haven.

She stared off across snowbound gardens, not meeting my eye.

"Maybe."

I said nothing, and let the silence pressure her into justifying herself.

"I mean, what if Diana doesn't want Kaothos to go back to Tullah?"

I snorted, even while I was thinking *yeah, but really, what if? Who wouldn't want that power?*

"What if Flint and Kane aren't what they seem?" she went on. "They turn up here and you know practically nothing about them—"

"I know more about them than I know about you." I stopped her. "So spare me the paranoia and tell me why you think I'm on the side of the angels."

"Gwen said to trust you," she said. "I trust her."

Again, that absolute confidence.

"Okay. So what else did... Gwen say?"

If I couldn't even decide what to call her, I was really mixed up.

"That you'd messed up with your search," Gabrielle said, "and everyone knew where Tullah was now. So she had—"

"That's odd, 'cause y'know, Yelena told me, when she called the apartment in RiNo, they said the Hecate had walked out without talking to anyone. And that was just after we finished our search."

Gabrielle twitched. Unlike the leader of her community, she had twitches and tells that I could read. I'd just caught a lie. By omission maybe, but still...

She squared her shoulders. "Gwen spoke to me before she left. She said not to tell the others."

"She doesn't trust them?"

"I don't know. There wasn't time to ask."

I could see the frustration in the way her jaw clenched. She had to know that her story was sounding paper-thin and yet she was determined to deliver it.

I could hear the crunch of Bian's footsteps in the snow, coming out of the gate behind us.

"So I'm to be trusted," I said. "Even though I messed up and let other people find where Tullah was. And Gwen has had to go out and fix things? Is that what she told you?"

"Kind of."

"So if she's got it all in hand, why do you need to come here and talk to me?"

"Because she said she couldn't do it all on her own. She needs you."

More twitches, more tells. A little doubt for a change.

"To do what?" I asked.

Gabrielle swallowed, took a deep breath. "To get Diana close enough to Tullah so that Kaothos can make the jump."

"Well, that answers the question we were just discussing down in the dungeon." Bian spoke from behind us.

"What?" Gabrielle looked confused.

"We were wondering how kidnapping Tullah could get Weaver access to Kaothos. What plan he'd come up with for getting the dragon. Now we have our answer. You come here and tell Amber to take Diana to Weaver."

"No, it's not like that!" Gabrielle said. "I'm not on his side. Neither is Gwen."

"Really? Let's see," Bian said. "The Hecate gets our attention by kidnapping Amber and letting her go, then gets an invitation to visit Manassah, because all she wants is to talk, apparently. So reasonable. But at that point Amber has some crisis with a working the Hecate claims comes from Weaver and that only she can help with, so we all feel indebted to her. Indebted so much that Diana invites her out to Haven. But once she's seen the setup here, the Hecate knows she can't persuade Diana and Kaothos to leave the dungeon, can't kidnap her, so she comes up with another way—use Amber to take Kaothos directly to Weaver."

Gabrielle's mouth opened and closed. Equal parts shock and outrage.

"But how to persuade Amber to do that?" Bian went on. "The Hecate can't, not once she's had to go and rescue Weaver while helping him to kidnap Tullah. But luckily for her she has someone who might be able to convince us. Someone young, bright and unconventional and loyal to the Hecate. Exactly the sort of person who would appeal to us, and who just happens to have been introduced to us."

"I'm not lying to you!" Gabrielle shouted.

"Of course not. It would be dangerous to lie to a roomful of Athanate and Adepts. Anyway, the Hecate would never let the rest of her coven in on her secret. In fact, she'd leave them with the absolute conviction that we're on the same side. Especially the person she'd selected to appeal to us."

"That's ridiculous," Gabrielle said, but for the first time a real hint of doubt had crept into her voice.

"Is it?" Bian raised her eyebrows. "What was the decision process the Hecate went through before she brought you along to Manassah that first visit? Seniority? Capability?"

Bian began crowding Gabrielle, making her step back.

"I specialize in substantiations," Gabrielle said.

"You're the best she has for that?"

Gabrielle's mouth snapped shut. Clearly she wasn't.

And Bian was right about another thing. We'd all taken a liking to Gabrielle. Even Bian. I didn't want the young woman to be part of any betrayal. I wanted to believe her.

"Hold it," I said, pushing Bian back. "This is all too complex. No one plans like that. Too many unknowns. Too many variables."

"You're not going to take Diana out of that dungeon," Bian said, her tone flat and final.

"I'm not suggesting I would."

Of course, Kaothos *could* reach out of the dungeon, whatever the rest of them thought. She'd spoken to me just before our peyote-fueled spirit walk.

I'd keep that quiet for the moment. If Kaothos wasn't talking about it, neither was I.

"I'm not lying to you," Gabrielle said. She was almost in tears. There was little of the brash and confident young Adept now. "You can check. Like you do with kin."

"You don't know what you're talking about, Gabrielle." I let my fangs show briefly and saw the flicker of shock in her eyes. "I don't think you're lying to us, but Bian has a point. *If* the Hecate wanted to trick us, she wouldn't send anyone who actually knew her real plans. She'd send you in blind."

Gabrielle just shook her head and looked down.

Bian put a hand on her shoulder. "I'm sorry, Gabrielle. Amber's right. All this magic stuff has made me paranoid. Maybe there's another explanation. Let's walk back, and you tell me exactly what the Hecate said to you."

I glared at Bian. Now she wanted me to be the bad cop.

We turned and began the walk while Gabrielle talked hesitantly.

"It was early morning and I was asleep. She woke me. She said you'd tried spirit walking to find Tullah. You'd used some kind of hallucinogenic inhibition suppressant. I mean, we know that kind of thing works, but it's not controllable. It's like you're lighting bonfires in the spirit world." She sneaked a glance at me, genuine worry on her face. "Not what you personally should have been playing with, Amber. Not while you were recovering from Weaver's working."

I shrugged as if I didn't care. Hard choices.

And yet, we'd screwed up because of what I'd agreed to do.

Maybe Tullah would have been safe for a while longer, high in the San Juan, hidden in the mill by her spells.

Gabrielle went on. "Gwen said Weaver was alert. Expecting us to do something. But it was worse than that; both Matlal and the Empire were watching as well. It was just because of that kind of thing that we said yesterday that we had to do a substantiation. You can keep that quieter, if you cut it right down to essentials."

"Nice of you to tell us all that," I said, but didn't press it.

"We didn't believe Flint and Kane would try a crazy thing like a spirit walk with drugs." She huffed. "We've been tracking them for ages and they'd never done anything like that before. Well, anyway, you did. They heard. Weaver, Matlal, the Empire. They were all watching, waiting for you to find something. In fact, I think they were holding back because they all thought this had to be a distraction."

Note to self: now that you know how, set up a distraction next time.

Aloud I said: "But Matlal and the Empire of Heaven didn't know what—"

"They know there's a dragon spirit," Gabrielle said. "They know where *you* are. They'd know *we* were here as well. They'd know about Weaver. They'd put it all together."

"I thought you had gone back to plan and rest," Bian said. "How was it that Gwen knew what was going on in the spirit world?"

"We'd done the planning. We were resting. Gwen is..." Gabrielle stumbled before going on. "She's different. Stronger. Her spirit guide is stronger, more independent."

"A bit like a dragon," I said.

"*What* is her spirit guide?" Bian said. "Why can't anyone else see it?"

"I don't know," Gabrielle replied.

Truth again, as far as I could tell.

"Okay, so somehow her spirit guide was alerted to what was going on, heard the noise of our spirit walk, saw that others were waiting in ambush, and woke the Hecate," Bian said. "And then what?"

"Gwen said she had to do something quickly. That Weaver was the least worst option. It was very dangerous. She made her own substantiation. She used it to go to him."

"What about helping *us*?"

Gabrielle was hesitant.

"I *think* she thought she couldn't," she said slowly. "I mean, it would have taken too long to get the rest of our coven to create a robust substantiation. She would be alone, at the limit of her reach, and she'd had almost no time to prepare. She's strong, but if she'd attacked all three of them alone, to defend you, she'd have failed."

Fair point.

"So you're saying the reason she made a deal with Weaver and helped him against Matlal and the Empire was that we'd have a better chance to rescue Tullah?"

"Yes. If either of those other two got her, you'd never get her back. We think Weaver's not so far away and he's not as strong as them."

"But he beat their attack."

With my help.

I'd keep that quiet.

"Two of them. At the limit of *their* range, and with help from Gwen."

It was consistent at least, even if neither Bian nor I could really judge the truth of her claims about the balance of strengths for substantiations in the spirit world.

I believed Gabrielle. But then I'd believed Gwen. Now, I wasn't quite ready to finally decide on the Hecate. She didn't make it easy, with the shapeshifting face and mixed mannerisms. One minute, a sweet face but disturbingly, no tells, then the next minute, that ice-bitch look and all predator body language. And keeping her spirit guide hidden, even from her own coven.

"Lay it out. How is she suggesting we get Tullah back?" I said as we got back to the gate.

Gabrielle licked her lips nervously.

"Weaver can't build a shield around Tullah strong enough to stop Kaothos under every circumstance. But Kaothos is still growing. She can't reach all the way through the spirit world or across the physical world to Tullah. You need to get her up close in this world."

"Where Weaver might have all sorts of traps set up that we don't understand and can't even sense." Bian wasn't buying.

"Of course he'll be setting up traps, but you have to trust me," Gabrielle said. "Get her close enough, and Kaothos can make Weaver's own traps eat him. Literally."

"How close?"

"I don't really know." She looked down miserably. "I don't think anyone does. Kaothos herself will only know when she's there."

"Wonderful." Bian closed her eyes and sighed. "Not persuaded yet."

I'd known that already. I could see Gabrielle's jaw tightening. She'd stand and argue the rest of the day, if she was allowed to.

"We need to think about the rest of it for a moment," I said. "The Empire of Heaven and Matlal. All they'll have seen is Tullah's kidnapping. No dragon present. But either they'll be intrigued enough to try and take

Tullah from Weaver, or they'll be watching us and waiting to spring traps of their own."

Bian nodded. "We have to talk this through with Skylur," she said, eyes flicking to me. "He's been asking to talk to you."

I could imagine the tone of that *asking*.

I reached for my cell before remembering it wasn't there. Yelena had taken it.

"Oh, shit. He didn't call my cell, did he?"

"He did," Bian said.

I winced. "What did Yelena say?"

"Oh, she was very polite. Told him to take a number."

"There are more calls?"

"David, for one. And your mother. Probably the same topic." Bian shook her head. "Then Alex and Jen. And Zane. And your shoemaker, I hear. You need to talk to the boss first. I'll go set up the conference system rather than use your cell phone."

She turned on her heel.

"What about me?" Gabrielle asked.

Bian turned back. "I can see you're telling the truth, as you know it. But for the moment, consider yourself my prisoner."

The sparky Gabrielle rallied and tried to show she wasn't scared.

"Going to tie me up in your dungeon, then?"

Wrong person to say that to.

Bian's eyes went all smoky. "I hadn't thought of that," she said, slowly. "What a good idea."

Chapter 59

The conference system in Haven was a windowless room with a huge screen on one side, and a conference table in front of it.

The two of us pulled up chairs and sat, and Bian dialed a number on a pad in front of her.

The screen cleared to show a luxury penthouse apartment with the lights of New York skyscrapers in the background.

The tone announcing the connection was still dying away when Skylur appeared and sat down.

He was wearing a suit. I'd seen him in different clothes before, and always I'd thought how unexceptional he looked. Until you saw the eyes. Today, in the suit, he looked like a very powerful man who was very angry.

"I've had the bare bones of it from Bian," he said without any greeting. "Update me, Amber."

"We failed to get Tullah back. We acted because of the concerns—"

"Yes, I know. It might become difficult to move Kaothos if we wait any longer, and you had some justifiable concerns that Weaver could track where Tullah was, given time."

"And we didn't entirely trust the Northern Adept League."

He caught my slight hesitation. "Which was justified?"

I spread my hands. "The coven itself... don't know. We have one of the coven here, and Bian and I think she's telling the truth when she says they didn't intend to betray us."

"She's telling the truth as she knows it," Bian added.

"What does the New York Hecate say?" I asked. "She's equivalent in rank, as I understand it."

"Indeed," Skylur said. "I haven't spoken to her face to face. In a telephone conversation, she said that she knew nothing of any intended betrayal. However, she also said that the dragon is of such significance that Hecate Gwendolyn Enkeliekki would commit any act to ensure the dragon is protected."

Bian snorted. "Protected from people *she* decides the dragon needs to be protected from."

"Yes, that *is* the problem, isn't it." Skylur sighed. "Wouldn't it be easier if the dragon just stayed with Diana?"

It would be easier for some people and not for others. I kept that to myself.

"Any reaction from the Empire?" Bian asked.

"No. They wouldn't show their hand this early, whatever they deduced from what happened." Skylur looked thoughtful. "They might even think we were running some kind of trap to draw Matlal out. And Matlal himself... we can't be any more vigilant, but I'll have to accelerate the project of sending Ops 4-10 troops to every House to ensure we're strong enough to defend ourselves."

Those troops weren't supposed to know that Diana and Kaothos were in the dungeon. I'd back Bian's attention to detail on security, but if just one of them had some inkling and it somehow leaked that we'd duped the Empire, the fragile construction which was the Assembly would fall apart. Skylur was balancing risks here.

"What about what you intend to do, Amber?" Skylur asked.

I explained our conversation with Gabrielle, who was now in the dungeon. Not tied up yet.

"I'm going to ask her to do the direction-finding working that the coven was planning on doing, that she says is quiet and safe. She'll have to find a way to work with our Adepts. I'm sure it won't be as good as the working the Hecate was intending to do, but I'll take that as long as it does the job."

"It does suggest the Hecate wasn't betraying you," Skylur said. "I mean that she left you the means to find Tullah again with Gabrielle."

"Or her plan from the beginning—" Bian began, and Skylur stopped her.

"Too many holes in that, Bian. Let's imagine Amber has a couple of readings on the direction Tullah is being kept in to triangulate from. Let's imagine that's a place, because Adept workings are better at defenses and traps than attacks." He clapped his hands together. "How wide is that area? What do you do then?"

"I think it'll be quite a large area," I said. "I think precision requires more power than Gabrielle can manage. So I'm going to need people on the ground, searching. Lots of them."

I'd been hoping for Ops 4-10.

Skylur knew that.

He thought carefully before answering.

"I won't empty Haven immediately. Use those you can, while you can. What about the werewolves?"

"I'll be getting right on it after this. But remember, they're also on alert."

"Because the Denver pack beat the Confederation last time, and the Confederation needs to show their strength to their own side," Skylur said. "I understand."

"It's now part of the Southern League, rather than the Denver pack alone," I said.

"Ah, yes, of course. I have someone from Felix and Cameron scheduled to visit me. An alpha from Los Angeles. Apparently he wants to transfer his territory to New York. Keen to get into the political scene."

Skylur allowed himself the smallest of smiles at the improbability of a Were eagerly getting into politics.

I snorted. Felix and Cameron had taken my advice.

Skylur glanced at the tablet on the seat next to him. An alert for his next meeting, no doubt.

"I authorize Bian to give you everything you need for this, Amber. Apart from more Athanate. My rules about Athanate visiting Colorado will have to stand. And we've just spoken about *finding* Tullah. Not about rescue. Call me again when you have a plan."

"Thanks," I said. "You might keep Diakon Flavia off our backs for a while as well. That would help."

"The infusion project." Skylur stroked his chin. "My Diakon doesn't know the real reason that Colorado is an exclusion zone, and I'm not about to tell her. No one else outside of your Houses knows about Diana and Kaothos. Not even Naryn or Tarez."

He sat forward and picked up his tablet. "If I remove the project overview from her and have you report directly to me, that's going to make her suspicious. Hmmm. Maybe I *will* do that."

The connection cut.

Chapter 60

Having retrieved my cell from Yelena, I found David's text as cryptic as it was specific: *Don't talk to yr family. My house asap.*

First, I got Gabrielle up from the dungeon and put her in a room with Flint, Kane and Alice. I threatened I'd never let them out unless they came up with a way the four of them could perform a safe and covert direction sensing to find Tullah. I gave them a couple of hours.

Then Yelena drove me to David's house in Wash Park while I called people back.

I got through to Alex's voicemail. Zane didn't pick up.

Jen answered. She was between meetings, and she was tired and short-tempered. Not with me. No, with me she was tired and sweet. What set her off was when I mentioned my mom's attempts to get me on the cell.

"I've just about had it with her," she snapped.

"Huh?" My response was short if not terribly clever.

"Look, honey, I'm sorry, but Alex and I have been playing an unending game of rock-paper-scissors to pick one of us to tell you, and I guess I'm it."

"Tell me what?"

"We both think your mother's a pain in the ass."

"Ahhh..."

"Anytime anything goes wrong, you have to sort it out. She's worse than Skylur, and that's saying something. Nothing you do is ever good enough. Meanwhile Kathleen gets a free pass."

"Oh. It's not really—"

"Trust me, honey, it is from everybody else's perspective. Alex and I will smile and be polite and never cause problems to her face for your sake, but we had to tell you at some stage. Kathleen needs help. Fine: give it. Do what you know is good for her, not what your mother says she needs."

"I don't know what to say."

"Think on it. I'm being called to the next meeting, honey. I'm sorry, I have to go. I love you."

"I love you," I answered and the connection was cut.

Yelena had heard every word.

"Is right," she said, and waggled her hand. "Like so. Not the whole right."

"It's a surprise," I said. "I didn't realize."

I could have used eukori to spy on my husband and wife, and then I would have known, but I wouldn't go down that route.

And yes, I guessed mom could be a handful. To a third party it wouldn't look good.

The wording of David's text seemed to loom larger. *Don't talk to yr family.*

Luckily, we were already at Wash Park and a couple of streets later, Yelena pulled up in front of David's old house.

The yard was covered in snow, and he must have come down here and taken the potted plants inside, because the patio was bare. The lights were on inside, and he was at the door before I'd even had time to knock.

"Come in," he said.

Taylor, Kath's fiancé, was just inside. "I'm sorry about the mess," he said nervously, holding his hands up. "I'll clean it up as quickly as I can."

The 'mess' was suitcases and plastic bags of clothes. The sort of thing you'd get when someone had to move in a hurry.

David and Taylor exchanged glances, then Taylor picked up one of the suitcases and disappeared into a bedroom.

"Where's Kath?" I asked anxiously. "What's going on?"

"Kath's fine. Asleep inside." David guided us into the kitchen. "Sit."

I sat on the stool next to his breakfast bar, and he put a mug of coffee in front of me.

"Kath's pregnant," he said without preamble. "She and Taylor have been 'released' by their company, and it turns out their rental house had a clause in it about continuing employment."

"Oh, shit!"

I nearly fell off the stool. Kath? Pregnant? A blizzard of fears swept over me. An alcoholic who was going to have a baby. An unemployed, homeless alcoholic, possibly in the process of breaking up with her fiancé.

All happening at the exact time I needed to be concentrating on getting Tullah, Tara and Hana back.

I got a grip before my mouth took off with a longer reaction. No one ever told me life had to be fair. It just was, and you found a way to deal with it.

And I sensed there was more.

I took several deep breaths.

David was radiating calm, and I trusted him.

I took a sip of the excellent coffee.

"Okay," I said. "I'm ready. Tell me the rest of what's going on."

"First, let me say this: I think this could be a good thing for Kath. Taylor say it's the shock that they needed."

"*They* needed? I understand the shock to Kath."

"Taylor's words: he's been acting like a kind of shock absorber, isolating Kath from the issues." He shrugged. "He hasn't been able to isolate her from this and that's made them both realize what he's been doing. His words again: they aren't as stupid as they've been acting."

I frowned. I could hope that was what was going to happen.

David went on: "Your mother is upset. She wants Kath to move into the house in Aurora, and she's talking about Kath's options given they're not married and—"

"No one is going to put any pressure on Kath about that!"

I was amazed by the depth of my reaction. It wasn't something I'd spent much time actually thinking about, so my response was unfiltered.

David ducked his head in agreement.

"Agreed. I've told the pair of them they're taking up Jen's offer of contract legal work. They're staying here at a nominal rent." He gestured. "The place needs someone to look after it, and I don't have the time."

"Thank you." I reached over and squeezed his hand. "Thank you, from the bottom of my heart. You're absolutely sure?"

"Of course."

I could see he wasn't quite finished.

"What else?" I prompted.

"Well, we have a problem with Tamanny staying at Manassah. Sooner or later she's going to walk in on something she shouldn't see."

He was right. What with necks being bitten and Scott possibly trotting around on four legs, let alone the frequent high octane sex, something regrettable was going to happen.

"Yeah..."

"I think she should move down here."

The surprises were coming fast today. I blinked.

Actually...

"What do they think about it?" I could imagine Kath's reaction to being told she had to be a babysitter, even if Tamanny was a fairly mature teen. Taylor wasn't that sort of man either, as far as I'd seen.

David smiled. "They like the idea."

"You mean they..." I stopped and lowered my voice to a whisper. "You mean they accepted because the package is a good deal?"

"No," David said simply. "I introduced them all, and they like each other. Tamanny thinks Kath having a baby will be the, quote, 'coolest thing ever'. Also, big news, Tamanny's new best friend is moving to Wash Park, just a couple of streets away."

"Best friend as in Emily Schumacher?"

I'd been worried about the Schumachers for a long time. Not that I was often at their house, but they were all connected with me, and Emily had already been kidnapped once by Peterson's troops. We'd had to erase that from her memory. Luckily, it didn't seem to have caused any lasting effects that time.

Maybe it was an illusion, but having them only a few minutes away from Manassah felt better than downtown.

"Yes, Emily," David confirmed. "You've been a little distracted, or you'd have understood how much this means to Tamanny. A little house, a family, a baby on the way, a friend close by and high school. It sounds like heaven to her. After all that shit in LA, she craves this normalcy. She needs it."

I could see that, now he'd laid it out. The last thing Tamanny needed was to live in Manassah. On the other hand, she was associated with me and that meant we needed her close by for her own safety.

David went on: "If they're here in Wash Park, we can easily keep an eye on all of them. In fact, I'd suggest buying another house nearby and leaving one of the couples from Ops 4-10 down here."

"If we get allocated any of them," I said, trying to keep it real. "Skylur's call. Whether we do or not, thank you, David."

"Just doing my bit," he said, with another little smile and a shrug. "You know. Tell me if I'm poking my nose where it doesn't belong... but I think the key to getting through to Kath is Taylor. However rocky things have gotten between them, she genuinely seems to trust his judgement."

I snorted. "How is that a good thing? I know Kath is irrational, but at least it's the sort of irrationality I have a chance of predicting. I don't know anything about Taylor, other than he loves ritzy nightlife like watching the ballet."

"You see, there's a hook already. He's very pro Jen because of her patronage of the Denver ballet, and if nothing else, Kath's not seeing Jen in such a negative light anymore."

It seemed that my House had managed to find a start to the solution for Kath.

And Taylor. I'd need to start thinking of them as a genuine item.

"Anything else you've managed to find out about him?"

David shrugged. "He's a hotshot in corporate law. The kind that can unravel company agreements and financial deals and tell you the exact closet where all the skeletons are hidden."

"Hmm."

I got caught up in trying to reimagine Taylor as an asset rather than a liability.

Yelena was *way* ahead of me. "Set Taylor to work on Weaver and Denver Adept community," she said. "Companies, partnerships. We want to know any property he owns."

It was an excellent idea.

I left Yelena to update David on why, and took the opportunity to sneak into the room where Kath was.

She woke and covered her face with her hands.

Taylor sat at the end of the bed and tried to comfort her by putting one clumsy hand on her leg.

I had to do or say *something.*

What?

I had too little experience at this kind of thing. I knelt by the bed and leaned over to kiss the top of her head.

"Congratulations, sis."

I could barely hear her mumbled response. "I'm not going to fuck this up."

"I know," I said. "Whatever you need, you got."

I couldn't make that promise. I really couldn't. I slipped my arms around her and hugged gently.

To start with, it was like hugging a piece of wood. A piece of wood that was leaking on my shirt. Then gradually, she loosened up a little.

"I really want..."

She didn't finish the sentence, and didn't speak again. I said very little—just little standard phrases. It all felt too raw, but when I left her ten minutes later, I felt we'd made progress, however small.

We stopped off at Manassah for a shower and change of clothing.

Both of us wanted to take more time.

I sensed Yelena through our half-open eukori; the phantom throb of her jaw. She wanted to exchange Blood. In return, she felt my confused, frustrated anxiety about Kath and the baby. But we both knew we had to rescue Tullah, and the first step was to find out where she was being kept.

Within fifteen minutes we were out and back on the road to Haven.

Chapter 61

Back in the Hill Bitch, it was time to try calling Alex again. I needed people on the ground to search for Tullah. Or wolves. Wolves would be much better.

I would use my pack as part of their training, but they weren't going to be enough on their own. There was the Denver pack, and I had a position in it, but not high enough to order groups of them around. However, Alex had that authority and he knew about Diana and Kaothos, so he'd understand the issue.

His cell was answered, but it wasn't Alex. It was a woman.

I could almost hear her gulp in response to my growl.

"I'll pass you to him, alpha," she said.

I could hear voices in the background. So, either some kind of pack meeting... or an orgy.

Hypocritical much? I mouthed to myself.

I wondered if the rumor mill had delivered any stories about Zane and me to Alex. And how I was going to deal with it.

"Amber." Alex's voice caught me, as it often did, sending tremors all down my body.

Despite the guilt, I couldn't stop myself. "Who was that woman?"

"Just one of your pack, assigned to answering my cell because everyone wants to talk to me."

He was chuckling. I had to leave it there.

Business, woman. Talk business.

"I need some of the Denver pack," I said. "I can tell you why, but I need you out of the pack's hearing."

"Hold on," he said. I heard him telling the others he was going to take my call outside, and the good-natured ribbing he got for it.

"Okay, I'm away from them. Shoot."

I brought him up to date, while he muttered and snarled at the problems this all threw up.

"So this substantiation thing seemed to go north from San Juan after they got Tullah? There's a lot of Colorado to cover going that way. There's groups of the pack in Grand Junction, and towns like Steamboat. We have patrols that check our borders, which can be used to search, if they can be told what they're searching for."

Wolves could smell a person from across a town if they were concentrating. I could get Tullah's clothes out to them. If Alex gave them orders, I wouldn't need to explain anything about Kaothos, just that Tullah had been kidnapped and had to be rescued.

"Where exactly are the pack's borders at the moment?" I asked. That was more of a problem. Borders for the Denver pack had always been a little vague. Now we were part of the Southern League and in open conflict with the Rocky Mountain Confederation. *Vague* was not acceptable.

Alex blew out a breath.

"Weaver doesn't have to take her far into Wyoming to be out of reach," he said. "Any Denver pack going past I-80 is asking for a response from the Wind River pack."

I drew a line in my mind between Rock Springs and Cheyenne that was the interstate's route. It wasn't far into Wyoming at all. Both Rock Springs and Cheyenne packs were part of the Southern League, but they weren't strong and their territories were small.

"What about west? Salt Lake?"

"No." Alex shut that down. "Salt Lake City, western Utah and most of Nevada is all officially unaligned. We don't want to do something that ends up with them joining the Confederation. If we need to go there, we'll need Felix and Cameron in on this. And they'll need to know why."

"Which will mean Skylur being willing to tell them."

"Yeah. Like that'll happen this year." I could hear Alex's frown. "Even within those boundaries, that's a lot of territory, Amber. We don't have enough wolves."

"I'm getting our Adepts to do a working that should cut it down."

"How much?" Alex said. "Even if you could get it down to one county like Moffat, that's what, 4,500 square miles? Towns we can do. Major roads. Railroads. The countryside... that's something else."

We were both quiet for a moment.

"You could ask Zane for help," he said, and my heart stopped.

Had he heard the rumors? Was this some kind of test to see what I said?

I kicked myself mentally. That wasn't Alex's style.

More importantly, this ducking and diving wasn't my style either.

And I was wearing his ring.

I'd rather have done this face to face, but I didn't have that luxury.

"Yeah. About him," I said. "He got... *we* got into some heavy petting at the warehouse, just before the challenge. There's bound to be rumors—"

"Pia called and told me about the working that Weaver used on you," Alex said. "Not your fault."

"Not Zane's fault either," I said.

Alex just snorted.

I could tell he was angry, but it wasn't directed at me. I hadn't realized how much it had been preying on my mind until I felt the flood of relief at his reaction.

"I got your back," he said.

"I got yours. I love you."

"Yeah, I know. I'm very lovable."

"Ass."

We laughed quietly. It felt good, even though he was over 500 miles away.

"I have family news," I said. "Your sister-in-law is pregnant."

"Oh, shit."

"That's what I said. David's got them at his house and... it's complicated, but it may work out."

"Well, that good to hear, but not entirely what I meant. If that research we did about the Farrell family curse was right—"

I felt like I'd been punched in the gut. How could I have forgotten?

"That's her first-born," I said. "The baby will die."

Then I said: "No. No. Not going to happen."

There had to be something I could do. Some kind of defense.

Hide Kath in the dungeon at Haven?

What if the curse didn't need to reach in and touch her? What if it was already inside her? Or inside me?

I could hear background noises from Alex's end and I had one last, difficult question. Despite how it made me feel, I asked: "Is it acceptable to ask Zane for a favor? I mean the alpha politics of it."

"He'll expect favors in return, which will be nothing to do with alpha politics. The alpha politics, I can handle. Hold on a moment."

Someone was talking to Alex about pack-owned businesses taking new orders and wanting to change their scheduled departure dates.

"I gotta go," Alex said, speaking quickly. "Call Zane. He can always say no. Take no shit from him. Whichever way, get Tullah back and let me worry about rumors. Love you. Bye."

Yelena was nodding as I put the cell away.

"It's like you tell me about when you were a soldier," she said. "David. Alex. Jen. Trust the rest of the people in your squad to be good enough to do their job. Concentrate on yours."

She'd heard what was said. She was trying to distract me.

"I suppose there's an old Ukrainian saying about it?" I asked.

"Oh, yes. Chase two hares and there will be nothing for the pot."

"That's not Ukrainian. Well, maybe it is, but anyway, it's the same saying in America."

"So? Sometimes is not *only* Ukrainians who are smart."

Back at Haven, I got Bian up to speed on what was happening and looked in on Mykala and Tove down in the dungeon with Diana.

They were both fine, but sleepy.

Tove woke up enough to give me a hug. I could tell from the scent that Rita had been down checking on her.

Mykayla demanded a hug as well, pretended to howl, cracked jokes about werewolves and sexual stamina, then flopped back down on the bed and was asleep in ten seconds.

I left them with Diana and headed up the elevator. It was time for my Adepts to try out their long-range direction sensing.

No, not to *try*. To *succeed*. We couldn't afford anything else.

Chapter 62

"We can do it." Gabrielle was caught up in her own excitement, everything else put aside.

"Good. Does it take time to recover afterwards?"

"Give us an hour or so before we go a second time."

"Perfect. We'll get more than that."

There was no point in running the working from the same place twice. If it worked, we were going to move some distance before trying again.

Bian had provided them with a huge wall map of the US. I looked down at where western Colorado met Utah, and felt the return of doubts. That was a big slice of country to hide in, even if he'd stopped there. There was nothing to say he wouldn't keep going.

I kept those thoughts to myself. "What about safety?" I asked.

"Actually, this will be more like a spirit walk. We'll be nearly invisible in the spirit world. I think this way is better than the substantiation Gwen decided to do."

I raised my eyebrows. I liked the confidence, but the Hecate got to be a big boss in the League for a reason. Was there something about this method that my group hadn't realized? And I didn't like that little word *nearly*.

It was cold. Gabrielle had decided not to use the room we'd used for the spirit walk to Erie. We were on Haven's flat roof, under a clear sky, in the middle of the night. This far away from the Denver light pollution, the stars were brilliant.

Other than the setting, Gabrielle told me that the preparation would be like the Erie spirit walk. We were definitely not going to be taking peyote. I guessed I was going to miss the fun parts of riding a blitzed coyote high over the Rockies, but I'd take that for a safer trip.

Gabrielle was muttering about having something of Tullah's to focus on.

"We're looking for my twin sister," I said. "Take it on trust, and I'll explain later. I don't need anything. Let's go."

"Oh. Okay."

They'd cleared an area in the middle of the roof. The map lay to one side, weighed down with ornate paperweights and a box that Alice had brought up. We sat cross-legged on a large rug they'd found.

Flying the magic carpet, eh? I kept that to myself, too.

Kane had found an actual drum in the mansion, and was drumming his fingers idly on it. He seemed eager to start as well.

Gabrielle sat behind me. She'd gotten a hairbrush and began to run it through my hair.

"Is this really part of it?" I was impatient.

"It seemed to relax you when we did the spirit walk," she said. "Is it okay?"

"It's fine," I said, but I could feel I'd made her nervous now.

I clamped down on my impatience.

Kane's drumming changed to a leisurely, steady beat.

Flint started humming.

Alice took the parts of a flute out of her box and put it together. Blew some experimental notes.

Sweet sound, but I was still eager to get going, fidgeting.

Gabrielle and Alice must have exchanged looks. Alice took a black velvet cloth from the flute box and walked around until she was alongside me.

She blindfolded me with the cloth.

"Kinky," Gabrielle said.

I laughed. "Until you've gone on a spirit walk by getting sweaty in a sauna with two naked, handsome men, don't use that word."

She laughed. Flint and Kane joined in, with a little undertone to their laughs. Oh, yes. We would probably never use peyote again for spirit walks, but I'd bet they'd come up with reasons we needed to use a sweat lodge. Fine by me. Even if nothing physical happened, like a good little Athanate, I fed on emotions, and lust was okay.

Alice snorted and returned to her flute.

She was much better than I expected her to be, playing a sort of improvisation on tunes I thought I should recognize, and weaving it cleverly around the beat that Flint and Kane provided.

Without really meaning to, I leaned back on Gabrielle and she started the gentle touches across my face, as she had last time. Again, I would have sworn that she was painting my face.

That tune Alice was playing! I knew it—the way it rose and fell, like a bird in flight.

Now it was the wind that stroked my face, and the wind was the music, and it was all one.

Turn. I heard a whisper. *Turn all the way around.*

I was a bird, a red hawk, riding the air currents. This wasn't like the crazy spirit walk where I snatched control from Gabrielle, or where Flint and I rode a crazy coyote into the heart of a mountain storm.

This is better.

This is a good team.

There was no transition either; there were no strange feelings as walls went all weird and transparent as we moved through them. We were all, together, simply a hawk, flying in the night. It was the most natural thing to lift one wing and wheel around in the sky.

And the other way.

Back we went, wheeling effortlessly. Beautiful.

I could see Haven far below. The lights of the town of Evergreen. Golden to the north. The dark bulk of Mount Evans to the west. Denver to the east, sparkling in the night.

Twin sister came the whisper. *Twin sister.*

It had to come through me. I was the one who knew Tara. On my own, I didn't have the power to reach out through the spirit world, but I felt the rest of them fitting around me like a jigsaw. Alice. Flint. Kane. Gabrielle. They'd provide the juice.

Around and around we circled, higher and higher, like a tune trying to find that perfect note that makes everything that went before fall into place.

It got to be too much. The air felt too thin. The sky was empty. We stooped, fell, but Flint caught me. Alice's spiraling tune pulled me back to rise again.

And again.

It was on the third attempt I heard an answering sound. The circle of my flight had grown wide. I was higher than I had been before. The first hints of tiredness from the rest of the team had joined the whispers in my mind.

The sound was gone before I could latch onto it. It was no more than a breath, a dream of a word, gone as quickly as it had come. A phantom that vanished as I looked.

There.

Around we went.

Don't try. Concentrate on being. Stay open. Listen.

Gabrielle's whispers blurred into the memory of one of my sensei's martial arts disciplines.

Don't think. Act.

There!

I didn't know where 'there' was.

Doesn't matter. Around again.

I struggled to rise, to complete my circle, to point the way I'd sensed it.

Tara! I called.

Hush. Gabrielle responded immediately. *Don't call.*

We were losing height. Losing focus.

There?

This time I wasn't sure. Now I was looking, *looking,* and it all broke up and floated away like mist.

Back. Back. Back. Down.

I was on the roof at Haven. I was lying against Gabrielle with my arms stretched out and my lungs laboring for air.

"No!" I said, sitting bolt upright. "I had her. I could hear her! We have to go back!"

Gabrielle's arms held me back. "It's okay," she said.

"You did well," Alice said. "It was enough for the first time. We have our direction."

"But where..."

Flint was already bent over the map. Kane helped me up. It was well past midnight. They both looked tired. They all looked tired. They'd designed a working that cost them heavily while it allowed me to fly around, as they say, free as a bird.

Flint took a pencil and drew a steady line across the map. It went west, but north as well. From Evergreen next to Denver out to Moffat county in the northwest corner of Colorado.

Onward.

Dinosaur National Monument.

Ashley National Forest.

And onward. Out of the Denver pack's boundaries.

Very obviously, *right* through the middle of Salt Lake City.

Damn.

Chapter 63

"I know I said we need to take a second direction, but I didn't expect this." Gabrielle looked up at Jen's Pilatus looming in the pre-dawn light next morning.

Yelena had gone ahead of us to Centennial, and the aircraft was fueled and prepped.

She was standing at the top of the steps watching us.

"Who's the pilot?" Gabrielle asked as we climbed up. She saw Yelena waiting, dressed in her biker leathers. "Not you?"

I laughed as Yelena let her fangs manifest in answer and Gabrielle flinched.

"Careful. Don't say anything bad about her flying or dancing. She gets grumpy."

Gabrielle laughed.

"We miss morning training and evening training. Again," Yelena reminded me.

Yes, we had. Morning training was just hard physical work with Yelena. Evening training was where she threw me all over the mats and treated me like a punching bag if I dared to slow down. She was obviously looking forward to our next session, which was probably scheduled for this evening.

Depending on how today went.

Our first reading had gone through Salt Lake, across the top of Nevada and California before reaching the coast, stopping in the neighborhood of the Californian town of Crescent City on Highway 101.

Assuming Weaver and Tullah were still in the country.

Gabrielle didn't think we had enough power in the working to reach as far as California or the coast. She was fairly sure that Weaver was in the northwest of Colorado, or Utah, and wherever he was, he'd put shields in place, which was why the contact was so faint.

Fairly sure. I liked that about as much as I liked her saying *nearly.*

Anyway, to work out where Tullah was on the map, we needed another direction reading. The further we moved away from Haven, the more accurate it would be when we plotted the result on the map.

Assuming Weaver hasn't moved her.

Yelena flew us west.

After a couple of hours' sleep last night, Flint and Kane had recovered easily. They had our map, and they were talking about how much the slightest error in the angle could result in hundreds of miles difference. They had lightly shaded the possible areas based on one reading. According to them, Weaver could be in Oregon, or Wyoming, or Idaho just as easily as Colorado or Utah.

Gabrielle and Alice slept.

I sat alone, staring into the distance.

If I was right, the power I sensed in me was from the Farrell family curse. The same power that would kill Kath's baby. Yet, I felt it had spoken to me. Given me a name to call it by. If there was an intelligence behind the curse, I could find it. I *had* to find it. And stop it. Maybe destroy it.

Which had to happen *after* I rescued Tullah, because I knew in my bones that somewhere in the possibilities that lay ahead of me, I'd need that power. It was the ace up my sleeve.

But it was also possible that once I'd used the power, really used it, that I wouldn't be able to destroy it. I'd need it, or I'd convince myself that I needed it, whatever the cost.

"Awesome!"

Gabrielle was awake, face pressed against the windows like a kid.

The scenery on the approach to Escalante airfield, in the south of Utah, was spectacular.

Once we'd parked, Yelena left to organize topping up the tanks while the rest of us stayed inside, performed the working again.

It was cramped. Gabrielle and I sat on the floor in the aisle. The others sat in their chairs.

Gabrielle had remembered to bring the hairbrush.

"My hair never got this much attention before," I complained as she started brushing again. "Keep brushing and you're going to end up pulling it out."

"Behave," she said, and slapped me gently on the arm.

Alice waved the blindfold, but I shook my head and closed my eyes. I reached out for them with my eukori.

For all their confidence about recovery times after the first working, I could feel the others were still tired, but we were getting better at this. Together we slipped back into the spirit world like a salmon diving into a river.

Wrong image.

We are the hawk again.

Maybe Gabrielle's spirit guide was making it easy to visualize.

This time, we were circling in the crisp morning sunlight above Escalante. Below us, the famous Grand Staircase. The petrified forest.

Higher and higher. Bryce Canyon to the west.

There!

We'd found her. Tara was waiting. She'd probably been waiting for us all night.

I could feel her, so carefully reaching out.

There!

Gabrielle wanted me to keep quiet, so I tried to think of love and hoped that somehow got through to Tara.

We're coming, Tara. We're coming.

The sense of her blinked and faded. Had she responded? Was she just too tired?

Lost.

We turned back, seeking the connection again.

But it wasn't Tara who was waiting this time.

I saw a glimpse, no more. A cold face. Cold eyes, blue entirely, without pupils. Hair like needles of ice.

Then blades. A thousand thin metal blades, woven together like feathers, dark as a raven wing, chopping down.

And silence.

What the hell was that?

Alice tried to quiet us down. Gabrielle and I turned one way and the other, seeking out that hesitant whisper of a connection.

TARA! I screamed it at the innocent sky.

I could feel the power boiling up inside me. More power than it would need. All it would take would be to reach down and—

Stop, Amber!

There was sudden panic in Gabrielle's voice now.

Stop. Stop. Back. Now!

I sank, but slowly, wheeling through the wide blue sky.

Tara?

But what I heard was the rattle of bones, a hissing and clinking and slithering that seemed to come from all around, while the sky suddenly darkened.

Back. Shhh. Back.

Then I was struggling on the floor of the aircraft, held down by a worried Yelena, who was looking into my eyes.

"Amber?"

"I'm okay," I said and she let go.

"What happened?" Yelena asked the rest of them. All were standing with shocked expressions on their faces.

"We got through to Tara," Alice said. "Then the connection was cut."

"By the Hecate," I finished, when Alice hesitated. I pulled myself upright.

I wanted to yell. Anger boiled up in my chest. I'd been stupid to trust the Hecate. And Gabrielle.

"Didn't look much like Wendy Witch to me," Flint said.

"Apart from the color of the eyes," Kane said. "And the hair."

Gabrielle didn't respond. Her face was pale and her eyes wide.

Alice waited a moment before she spoke. "I think we came close to discovery by one of those substantiations that the Hecate warned us about."

"The Empire? Matlal?" I asked.

"I couldn't tell." Alice shrugged. "Are we in danger now, Gabrielle?"

Gabrielle shook her head.

Unless I was being duped again, Gabrielle's reaction showed she had really believed the Hecate was on our side somehow. I sensed she still believed it. I was going to need to talk more to her, but later. The connection had been cut, but not before we'd got a direction from it.

The only problem was we'd given away how we were searching.

Ignoring that, Flint spread the map on the floor of the aircraft. He started to draw his line north from Escalante.

And east of Salt Lake!

The lines from the two directions crossed in the Ashley National Forest.

Not as bad as Salt Lake City, but still in Utah. The Ashley was part of the wilderness area that started fifty miles or so east of the city, but which the Salt Lake pack might regard as part of their territory.

Flint marked the possible errors on the second reading we got, so eventually there was a rough diamond shape around the point where the two direction estimates crossed.

"That's still a lot of territory," Alice said.

"At a guess, 1,500 square miles," I said. "Maybe 2,000."

That was a lot better than the 4,500 of Moffat County that Alex was talking about, but most of the Ashley was rough going. We were definitely going to need more feet on the ground. Or paws.

Yelena came back in and looked over my shoulder.

"You make it narrower, smaller error, by going closer," she said.

That got a reaction from Gabrielle, who shook her head quickly. "This working is very quiet, but it's still detectable, and the effect isn't linear. If we halved the distance, we'd be four times more noticeable."

"*If* Weaver is watching," Yelena said.

"Even if he isn't, there's something else prowling around out there."

"Okay." Yelena shrugged and made her way forward to the pilot's seat. "Back home, Boss?"

"No," I said.

The territory was too big, and I had to assume Weaver was going to do something now he knew we were searching. His options came down to moving to hide somewhere else, or speeding up his plan. It would be much more difficult to hide and move at the same time, so my guess was he would speed up his plan.

He'd try and break Tullah to gain access to Kaothos. However strong Tullah was, no one holds out for ever.

I reckoned we had maybe the rest of today and tomorrow. But no one on site today, so only tomorrow. To cover 2,000 square miles. So I did what I had to and texted Zane.

Need to ask a favor. Urgent.

To my surprise, he sent a reply immediately, but it wasn't really good news.

Busy. El Paso. Thanks for that. Come ask F2F.

I got the meaning. I reckoned Cameron had followed my advice and gotten Zane to prepare a replacement pack for El Paso by moving one of the New Mexico sub-packs a little further south. Even if he wasn't really pissed by the extra work, he was certainly pissed that I'd failed to answer his calls.

Now that he knew I wanted something, he was going to use that for his own ends.

Fair enough. Two can play that game.

I went and sat up front, and played with Yelena's aviation GPS to see what was available down near El Paso, but away from the city itself.

After five minutes, I sent Zane another text.

Doña Ana airfield. Noon. Important.

Chapter 64

Zane was waiting in the small, neat terminal at Doña Ana when we landed.

I was half expecting him to have a posse of the local sub-pack around him, but then again, maybe not this time. Maybe he didn't want witnesses. He didn't even have his usual Albuquerque sidekicks, Haz and Bode. He was alone, dressed in khaki cargo pants, skinny T shirt and tailored brown leather jacket. He slouched on a seat as if he couldn't care less whether I was here or not.

He'd let his dominance off the leash as well, but unfortunately for the image he was trying to project, there was a subtlety to it today, as if it was obscuring what he really felt. He was also trying to frown, to show me how angry he was, but he couldn't hide the way his brown and green eyes were devouring me.

He looked good, which was not the frame of mind I was supposed to be in, considering what I had planned.

And my wolf came out to play, shoving back against his dominance to see what he'd do.

Oh, crap. Stop this.

I sat next to him. Yelena ambled around the terminal building, never quite out of sight, but giving us space.

Our shoulders touched. I was very aware of the heat of his body, and equally aware the reverse was true.

The man wasn't going to start talking first. He continued to glare into the distance, his proud features set firm.

Against a prepared opponent, be sneaky. Do the unexpected. Take control of the fight.

I was pretty sure my old Ops 4-10 instructor, Ben-Haim, hadn't meant this kind of fighting, but all advice is worth considering.

And to that advice, I would add Dominé's warning, given just before I'd met Zane for the first time: *Don't be prey.*

I leaned across, pushed Zane's dark, coiled hair out of the way, kissed his cheek and then let my Athanate fangs out.

"Mierda!" he said, twitching. His voice was usually rich; now it was as hoarse as old crow.

Score one.

"Bruja!" he swore. *Witch.*

"Yeah, I know," I said. "All my fault. Making poor Zane go crazy. The thing is, mi corazon, I really am a witch."

He snorted and his eyes traveled up and down my body. "A witch. Makes sense, I guess. That's how you do the ritual thing with the halfies?"

I nodded.

"A witch as well as a wolf and a snake?"

I could have done without the *snake* nickname for Athanate, but I nodded again.

"And so?" he said, pushing back.

"Not even a little bit afraid, guapo?"

"No."

I was listening to his heartbeat, inhaling his scent. He wasn't lying. If anything, he was more aroused than when I'd sat down. He'd enjoyed being called handsome, too.

"I need..." despite everything, I couldn't stop myself from chuckling and drew it out. My voice had dropped half an octave. "I need a favor."

He snorted again and wrestled his voice back to the way he wanted it to sound. Casual and in control. "You don't write. You don't call. You don't answer your freaking cell. You fly all the way down south and it's because you want something only I can give you? Am I surprised?"

I bit my lip to stop answering *that isn't surprise in your pants.*

Instead I said: "It's hard. To explain, I mean."

"Try me."

He'd stopped frowning, and now he was playing word games with me.

"There's a woman who's been kidnapped, that I need to rescue," I said. "This is all about Adept politics..."

"Power, you mean. And whenever the people in power need someone to be rescued, they send you, like they sent you down to Albuquerque last time to talk to the crazy werewolves."

"They didn't send me, and anyway, look what happened."

"Yeah, you came down without a single fucking clue about the situation in New Mexico! You nearly blew up the state, nearly got killed by us, nearly got killed by rogue Athanate, got us into a war with the Confederation—"

"Rescued the person I went to rescue, and a couple of others, tripped up the rogues, got Cameron and Felix in bed with each other, literally, *and* helped a halfy change, too. The Confederation was already at war with you, unless you were going to just roll over, which you weren't. And we met, as well. All worked out okay."

I got a bleak stare for those last comments before he spoke. "How insanely stupid is it this time? Come on, tell me she's being held in Confederation territory or something."

I winced.

"Shit, woman! I'm right, aren't I? You want some werewolves to go attack the Wind River pack or something."

"No. Not that bad. We think she's being held in Ashley National Forest."

He just shrugged—he didn't know where that was.

"The wilderness area where Colorado, Wyoming and Utah meet."

He looked at the ceiling. "So, not just knocking on the Confederation's door, but pissing off the neutral neighbors in Salt Lake as well. No. The answer is no, Amber."

"Hear me out. Please. This is really important."

I didn't say: *Help me, Obi-wan Zane-obi, you're my only hope.*

Nope. Not going to say that. Even if it was kinda true.

"If it's too close to Wind River territory, or the Salt Lake pack gets itchy, we pull back unless Felix and Cameron give us a green light—"

"Which they won't until they're good and ready," he interrupted, "*and* convinced it's worth it, to them. So, tell me, is it?"

Getting Kaothos back to Tullah *was* worth it to the wolves, but I couldn't explain why to them yet.

"Yes," I said and left it at that. "First we need to find out exactly where it is, and I can't get enough spare wolves from the Denver pack. It'll take weeks to get my new pack from El Paso to Colorado. I can't drum up enough Athanate, either."

"What about the Adepts? Aren't there any who will help?"

"A handful. Not enough. And better at defensive fighting anyway."

"So you come down to ask the crazy wolves who hang out in New Mexico and haven't got anything better to do."

"What have you got on your hands, apart from setting up a new pack in El Paso?"

"The Sonoran pack are pushing in on Arizona," he said, with a jut of his jaw, "and the Tucson pack are our allies. We're helping them."

"And that takes a lot of your resources?"

He was bullshitting. A year ago, it'd been the New Mexico packs on their own, keeping everybody out of their territory by their reputation of being both crazy and deadly. The Denver pack to the north, Tucson to the west, El Paso to the south, and Amarillo to the east. Maybe Mexican packs as well.

All of those US packs were now allies in the Southern League. That *had* to have freed up a lot of foot soldiers. Or paw soldiers, technically.

"Yeah, okay," he conceded. "Let's imagine, *theoretically,* we help you find this kidnapped woman, and she's not in Salt Lake or Wind River pack territory. What then? You want my wolves to attack? What would we be facing? Adepts? A mix of Athanate, Adepts and Were like at Carson Park? Guns? Magic?"

"Won't know much until we find out where it is, and I'm not going to jump into any confrontation without all the bosses being on board."

"So just hunting the location?"

"Unless the bosses say otherwise."

Or events overtake us.

"Who have you spoken to?"

"Skylur. Alex. Haven't spoken to Felix and Cameron yet... unless you think it's necessary."

Big boy like you doesn't need to talk to the bosses.

"Don't try that pop psychology bullshit on me," he said.

"Okay. Sorry about that. But let's say, *theoretically,* you're going to lend me a hundred wolves—"

"Not going to happen."

"Seventy-five."

His eyes narrowed and his jaw muscles rippled before he spoke. "Maybe."

Maybe was good. *Maybe* was halfway there.

And despite what Alex said, Zane wasn't going to ask me what he was getting in return. He was either arrogant enough to believe that he'd get it anyway, or smart enough not to say it outright to me.

"Could you get them up to the town of Vernal tomorrow, ready for several days out in the wilds?"

"Shit! Not only have you taken my best lieutenant and landed me the job of shifting the White Sands pack down to El Paso, but you want me to whistle up seventy-five werewolves and ship them to the other end of Colorado, and you want it done tonight. Who's paying for this, by the way?"

He was down to arguing over details now.

"Bill me for the costs."

Skylur had said *everything you need for this, apart from more Athanate.* Transporting werewolves to help out had to come under that.

"As for your lieutenant, Rita," I went on, "she told me she volunteered and it was Cameron who raised the option. And lastly, cariño, I can help you with the White Sands thing."

"Oh, yeah?"

"Yeah. Instead of sneaking around El Paso as if you were planning to invade enemy territory, hand the work to Alex. We're all one pack now, remember? Cameron's words were: *one pack, New Mexico and Colorado*. Alex has got to be down here anyway, so why would it need two of you?"

He scowled. He didn't refuse, and his grimace showed how unhappy he was that he hadn't even thought of it that way.

"Why would I want to work with Alex?"

"Because the bosses said you have to, and they appointed me to make sure it happens."

He grunted at that. It *was* what Felix had said: *to ensure the two parts of the pack work seamlessly and without friction, we appoint Amber Farrell as liaison.*

"Mi corazon, the last thing I need is to be traveling back and forth between the two of you, interpreting your snarls into diplomatic language that doesn't get the other's hackles up. None of us has time for that, and it would weaken the defense against the Confederation."

He didn't like it, but he knew I was right.

This was *exactly* like sparring in the gym; while he was off balance, I pressed my advantage.

"Which is why I called Alex and told him I was meeting you down here. He should be along any minute. By the end of the day, you'll have agreed on a way for White Sands to move in while the old El Paso are moving out. Houses can be traded, businesses handed over. Less hassle, less waste, less inefficiency. You'll be free to look after more important things. Win-win-win."

Zane actually snarled, loud enough that someone wandering through the terminal stumbled and looked around to see where the rabid dog was.

Alex's reaction hadn't been that different when I called him on the way down, but I'd worn him down. Eventually, he'd given me the address of the pack's house in Vernal. He'd agreed to order the Denver pack's patrols in the area to incorporate the search for Weaver's hideout, promised to send me twenty-five reliable El Paso werewolves to help... and he would order them to coordinate with New Mexico pack members that Zane was going to send me.

If you get any, he'd said.

Snarky bastard. Well, I'd done okay on that count.

Meanwhile, Alex had arrived here early. I could tell he was outside, and there was nothing wrong with Zane's werewolf senses.

He leaped up off the seat.

"It's only Alex," I said. "You're both alphas, but you're also lieutenants on equal footing in the *merged* pack. There's no call to snarl at each other. You have to meet him sometime, Zane, and I wanted it to be while I was down here in El Paso."

Alex came prowling through the doors, with that sort of stiff-legged gait male alphas all seem to get around potential rivals.

He had his dominance dialed down; not completely off, but not challenging. That was as much as I could ask for.

Zane struggled to dial his back down as well, looking as if it was going to choke him.

We all met up in the middle.

El Paso and the surrounding area was, temporarily, Alex's territory. Zane was thinking clearly enough to acknowledge it, and spoke first.

"Deauville. Hello," he said and put his hand out.

"Quivira," Alex answered and they shook briefly. "Welcome to El Paso."

Oh, he'd had to force that out.

"Wonderful," I said, and gave them a bright smile. "We'll be on first-name terms in no time."

That got the lip-twitch type of silent snarl from both of them.

It didn't go badly, after that start. Both Alex and Zane had a job to do, and I was right, they were doing it the wrong way. Leaving Alex in charge of changing the White Sands pack for the El Paso without a break was much better.

An hour or so later, I decided they wouldn't be at each other's throats without my presence, so I was getting ready to make my excuses and leave.

Alex got a call he had to take, leaving me with Zane for a minute.

Zane hadn't said a thing about us, and he was too proud to start it.

"Tell me, guapo, what you're thinking about us?" I asked. "You and me."

"That we got some unfinished business," he said.

"Really?" I chuckled. I looked at him the way Bian might, and ran lazy fingers through my hair. Totally worth it for the effect on his heart. "I imagine once I leave, mi corazon, one of the things you're going to talk about is what happened at the warehouse before the challenge."

Zane's eyes bulged. That was not what he was expecting.

I went on. "Alex is going to tell you I wasn't in my right mind. That I was under the influence of an evil Adept working."

"Were you?" He looked hard at me.

"A little." I couldn't help teasing him. "But hear me out. If I was a pure werewolf, I'd be mated to my co-alpha. You and I wouldn't be having this conversation, and I wouldn't be having very wicked thoughts about you."

His nostrils flared. If he were a bull, he'd be pawing the ground.

"But I'm a hybrid, and the snake side of me does things a little different. The snake side of me tells my wolf that having two alphas in my bed would be a really great gig."

He couldn't tell if I was bluffing or not. He wanted it to be true, and he knew he wanted it so badly, he was working through all the reasons I might be tricking him. Overthinking. Same kind of mistake he made playing cards. He couldn't forget that I'd beaten him at poker, and the suspicion that I'd done it with a real cool hand ate him from the inside.

"Claro, guapo." My voice went all growly and I wasn't putting it on. "You want to get in my pants, you got to get in my bed. You want to get in my bed, you got to get an invitation from my husband."

"Mierda. Like he'll do that!"

"You don't know that, but I'm telling you what'll happen any other way. *Nothing*. How you two work together down here will set up the future."

Alex was coming back. I stood up.

"So, in addition to the twenty-five from El Paso, seventy-five New Mexico wolves, with their tails up, knocking on my door in Vernal by 7 a.m. tomorrow, and I will love you forever."

I kissed Zane on the forehead.

"I'm going to leave you two alone, 'cause I'm a fool like that," I said.

I kissed Alex. On the mouth. Not as deeply and as long as I wanted, but enough to get everyone's Blood racing.

I was bad, because my Athanate was *loving* this.

Chapter 65

I was still thinking about Zane as the Pilatus took off and Yelena pointed us back toward Denver.

Yes, I had gone down to Doña Ana intending to flirt with Zane and get him to loan me some werewolves to hunt for Tullah. All fair. It wasn't like Zane was an angel. There was nothing I'd done that he wouldn't have.

But I'd gone way overboard. I'd never really been any good at fluttering eyelashes, but I suddenly seemed to have learned hardcore flirting.

Why was I teasing him like that? Results?

What I'd said was true; if I were pure werewolf, Alex and I would be exclusive—that's what true mating did for werewolves. Which wasn't to suggest ordinary werewolf love-matches were any less for not being true matings. Given the disparity in numbers, most female werewolves had a couple of male werewolves as lovers, if they were so inclined.

My wolf wasn't that interested in my Athanate House, or my needs for Blood and kin, even though she enjoyed the benefits. My wolf would have been content with just Alex.

Or had that changed?

Why *didn't* it feel as if this stuff with Zane was a purely Athanate thing?

I'd teased Zane when I'd visited Albuquerque with Tullah. He'd teased me back when he'd visited Denver with Cameron.

But neither of those came anywhere close to the burning lust at the warehouse, or the way I'd just been acting with him.

Blame it all on Weaver's working which lowered my inhibitions?

What if it was more than that?

Nothing was going to happen, obviously. *Obviously*. Alex wasn't going to become such good friends with Zane that he'd invite him into our bed. No, nothing was going to happen beyond werewolf levels of teasing and flirting.

Yes, but what if this was something my wolf wanted—or needed?

A mated pair of wolves gained dominance from their bond, more than just the simple addition. One plus one ended up with four. What if three werewolves mated? True mating. One plus one plus one—how much would that make on the dominance scale? Nine?

And if Zane was out of the question, what about, say, Billie, down in LA? Much more acceptable to Alex.

What about both? Four alphas? Level sixteen dominance?

I'd never had these thoughts before. Since Weaver's working had been let loose in my mind, something had changed and it wasn't just about libido.

Using the aircraft's cell phone facility, I called Amanda.

"Yes, Flint and Kane are fine. I'll hand you over to them in a second," I said to her. "I just wanted to know if the doctor was in this morning."

"Of course, Boss."

"And this is covered by client privilege stuff?"

She laughed. "That's lawyers, Amber. Psychiatrists say patient confidentiality stuff. But yes, I won't talk about what we talk about to anyone else. I'm alone at the moment, and I'm just closing the door."

"Good enough for me. Okay, when Athanate blur a person's memory, it gets more difficult the more there is to blur because everything's connected up, right?"

"More or less."

"So when an Adept designs a working that affects a part of someone's mind, we're not talking about surgical precision."

Her answer came a little slowly as she realized where I was going. "No, we aren't."

"Something that is nominally targeted at inhibitions, or lowering resistance to compulsions... that could affect a whole bunch of other mental stuff."

"Probably. Are you asking whether Weaver's working has changed your behavior in other ways?"

"Yeah. If my aversion to politics got stored in my brain in the same place as my inhibitions..."

"You running for governor?" She laughed again. "I see what you're getting at, but you already identified the problem with this theory. There is no single, isolated part of the brain or mind where an aversion to politics would be stored. But, on the other hand, and pointing out I'm not an expert on Adept workings, I can see that a working attacking inhibitions may very well affect aversions."

So having had a lifelong aversion to politics, now maybe I going to be interested in it?

I shuddered.

I really didn't want to be involved, unless it couldn't be avoided.

"Thanks for your help, and I'll pass you to Flint."

I handed the cell over and settled back.

Weaver's workings were subtle and powerful. To make me more susceptible to his compulsions, he'd devised a working that undermined inhibitions, but might have affected me in dozens of other related ways as well before the Hecate had stopped it.

What crazy things was I going to do?

Like starting to build a werewolf political base with enough dominance that Felix and Cameron might see it as a threat? And using their own packs to do it. That would play well when I next saw them. In Louisiana. In a couple of weeks' time.

No.

But as if my thoughts straying to the Hecate saving me from Weaver's working had summoned Gabrielle, she arrived, bringing me a coffee from the galley.

She wouldn't meet my gaze.

"Sit," I said and she sat next to me.

"Gwen's not like that," she said before I got a chance to open up the conversation.

"What other explanation could there be?"

"I don't know." She sounded miserable.

"You're so sure of her, but she doesn't trust you enough to tell you what her spirit guide is. She doesn't share what the League's plans are, let alone what she's planning."

Gabrielle had no answer.

I was angry because I'd talked myself into trusting Gwen, and now she'd obviously betrayed us. But I still couldn't quite see why. She'd made the decision that kidnapping Tullah was more important than being allied with Kaothos?

I couldn't understand it. But now I had a general idea of where Tullah was, and maybe enough werewolves to go looking for her. If I found Tullah, maybe I'd find answers to why the Hecate had done what she'd done.

Meantime, I needed to think more about Tullah.

"Okay, clearing your mind of what the Hecate has or hasn't done, what do you think Weaver can do, now he has Tullah?"

"It's obviously some kind of trap for Kaothos, using Tullah's connection. I can understand how he might force Tullah to make that connection, but I don't know how he could create something strong enough to hold Kaothos."

I asked the question that had been giving me nightmares.

"What if his first step is to do something to Tullah's mind?"

She looked sick. "I don't think that would work. All that he really gets from Tullah is a connection to Kaothos. And if the whole Denver community works together they can make a trap."

"Not strong enough to hold Kaothos?"

"Not for any length of time. Even if he's making them all work under a compulsion, he'd never have complete control over everything. The moment someone makes a mistake, Kaothos would get out."

I thought about control, and the Hecate's coven that had slipped enough for Kane and Flint to break the working. Then I thought about a coven keeping control of a dark magic spell over years and years.

"So tell me about soultrees," I said.

"I'm not supposed to talk to you about them," she replied, biting her lip before continuing. "But anyway, I don't know much. It's kinda not encouraged in the League. People think it's a bit shamanic. I think only the really old covens have them. The French Canadian covens call it Cœur de Lune."

"Moonheart?"

"Yeah. I love that name. I talked to a woman in a coven which has one. I think they're a bit like a reservoir for the coven. A repository of every member over time. Everyone shares a bit of themselves with the soultree and gets a bit of everyone else in return."

"And an old soultree would be powerful?"

"It's possible."

"More powerful than the individual members? And self-aware enough to act independently?"

She blinked. "I'm not really supposed to talk about this outside the League."

"Which means the answer is yes," I said.

"Theoretically," she replied carefully. "But I'm pretty sure Denver doesn't have a soultree, if you're thinking about how they'd try to trap Kaothos."

It wasn't the only thing I was thinking about.

Even if my experience was limited to my family curse, it seemed Gabrielle wasn't any more of an authority on soultrees than I was, so I let her go. I called Bian to update her about the results of the triangulation and to organize Ops 4-10 to head out for Vernal under Annie's command.

All the time, the back of my mind was still churning around what little I knew of soultrees.

I had to assume that Ash, if that was her name, was the soultree of the Irish coven responsible for the curse laid on my great-grandfather's family:

that all the first-born would die. A curse that was an enormous and complex working and required great power, over years.

Which meant Ash had to be an old and powerful soultree. Probably very powerful.

I held my cooling cup of coffee and tried to focus my mind on workings the way Tullah had suggested, but first, I reached down inside me until I got the sense of connection to the darkness there.

Imagined I was speaking to someone called Ash.

Asking about taking the power directly into me. Quietly.

The coffee heated up in an instant.

No one else noticed. I didn't need to pull this power through anyone else. And for simple things, it responded.

I cooled the coffee. Heated it back up. It was much quicker and easier if I touched the mug, but either way, it worked. I knew from Tullah that cold, heat and fire were standard magical workings, and even if my control wasn't up to creating fintyne, the Adept magical equivalent of napalm, heating and cooling might be a very useful working to have.

So... I had some strange arrangement which *seemed* to allow me to use the power that fed the curse. Was Ash actually directing the curse, or was Ash only the power?

If Ash was directing the curse, I couldn't see why she'd be allowing me to use the power. So, assuming that Ash was the power and the coven, who directed it, didn't become aware and stop me, I could presumably use this against Weaver somehow.

Unless it was a trick. Intended to make me depend on it, and then vanish at the critical moment. Or using the power was all part of the curse and it would backfire on me some other way.

If I used the power, could I direct it *away* from Kath and her unborn baby?

Or if I tried that, would it cut my access off?

I ran fingers through my hair and sighed. Too many questions. I had no time to experiment and so I couldn't rely on this ability. I had to go against Weaver with what I knew I could depend on: guns and physical violence. And I had to put off the issues of Kath and resolving the curse for another day.

Chapter 66

The Arapaho, in flight in the early, *early* morning of the next day, wasn't the ideal place to get a call from David.

Jen's Pilatus had a smart-comms capability that allowed passengers to use internet and cell phones. In contrast, the Arapaho had standard aviation radios. Not even a connection to the Ops 4-10 tactical network.

David's call was probably connecting through the cell phone towers at Vernal and it was at the edge of their range. The quality of the connection reminded me that we couldn't use cells in the Ashley Forest, and we didn't have enough Ops 4-10 TacNet headsets for everyone. Coordinating this search was going to be a bitch, so naturally, that was going to be my job.

"Amber?" David's voice was faint.

"Yes."

"Taylor found data on Weaver you need to see."

"At this hour?" It was 5 a.m. I hardly expected my sister's fiancé to be putting that kind of effort in, but clearly David had other ideas.

"We've been working all night," he said. His voice faded out and came back. "... wrapped himself up in a string of companies, but as far as Taylor's concerned, it's amateur hour."

"Good to know."

"Yeah. Hardly any untraceable offshore cut-outs or traps like that." Even as his voice came and went, David sounded almost offended that Weaver had thought his commercial structure was secure. "... doesn't pinpoint... land purchases... emailing you a list... especially... got a deep interest in something up there."

"You're breaking up, but it sounds like good news so far. Keep working. Anything that can help us find him quicker is gold at the moment."

The link cleared and David's voice came through stronger.

"We'll call again when we find more," David said.

Vernal was coming in sight as he ended the call.

He'd meant he'd call *if* they found any more.

It was frustrating that he couldn't just tell me where Weaver was, but to cut the territory down to a list of properties was a huge improvement.

We only had a day, but we could do this.

I had to keep believing that, in spite of the chill in the pit of my stomach.

Kane flew us directly to the Denver pack's house on the edge of the town. The house didn't have a heliport, but the backyard was more than big enough for the Arapaho to land.

Annie and Ops 4-10 had beaten us here. She'd driven a truck convoy through the night to deliver the Hill Bitch, a bleary-eyed group of my trainee werewolf cubs and five squads of Ops 4-10.

The Ops 4-10 troops looked ready for anything. The cubs, not so much. We'd keep them away from trouble if we could. It would be a good exercise for them, and maybe an opportunity to prove to Ops 4-10 they weren't a complete waste of space.

The local Denver pack patrols had turned up overnight. They were agitated, their Call bubbling beneath the surface, impatient to be out hunting.

All the senior Denver pack lieutenants were with Felix down in Louisiana, so I didn't know the guy heading up the teams. He came across and shook my hand.

"Nathan Woodside, ma'am."

"Amber, please. Good to see you, Nathan. Thanks for getting the patrols here. You understand the situation? Tracking down where Weaver has Tullah is really important."

"Tullah's part of your House, which I reckon means she's part of the Denver pack," he said simply. "For us, it's like that bastard kidnapped a sister. Don't worry, we'll find her."

The chill wind caught my eye and I had to turn away, just in time to see a couple more SUVs come in.

They were the first of the El Paso and New Mexico werewolves.

Zane and Alex had chartered a plane and flown them up to the closest airport, Roosevelt Municipal, about twenty miles away. One hundred of them had come, but there were only a dozen crammed into the two SUVs and nothing on the road behind them.

Annie came out from the house listening to her cell phone. Bad news: they'd run out of SUVs and trucks to rent in Roosevelt. They'd been able to rent some town cars as well, but there was heavy snow on the road. Five werewolves can lift a car out of a ditch, but we'd need truck levels of clearance on the snowbound roads and tracks in the Ashley.

Nathan's local Denver teams called in favors. Another five trucks in half an hour. More would try to get to us from Grand Junction, but that was hours away and those highways were snowed in too.

It was all happening unbelievably fast, given how short a time we'd had to work with, but also impossibly slowly, given the task ahead of us.

"We can use the trucks we have like shuttles," Nathan said. "Dropping some off and coming back to collect them later. That'd work around ranches, but obviously, we can't run four-footed through towns or anything."

"Work on plans," I said. "If we have to, we might use the Arapaho to drop groups off."

I handed over some of Tullah's clothing to Nathan. It'd all been washed of course, but werewolf noses would still be able to get her scent from it. Then I rushed into the house to find a computer and printer, leaving Annie and Nathan in charge of making sure everyone got into a team and each team had a piece of clothing to work with.

I prayed that the list that David and Taylor had sent broke the vast search area up into more manageable pieces. The problem with the trucks meant time was slipping away.

The email summary David had sent was long, but it included maps which had been marked with coordinates and property boundaries. All of them were well away from towns, which was good in that the local population wouldn't be involved, but bad in that the access tracks to them wouldn't be well maintained.

I set the printer to producing copies and took the first set out to Annie.

"These are known to be used or owned by Weaver," I said. "Prioritize them. Use them as center points for search patterns."

"Got it," she said. "We can send some of the SUVs back to Roosevelt with just a driver to pick up the teams there and head out to these sites further west." She ran a finger down the five furthest properties. "Any place on the way they find suitable vehicles to rent, the driver drops them and returns."

"Good."

A few more of the New Mexico and El Paso wolves turned up in cars just as I was heading back in to pick up more maps.

I hesitated, then made myself keep going.

I wanted to be there to greet them. Damn, I wanted to go out and run with them. But the most useful thing I could do at the moment was direct the search, and I needed to be here to coordinate the next step with Felix, Cameron and Skylur if... *when* we found Weaver.

The next set of maps I thrust into Kane's hand.

"Fly down toward Salt Lake, passing over these properties on the way," I said. "Check for unusual amounts of traffic, unusual heat signatures and so on, but don't circle over anything suspicious. Annie will make some calls while you're in the air, and if there are SUVs to rent down the road, ferry some of the troops from Roosevelt to pick them up. Then stop at Roosevelt on the way back and make sure your tanks are full. If we need to get somewhere in a rush, the Arapaho is it."

"Understood." He trotted back to the helicopter.

Annie and I distributed the remainder of the maps, and the group started to divide up into teams.

It was moving forward, but so slowly.

Back inside, there was an email from Abel Mathis, the Rock Springs alpha. More werewolves on the way to help and would I please call him about pack territories in the Ashley.

That was important.

"I guess it was too much to hope for that the Salt Lake pack wouldn't use the Ashley as part of their territory," I said to him.

"We're civilized," he said. "We both run in there and we manage to get along. I've called the alpha, and he says they haven't anything planned, but there'll be some wolves out there anyway. Best you take my Rock Springs guys and make sure there's one or two in every team you put out there, especially with New Mexico or El Paso wolves. Salt Lake'll recognize Denver, but not the others."

"We'll do that, thank you, Abel."

"Also, most of my guys will be coming down in their trucks with plenty of room to spare." He laughed. "Knowing the area, I'm guessing you kinda overloaded the capacity of the local economy for renting."

"You got that right."

I felt a rush of gratitude for his support—and his valuable knowledge of the local Were situation. All without exact knowledge of the importance.

"My boys will be there any time now," he said.

"Thank you again, and I'm sorry this is all so secret. It's really important. When I'm cleared to tell you why, I'll call you."

He was silent for a second.

"Appreciate that, but you need to know, Amber..." he stumbled a bit using my name, as if it made him embarrassed. "The Denver pack turned the Confederation around when they steamrollered us. And you yourself... well, my youngest brother was at that ritual at Bitter Hooks." His voice went very quiet. "Truth be told, there ain't that much to the Rock Springs pack, but you call, and we'll come."

We ended the call. I wiped my eyes and went outside with more maps. Annie and Nathan were getting some order in the melee. I updated them on the call.

Nathan looked much happier.

"Once Rock Springs arrive, we'll have enough trucks to get everyone where they need to be," he said.

Annie gave me the master TacNet headset.

"Your callsign's Alpha 6," she said. "I'm Hotel 6. I'm going to reorganize the teams and objectives based on Rock Springs pack members and trucks. I'll give you a copy when I'm done."

The pair of them ran off and the group began to seethe again as new instructions were made.

There was tension in the air, but also an excitement, and a Call.

Run! Hunt!

Chapter 67

A couple of hours later, the last of the trucks had left, having churned the yard into a sculpture of freezing mud and snow.

I'd had to fight the urge to join them. Instead I was studying Taylor's list on the computer screen. What Amanda would probably call displacement activity.

There were about twenty companies, all controlled by Weaver. Through them, he owned ranches in the foothills, leases in the park itself, a couple of stores in the towns. There wasn't any pattern to the locations other than they were scattered along the line of the Uinta Mountains as far west as the town of Hanna, and as far east as the Whiterocks, not too far from Vernal.

Something tugged at my memory reading those names, but it refused to surface.

I had a copy of Annie's plans on one of the maps, with the team that had been assigned to each of the properties, their callsigns and the team leader's name.

No one had even called in yet to say they'd arrived.

Frustrated, I did searches on the internet. If there was anything there, it was well hidden in millions of hits. Too much. The search parameters were too wide. The same as our physical search in the mountains.

Outside, I heard the Arapaho return.

If he'd seen something, Kane would have called ahead, so I blocked the noise out and stared at the screen as if there was a magic pixel there that would reveal where Weaver was.

"If it were you, which of those would you go to hide in?" Scott's voice startled me. He'd picked up one of the maps showing Weaver's properties and he was talking to Flint.

Alice and Gabrielle were sitting down listening. I'd held them back from joining the hunt on the basis that, if Weaver were alert, he might notice Adepts sneaking around his backyard.

Yelena had stayed as well. She'd told me she wasn't going to leave my side until we'd found Tullah, which I guessed meant she was there to stop me from doing something stupid.

"Why didn't you join in, Scott?" Alice asked. "Chasing the cubs through the forest."

Scott smiled. "They'd probably prefer that, which is why I left it to Rita."

Actually, I'd kept him back as well.

I turned away from the screen. Computers can only achieve so much, and it was better to leave David and Taylor working on the data. I had a team here, so I should use them.

"I know everyone's tired, but I need your help," I said. "Can we kick this around, please? Starting with Scott's question. If Weaver's at one of his properties, which one is it likely to be and why?"

"Which would be easiest to put a shield around?" Yelena asked. "That's where I would go."

Flint nodded. "Not something you do in a hurry, if you want a strong shield."

Kane spoke from the door as he stamped the snow off his boots. "Also, not easy to maintain. Tullah used the snow covering to bind a working around the mill in the San Juan. Alice uses the water running down the walls in the dungeon at Haven in the same way. What's Weaver going to use? Which of his properties is covered in snow?"

Good question, but easy answer, unfortunately.

"Probably most of them," I said.

The town of Vernal had a foot or so in the streets. The higher you went into the Uinta Mountains, the more snow would have fallen. Covering a ranch was nothing.

Dead end.

"Okay. What clue might there have been in Weaver's house?" Alice said when it went quiet.

She was speaking in the past tense. Rather than allow any traps we'd missed to go off and injure someone, Weaver's house had suffered a catastrophic accident and thoroughly blown up, courtesy of Annie.

We kicked around whether there would have been a clue there at all. Had he put the traps in the house so we wouldn't find clues? What about the books he'd taken from the shelves in his study? Were they significant? Taken because they were clues, or did he want some reading matter in hiding? Or, as Yelena pointed out, the books might be a false trail.

It was academic; I couldn't remember which books were gone, only that there had been some missing from his study.

Another dead end.

"Could a magic shield prevent werewolves from picking up a scent?" Scott asked.

Flint and Kane shrugged.

"Maybe," Flint said. "Not straightforward."

"Need to work on it to answer that," Kane finished.

My oath stirred with frustration. As rapidly as we'd moved, this was taking too long.

Need to find Weaver's hideout. Need enough time to organize an assault. Got to finish this today.

It was late morning already.

I needed to *do* something. We were running out of time for Tullah, and that meant for Kaothos too, for me and Hana and Tara. I could feel it.

I took the original map we'd made from the direction-finding workings and taped it to the wall. I marked Weaver's properties. About half of them were inside our estimated area.

Annie knew that, and those would be her top priorities. Within the hour, we'd start crossing the closest ones off the list, but the furthest away might take all day.

We stood and stared at the size of the problem on the map, and drank the coffee that Gabrielle brought out.

My mind strayed back to the flicker of memory that had tugged me earlier, as I read the list of properties. Something about that, and Weaver's house…

I closed my eyes and tried to visualize when I'd last seen Weaver, in his study. I tried to remember everything Weaver had said to me, everything I'd seen.

"Looking for something," Flint murmured, so quietly I almost missed it.

He was staring at the map. Alongside each property, he'd written the date it had been purchased. They ran left to right. West to east.

I blinked. He wasn't making a stupidly obvious comment that we were looking for something. He was saying *Weaver* had been looking for something. He'd started by buying a property in Hanna, and worked his way east along the Uinta Mountains.

"Oh, shit!"

My jaw dropped. That nagging memory had finally surfaced. A legend. One that linked everything together.

They were all looking at me.

"Thomas Rhoads," I said.

It clearly made no sense to any of them.

"Weaver's house." I was having trouble stringing words into sentences as the enormity of it hit me. "The artwork."

"What about the artwork?" Kane asked. "Besides the gold paint and bad taste?"

He frowned and then his eyes widened. "Mining!"

"Mining," I echoed. "Every single artwork was about mining."

"He's been looking for gold?" Flint asked incredulously.

"In a manner of speaking. I say he's found a legendry lost mine and he's down inside it, right now," I said, conviction gripping me as I spoke. "Water on the walls? A focus for workings? Got all that. Along with all the hills up here, there are a million lakes or something."

I moved in front of the map.

"And they say, what you're looking for is always in the last place you look." I took a marker and made a ring around the property Weaver had bought last, over two years ago.

"Somewhere in the vicinity of this ranch, he found the mine," I said. "And it's not just any mine, so there's no way he'd leave it unguarded or unprotected."

"What on earth is it?" Alice asked.

"In the 1850s, a Mormon by the name of Rhoads made some kind of deal with the Ute who lived here. They told him where to find gold in the Uinta Mountains, and that he did. He was the wealthiest Mormon of his time, and all of it was from the gold he brought out of these hills. His son was so rich, he offered to pay off the US national debt if he was given a lease to mine all the Uinta."

"But they didn't give it to him?"

"No. If I remember the story correctly, politics prevented it, and the knowledge of where the mines were hidden died with Rhoads' son and the Ute chiefs who dealt with him."

"Now Weaver has found the mines. And that," Flint tapped the map, "was the last place he was looking."

Kane was holding the map with Annie's scribbling on it. "Good news: it's the closest to here. Bad news: that's where your cubs and Rita have gone."

Chapter 68

"Hotel 6. Hotel 6. Alpha 6."

The TacNet was an incredible piece of equipment. Just not in this particular wilderness.

"Hotel 6," I heard, followed by a wash of static. She knew I was trying to talk to her, but nothing else.

The cubs had been sent to the easiest, closest location, so when it came to rationing out the TacNet headsets, they didn't get one. Cell phone coverage should have reached them. I tried calling Rita and got no answer. I left a message to bug out and call me.

I called Bian and asked her to update Skylur, and I was on the point of calling Felix when I stopped myself.

We didn't actually *know* Weaver was there. If he wasn't, I was wasting time talking to Felix and Cameron. If he was, the cubs might be in danger and any delay in pulling them back was unjustified. We weren't going there to engage with Weaver yet, just to scout.

"We'll get up in the Arapaho and see if that solves our problems connecting to Annie. We might be able to contact Rita as well."

"Noisy," Yelena said.

"We'll keep well away from the actual ranch. There are always mountain rescue helicopters flying around here. Vernal is the local emergency hospital."

I was making some of that up, and Yelena knew it.

"One mile," I said, to appease her. "No closer."

"Nautical or statute?" Kane asked innocently as he trotted off to the helicopter.

Yelena's eyes narrowed, but all she did was mutter in Ukrainian and pick up the Ops 4-10 light recon pack. So did I. Whether or not we were intending to fight, we weren't going to be unprepared. This was all enemy territory, potentially.

"It's the right move," I said, as we took off ten minutes later. Kane was flying, with Flint navigating. Alice and Gabrielle should have remained at the house to coordinate, but I had the TacNet headset and I wasn't leaving it behind, so they came with us.

"Hotel 6, Alpha 6." I tried the headset as soon as we were clear of the house.

"This is Hotel 6. Situation query." Annie came through.

"Alpha 6. New information. Site..." I had to glance back at the map for the designation. "Site Oscar now top priority. Attempting to recall Team Oscar. En route by helicopter. ETA 5."

"Hotel 6. Roger that. In contact with Team Mike. Will redeploy to assist you."

"Affirm. Vehicles remain one mile from site center."

There was a wave of static so long I thought I'd lost her again, but she came back.

"Query redeploy all teams."

I was working on a hunch, not solid data.

"Negative," I said. "Not at this time. Continue assigned tasks and listen out."

"Will do."

Yelena was trying the same with Rita by cell phone. She shook her head when I looked up. Not getting through.

I leaned across and spoke over the noise of the rotors. "Maybe the sound of the helicopter will make her stop and investigate."

Yelena pursed her lips. "Maybe." She waved out the front where we were heading. "This is not good."

It wasn't. It really wasn't.

In Ops 4-10, mines, tunnels or caves had been one of our nightmare scenarios. Inevitably, there were no maps of the underground passages and no way that normal GPS or surveillance would work. We'd needed to assault a couple in my time, and they'd been the most difficult targets. No idea how many enemies, no idea where they were underground. In this case today, no idea how they were armed, either.

Of course, if all we needed to do was destroy Weaver, the task would have been simpler. There are bombs that would do that quite effectively. But we needed to get Tullah out. Maybe Rita and the cubs, if they'd been caught.

It was nearly impossible to attack an enemy dug into a mine without harming hostages. Getting all of them out safely would be completely impossible.

Sneak attack?

Trick Weaver into abandoning the mine?

I was still spinning through a very poor set of options when Kane landed the Arapaho.

He'd found a frozen mud bank made by a bend in a stream, which offered a good flat surface. We were about a mile southeast of the ranch and hidden from it by ranks of lodgepole pine and mountain spruce, and a series of low, bare hills. The track up to the ranch was nearby, and there were places around here that Rita might have hidden their truck while Team Oscar checked out the ranch.

Yelena refused to consider me moving beyond the first of the bare hills we came to.

"You have headset to talk to others," she said. "You are coordinating."

I had binoculars, so I could see the ranch, and if I stayed lying flat, behind the summit of the small hill, I would not be seen.

Every time recently I'd ignored her warnings, it seemed I'd gotten into trouble.

And it was okay, really. We were here to get Rita and the cubs back first. It wasn't as if this was going to be an all-out assault on the ranch or the mine. Yet.

Not that we even knew where the mine was. It'd stayed undiscovered for a hundred and fifty years. We weren't going to stumble into it.

Get the cubs out. Check if this place had seen any visitors in the last couple of days. They could do that without me.

Under instruction from Yelena, Scott changed to wolf and tore off through the snowy pines to see if he could catch a scent or find tracks.

Under protest, Kane had remained with the Arapaho. Gabrielle stayed with him to work a couple of cell phones: one to keep trying to contact Rita, the other to talk to Team Mike, who were saying they'd join us in twenty minutes.

Alice was sent after Scott, to call on her cell if he found something.

Flint and Yelena took off at a trot through the trees toward the ranch.

I used the TacNet to update as many teams as I could get through to while I watched the ranch through the binoculars.

No trucks outside. No smoke from the chimney. No clearing of the snow away from the doors.

The track that went up to the ranch had seen some use, but at that distance, I couldn't tell how long ago, and I had no information about when the last snowfall had been.

The Denver pack patrol would know that, so I was about to call Team Echo and ask when something stopped me.

Something was wrong.

Had I heard something out of place?

I looked back at the frozen stream where we'd landed. It was about half a mile away.

The Arapaho sat on the bank. The engine was off, the doors were closed and I couldn't possibly hear Gabrielle talking on the cell, not even with my hybrid hearing.

The stream was frozen over. No possibility that was making any noise that I'd hear at this distance either.

A flock of doves burst out of a stand of pine about a hundred yards away to my left, startling me. They arced away in a frantic flurry of wings.

What had spooked them?

That was the opposite direction from the one Scott had taken and a long way from where Yelena had gone.

A fox broke cover and ran away, leaping clear of the snow to go faster.

And down there, next to the ranch, deer I hadn't even seen suddenly bolted across a snow-covered field.

I took the safety off my MP5 and turned in a slow circle.

Nothing.

My imagination?

I *could* hear something.

A distant hum, like electricity pylons. Then a grinding sound.

And then, I felt it, through the ground.

Earthquake?

No. A hundred yards away, the trees weren't stirring. There was snow on the boughs that wasn't falling.

I staggered up like I was drunk, unable to keep my balance.

A substantiation?

I looked upward.

Blue sky. Morning sunshine. No weird clouds. No clouds at all.

It was at that point the earth opened up beneath me. I fell, and the last thing I saw, high above, was the bright sunlight and the blue of the sky being eaten by the Fenris wolf, with jaws of dark earth and teeth of rock.

Chapter 69

"The bitch is coming around."

If I could hear that, I guessed I had to be alive, whatever it felt like. The words were oddly muffled.

Dirt in my mouth. I tried to spit to clear it, had to roll over and vomit abruptly. I was covered in cold, wet earth. Mouth, nose, hair, eyes, ears—everything invaded with mud. It'd torn away the MP5, the TacNet and the rest of my equipment, ripped my jacket and T shirt off.

I was soaking, *freezing*. I'd been handcuffed, with my hands in front of me. There was some kind of collar around my neck. It was heavy and ominous.

Someone threw water into my face and another voice spoke. A reprimand.

I could hear a bucket being put down in front of me.

There was water inside; enough to clean my eyes and ears, wipe the mud and vomit from my mouth.

"Everyone looks upward for substantiations," Weaver said. "Up in the sky. Never down in the earth. Foolish."

"There are people who are looking for you, and they aren't fools," I replied and coughed up more dirt. "Now they'll know where you are."

We were in a small room, no more than five by five. The walls were rough-cut from rock. A camp bed was pushed against one wall. Electric cable came in by the door for a single light tube on a stand. Pipes also came in, next to the door, ending in a faucet, a sink and a toilet. All the comforts of home.

Weaver and another man were standing watching me. They were between me and the door.

"Oh, they'll figure it out and your little troop will gather and finally decide to make some attempt to get into a mine where they can't even find the entrance," Weaver said. "It'll be far too late by then."

I didn't like the sound of that, but I kept my mouth shut.

"Get up," he said.

I took my time, checking for any damage.

There seemed to be none, and I still had my boots, and my pants. Small mercies. I clenched my calf muscles on the right. Ahh. And one thing these assholes had overlooked. My hidden knife. Amateurs. Good.

The other man spoke: "That collar you're wearing will deliver enough electricity to fry your neck." He held up a small controller. "It also contracts."

He demonstrated the contraction, and I choked before he wound it back enough for me to breathe.

Bastard.

"Feel free to give me problems," he said. "I'm looking forward to your death being slow and painful. Or terrifying. Both work for me."

"I hope there'll be no need for that, Celum," Weaver said. He took his jacket off and draped it across my shoulders, buttoned the front. Patted my shoulder. "No need to make this any more uncomfortable than it is. In the final analysis, we're all going to be on the same side."

Celum and I would not be on the same side. *Ever.* Even with my nose still blocked with mud, I was getting a scent off him. El Paso.

You can take over a pack, but sometimes you can't take everyone in the pack with it. I guessed he'd be one of Caleb and Victoria's former lieutenants, maybe one of the oldest ones. Whatever anyone else did, he wasn't willing to accept the change of leadership.

Either Celum was going to die today, or I was.

"You'll want to see Tullah," Weaver interrupted my thoughts. "Follow me."

At the level we were at, the mine was a collection of caverns connected by tunnels. Somewhere they had a generator, because they had electric light down here.

Which meant a vent to the outside.

If there was a way out, there was a way in. Ops 4-10 infrared scopes would see the heat from the vents. So could wolf eyes.

I just had to stay alive and prevent whatever it was that Weaver was planning.

We dropped a level down a steel staircase.

Weaver had put a lot of resources into this.

"Find any gold?" I asked.

Weaver laughed. "I guess my hobby is obvious. Yes. These tunnels go for miles. No huge motherlodes yet, but even the old tailings are worth processing."

We walked down another staircase.

"That was how you found me, eh?" Weaver said. "Quicker than I planned, so it's lucky you led us to Tullah first. Without that, things would have been difficult."

"Without the Hecate, it would have been more than difficult," I said.

He laughed it off. "Your Adepts did manage to surprise me, but we were never in danger. We got rid of you and both the other substantiations quite easily. The Hecate was handy, but not essential."

Well, I wasn't going to argue with him. Let him delude himself and underestimate others.

I hadn't seen anyone else in the mine yet, but I could *feel* them down below, and the further we went, the more my skin began to crawl. There were some serious magical workings down here.

The rough-cut tunnels disappeared behind plain plastic boarding.

It was warmer, and hidden behind the boarding there were pumps working. Water flowed through pipes.

I remembered it as a hazard of mining in the Uinta Mountains. There was water everywhere. And of course, I'd bet he was using it to bind a working, hiding what he had down here the same way that was used in Skylur's dungeon.

In confirmation, we came to an open archway that was closed off with a sheet of water dropping from the top and collected in a trough at the bottom.

"Through quickly, please," Weaver said. He flicked a switch and the water stopped long enough for Celum to push me through.

No electricity on this side. A couple of old miner's lamps sat on the floor inside. Weaver picked them up, gave one to me.

I could feel the water all around this area, like a cocoon. I could feel the working in it, blocking us away from the outside world.

I could feel the growing power and I stumbled down more steps into the gloom.

A wide circular pit, making me think of a huge crucible.

Seating still being built around the ring.

Bare concrete floor.

Tullah lay in the middle. She was naked except for a collar like mine around her neck. Hers was fastened by a chain to a hoop set in the floor.

I fell to my knees. Her skin was cold.

"Tullah?"

She didn't stir. The light of my lamp gleamed on the sweat coating her. I found a weak pulse in her throat.

"She hears you," Weaver said. "She's recovering at the moment. Not really been subjected to anything too painful. Not yet. Whether that continues is up to you."

Chapter 70

"So here's what we'll do," Weaver said while I sat on the floor cradling Tullah's unresponsive body.

"You call your mentor in Denver and persuade her to come here. It's as easy as that. No one gets any more hurt than necessary. You and Tullah can go back and get on with your lives. I know you Athanate and Were are becoming frantic over humanity discovering the paranormal, but you can all stop worrying. I will handle it, with the dragon."

Above the pit Tullah and I were in, there were broad steps completely encircling it, like an amphitheater. They'd started to install seats, but it wasn't complete. Tools and iron support bars lay stacked on one side.

Weaver walked around the first step until he was opposite the door we'd used to enter, then sat down, his lamp at his feet.

The uplighting wasn't flattering. It made him look demonic, but he was probably way beyond that type of petty consideration.

"I have no biases against humanity or paranormal races," he said. "We can all live together. Life will be immeasurably improved for everyone. Well, almost everyone. It'll need firm direction, of course, that's a given. Nevertheless, within my guidelines, countries would continue to rule themselves, without wars, without abuses of their populations, paranormal or otherwise."

He chuckled and shook his head. "I may become the only universally loved ruler ever. Not at first of course, but when the benefits become apparent to the billions of marginals, the disenfranchised, the poor and subjugated people all over the world. The sort of people whose lives mean nothing to monsters like Matlal, and little more to the Emperor of Heaven."

I was barely listening. He had me at 'firm direction'. In the negative sense.

I was trying to gently ease into Tullah's mind with my eukori, but there were barriers I'd never sensed before.

Whatever Weaver had tried, it seemed she'd put up a barrier that had defeated him.

And there was no way, even if I called Diana, she was going to agree to hand Kaothos over to him. Not that it seemed Weaver had any way to achieve that without getting himself squashed like a bug by Kaothos. Yes, he'd grown in power, but stronger than Diana? Strong enough to bind Kaothos?

No.

Others were coming in through the water-door behind me. They were walking around the circle and taking their seats in silence, making us the ominous center of attention. Each one added a *weight* to the feeling in the pit. My skin crawled.

"Now Altau, he has the right idea, but he lacks something." Weaver pursed his lips in thought. "The *drive,* the single-mindedness to see it through."

The irony of that statement completely escaped Weaver. He was what—fifty years old? Skylur had watched over the Athanate for *thousands* of years without rest, making untold sacrifices in a single-minded mission to ensure their survival.

In service of that mission, he could be one of the most cold-bloodedly ruthless people I'd ever known.

And yet… he still lacked the callousness, the ability to murder millions, which would be the first outcome of Weaver's reign.

"But even worse, Altau does not have the competence in his organization. Look at you two! A half-witted, disloyal Adept who refused to admit she was hosting the dragon, and then proceeded to lose it. Not to a stronger Adept, though that would have happened in time, but to an *Athanate.*"

"And as her friend, did you offer counsel? Take her to Skylur? Suggest any sensible options? No. You blundered around in the dark, driven mad by your hybrid nature, until you precipitated the confrontation where the dragon moved unpredictably."

I was getting tired of this, but he loved the sound of his own voice. I guessed I was condemned to listen until the rest of the coven had come in.

They weren't the Denver coven. They were the same bodies, but I *knew* some of these people, back when Tullah's mother had been leader of the coven. Tullah had told me tales of looking after their children on camping trips in the Rockies, of parties and barbeques. She'd complained about all their fussy rules about not using magic.

These weren't the same people. They couldn't be.

They looked... absent.

Compelled.

The weight continued to build. At some critical point, it'd formed a shadow, a visual distortion behind Weaver.

It came to me that each member of the coven was part of that *thing.*

Which, in Adept terms, meant that the *thing* was part of them as well.

What had Diana said to me about the Taos Adepts? *The fish goes rotten from the head.*

The lock on Diana had bound the Taos community into the evil that might have started with their leader alone. For the Taos Adepts, that lock had become their soultree.

What I was seeing behind Weaver was the soultree of the Denver coven.

Evil, given a foothold through Weaver, had propagated throughout what had been the most benevolent of Adept communities. That was where he had gotten his extra power from.

I felt sick to my stomach again.

"It should have been mine from the outset," Weaver was saying, leaning forward for emphasis. "All of this could have been avoided. It was intended for me."

He leaned back, and in the yellow glare of the lamp, the shadow seemed to settle around his shoulders, as if it was possessive.

The hairs on the back of my head stood up.

A soultree could be more than just a passive, inanimate concept, a shared space for aura.

I knew that; Ash wasn't inanimate.

It'd happened here, too. Instead of being a sort of central repository of their ideals and aspirations, and a common resource, the Denver community soultree had turned into the agent of their corruption.

Taos Adept community. And then Denver.

Once might be a coincidence. Twice is not. I could hear the voice of my old Ops 4-10 instructor, Ben-Haim, as if he were standing beside me.

Matlal was behind this. He had twisted the Denver community, just as he had twisted the Taos community. I didn't know how, but I knew it was him.

I'd forgotten Celum, until he bent down beside me and whispered in my ear. His voice was soft as a serpent.

"I'm looking forward to you refusing his offer," he said. "So I get to play with you. And if you think that's bad, I'm going to hand you over to an old friend of yours afterwards. I'm sure you'll remember Mirela Tucek. When she starts on you, you'll wish you could have stayed with me."

I remembered Tucek. She'd called herself Mother Tucek, and had run a 'convent' in Taos, full of Carpathian nuns. She'd killed for fun in front of me, and it was she who'd been responsible for Matlal's escape.

She was a link between Matlal and what happened to the Taos Adepts.

And here in Denver? I took another long sniff of Celum. El Paso, for sure. Beneath that? I couldn't be sure, but there are no coincidences. Celum was obviously familiar with Matlal, through Tucek, and he provided a connection to both the El Paso alphas' challenge *and* Weaver.

"You know they've gone all Aztec down there in Yucatan. After we've had our fun, I'm going to watch Mirela open you up and dig your heart out of your chest."

My stomach churned. His voice had gotten hoarse. He was actually aroused thinking about it.

He'd gotten louder as well.

"Enough, Celum," Weaver said. "I don't think we'll be doing that. Outside of strict need, all this fascination with pain and terror is unwholesome. There's no call for it. And I'll have no requirement to keep Matlal happy either, when I have the dragon."

Celum said nothing.

I wasn't going to foul my eukori by looking into his mind, but I didn't need to. Celum hated Weaver and he'd kill him, if he got the chance.

More members of the coven, at least the ones that had survived Weaver's takeover, had come in and sat in their places. The shadow behind Weaver had grown with each addition. It was dark and thick as an oil fire. To my paranormal senses, it reeked. And it was growing, more than the addition of each member.

"Do you agree to call your mentor?" Weaver asked me.

I shook my head.

He sighed.

"Then we must revert to the plan to lure the dragon here and precipitate a move. Unfortunately, there needs to be great duress both for the lure and the move. In plain words, pain for the hosts, and pain for the dragon. Enormous, unbearable pain. Are you sure you won't reconsider?"

"Don't." Tullah stirred feebly and breathed as I held her against me. "Kill me. Don't let that creature trap Kaothos."

Weaver's plan fell into place at that point.

Weaver wasn't intending to displace his own spirit guide with Kaothos. He'd deliberately twisted the Denver soultree with the specific purpose of capturing the dragon. That's what Tullah meant by 'creature'—the foulness that had been the soultree.

I didn't understand the mechanics, or whether it'd work. Weaver was convinced it would. Weaver believed that Kaothos would be trapped in the soultree and Weaver would control the soultree.

I shook my head again in answer to Weaver's question of reconsidering. There wasn't any point calling Diana anyway. She wouldn't fall into this trap, whatever I said.

Weaver shrugged.

The shadow stretched out from behind him, formed a snakelike arm.

This was very, very bad.

Tullah cringed.

The snake slithered down the step and crossed the floor slowly. The way it did that—it was nothing to do with a restriction on its movement; it was enjoying our fear.

"Kill me," Tullah said, shrinking away from it, but at that moment, Celum ripped Weaver's jacket off me and snapped a chain onto my collar. He pulled me back so I couldn't reach her and then he fastened the chain to a hoop.

"Can't have you killing our little star," he said. "Not until we're finished."

He quickly stood away from me as the shadow snake approached.

It ignored Tullah.

It rose and struck at me.

Chapter 71

"Not that bad, was it?"

It wasn't, but I wasn't going to tell him that. The soultree's strike was a stronger version of Weaver's covert working that he'd hit me with at the club and afterwards at his house. It was like static electricity. More shock than pain.

The payload was the same.

Weaver had gone back to his favorite weapon; a working that attacked my mind. Except I was ready this time, even if I hadn't realized I was. With a kind of sick fascination I found I could visualize what it was doing and how it was succeeding, like a psychedelic shimmering trying to creep through my head, some bizarre aftershock of Kane's peyote trip.

It *was* fascinating.

Not only was it not quite what Weaver thought it was, but I found I had defenses against it.

That was a wild card in my hand. It might give me an edge, but I couldn't see how, yet.

One last person entered the room through the water-door behind me. Not one of the Denver coven. I could feel a ripple of fear down the seated ranks of Adepts and I knew who it was.

Gwendolyn Enkeliekki, leader of the Michigan and Ontario Adepts, and Hecate of the Northern Adept League, stalked around the raised circumference of the pit like a jaguar.

She was as I'd first seen her. Hair like ice. Eyes like electric blue neon. Dressed in a black leather duster and thin gloves.

Weaver seemed to be the only one not actually scared of her.

A couple of Adepts to Weaver's right hurriedly moved, and she sat in the vacated space. She peeled off the thin gloves, her movements languid and precise, her eyes fixed on Celum.

"You have a job, Celum," she said, "and it doesn't involve your perverted hobby of torture. It involves protecting the mine."

"There's no threat," he said.

"No? Several groups of heavily armed troops, including former Special Forces colleagues of our prisoner, are above us as you stand there, wasting time."

"So what? They can't find the way in!"

"Their equipment includes explosives perfectly capable of removing twenty feet of topsoil, if correctly placed, and collapsing the mine around our ears, if not. Take your scum pack of outcast wolves and persuade the visitors to fall back until we have the dragon."

Celum squared his shoulders and tried to stare the Hecate down. "You can't order me around," he said.

The Hecate didn't answer. She simply looked at him and the temperature of the room plummeted. Even the obscene shape of the soultree seemed to shrink in on itself.

"Go," Weaver said hurriedly. "Give me the controller for the collars first."

Celum stomped to the front and handed it over with ill grace.

He didn't like the Hecate, and he didn't like Weaver. I wondered if there was anyone he did like.

"Harrison," Weaver called out to one of the Adepts behind me. "Go with him and run the tunnel substantiation. Let Celum and his wolves come up behind the troops at our front door."

There was nothing I could do about that immediately, but if Annie was here, she'd never get caught off guard like that. If Annie wasn't... I tried to remember who was in charge of Team Mike.

Besides all that, the Hecate was lying, unless Annie hadn't told me what the Ops 4-10 squads were carrying, but I allowed nothing to show on my face. It seemed no one dared challenge the Hecate's statements about the troops carrying explosives.

With Celum gone, the room temperature returned to normal.

"You're a bit early," Weaver said to the Hecate.

"On the contrary, I'm just in time," she replied. "Celum needed to be sent to do his job, and I needed to come here and prepare to open a bridge to the dragon."

"You said it would be much easier if we could use Farrell."

"And I meant it. It's Farrell's Athanate mentor who's hosting the dragon. Far easier to use that connection to build the bridge than one between a former host and spirit guide. It would have been even easier if she'd brought Diana to Vernal with her, but she didn't."

"Is the former host redundant then?" one of the Adepts asked.

"No," the Hecate replied. "She remains the lure, and it's her pain that the dragon will be subject to."

"Speaking of which..." Weaver ran his finger over a button on the controller and Tullah jerked. She tried to stay still, but no amount of self-control could stop her hands from reaching for the collar.

I strained forward, but the chain holding me was already taut. I tried to shout for him to stop, but the collar was choking me and my voice was a near-silent rasp.

They ignored me.

"Build it slowly." The Hecate put a hand out and touched Weaver's arm. "It does no good to knock her out. The correct timing on this is vital. I will open that bridge after Farrell's resistance reaches its critical point. Your conjunct spirit," she waved at the shape behind him, "must be ready by that time. At exactly that point, the former host must be in excruciating pain. Not unconscious. Fail any of that, and we're in a world of trouble."

"It's all going as planned," Weaver said. "The conjunct will reach full power in..." he looked at his watch, "seven minutes and forty seconds exactly. The pain for Tullah will escalate smoothly throughout that time. Farrell's ability to resist my commands will be destroyed long before that. She's barely recovered from the earlier working and this one's more powerful. She'll do exactly what we tell her."

Either the Hecate was an evil, perverted bitch who enjoyed ensuring I knew what was about to happen to me, or Gabrielle had been right all along, and she was feeding me information in the hope I could do something about it.

If I couldn't, what would she do?

Sabotage it herself?

Skylur had passed along the message from the New York Adepts. They'd said the dragon was of such significance that Hecate Gwendolyn Enkeliekki would commit any act to ensure the dragon was protected.

I felt a chill pass through me. I suddenly saw that 'any act' probably included dying. Me, Tullah, everyone here, including the Hecate herself.

My nose flared, and I tasted the subtle scents of the room. The Hecate hadn't completely lied. There *were* explosives that threatened us. She had them.

They were continuing to talk. It was a low-voiced, private conversation. It seemed Weaver had forgotten about my hybrid hearing.

It was good enough to hear them discussing the fact that the Hecate's input was key. None of the other Adepts had the power to reach all the way to Denver and breach the shield around the dungeon. The conjunct could do it, theoretically, but it was tricky to try that, channel the pain from Tullah to lure Kaothos out *and* then draw Kaothos back here and capture her within the conjunct.

"I'm sure you will develop the level of power to spirit walk that far," the Hecate said. "It's mainly a matter of overcoming your self-limiting beliefs."

Weaver thought she was flattering him.

She was talking secretly to me, and giving me the faintest outline of a plan.

Get Kaothos here *before* the conjunct was ready to trap her. And knock Tullah out so she couldn't distract Kaothos when I did. Obviously, I needed to disobey Weaver's commands.

How to do all that?

The Hecate had told me; I needed to overcome my self-limiting belief that I couldn't spirit walk all the way to Denver.

The Hecate had to know what Weaver's workings were doing to me. Yes, they were attempting to dismantle my ability to resist his demands. Good luck with that. But it was no precision surgical strike. It was about as subtle as a grenade, damaging inhibitions and increasing suggestibility.

His previous attempt had done all sorts of things he probably didn't know about.

He probably anticipated the reduction of sexual inhibitions. He didn't even know about Ash, and that whatever else it had done, his working enabled my connection to Ash.

And I'd spirit jumped all the way back to Ireland.

If I could do that, I sure as hell could spirit jump to Denver.

All I needed was a base to launch from. Being chained to the floor in a room which was magically isolated from the rest of the world wasn't that base.

But I had other skills Weaver didn't know about. My Carpathian Athanate heritage. I could connect my eukori to other paranormals and harness some of their power.

Step one was to get out from behind this magical shield.

Step two would be to connect with my House outside.

Step three would be to spirit walk all the way back to Denver.

I'd need to tap into Ash's power to do that. I needed to really open up and let that power in. I didn't care whether that was good or bad. It could suck my soul out of me for all I cared at that moment.

That was my plan. Get Kaothos and she would put an end to Weaver.

Only everything had to go right, or nothing would.

With my desperation driving it, my Carpathian eukori probed the barriers that had been raised in Tullah's mind, achieved a spark of a connection. I willed her to meet my eyes, no matter how much pain she was in.

I could feel that pain. The collar was pulsing electric shocks into her system. Linked through eukori, I shared those and their brutality made me gasp.

For a moment, I thought I was too late for Tullah, that there was nothing left.

Then I caught a tiny spark; the smallest glimmer of the old Tullah hidden deep inside her. I needed to draw that to the fore. I needed her with me.

She looked, and I saw myself as she saw me: a wild figure, mud-caked hair, muddy warpaint covering the top half of my face, eyes staring like a demented woman.

"It's only at times like these, Apprentice," I said, my voice ragged, "when you've got nowhere left to go, that you draw to an inside straight."

"What's she saying?" Weaver frowned and peered at me.

I ignored him. Ignored the workings attacking my mind. Ignored everything around me but Tullah.

I forced the words out. "Remember what I taught you about drawing the inside straight. Tell me."

Her eyes were dull with the pain, but her lips moved.

"Outside straight good. Inside straight bad. Bad odds. Never take it. Unless no option."

She was a mess, but answering me brought that fierce glow back to the surface. She was fighting back.

Helped by Tara. I sensed my twin, but I couldn't see clearly. Tullah's mind was dulled with the pain already, and every second it grew worse.

Sharing eukori would help with the pain, but that wasn't the purpose.

It'd give us more power than I had on my own. It would also expose Tullah to the effects of Weaver's spell on my mind. It would be a race between our spirits breaking out of the crucible and Tullah's resistance to Weaver failing.

"If fail..." Her eyes closed as the shocks grew worse. Her voice faltered. Her lips continued to move, mouthing the same words over and over. "Promise. Fail. Kill me. Save Kaothos."

I could. If we were tightly bound, linked with eukori, I could stop her heart. It'd probably stop mine as well.

I would. She sensed that and she lowered her barriers. I gathered her fully into my eukori, bound her to me as quickly and completely as I could, and we reached out.

We met the slick water-bound shield that covered this room.

There wasn't even a single electric cable that pierced that shield, and like the construct, the shield was getting stronger every second. Tullah and I slammed against it and couldn't pierce it.

There was no other power I dared use in this room. No Ash. I tried and there was nothing there. The shield held.

If only I'd done it earlier. If only I'd tried when people were walking through that water-door.

Drawing to an inside straight was a fool's game. We couldn't even get out of this room.

And as Tullah said, we couldn't let them use us to capture Kaothos.

But our attempt hadn't gone unnoticed.

An aura like cold smoke seeped around us. I could taste who it belonged to.

Was she on our side? Would she help?

Or would letting her in allow her to prevent us from escaping?

Or worse, if we got out and called Kaothos, would we find this was all another elaborate trap for the Hecate's own ends?

Maybe. Maybe not. We had no other options at the moment.

I pulled my second inside straight and let her in.

Great wings around me, lifting me up. Cold. Cold. Blue.

The water-door stuttered.

A fraction of a second without the continuous sheet of water enclosing the entire room. A tiny break in the working. It was enough to reach out, but would it be enough to spirit walk?

Tullah was suffering too much to help.

The Hecate wasn't there anymore.

My eukori shot through the water-door, through the empty mine.

I needed an anchor out here, a relay. Something to attach myself to, so I could gather myself for the next leap. All in that closing fraction of a second.

Kane!

The crazy coyote had found the generator's vent and was scrabbling his way down the shaft into the mine. He was using some shapeshifting illusion to pass himself off as one of Celum's werewolves, in case he met anyone. Creeping behind him was Flint.

Stupid boys.

I couldn't project words with simple eukori, but we both knew what the other was thinking.

You're welcome, Boss.

I latched onto them and they gave me the strength to keep the tiniest pinhole in the water-door while my eukori raced up the ventilation shaft to find Yelena, Rita.

Relief. Fear.

I had no time. I needed the soultree's power. I didn't even have time to warn anyone. The best I could do was to reach slowly. Try and limit the shock.

Ash! Ash!

The Irish soultree's power seethed and started to rise through me, and through everyone connected to me. Dark. Seductive.

But it rose too slowly, as if being held back. Three spirit anchors fought against me. I screamed. I had no time. No time. *No time!*

Kane understood.

I sensed him hesitate and shudder at the feel of Ash's magic. Sensed him tremble on the brink. If he cut me out, the water-door would probably close, leaving me trapped in the pit.

But what I was asking him to do was to put all his strength into blood magic.

My eukori link stretched, grew pale and insubstantial as mist.

The presence of Ash, that sense of *power*, receeded.

Despair flooded me.

And then Kane shook himself and fed his power into our link. Somehow, without words, he warned the others.

Thank you!

I sensed what I needed to do and *pulled* with everything I could. Poured pain and anger down at what was holding Ash back. Pulled again. Mercilessly. Felt the shock. Felt the spirit tethers break, and I wrenched Ash's power into me.

Pain!

Like molten lava through my veins.

Bubbling up. Weaver's workings snuff out in my head. What damage is done, is done.

The workings in Tullah's head are more difficult. They slow. Stop. That has to be enough for the moment.

My surroundings disappear. I'm in the mine and I'm outside and I'm on the ground and I'm in Ireland and I'm in the sky and I'm soaring south and east over the Rockies like a missile, screaming anger and pain into the sky.

"She's spirit walking! She got out! Stop her!"

Somewhere, far away, there is a great alarm. People shouting. Running.

Doesn't matter. All so slow.

I arc down.

Denver. Evergreen. Bear Ridge.

Finally, Haven.

Where I have come from there's a silken thread in the sky and I pull it after me, down the secret elevator, through the tiny gaps in Alice's working, down into the dungeon.

Diana leaps up in shock. What's happening?

Kaothos speaks: Amber Farrell? Is that you?

Her voice rocks the dungeon.

Yes, it's me. Quick.

She manifests in a panic, her body filling the room, shattering furniture and pushing Lyssae off their pedestals. Screams and fear.

I slap my silken thread on the dragon's snout and point. Follow it. Up, back. Tullah. Hurry! Now! Go. Go. Go!

Kaothos is slow. So slow. It's as if she's a part of Diana now. She can't get free.

It's tearing Diana apart. Tearing them both apart.

Pain.

Everything is painful.

Except death, maybe.

And that was when someone back in the pit must have picked up a miner's shovel and hit me over the head with it.

Chapter 72

Light. Dark. Light. Dark.

The contrast was too painful to open my eyes just yet. I was shuffling forward, swaying.

Hot. Cold. Hot. Cold.

Scrape of soft shoe on stone.

That was good, right? Hearing and feeling means I'm alive. Even the pain in my eyes is proof I'm alive.

I put out my hands to feel my way and cracked an eyelid. I touched nothing, but the light stabbed in like needles.

Blurry.

Light. Dark.

Hot. Cold.

I was shuffling along some sort of corridor.

Oh, my God, I'm in a hospital. An asylum. I've gone crazy. I'm full of drugs. It was all a hallucination.

No.

Stone floor. High ceiling. Windows at regular intervals. No, not windows. Arches. Weathered stone arches, like an Old World monastery. Not an asylum.

Cold and dark in the shade. Light and hot in the sun.

Where the hell?

I opened my eyes a bit more. The corridor went on and on, angling smoothly to the right, so I couldn't see more than about fifty paces ahead. Outside, featureless green grass stretched away to a dark line meeting a chalky blue sky at the horizon. Weird as hyper-realistic art.

"Am I dead?" My voice belonged to someone else. It creaked.

No, replied Speaks-to-Wolves from behind me. *Not yet, anyway.*

"Thanks so much for the boost, great-grandmother. Wonderful turn of phrase."

I felt the sigh and the rolling eyes. But a little laughter behind that as well.

If I'd brought you up, you'd have more respect for your elders.

"You once said you wanted me to have Coyote as my spirit guide. I don't think he does respect very well."

You have Coyote now. And Raven. Not exactly as spirit guides, but similar.

"I need all the help I can get, and I'll take it where it's given. Where the hell am I?"

It doesn't matter where this is, and I can't explain it to you.

"It does matter. I have some friends that need my help."

I turned around, but she was just a shape of light and dark, standing next to me. I could see we were dressed in buckskin and moccasins. I felt my cheeks and forehead; a bar of dark war paint crossed my face.

Your friends will be there when you get back, Speaks-to-Wolves said. *Time isn't the same here.*

"This is the spirit world? I'm having a time-out?"

No. You must concentrate on why you're here, not where you are. You have a really important choice to make. Everything there depends on what you decide to do here.

I grunted. "And according to you, I get no help from anyone else to make my decisions."

Yes.

"If time doesn't matter, it would really help me... in a different way... to understand where we are."

She sighed and laid a hand on my arm, stopping me.

It seemed like a real, flesh-and-blood hand.

I couldn't see her face. I'd seen her before, in the shape of a wolf and as a woman, but today, she was a phantom in the darkness between the arched windows, apart from her hands, which she stretched out in the bright sunlight.

She put them together, slipped finger over finger.

What do you see, there on the floor?

I looked down at the shadow of her hands.

"Wolf."

As soon as I said it, there was the whisper of hand slipping against hand.

"Rabbit. Eagle. Elk. Cougar. Hey, that's really good, that one."

And yet they are none of those animals. They are hands.

Humans see the shadows in their world and name them, but none can imagine, from the shadow, what shape in the light causes them. We are standing in the light, but the only words I can use are words you have for the shape of shadows. We are not in the physical world, or the spirit world.

We are where the shapes you have names for, come from.

Strangely, it did help. However chilling and obscure it was.

I started walking again.

Warm and light in the sunlight. Cold and dark in the shade.

"So what do I have to decide?"

Speaks-to-Wolves sighed again.

What will you do with Kaothos?

The question shocked me enough that I stopped in the shadow between windows.

"What? I'm not doing anything with her at all, other than guiding her to Tullah."

Your spirit bridge through the sky leads to you. She will come to you first.

"And then on to Tullah."

Maybe. If you let her go. The problem is, Tullah will be unable to do anything until she recovers from Weaver's workings. As well as that, spirit guides and hosts develop over time. Kaothos has been greatly changed by her time with Diana. In the same way, Tara and Hana have been greatly changed by their time with Tullah.

It was cold in the shadow. I edged forward until the sunlight warmed me.

"Still..."

Kaothos might be a better fit for you. Tara and Hana might be a better fit for Tullah.

"No!"

Are you sure? You can barely imagine the power that Kaothos will develop over time, given a host who can direct and use those powers. You are more experienced than Tullah, much better placed in the coming events of Emergence. Think of what you could achieve...

I was thinking all right.

That power. Even more power than Ash, and not full of pain and hatred. A force for good.

That's exactly right. A force for good.

There was a sweetness to it, a rightness, that tasted familiar. Beguiling. A taste that would never cloy. Addictive.

But was Kaothos good?

"The Hecate said... implied that dragons can't be good. She said the name comes from drac which means devil. Was she just trying to confuse me?"

I don't think she was trying to confuse you. What did she mean? Think it through.

I frowned.

Drac was a name. A name humans came up with. A name for shadows, without knowing the true nature of what stood in the light.

Diana again, explaining about people calling Athanate monsters: *The monster's inside you. It has always been. The Athanate powers do no more than tempt it from its lair inside your head. What happens next is up to you.*

I blinked. "There are no devils, but we make them," I said.

Speaks-to-Wolves nodded, a movement of light and darkness.

Kaothos could be a devil, if we made her so. And dragon spirit guides *had* been devils, in history, because that's what humanity had made of them.

"And power... the use of power is what defines them. The greater the power, the more the temptation to go wrong."

Yes, daughter. And the easier the corruption.

"But how to use power without becoming a monster?"

There are ways. A guardian angel. A sacrifice of the self. Both.

"Well, there are no guardian angels. And besides, my old Sergeant always asked who guarded the guardians."

A wise man. Yet they exist, where such names are given.

"Whatever." Did she mean the physical world? I couldn't unpick her puzzles now. "Which leaves us with sacrifices."

Who wielded a lot of Adept power? What had they given up?

The Hecate? I couldn't think what she might have sacrificed; I didn't know her well enough.

"All I can think of is Tolly in his library. Content to sacrifice his sight to be able to read what no one else can."

A small example, but yes.

"What would I sacrifice to wield a dragon's power?" I spoke without meaning to. "Or Ash. Even for a minute."

Posing the question in my mind, I saw the appalling, seductive temptation to choose *others* for the sacrifice. That's how you set out with good intentions and became a monster.

But Speaks-to-Wolves swept on to answer my question.

A great heart knows what to offer, my daughter. Strength for strength. Measure for measure. It's all about the soul seeking balance. A sacrifice may or may not be known at the time, for this decision belongs here, in this true realm, not in the physical world, and time is not the same between them.

It almost sounded as if she wanted me to take Kaothos.

"Whoa! Hold on. If it's such a good idea, why doesn't Diana want to hold on to Kaothos?"

She does.

"Yeah, but she let go."

Yes.

To help me think, I walked on, along the corridor, through light and dark.

Did letting Kaothos go count as a sacrifice? Yes. And no, because Diana chose *not* to wield the power.

Diana was better placed than me to influence Emergence and prevent it from turning into the apocalypse. But she'd decided *not* to hold on to Kaothos. Had she decided she had nothing sufficient for the sacrifice, and wouldn't contemplate sacrificing others? Or another reason?

Or did Kaothos not want to stay?

No, their parting had been slow and painful, but they were *both* pulling apart.

Because Diana didn't think there was such a thing as a force for good? Or that one person could be?

No, those guesses didn't feel right.

Then it came to me. For Diana, it wasn't about the sacrifice. It was about the power concentrated into one person. A person that others believed in, uncritically. That others looked up to. That wielded absolute power. *That's* what Diana didn't want.

Speaks-to-Wolves had it wrong, this time.

"I *do* have a guide for this decision."

Diana? If you chose to follow her...

"Diana wouldn't keep Kaothos, despite the temptation. I'm certainly not in Diana's league, so there's no way I'll keep Kaothos. She belongs back with Tullah. Which means Tullah must choose what to sacrifice or we need..."

Guardians. Tullah needs protection and guidance. Starting with physical protection, because she's vulnerable as she tries to host Kaothos again.

"Am I her guardian angel, then?"

No, daughter. Not exactly. Not in the long term, where such considerations are measured.

The light flooding in the windows got paler. The dark in between got lighter.

I needed to ask so much more. I'd used Ash's power to call Kaothos. What was my sacrifice for that?

A sickening thought came to me. What were the sacrifices that had fed Ash's power? What did Ash feed on?

Not Kath's unborn baby. Not that. *Please.* Not that.

I saw Speaks-to-Wolves clearly as the light and dark blended. There were tears, like a spray of priceless diamonds, carelessly cast on her cheeks.

And then I was gone.

Chapter 73

PAIN.

Kaothos crashed into my body like a runaway train.

Tullah, linked through eukori, was completely unconscious.

Better. That way she avoided some of the worst aspects of spirit guides moving between hosts.

"Stop chewing coal and get on with it, you stupid lizard."

My voice clearly still belonged to someone who'd abused it with a long life of smoking and drinking.

Traffic jam, Kaothos said. *Sorry about this, Amber Farrell. Profoundly sorry...*

Incredibly, the pain doubled.

I screamed. The sheer shock of it made me leap to my feet.

One of Weaver's Adepts was coming at me, swinging a slim iron construction rod. My sudden movement saved my head from being split open. I took the blow on the thigh. The pain was nothing in comparison to what I was feeling from Kaothos.

And meeee!

"TARA?" I screamed it like a war-cry.

I'm back. With Hana. Punch that bastard already will you?

The Adept had put all his weight behind the rod. He was off balance and unable to get out of my way. Years of training, culminating in being beaten up in the gym regularly by Yelena, took over. I struck out, without thought. I broke his jaw. Then his elbow. Then his knee.

Oh! Nasty.

Her vacation being hosted by Tullah hadn't improved her wit, but the violence made the next rank of attackers think twice.

I wasn't looking at them. I was looking at Weaver.

The bastard had the controller for the collars that Tullah and I wore.

But he wasn't using it. He'd started another working.

"Kaothos?" I called out.

Nothing.

The dragon had her work cut out for her, reviving Tullah.

I felt the working that had been shielding the room change. It was as if we'd slipped sideways and spun away into the deeps. My skin crawled. The whole room was now a substantiation. We were adrift in the spirit world.

Oh, crap.

I raised the iron bar in my hand. I was still chained to the floor, but the bar would make a reasonable spear to kill Weaver. Then I was down to the knife hidden in my boot against fifty or more Adepts.

I had no time to throw the bar before the Adepts all collapsed.

Huh?

Something Kaothos had been able to do?

No. Hold still.

Tara spoke from behind me.

I ignored her and twisted around.

A wolf stood behind me. Not a normal wolf, or even a werewolf. A wolf who breathed fire. A wolf biting the chain that held me, whose saliva dripped and made puddles of smoke on the concrete floor. A wolf whose fur seemed to be ablaze.

"Hana?"

Tara-Hana. Both. One. No time. Weaver's going to take the whole coven's energies into that thing. He'll try to do the same with Tullah and Kaothos.

The chain parted. I spun back.

Weaver had merged with the corrupted soultree and become truly monstrous. His legs and arms had been absorbed into a squat blob. Only his face remained, stretched across the shimmering construct, and bloated beyond recognition. On the benches, the unconscious Denver Adepts were sliding across the floor and being sucked into the growing mass, one by one. With each one, the soultree's bulk bulged and stretched like a membrane of thin rubber. Faces appeared in the membrane, mouths open, silently screaming in horror and then they burst out, changing shape into writhing, fanged serpents.

In seconds, the whole body was a mass of serpents, corpse-gray and glittering. Slime dripped of the construct and an oily mist from it began to creep across the floor.

Weaver's distorted mouth opened as the soultree advanced on Tullah's body, but all that emerged was stinking smoke.

The snakes reached out toward us.

Was I too late? The Hecate was already crouched over Tullah.

The closest snake stretched.

A blade flashed in the Hecate's hand. The snake snatched itself back, slime spurting from a cut. The snake's scream was like a rusty saw cutting my flesh.

I reached the Hecate's side with the knife from my boot in one hand and the iron rod in the other. Just in time. Hit one snake. Stabbed another.

The firewolf made it three defenders, facing all ways. We needed to because the snakes were growing. The construct was an obscene heart pulsing, and with each pulse, the snakes reached further around the room, surrounding us with their gaping mouths and fangs like icepicks. All of them shrieked that horrific noise.

I slashed and stabbed and struck out.

"A working, Hecate?" I managed to grunt.

"Fight and cast. Same time. Difficult," she grunted back.

The snakes quickly learned to keep away from Tara. I couldn't look around, but the stench of frying snake-flesh was as appalling as it was heartening. The things could be killed.

Of course, keeping away from Tara meant they concentrated on me and Gwen. Neither of us had blades long enough to easily kill. If I'd had more space to swing, the rod would have been dangerous. Even better, if I had a sword. Actually, if I had a machine gun that worked down here.

If, if, if.

A fang slashed my arm and the wound sizzled.

Acid. Shit, I hope they can't spit like cobras.

The Hecate swore. It sounded Scandinavian.

Ash?

I tried again.

ASH?

Nothing. The substantiation had cut my link to the soultree.

I had no reserves of power to break out. Like the Hecate, I had no ability to do anything more than fight off the next snake.

And we were losing. The snakes were still growing.

"Beware above," I said.

That's where they'd come at us from next. Too many angles. That was what was going to kill us.

"Hold them, Amber!" the Hecate shouted. "Whatever you do, keep them away from Tullah."

I felt her back press against mine, and then it wasn't pressing. It was slipping down. She was falling.

"Gwen!"

No response.

I couldn't even spare the time to look.

I stepped over her body, trying to protect them both.

Tara howled a warning.

They struck at me from above at the same time as some came in low. Three of them bit me. Arm. Leg. I knocked one away that was going for the

Hecate. Another attacking Tullah. I stabbed too hard at that one. The snake jerked back with my knife in its eye. I didn't have time to reach for Gwen's knife. I took the rod in both hands. At least I had more room for a full sweep. Not too much, or I'd overbalance.

Swing.

A satisfying crunch of a snake's skull.

After the pain of the bites, my wounds were going numb. I couldn't feel my right leg. My left hand was getting weaker.

I swung again, but the weight of them against the rod pushed me and I fell to one knee.

Smashed the skull of another going for Gwen.

There were too many of them.

I struggled up to stand over Tullah and Gwen. Couldn't fall, or it was all over.

The snakes were poised above, wary of the rod, but gathering so thickly I could barely see the roof of the crucible.

And then, all together, they lunged at me.

A wheel of fire burst in front of my eyes.

The screaming redoubled. I couldn't think in all the noise.

My hand found Gwen's knife. Stabbed a snake head.

There were half a dozen snake heads lying on the floor in front of me, twitching.

Decapitated.

Not by a wheel of fire. By a sword. A burning sword. Six foot of longsword with flames that leaped further from it the faster it was swung.

Swung by a seven-foot-tall woman in mail and leather.

I blinked.

Hallucinations? Poison in the snake bites?

The woman was screaming, and she was screaming even louder than the snakes as she swung again.

There were still too many of them. They filled the room and they came at us from every angle, suddenly desperate, heedless of any damage we inflicted.

They swarmed Tara.

They wrapped themselves around the tall woman's arms.

The woman's back flexed, bulged. Wings erupted out. Not soft and feathered. Sharp. Not really wings as such, unless you count metal blades as feathers.

The wings sliced off snake heads, tried to cover me and Tara and Tullah, but the press of snakes was too much. The wings couldn't get free.

We were still going to disappear under the wave of attacks.

As the least threatening of their opponents, the snakes had left me alone for a second.

I changed my grip on the iron rod, rocked back, and then threw it like a spear with everything I had behind it.

Straight at the part of the soultree that looked like Weaver's face. It hit in the eye, punched right through into the shaking bulk.

But it didn't kill the soultree.

The winged woman twisted and her lethal wings cut more snakes, but it wasn't going to be enough.

The whole soultree raised above us, started to topple. It was going to swamp us and I knew once inside that bulk, we were finished.

Weaver's face was above me, the rod emerging from his eye.

I reached up and grabbed it. That made the construct stop, but then its flesh started to flow down the rod like melting fat.

ASH!

Almost as if it were part of me, I could feel something punch through the working that surrounded the pit. Broke the substantiation.

And I *reached* out. Found Ash. Pulled.

The end of the rod began to glow. I could see it inside the monster. I could see flames consuming it from the inside out. I pushed the rod, swept it in circles, trying to hit something vital with the incandescent end of it.

Too late. It had my hands. They went numb.

Tara leaped and bit and tore.

The winged woman got her sword free.

The monster's liquid flesh ran down my arms.

I fell back to my knees again, struggled up against a crushing weight.

I couldn't breathe. Couldn't see.

The room was full.

Movements.

Noises.

Glimpses of the pale corpse flesh of the snakes... and the green, gleaming scales of the dragon.

"Kaothos?"

She didn't answer.

The crush eased.

I fell over.

The screaming had stopped. There was a thud, an impact, like a train hitting the buffers.

Then all movement stopped.

There was no substantiation cutting the room off from the rest of the world.

No isolating spell.

No monstrous soultree.

No sound.

No Weaver.

No Adepts.

No snakes.

No seven-foot woman.

No Tullah.

No firewolf.

No Kaothos.

Just me, kneeling beside Gwen's body, and somewhere far away, my House, Ops 4-10 and packs of werewolves digging their way into the mine and slaughtering the defenders.

A parting whisp of understanding from Kaothos floated through my head, and the craziness all finally began to make a strange kind of sense to me. Even the Hecate and the winged angel with the flaming sword.

Chapter 74

Gwen was lying where she'd fallen, crumpled like a discarded coat. Her face pressed against the concrete.

I knelt and touched her shoulder gently.

"I'm sorry," I said. "Okay to give you a hand?"

Her face was pinched with anger.

"Nothing I can do about it, is there?" she said.

I took her waspish comment as a *yes*. "Anything I need to be particularly careful about, moving you?"

"No."

I lifted her out of the pit and onto the step where the first row of Adepts had sat. Despite her denial, I took care to support her neck while I did. I straightened her legs out, and crossed her hands on her chest. Then I tugged her coat until that was straight and tidy too.

She was bleeding from cuts on her head.

I licked them clean. My aniatropics would heal them quickly in the same way she could have, if she'd had her spirit guide.

"Bit of anti-snake venom in that as well," I said.

She ignored that, staring at the ceiling. Without her spirit guide, her eyes had reverted to hazel. Her hair had relaxed into its natural wavy brown and framed her angry face. Angry, and now *more* angry because she felt somehow ashamed as well, as if she'd been diminished. She wouldn't meet my eye.

"You knew," she said. It was a statement.

"I suspected something." I reached out a hand to untangle her hair, and stopped. "May I?"

Her jaw worked. Then she nodded once—no more than a dip of the chin.

My fingers ran through the soft, wavy hair, combing it into some kind of order.

"Every time you took a break from your spirit guide," I said, "your hair and your eyes would change."

"That's not what—"

"No. Of course not. It just made me alert to the changes in you. The thing that really made it clear was your body language. You don't fidget when you're like this. At all. No tells, no tics, no twitches. And then I thought back and noticed your spirit guide only ever left you when you were sitting down securely. Made me start to wonder. It all seemed to make sense when your spirit guide joined the battle after you collapsed."

"Is she allowed to come back..." Gwen swallowed and her eyes glistened. She kept staring at the ceiling. "Please..."

"Shh. You don't have to ask. Your spirit guide will be coming back. I should have said that right away. I believe Kaothos is having a bonding and sorting session with them all. Mine included."

"Thank you," she whispered.

"I can't keep calling her your spirit guide. What's her name? The angel with the flaming sword?"

"Bryn," Gwen said. "Short for Brynswere."

"And she's a..."

"Valkyrie. Yes."

Valkyrie. Someone had said something to me recently about light and shapes and names. Or was that a dream? Was valkyrie as accurate a name as vampire? A sort of mixed bucket of myths and superstitions, a set of vague guesses at a truth.

Regardless, something that was *not* a standard spirit guide.

"A dragon and a valkyrie. That makes two guides who are... different, and have come together."

"Three unusual guides. Or have you forgotten your firewolf?"

"You're right. But I'm not worried about Tara," I said. "Bryn... this isn't a Saint Georgina and the dragon situation, is it? I mean, she helped Kaothos. She protected Tullah."

"Bryn would never harm Kaothos, or Tullah. She believes her role is to protect and advise the dragon. She thinks that's what went wrong with dragon spirit guides before—they had no one to protect them from misuse."

"A guardian angel," I said and frowned. I'd had another dream about that, hadn't I? Something about a corridor and a conversation about guardian angels.

Weird.

Aloud, I said: "I think Kaothos might like that. Might *need* that. Someone she can talk to about spirit guide things and difficult decisions. I know my advice hasn't been much use. I've caused Kaothos more problems than solutions."

"You haven't, and besides, you were doing your best with what you knew," Gwen said. Her jaw worked again. "Bryn thinks a lot of you."

"Hmm. I don't want to pry, but why doesn't she... ah... fix you?"

"No!"

"If she doesn't want to, I could heal you." I leaned over her. My Athanate glands were working, and I could taste the flavors of the aniatropics. I bared my fangs.

If she could have, her whole body would have tensed up. As it was, an expression of horror slipped across her face.

I put the fangs away quickly.

She didn't seem to be the sort of person who was fang-phobic, but you couldn't always tell.

"I'm pretty sure I can repair nerve damage. And if I can't, Bian could." I stroked her hair away from her throat. "Such pretty hair. The damage is near the top of the spine, isn't it?"

"Yes." The word seemed torn from her.

"Is that *yes* I can repair it?"

"No! Don't bite me. Please. Yes, the damage is at the top of the spine. Yes, you could probably fix it. No. I don't want you to. It's part of what gives me my power."

"Let me get this straight. Without Bryn, you have no feeling and no control of your body below the neck, and you have to stay like that so your magic mojo works?"

"Yes." Her lips became a thin line, pressed together.

"A sacrifice," I muttered. There was something about that in the strange corridor dream as well. "A balance in your mind, so you can use your power without falling prey to the temptation to misuse it."

"Something like that."

Something that felt right to her, and actually served the purpose, but wasn't necessarily right, or the only solution.

I kept that to myself.

"Well, I'm not going to fix you against you wishes," I said. "But I'm going to have a long talk with Bryn."

A shiver of magic ran across the skin of my arms, but it wasn't Bryn returning. It was my firewolf.

"Tara!"

Amber!

Then the firewolf shimmered and became human, almost a mirror image of me, but fully dressed and without the all mud. I'd always imagined my twin sister would look like me, and she did, but she was still her own person, not just the image in the mirror.

She hugged me, and an old, old pain eased deep inside.

Our tears were interrupted by Gwen.

"One is bad enough," she said, with a hint of laughter in her voice.

Tara stuck out her tongue.

"Bryn will be along shortly," she said. "Until then, lie there quietly like a good little girl."

I was trying to form *how* type questions, but Tara anticipated them.

"We're together. Me and Hana. Something happened when we moved to Tullah, which we totally didn't mean to do or expect to happen. We just woke up there, and we'd merged. Not only merged but we kinda adapted to the space left by Kaothos. We're not that strong, but we gained some dragonish abilities with fire."

She changed back to wolf, raced around the circular pit and belched flames.

Then she leaped at Gwen. She changed mid-flight and came down human, looming over the Hecate with her weight braced on her arms and her face inches above Gwen's.

Gwen blinked.

"Congratulations," Tara said.

"What do you mean?"

"You get what you wanted; you and Bryn are best pals with Kaothos. You get to be the dragon's advisors and protectors."

"Why am I waiting for the other shoe to drop?"

"Because you're as paranoid as Amber." Tara rolled her eyes. "Oh, yeah, and you get to be part of Amber's House and you get to set up a new Denver coven, with Gabrielle, Alice, Flint and Kane of course. And Amber's got to be in your coven, just as you're in her House."

"What?" Gwen's eyes bulged.

"Hey! What's happened to the Denver Adepts?"

"Oh, complicated. Kaothos will explain."

She disappeared and I felt the weight of her in my head, missing for so long.

Missed you, sis. Really, really missed you.

Another shiver of magic and a seven-foot valkyrie stood in the center of the pit. Her head was bowed, the blade clenched in her left fist. The longsword wasn't burning now, but the woman still radiated scary vibes.

"Bryn!" Gwen called out.

I stood up. Even on the raised step above the pit, that didn't put me eye to eye when she looked at us.

Chilling blue eyes. Hair like ice. Gleaming mailed armor from her throat to her knees, and over her arms. Blue tunic underneath. Leather pants and boots. Golden winged helmet. No wings sprouting from her back.

She held the sword against her chest and it shimmered and shifted. When it stopped shimmering, the sword had gone and it was replaced by an image of it on her chain mail. She moved to sit on the lower step, one hand resting on Gwen's shoulder.

I sat back down.

"Thank you, Amber Farrell, for protecting Gwendolyn," she said.

"Thank you, too. You saved us."

"I think we might share those honors with each other and with your firewolf." She stretched her hand out toward my face, then paused. "If you permit?"

I hadn't any idea what I was supposed to be permitting, but I trusted this crazy spirit guide, all seven foot of her, so I nodded.

Her cool fingers slipped underneath the edge of the collar, gently tugged, and then I could feel the coolness all around my neck.

I put my hands up. No collar. It was dangling from her fingers. It had been sliced through.

"Neat," I said, and shivered.

Yes, neat. Also scary.

She rolled her shoulders as if she was making herself more comfortable, and wings erupted from her back.

I gasped. They were beautiful. And deadly. I hadn't had much time to examine them before, while I was just about to die, so I took the opportunity now.

There were no handles to the blades, no obvious way they connected. Each blade was a thin, slightly oval shape and looked razor sharp. They were glossy, each tucked into the next one like a feather would be. I couldn't decide on what color they were. It was like the inside of a seashell coated with mother-of-pearl. Lustrous. Pink? Violet? Iridescent. They seemed to change color depending on the angle I looked at them from.

Bryn pressed the collar against the edge of the right wing, and wiped upwards with her hand. The collar disappeared and fresh new blades appeared.

The wing shivered as if settling into place, and she extended and contracted it to check that the blades were sliding smoothly against each other.

I made a guess: "These were all weapons?" Cautiously, I put fingers out to touch the blades, alert and ready to hold back if it caused some kind of offense.

"Yes," she said. "I collect weapons from battles. Usually from the dead."

I wasn't going to count, but that was a lot of battles or a lot of dead people. Not only was the paranormal stranger than people thought, even paranormal people, but it seemed it was bigger as well.

She didn't seem offended by my touch on her wing, and the sensation was pleasant. The blades seemed to tingle beneath my fingers. They were firm, and it felt as if they were alive somehow. They were warm, very smooth. The sort of surface I wanted to stroke just for the feeling of running fingers over it.

"That's crazy cool," I said.

The corners of those blue eyes crinkled. Bryn was obviously very amused.

"What?"

"You are not to know of course, but caressing a valkrie's wing blades is very sensual. A declaration of desire."

Beside us, Gwen cleared her throat.

"If you've quite finished seducing my spirit guide, I'd like to get up," she said.

"Finished?" I said. "I've barely started, but go ahead."

The little demon that used to live in my throat and say inappropriate things at awkward times seemed to have returned with Tara. *What a surprise.*

Bryn smiled lazily at me as her blue eyes looked me up and down.

Her wings folded back with a *snick*, then she disappeared.

Gwen sat up, restored to her slinky self. "It was getting boring. Choice of looking up your nose, or staring at the roof," she said, putting on her gloves. "You realize, you really need a shower. And a shirt."

Chapter 75

Weaver's werewolf defenders, including Celum, were slaughtered. It was as if there was a stench that attached to outcast wolves, and getting themselves together in a group had made it worse. The werewolves of the Southern League had no mercy on any of them.

Kaothos returned the Denver Adepts who'd survived, except they weren't the Denver Adepts anymore. They were a group of humans who'd once been Adepts. Kaothos had absorbed their corrupted spirit guides, taken all their power.

The former Adepts were welcome to try and seek out new spirit guides, but there was only one community that would accept them, and that was now the Denver coven of the Northern Adept League, headed by the Hecate Gwendolyn Enkeliekki, former Hecate of the North, former leader of the Michigan and Ontario Adepts, who Flint and Kane still referred to, even in her hearing, as Wendy Witch.

I spoke to Kaothos at length when she returned to Haven with Tullah.

Power is power the dragon had said to me. *The evil comes from the use of power. The two can be separated.*

That helped.

The mine was destroyed by Kaothos, and the gold that Weaver had extracted was turned into funds that went towards education and hospitals in the Uintah Basin.

The rest of Tullah's family and her boyfriend, Matt, were recovered from their desert hideaway down in Arizona, and for the moment, they were staying at Haven along with Gwen and Gabrielle.

Skylur received a long formal enquiry from the Empire of Heaven. Stripped of its diplomatic language and polite terms, it was essentially *what the hell have you been doing in Utah?*

The spirit world had been churned up in a way no one had ever seen before. The predatory substantiations of the spirit world had risen from the deeps and were circling like sharks. No one was dipping their toes into the waters just at the moment. Gabrielle had become a bit tight-lipped about Adept secrets, but she'd muttered something in my hearing about seeing a legendary and terrifying substantiation called the City of Lost Gods when she'd peeked into the turmoil.

Skylur's reply to the Empire was possibly as great a masterpiece of diplomatic stonewall as existed in Tully's archives. It boiled down to

What? Us? We thought it was you carrying on with substantiations in our territory. Very dangerous, you know. Irresponsible even.

I hadn't had a lot of time with Gwen and Bryn. Formally, they were in my House, and the Adepts in my House and I were part of Gwen's coven, as Tara had said.

I'd need to test out exactly what that meant before it became an issue in a critical situation.

In the meantime Mykayla, Rita and Tove were back with me at Manassah. Mykayla was still pretending to be about to change into a werewolf, but her progress so far was that she'd developed a set of Athanate fangs and blooded them.

Taylor, Kath and Tamanny were settled in David's house, and I had to call my mom soon and explain my reasoning.

In the meantime, I was having a delayed vacation until the next halfy ritual in Louisiana, intending to enjoy it with my House and my family as much as possible.

Except for one remaining task.

Epilogue

It'd been a *grand soft day* in the words of the tourist agencies, which meant fog, and a rain so fine you needed gills to breathe.

And it had been a grand soft night earlier. But now the fog was shredding like streamers and the moon was up, cold and merciless, which only made the midnight shadows darker. The fog chilled my face and left it damp. It smelled of the Atlantic.

Each place has its own quality of silence, and there was a hush in this isolated Irish coastal village like a breath held too long.

I'd come down off the trail along the peninsula's ridge, past the brooding Stone Age circle, through a small patch of woods to emerge at the top of the waiting village.

No lights. Not a single window, streetlamp or porchlight.

I followed the winding path which merged into a dirt road. I passed long, low houses hunched in the darkness to either side, surrounded by hedges and gray stone walls, wrapped in tatters of fog and shrouded in silence.

There were watchers, of course. A dozen eyes or more followed my silent progress. I could feel their presence, the weight of their regard. My skin crawled.

No voice called out. No hail. No challenge.

No welcome for a daughter come home.

At the shadowed heart, where all the village's wandering roads met, the vision that had haunted my dreams emerged from the mists, and became real.

The village had built the small church, many years ago, within the arms of their sacred circle. No spire: instead a strange, circular tower with a conical top. Tall slot windows were cut into the front of the church. They were too narrow and they reminded me of wounds. The front door was almost hidden between wide buttresses which stamped down into the damp earth. The church's walls and the roof over the nave formed an arch, like an upturned boat. All built in thin, gray stone, except the corners of the walls, which were large, paler rocks, rough dressed. Every stone was crusted with moss and lichens.

And the sacred circle itself: the trees.

Rowan. *Beloved of Brigid* whispered a voice in my ear. *She offers protection from magic.*

Alder. *Faith above all. She summons the spirits of the air.*

Hazel. *Healing and knowledge.*

Oak, and in its branches, mistletoe. *Nobility, and sacred sight.*

The trees ringed the churchyard like sentinels.

All but one: the towering ash tree in the center of the graveyard.

"Hello, Ash," I said, standing by the lychgate, messenger bag over my shoulder. *Tree of dreams, tree of life, soultree of the Threefold Spiral Coven.*

Hello, Amber.

My skin prickled.

I passed through the gate and into the cemetery. The older graves were on the right. Less uniform, to the point there was an unruliness about them. Celtic crosses. Plain, pale slabs. Black marble. A cherub. A weeping angel. The crucifixion.

I turned there. My fingers ran across images and letters on gravestones, reading in the darkness like Tolly. Reading the words and names, and feeling beneath. Images floated up out of the deep. Sounds. All unformed, blurred by the years, like the carvings on the standing stones of the circle on the ridge above the village.

And among the tangled, dangling lines of a thousand untold stories...

Ó Fearghail.

Children of valor. Farrell, in the modern spelling.

Two, side by side. Alone. I caressed the dates.

I'd found great-grandfather Padraig's parents. The last of their line in the village. The only ones buried with stone markers in this cemetery.

All my other Irish ancestors in this rich earth would have been buried wrapped in linen, with the grave unmarked, its place known only to those that held them in their hearts; their memories to fade away softly and silently, their bodies to nourish the sacred circle.

But it wasn't my family's graves I'd come to find.

Across the path, there were new graves. Three of them, in front of the ranks of death.

The gravestones were smooth granite. The words few, eloquent in their grief. No images.

My fingers raced across the letters. All three had the family name in the old form: *Ó Súileabháin.* Children of the dark-eyed one. Sullivan. My fingers ran on.

Mac: Son.

Iníon: Daughter. Two of the gravestones.

I closed my eyes, rested my head against the unyielding stone. Two daughters and a son had died.

They didn't just die, the shadows hissed. *You killed them.*

"Yes, I did," I said, and the shadows moved, split into seven separate shapes standing in a semicircle about twenty yards from me. The Adept elders of the Threefold Spiral Coven.

I stood slowly.

"I killed them, and even though I'm sorry, I'd kill them again in the same circumstances."

The cold wind off the Atlantic whispered through the trees, and carried away the last strands of fog.

I opened the messenger bag and carefully took out a wreath I'd made for these graves. It was round, like a normal wreath, but I'd woven the base from green splints—woven them in and out and around each other to form a twisting Celtic knot with no beginning and no end.

"There's willow, and hazel, and aspen," I murmured, as I knelt again in front of the middle grave.

For sorrow, whispered one shadow and floated forward a step or two.

I put the wreath down gently.

"Daylily," I said, and touched the three flowers in the center.

To forget, whispered another.

No, whispered the others. *We will remember.*

"And a crest of cattail rushes bound by olive twigs."

Peace. The first shadow came closer, still floating, but swaying like an old woman walking.

"For peace," I said.

Padraig Ó Fearghail, he—

"I don't care what he did," I said, and rose again.

An oath was made—

Handfasted—

A word was broken—

It is our bond, or we are nothing.

It is what makes us.

"It's not what makes you," I said. "It's what you've made yourselves."

A woman in the middle of the arc threw back her cowl.

"You're arrogant, to come into our place of power and challenge us," she said. "Farrells were always so."

"Foolish child," a second joined in.

"I've already challenged you, and won," I said, and gestured at the graves as the wind stirred the tall ash's branches. "You left these to guard your soultree, but I had a need, and when I called, the soultree came to me. I did not will their deaths, but knowing it, I would do the same again. Your curse has returned to you."

I felt them try again to pull the threads of their soultree away from me, but their hearts weren't in it. They knew the truth of it. I could call on their own power to defeat them.

"Because of something my great-grandfather did or didn't do, this coven wove a curse. A working that killed firstborn children of the Farrell family. You weep over these graves and you won't shed a tear for the unnamed babies who never saw the light of day."

"You lived." It was the old Adept who'd come closest who spoke. "The curse has burned itself out."

"No."

Tara manifested as a wolf, clothed in flames, and there were no longer any shadows to hide in.

They cringed.

"I lived because my twin died for me. And now her spirit has merged with my wolf guide, and your curse has returned to its origin to seek its threefold price."

The old woman fell to her knees.

"I'm eldest," she said. "Let it fall on me."

"An old woman in exchange for all those children?"

One by one, the other elders took stumbling steps forward and knelt.

And I knew it was because there were other children, all Sullivan blood, all children of the dark-eyed one, hidden in the village, hearts beating in terror, ears straining to hear their fate. Innocents, all bound into this obscene working. All targets for the returning curse to burn itself out. And just as an Athanate Mistress might offer her death as *korheny*, a sacrifice to save the others of her House, the elders knelt in front of me to plead for their children.

But if there was no coven, there was no curse left; it wasn't my fault they'd bound the entire family into their working.

No coven would mean every person in the village with a drop of the Sullivan blood.

No curse would mean life for Kath's unborn child.

I took a painful lungful of Atlantic air and my breath plumed in the night.

This was Tara's call. They'd killed her.

"It was the way," said the Adept who'd shown her face. "We were raised into the coven. We swore two oaths of entry: loyalty to the coven and the curse."

Around me, a blur of memories rose from the ground like mists. Year after year. The midnight before the ancient feastdays. Young men and women, shivering in the darkness. Hands held out. The swift cut of a knife. Blood on the ash tree. Solemn vows.

...and death to the firstborn of Ó Fearghail.

"You could have set it down at any time," I shouted. "One person to stand up and argue."

But I knew it wouldn't have been that easy.

"It defines us," the eldest said.

She was right. Something done or said out of habit became part of what you are. A habit became a tradition. A tradition became a rule. And the rule defined you.

Until the greatest of them saw the glimmer of hope and took a step.

Their own soultree wanted to be free, even at the expense of the coven that gave it being.

I stood over their leader and took a grip on her hair, forcing her head back.

"I will define you," I said and my fangs manifested in the shimmering light cast by Tara's flames. "Accept my decision or die."

A sob from the end of the circle.

I ignored it.

The woman closed her eyes.

"I accept," she said, and her lips moved silently to words in the old tongue, greeting death.

I sank my fangs into her throat and let my eukori leap from Adept to Adept, out of the graveyard, down the silent streets, through the darkened houses like summer lightning, gathering them all, old and young, into one awestruck Carpathian communion.

And when I held them all, I let Ash in, and let the soultree gather what I wanted from the coven: the fuel for the curse.

I had a place to hold all that anger and hate. I had a use for it, better than theirs. Fed by Ash, I took and took.

When there was no more left to take, I let my fangs slip from her throat. But I wasn't finished.

"I bind you." I called out the words Alice had given me. "I bind you, all here and all to come, to a new purpose, with an oath on the heads of all your children, all of them: the dead, the living, and those yet to be born."

The chill Atlantic air stirred. Fog began to creep into the village again.

We hear, the shadows whispered.

"There's an Athanate House called Ó Ruairc."

"We know them," whispered the oldest. "The Healing House."

"They have children there, brought up as blood slaves by Basilikos, their minds twisted and tortured so that Ó Ruairc can do nothing with them. That is what will define you from this moment forward: that there will never be a soul you cannot heal, if you die trying. You will swear this."

"We swear," said the kneeling elders, and the shadows echoed.

"You will never speak to outsiders of this."

"We swear."

And then I dismantled the Carpathian communion, gently pushing Ash back.

I took the last offerings from the messenger bag and laid them down in front of the new graves.

"There's seedlings of birch," I said.

Alice had told me that it was the month of the birch in the old Celtic calendar.

"For new beginnings," murmured the eldest.

"And yew," I said, remembering the words of Felix's sister, Martha, in the quiet cemetery behind the ranch house at Coykuti. "A friend once said to me that the yew tree lives off itself, makes itself new from all it has ever been. In the same way, you'll always be all the things you've ever done, but that means you'll be all the things you ever will do, too."

Then I turned and walked away.

Tara disappeared and I felt her settle into my mind, neither happy nor unhappy, but satisfied with the way it had gone.

There were whispers behind me, spreading quickly out from the churchyard, jumping from house to house. Lights began to come on.

You lit a flame, Tara said. *I wonder how it'll burn.*

It will burn, or their children will die, Ash said.

"You must go back, Ash," I said to the night. "I have unbound you. You're the soultree of the Threefold Spiral Coven again."

I am, but I may also be with you.

"I can't pay the price. For all my words, Ash, I'm not sure I could do it again. Three innocent young lives in exchange for using your power."

Think on these three things, Amber Ó Fearghail. Think on their claim to innocence. No Ó Súileabháin child who put their bloodied hand on me and spoke the words was innocent.

The fog was gathering thickly again now, blown in off the Atlantic in great banks, like waves crashing against the headland.

Think on what would have happened if you hadn't used my power.

I thought.

There was silence but for my steps.

"You said three things."

Think on my belief that it was my sacrifice to use your power, and not yours to use mine.

"Huh?"

But Ash was gone.

Made in the USA
Monee, IL
31 December 2020

56043421R00246